NIGHT OF THE JAGUAR

NIGHT OF THE JAGUAR

Joe Gannon

Minotaur Books
New York

This is a work of fiction. All of the characters, organizations, and events portrayed in this novel are either products of the author's imagination or are used fictitiously.

www.minotaurbooks.com

Design by Omar Chapa

The Library of Congress Cataloging-in-Publication Data is available upon request.

ISBN 978-1-250-04802-8 (hardcover)
ISBN 978-1-4668-4831-3 (e-book)

Minotaur books may be purchased for educational, business, or promotional use. For information on bulk purchases, please contact Macmillan Corporate and Premium Sales Department at 1-800-221-7945, extension 5442, or write specialmarkets@macmillan.com.

First Edition: September 2014

10 9 8 7 6 5 4 3 2 1

To Valentina Barbara Pearl,
luz de mi vida, reina de mi corazón,
and
to the people of Nicaragua, who deserve so much more

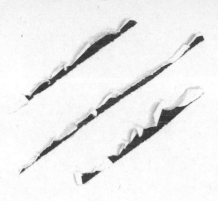

ACKNOWLEDGMENTS

This is a work of fiction, not history. Events and people from the real Nicaragua of the 1980s have been altered or invented to meet the needs of the story. Only the glory of Somoza's overthrow and the terrible costs of the Contra War are real.

I must effusively thank Matt Rigney, whose keen eye read every word, whose singular mind pulled more out of my fuzzy head than I thought was there, and whose stellar friendship kept me going. I owe a great debt to Sterling Watson, author, friend, mentor—*il maestro di tutti maestri*—who taught me to kill my darlings, and without whose help and encouragement this novel would never have seen the light of day. Thanks to all of Mrs. Pine's Kids—the students, faculty, and staff of the Solstice MFA program.

I am grateful for the works of nonfiction I relied on to jog my memory, especially Omar Cabezas's *Fire from the Mountain*; as well as Stephen Kinzer's *Blood of Brothers*; Christopher Dickey's *With the Contras*; Forrest D. Colburn's *My Car in Managua;* and Gioconda Belli's *The Country Under My Skin*.

I am most deeply indebted to the poetry of Pablo Antonio Cuadra and the immortal Rubén Darío, which was the first inspiration so many years ago.

Thanks also to the Smith College art library, which let me have a carrel of my own. And finally, thanks to MN, who helped me through from red to blue.

Disdaining kings, we give ourselves our laws
to the sound of cannons and of bugle calls.
And now, on the sinister behalf of black kings,
each Judas is a friend of every Cain.

—*Rubén Darío, "To Columbus"*

NIGHT OF THE
JAGUAR

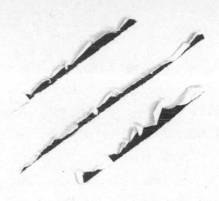

PROLOGUE—THE JAGUAR

June 21, 1986

"Say the first part."

Enrique Cuadra smiles in the dark. He turns his balding head—gleaming under the full moon—and studies his cousin's profile. The hawkish nose and high cheekbones—El Indio. Epimenio can barely write his own name, but he never tires of the poems, and asks to hear them each night once they make camp. The three days they've spent tracking the jaguar have taken them high into the selva, the mountain forest that runs from southern Mexico, through their home in Nicaragua, and all the way south to Peru. They've only covered ten miles as the crow flies from Enrique's farm, and then circled, looking for a sign. Any further out and they might run into the Contra. Enrique knows a lot of the hungry, hard-eyed young men who have joined the counterrevolution. They are led by some of the old dictator's Guardia, but the foot soldiers are local boys mostly. He should be in no danger from them. But they would take his shotguns.

Three days away from the coffee finca is more holiday than Enrique's had in years, and he enjoys Epimenio's company. There is an ease between them that is rare between padron and peasant, even when they are related. They spend most of the daylight tracking in companionable silence, then make a small fire, warm a few of the tamales Enrique's young wife prepared, and enjoy the first hours of night talking quietly, like this. Epimenio is fascinated by the notion that he could walk this mountain chain all the *way north through Central America and Mexico, America, Canada, and on to the top of the world. He marvels that there are Americans even there, in Alaska. Enrique explained that Americans have a powerful hunger to be in many places, some of them far from home.*

"Say it, Enrique."

"You know it as well as I do," *Enrique says.*

"Only the words, you know how to, you know . . ."

"Recite it."

"Yes!"

Enrique sits up. "'Rain, the first creature, even older than the stars, said, "Let there be moss aware of life." And this was jaguar's skin. But lightning struck its flint, and said, "Add sharp claws." And a soft tongue licked the cruelty sheathed in its paws.'"

Epimenio Putoy lies on his back in the cool mountain air and smiles. He looks straight at a moon so full his cousin could read the poem from a book—if he needed a page clearer than his memory. It is Epimenio's favorite passage. He has heard it many times on the porch back at Enrique's farm. But out here, high in the Segovias, the two middle-aged men stretched out on horse blankets, the fire just dying embers, their shotguns near to hand, the very creature itself somewhere out there in the Nicaraguan night, Epimenio feels a thrill that the poem never brought before.

"Do you think that's true, Enrique? Can you make skin out of moss?"

"You can if you're a god."

"But there's just one God."

"One God with many names, many gods with one Name. We can't know."

"Father Jerome wouldn't like that."

"Father Jerome knows what he knows, and we know what we know."

"And the jaguar knows what she knows."

"And the jaguar knows what she knows. But you're sure it's a she?"

"She walks a little crooked when nursing. Her paw fits into the closed hand." *Epimenio makes a fist.* "The male's fits into the open hand." *He spreads his fingers.* "But either way, it's true. The claws are cruel."

"Cruel to the cow when she killed it. But she doesn't kill out of cruelty. She's nursing little ones of her own, verdad?"

"True. Now say the next part."

"'Then the wind, blowing its flute, said, "I give you the rhythmic movements of the breeze." And it rose and walked like harmony. And jaguar ruled the kingdom of death, undiscerning and blind.'"

Epimenio looks at the moon; he mouths the last lines to himself. "What does that mean, 'undiscerning'?"

"It means indiscriminate. But in the poem, it means not to care what you hurt."

"But you said she's not cruel."

"Not the animal we hunt. The jaguar in the poem is a symbol for powerful things. Kings, dictators, emperors. Those who do not care what they hurt, they . . ."

Epimenio springs up, flicks his blanket over the embers to smother them, and crouches stock-still. Enrique rolls onto his belly, silently lifts his shotgun. He snaps the safety off; the usually small metallic click is like a thunderclap in the silence. Enrique peers into the dark. The waxy leaves of the dense selva reflect only the moon's silvery sheen. The clearing seems to be an island of light in a doomsday-black sea. He feels exposed, as if caught in a searchlight. Enrique belly-slides next to his cousin, holds his hand up like a claw. Jaguar?

Epimenio wags his index finger, points his thumb at his heart, and wiggles two fingers like legs. No. Men.

Enrique closes his eyes and listens. After a moment he hears something, something mechanical. The faint whine of an engine. A plane? He points to the sky, nods, and points to his ear: I hear the plane. Epimenio wags his index finger, points into the darkness, and wiggles his two fingers again: No. Over there. Men.

Enrique closes his eyes. Listens. Listens. And then, yes, he hears them. Distinctly, but far away: men's voices. Laughing.

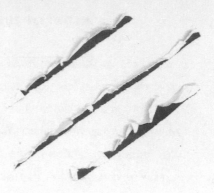

1

Managua, July 2, 1986

1.

Captain Ajax Montoya had a pain in the ass.

As he drove along the carretera playing Russian roulette with the potholes in the decaying city's streets, it occurred to Ajax that life since he had come down from the mountains was a series of pains in the ass. A chain, a sequence, a succession. He had an abundance of them, a plethora, an actual cornucopia of them. *How doth my ass ache?*—he could shout out the goddamned window of his broke-ass car if the window worked—*Let me count the goddamned ways.*

The shrapnel lodged in his tailbone where a mortar round had sown it was the first, original, and perpetual pain, always with him like a schizophrenic conscience that can't stop muttering to itself. That pain was aggravated this morning, like warm breath over hot coals, by the chrome-plated Python holstered down the small of his back. But the aggravation put him in the right frame of mind to deal with the cigarette smugglers. And those sons of bitches had better hope he found them before he smoked his last butt.

He'd had been up for five straight nights reading his thesaurus and smoking one Marlboro Red after another. It was all he had left now—now, nowadays, at the present time, currently. He'd been stone-cold, cold-turkey sober for five days. And that was maybe the biggest pain in the ass he'd had since he was last sober. Four years ago, almost to the day. His impulsive sobriety was accompanied, not surprisingly, by an inability to sleep or to fight off that parched inner voice—demon, fiend!—constantly begging, demanding, imploring *Gimme! Gimme! Gimme! Gimme just the one drink!* Which was why he had taken up reading the goddamned thesaurus all night long in the first place.

He'd begun by reading the dictionary as an antidote—a remedy, a tonic—to that shrill, sleepless voice, but had discovered that he preferred the thesaurus. The dictionary, Ajax found, with its multiple, even contradictory meanings only disoriented him like these Managua streets, which lacked not only identifying street signs, but *names,* and so could only be navigated by landmarks, many of which no longer stood, and so were only known to lifelong residents, one of which he wasn't.

The thesaurus—alternately, conversely, on the other hand, with its long lists of alphabetized synonyms ready to roll off the tongue— the thesaurus seemed more a poem to be recited. He had learned long ago in the mountains that he didn't have to understand a poem to be soothed by it.

Ajax had endured some memorable pains in the ass up in the mountains during the long years of the insurrection: gunshots, jungle rot, malnutrition, malaria. To say nothing of the spies and traitors who had to be endured before they could be found out and executed. Then there had been the loneliness—loneliness as immense and un-broken as the sierra itself. And the boredom, which in the early years had only occasionally been interrupted by bloody, thrilling firefights with the Ogre's Guardia Nacional—and he'd really not cared if he was shooting or being shot at. Then there had been the hours of mind-numbing indoctrination they'd had to absorb and discuss to help forge the New Socialist Men they were supposed to become, in the Worldwide Revolution they were supposed to be part of, even though they'd mostly lived like mice in Cat City.

He'd joined the Frente Sandinista in 1969 when he was only eighteen. That was in what would charitably be called the Sandinistas' *quixotic phase* as they faced off against the longest-ruling dictator and the biggest army in all of Latin America. Ajax had fought alongside them for the next ten ghastly years until the impossible had happened that impossible day in July 1979. Forty-three years of despised, dynastic tyranny fell in a matter of months, and the cruelest army in Central America collapsed into nothingness. General Somoza, the ageless Ogre, was overthrown!

Yet during all those hellish years, no matter how hard the march, how short the rations, how endless the rain, how well-armed the enemy, not once—not once in ten years—had Ajax ever doubted himself, his compañeros, or that he would see Victory or Death. Meaning, no matter what, he had always known what was what. Which was why it troubled him—vexed him, frightened him—that on his third day of sobriety he had begun to lose his mind.

Now, at thirty-six, Life—La Gran Puta of all Putas—presented him with the ultimate dilemma, irony, paradox: remain a drunk and lose his soul, or keep his temperance but lose his mind.

He hit another pothole and the shock shot a needle into his coccyx. *Shit-eating fucking sons of bitches!* This pothole Russian roulette was worse now, in the rainy season. The ruts, plentiful as splinters in the Risen Carpenter's ass, were full of water from last night's tormenta, so he couldn't tell which was a puddle or a pool. His rattletrap Lada magnified the hurt. Its suspensionless frame telegraphed through its springless seat directly to his ass every jolt, pothole, fissure, and bump of the weary city's exhausted streets.

And he had those streets mostly to himself.

The Soviet tanker bringing the month's fuel shipment was late, again. The gas had dried up yesterday. No oil meant no buses, no buses meant few workers, and few workers meant almost no sidewalk vendors or street hawkers. Why bother? Managua could still seem an alien place to Ajax. He hadn't come home to Nicaragua until he was nineteen, and had never set foot in Managua before the revolution had triumphed in '79. He was thirty by then. He'd had seven years to put the city on like a glove, like a skin. Let it in. But he still felt a stranger in it. It was a city of almost a million souls in a country of four million, yet the city center was empty not only of citizens but even of buildings. The terrible earthquake of '72 had toppled a critical mass of the homes and businesses that made the city the city. Much had never been rebuilt—despite the world's generous response—because General Somoza, the last of the Ogres of that name, had hoarded the donations like bones to make his bread. So now Ajax passed through neighborhoods of tidy homes, a hotel or a restaurant, but then block after endless block of empty lots, framed by snaggle-toothed walls overgrown with weeds, where young boys now tended cows.

The horizon, too, as he sped toward the cigarette smugglers, was empty. For a full 360 degrees only four points stood more than a story above his head. The Government House and the InterContinental Hotel in the dead center of "downtown," were paired in perfect symmetry with the twin cones of Momotombo and Momotombito—the two volcanoes on the far side of Lake Managua that waited patiently like unexploded ordinance. Ajax wiggled his ass, looking for some relief as he pushed the accelerator—and counted the usual six seconds until his Lada actually sped up.

Earthquakes and volcanoes, it sometimes seemed, were two of the few assets his piss-poor country had in abundance. The only stable things in Nicaragua were the stars, and they were too far away to be of any help. He fished a cigarette out of his last pack. He *had* to get to the smugglers. Instead, he got the radio call he'd been waiting two days for.

"Ajax, Ajax, Ajax. Copy?"

"Copy, Darío. Go"

"We got him, Ajax. Positive ID."

"Where?"

"Barrio Jorge Dimitriov."

"Any sign of the priest?"

"Neither dead nor alive."

2.

Fifteen minutes later, Ajax squatted inside one shack, observing another about twenty yards away. He pulled the .357 magnum from its hand-tooled holster and slowly rolled the Python's chrome cylinder over his open palm. With the hammer half-cocked it turned smoothly. He could feel the chambers silently clicking as they rolled past the barrel, like tumblers falling in a big lock. It helped him to think, always had.

The people in Jorge Dimitriov were among the poorest of the poor—barrio kids, farmers displaced by the war in the northern mountains, and decommissioned soldiers. This was why the soldier Ajax had been searching for took refuge there. You could hardly call it hiding, Ajax thought. The shack he was in was as locked down as a wooden hut could be, its flimsy shutters sealed tight, with wisps of incense smoke curling from cracks in the mismatched slats. The soldier inside must be burning piles of it: smoke signals calling Ajax to him.

"Smells like a priest's whorehouse, doesn't it?"

He turned to see his new partner, Lieutenant Gladys Darío, only twenty, crouching next to him. Gladys had missed much of the battle against the Ogre and so sometimes overcompensated with foul-mouthed blasphemy.

"There aren't any whorehouses in Nicaragua, Lieutenant. Don't you read *Barricada*?"

"Oh, right, sorry, Captain."

New to the homicide squad, and fresh out of a Cuban police academy, Gladys favored clean, crisp uniforms and was an eager Sandinista believer of the stripe Ajax increasingly found a pain in the ass. But she had two great assets: she was a dead shot, which, while not really necessary to the job, was a trait Ajax admired in anyone, and she actually believed being partnered with the "great Ajax Montoya" was a blessing. Ajax figured she had really pissed someone off, or was spying on him. The latter possibility was one reason he'd agreed to sober up. An old friend had warned him that the Frente—the Sandinista Front, both as ruling party and government—had overlooked all the missed assignments, no-shows, and glassy-eyed insubordination it was going to. If the Frente wanted to make a move on him, Ajax had vowed, they could do it for any reason they liked. But *not* because he was drunk on the job—or insane.

Still, he liked Gladys. She had close-cropped hair—kind of butch, he thought—but an unlined face that made him feel good when she smiled, even if she was taking notes.

She wasn't smiling now.

"What's the matter?" he asked.

"Seguridad is here."

Ajax shot up off his haunches and looked out the door. A squad of Russian-trained sharpshooters from State Security took up concealed positions around the soldier's refuge. He froze Gladys in an accusation: "How did they know?"

"We got orders at formation this morning. You weren't there. The major said to notify State Security when we found him."

"The major is a moron."

"The perpetrator was from the Seventeenth Light Hunter Battalion. They're a MINT unit."

The Ministry of the Interior, the MINT, was an octopus with a tentacle in too many tamales, including State Security and its own combat units fighting the Contra.

"Gladys, his name is Fortunado Gavilan." Ajax returned the Python to its holster and handed the rig over to her, ivory handle first. "Don't ever involve State Security in our business again."

She looked at the gun. "Captain, are you crazy?"

He regarded her for a moment. Did she know his history with

State Security? Did she sense his confusion from the hallucinations he'd been having? Or had he told her and forgotten?

"I won't need the piece, Gladys, he's done killing."

She seemed to straighten up into a formal pose. "Captain, regulations say no officer is allowed to enter the presence of a dangerous suspect without protection."

"Jesus, you sound like a condom ad from the Health Ministry."

He shoved the Python into her hands.

"Ajax, please, he killed his girlfriend. The priest could already be dead, too."

"Gladys, he's shell-shocked. This is not an arrest. It's a rescue. Give me the wire." Ajax felt a burst of adrenaline flutter his heart and turn his stomach. My God, how long had it been? "Just sit still until I bring them out."

Ajax stepped out of the shack. He signaled the sharpshooters, who lowered their rifles. He stole around the back of the soldier's hut. He slid the wire inside the shuttered window, turned the simple wood latch, and slipped soundlessly inside.

He crouched on the floor and covered his shut eyes for a count of five to help them adjust. Opened them in the darkness. The musky incense clogged his nose, so he had to smother a cough. He was in the back of a two-room shack. He made out a few shapes: two simple cots, a packing-crate table, a woman's plastic brush and comb. On the wall was a scrap-wood shelf, holding only a prized bottle of imported Jergens hand cream, looking a saint in its niche.

The hut felt empty. He stood, took a step further inside. The window he'd come through was framed by a halo of sunshine. A few panes of smoky light seemed to hang on invisible wires where the sun bled down from the roof. Ajax moved soundlessly into the other room. The door was barricaded. Piles of incense smoldered on the dirt floor. This room seemed empty, but he could sense, if not see the soldier.

"You came in so quietly I thought you were an angel."

The soldier materialized out of a corner, as if passing through the wall from outside. Ajax stumbled backward and went down over a table flat onto his back. Fortunado Gavilan stood over him. He was dressed in camouflage pants, bare-chested, a bottle of rum in one hand, an AK-47 in the other. He pointed it at Ajax. "You aren't. Are you?"

Ajax cleared his throat, struggled to control his voice. It had been a long time since police work had involved Ajax in real danger, and madness was the most dangerous of all. "No compa, I'm no angel. Just a soldier like you."

The soldier leaned toward Ajax, studying him in the gloom. Ajax looked up at a dark, miserable, mestizo face. Close-cropped black hair and heavy brows. He'd seen the face many times before. An old man's exhausted visage on a very young man's body, the pitiful, pitiless look of the combat soldier.

"Sorry about the smell." He bent down to blow on the embers of incense. "Did you see any crows outside?"

"No."

The soldier trudged on leaden legs to one of the cots and sat heavily, knocking over an empty bottle of rum. There was a pile of them at his feet. He laid the AK across his lap and raised the bottle as though to drink. Instead, he poured rum over his head and shoulders. Massaged it thoroughly into his arms. He bathed himself again. He didn't even flinch when it cascaded into his eyes.

"Sorry about the smell. The priest said the incense would help. But it does no good. That's how they find me, see? The crows. By the smell. That carrion smell." He opened another bottle of rum, doused himself. "I can't get that smell out."

Ajax got up, drifted to the cot, squatted on his haunches in front of the soldier, inches from the rifle. "I can't smell anything but the incense. A friend says it's making the whole barrio smell like a priest's whorehouse."

The soldier smiled, almost chuckled. "You better watch that. God will get mad." He rubbed his eyes, but only one hand at a time, the other resting on the rifle. "I need to sleep. But that's when they come. My friends. The crows." His head drooped then snapped up. "Do you think God sees everything? Everything everyone does? I mean there must be millions of people in the world, right?"

"No. He doesn't see. He's too busy."

"That's what I told my novia. My girl. *That's* why He sends the crows!" The soldier dropped his head to his chest. He seemed asleep, but his thumbs made small circles on the stock of the AK. "Can ghosts hurt you? I mean can they get mad at you? Even if maybe it's not your fault?" He raised his eyes to Ajax's. "I mean, they were already dead. It was the only way to get them in the same hole. I was gonna bury them. I wanted to, but I lost them in the river. My friends understand that, right?"

Ajax understood the soldier was reliving the torture he'd been put through; he'd read the boy's file. There had been dismemberment, body parts carried on the soldier's back. He touched the soldier for the first time, patting his knee. "Your friends understand everything. And they forgive you. Besides, the dead don't have the same worries as us. Once they're dead, their concerns from life disappear."

"Yeah. Yeah. I hope so."

Fortunado's head dropped, then snapped up again, a look of alarm overcoming his tortured features.

"Shhh." He raised fingers to his lips. The AK was finally free of his grip, Ajax's hand still on his knee. "Listen. Do you hear?" His eyes roved over the soot-dark ceiling. "Did you see any crows outside?"

"No. Nothing."

His hands dropped to the AK again. "When I escaped the Contra—you heard of Comandante Krill? Real shit-eater. But it was the crows that helped me escape. *They* led me to the river. I would never have found it. That's how I got back."

"God and Nature are with the Revo, hombre."

"No! Then they turned on me. Shouting, 'He's here! He's here!' That's how the ghosts found me. Them fucking crows reported to God and God said, *'Punish Him! Punish the coward! Punish the traitor!'*" The soldier beat his head with his fists, the moan of an animal in agony rising out of him until Ajax feared it would spook Gladys into rushing the barricaded door. The soldier scratched at his scalp, leaving long red welts. Ajax grabbed his wrists, wrestled his hands down, the rifle no longer his main worry.

"Stop it! Stop it! Look at me!"

But the soldier tore his hands away, attacked his scalp again as if he would rip open his head and tear out his mind. "Leave me alone! Leave me alone! Get out! Get out, get out, get out!"

Ajax recoiled at the soldier's torment but fought to wrestle his hands away from his head. Fortunado fought him, his eyes roaming madly over the darkened ceiling.

"Get out! Leave me alone! I was trying to help them. Help!"

Ajax took an accidental head butt to the nose. The pain, as always, made him stronger and he grappled with the soldier's hands.

"Compa, God doesn't punish soldiers. Look at me! Look at me. Hombre! Corporal Gavilan look at me!"

Ajax pinioned his hands. The soldier calmed himself, or just gave up. But Ajax could see up close now the black eyes swimming in blood-red pools. The cracked lips and hard-caked spit at the corners of his mouth—Ajax had been told by the psychologist—were symptoms of the dehydration that accompanies sleep deprivation.

Ajax released the soldier's wrists and slowly laid his hands on his cheeks. "Compañero. You did no wrong." Ajax rubbed the soldier's head, massaged his temples. "Compa, your friends have already forgiven you. You've got to forgive yourself, man. God does not punish soldiers." He raised the boy's head to look into his eyes. "That's what officers are for, right?"

The soldier's eyes stopped swimming. They finally looked into Ajax's eyes. He let out what seemed a wail of pain, but was really a high-pitched laugh. He dropped his hands back to the AK. "You're funny."

Fortunado doused himself again with rum. This time Ajax saw him wince as it poured over the new scratches in the boy's scalp.

"You want a cigarette?"

"Sure."

Ajax shook a Red loose from his pack.

"Marl-burros! My favorite."

Ajax lit his Zippo with one hand. His other twitched to seize the rifle. Instead he lit himself one, too.

They smoked for a while.

Then Ajax made his first try. "You know I found a great place for you to get some sleep. Good chow, too. Lots of free beer." Instantly he knew it was a mistake. The soldier sat up alertly, peered over Ajax's shoulder into a corner of the room. Listened intently to something. Someone? When his eyes returned to Ajax, they were full of suspicion. The soldier crushed out the cigarette, leaned close, put a hand behind Ajax's neck and forced their foreheads together.

"Are you a ghost talker? Do you see them? Speak to them?"

"No, compa. I told you."

Fortunado's eyes turned back to the corner. He listened. Ajax knew they were not alone. He reached slowly for the AK, but the soldier suddenly held it tight and gripped Ajax's neck.

"He says you're a liar. He says you talk to him and he talks to you. He says you're a snake and you brought the crows with you!"

Ajax pushed back, grinding their foreheads together, his neck muscles straining. He laid a hand on the AK. "Well, he's a cock-sucking, motherfucking, bitching, bastard, son of the Great Whore, shit-eating liar." Ajax poured all of his heart and soul through his eyes into the soldier's bloodshot windows, desperate to reach some final thread of a man. "And so is his mother."

The soldier flicked a look into the corner and back to Ajax. He released a stale, stinking breath into Ajax's face. "I don't like him either. He's always making trouble. Telling me things. Making my friends angry." He loosened his grip on Ajax's neck and the AK.

"That's right compa. *He* brought the crows. Look at him. You know he did. Let's leave that sick fuck here." Ajax slid the AK onto his own lap. "Let's just go. You need to sleep. I'll stand guard over you. No ghosts. No crows."

"You swear it?"

He raised his right hand. "*Te lo juro.*"

The soldier picked up the destroyed cigarette, assessed its salvagability. "Got any more?"

"Sure."

"I should get in uniform."

"I'll get you some water."

The soldier fumbled for his clothes. Ajax stood, took a breath and turned, half expecting to see someone standing in the corner. For a weird moment he knew there would be, but . . . but what? That would be crazy. He slung the AK over his shoulder, spotted a gourd water jug on a table in the corner, and tried to pour some into a scarred plastic cup. His hands shook too much. As quietly as he could, he panted to catch his breath. His heart raced and his stomach churned. He poured a cup of water, gulped it down then poured one for the soldier. It was then he noticed a bulging pile of wet rags and newspapers heaped under the table. *Damn.* He looked over his shoulder, lifted the rags with his boot. Underneath he could just make out a head, gray hair matted with blood. The priest's rosary still gripped in his hand. *Pobre padre.* The kid might be battle crazed, but the bishop and the antigovernment press would have a field day with this. His poor girlfriend would be forgotten.

"How do I look?"

The soldier had on his fatigue jumper and bush hat.

"You look like a soldier."

"Got another Marl-burro?"

Ajax shook out a Red, lit it, tucked the pack into the soldier's breast pocket, buttoned it.

"You keep them. I'll get more."

"You buy them on the black market?"

"Well. Let's say I get them from the black market."

Ajax gave him the jug of water. He drank it down in great gulps and poured the rest over his head. He took a long drag and slowly blew a trail of smoke to the ceiling, seeming to notice something in the dark. He looked Ajax in the eye, gently touched the red-and-black Policía Sandinista insignia on his shoulder and whispered, "Ajax. I know why you're here. I know what I did."

Ajax knew it was now or never. He took the soldier by the arm and quickly kicked away the barricade from the door.

"Come on, Fortunado. It'll be all right. *Te lo juro.*"

"I know."

He stood with the soldier in the doorway. The sunlight blinded him but the soldier hardly blinked at all. Ajax eyeballed Gladys and saw her check her Bulgarian-made watch. He was not sure how long he'd been in there. Gladys turned toward the sharpshooters, now mustered in a line, and said something that made them snap their rifles to the ready. She turned to Ajax and touched her wrists together. Chica's got a thing for standard operating procedure, he thought, but he was damned if he'd handcuff someone already so caged. He adjusted the soldier's AK over his shoulder to show her he had it under control. He signaled Gladys to be at ease. She and the sharpshooters obeyed.

Ajax shaded his eyes, an old habit. Reconnoiter before moving from shade to light. Then he stepped fully outside with his arm around the soldier's shoulder. Slowly they walked out. Gladys frowned when the soldier took a drag on the Red. Ajax nodded at her and walked steadily on. They had cleared out the neighboring houses and the barrio was very quiet. He heard the soldier take another drag, and exhale as quietly as . . . as quietly as . . .

He was distracted for a moment, a sound, something. Something changed. The noise didn't register. The soldier stopped, looked up, plucked the Marlboro from his mouth and ground it out. Then Ajax heard it again—a single crow caw. He turned to the soldier, wanted the soldier to look at him one last time. Later, he was sure he could've fixed it if the kid had looked at him. He tried to throw a bear hug on Fortunado, pull him down. But the moment had passed and all Ajax got was a punch—a pile driver to his solar plexus. He dropped like a stone to the dirt.

"Listo!" Gladys yelled.

Ajax heard rifle butts snap to shoulders and saw the soldier's legs pump toward Gladys. And although the breath was knocked out of him, he knew what was happening. The soldier had not gotten himself dressed, but armed. He was drawing the pistol he'd secreted under his jumper and swinging it up at Gladys. He knew that the soldier was not giving himself up, but facing his tormentors one last time. The rifles went off like a single shot. Like a firing squad might. And at that sound a crow leapt out of a tree. Circled once. And was gone.

Ajax writhed in the dirt, suffocating. Drowning. The soldier's fist had created a vacuum in his lungs. Stranded on hands and knees, he could only heave as if trying to vomit air. Boots rushed around. But all was silence, except the blood pounding in his head. And then hands rolled him onto his back. The sun blinded him, caused a small explosion in his lungs, which suddenly filled with air.

"Ajax are you all right? Are you shot?"

He shoved Gladys's hands away. Looked around with swimming eyes and saw the soldier sprawled on his back. He rolled onto hands and knees, crawled to the boy, swatting at the robots' legs. "Get away, you fucking *asesinos*!" Assassins! "Don't touch him!"

Fortunado's arms were flung akimbo. Holes in his chest pooled blood. The sharpshooters would be proud of such a tight grouping. Ajax put a hand over the one hole in the soldier's forehead, to cover the goo that had blossomed there. His face was in repose. His eyes were open, and to Ajax's amazement they were no longer bloodshot. Yes, that's what had alerted him. The soldier's eyes had cleared. He patted the boy's chest affectionately. Felt the little box, and retrieved the bloodstained pack of Reds. A neat hole was drilled between the M and O, like a carnival trick shot. The package now spelled M ORO.

Then he heard the cawing of crows. He saw them in the tree. The last thing Fortunado Gavilan had seen. He snatched up the soldier's AK from the dirt. For the first time in years, the blood rage returned. He opened fire on them.

2

1.

Ajax lay on the hammock in his tiny, wet garden, looking at the stars, thinking, *It must be Wednesday.* Because the stars were all he could see. His barrio was without electricity on Wednesdays. No water on Mondays and Thursdays. No lights on Wednesdays. But at least he had both on the weekends.

Like that did some good. *When was the last time you had someone here on the weekend? You're a fucking monk.*

He noticed that he was spinning the Python's cylinder but wasn't sure how long he'd been doing it, nor how long he'd lain in the hammock talking to his pistol.

He sat up, rubbing his tongue over his lips, saliva building in his mouth. He could kill for a glass of Flor de Caña. Nicaragua exported eighty million pounds of coffee beans a year. Yet the coffee in the mercados was shit. But the rum, the Flower of the Cane, was famous in Latin America for its delectability. As if the poorest province of France produced its finest wine.

Ajax exhaled a breath as long as the day had been. "If those crows hadn't been there I could've saved that kid."

If you'd put cuffs on him you would have. Gladys knew it and you noticed how she didn't say anything?

Then he had another thought: *Gimme! Gimme! Gimme! Gimme! Gimme just the one drink!* He spun the Python's cylinder, pointed it into the air, and pulled the trigger. Click! An empty chamber. "Eighty-six," he muttered, disappointed. Damn, he'd been sure he'd hit it the eighty-sixth time.

Ajax dropped the Python next to the Makarov 9mm he'd retrieved from the soldier. Then he rose, and walked automatically through the dark. The house was almost the same as when he'd been assigned it in '80 after joining State Security. He hadn't been in it long when he'd moved into Gioconda's house with its yard and pool for all her entertaining. He'd moved back two years ago after the divorce. Horacio, his old mentor and only regular visitor, liked to tell him he lived in a cave, like a bear with furniture. But at least he had furniture. The only major changes to the small house were the wrought-iron bars he'd installed over the windows, and the jagged glass cemented on top of the wall that surrounded his little garden. He'd mixed the cement himself and smashed more bottles than he'd needed. (That they'd been empties from his wedding party had had nothing to do with it. He'd just gotten into a rhythm.)

There was no need of light. Garden to sala to kitchen to bedroom to office, all paths were well worn. He *was* like a monk in his monastery. Or a prisoner. But a monk was not a prisoner, he reasoned. If you willingly went into the monastery you were not a prisoner. Wrongdoers got life sentences. Monks were devoted to a cause. The Knights Templar were monks and warriors and you wouldn't call them dickless, not to their faces anyway, even if they were celibate.

Gimme, gimme, gimme, gimme just the one.

Ajax turned left and went into his office. It was really a second bedroom—might have been a child's bedroom. He sat in the comfortable leather chair *she* had given him back when she was mostly a pretty face but he was the great man. He opened a big desk drawer and stared through the darkness into it. He thought of it as the Dead Drawer. There were only four objects in it, like relics that, if laid out just the right way, offered clues to the loss of some bygone tribe. He removed The Needle, wrapped in oil skin to protect the blade, and set it aside with no more thought than you would give an old shoe. Then his fingers touched the finely framed photo she'd given him. A picture of the one perfect moment in his life—the afternoon of July 20, 1979. The day that divided his life into the Before of "All was possible" and the After of "Life is a double-dealing bitch."

He ran his fingers over the glass, closed his eyes. The image showed Ajax before a wildly cheering throng of people in what was now the Plaza de la Revolución, but was then still the Ogre's Plaza de la Republica. Ajax stood on a platform, front and center, held an American sniper rifle over his head, the ivory handle of the Python visible on his hip. He was surrounded by his smiling compañeros. The look on his face was not one of triumph, but of joy. There was a watch on his wrist. Through a magnifying glass he had once tried to check the exact time. But it was obscured. She who had given him the watch stood at the back of the platform, her face just barely visible through the crowd of scruffy, fatigue-clad men and women. She was the only one not in fatigues. She stared at the Ajax the crowd adored. On her face was a look of hunger, but also of admiration. A look frozen for all time as incontrovertible proof that she had once adored him. No matter what bullshit evidence would later be introduced that *he* was cold, distant, and unable to live in the present.

Ajax dropped the photo carelessly onto the desk and fumbled for the third object, a small makeup case. Through the plastic he could feel the tube of dark red lipstick. The brush still woven with strands of her chestnut hair. The nail file, long like her fingers. And, most precious, the small bottle of perfume. She'd worn the perfume the night of the photograph. His head had swum with the fragrance as she had torn at his clothes. He'd just been able to drag her into the back of a truck before she took him like some ravenous marauder, took him with such intensity, such unhinged abandon that it had been as if the people's delirium at the Ogre's overthrow had been channeled into her, the suffering and sacrifice of the guerrilleros channeled into him, so that when he'd entered her their bodies had become something new, some Adam and Eve, and the long stream of orgasms she had milked out of them both, her nails bloodying his back, had purged the suffering of the past, celebrated the unimaginable triumph of the present, and consecrated an unwritten future.

Ajax had found it a little frightening.

It had been, after all, only his third or fourth time, and he'd been nearly thirty. But she'd shown him, coached him, taught him. As was her way. He had wanted their child to be conceived that night. The very constellations in the sky were new. The Ogre had been overthrown. Decades of merciless dictatorship staked through the heart. Those who had been its slaves were now masters. And they would create a new world without slaves. Or masters.

But the clock had already struck. Ajax did not know it then, but the day and the moment were gone. The constellations were not new. They were the same ones Ajax had looked at this very night. Only the Ogre would not come back (would be denied even exile, and sent to welcoming Hell on the nose of a rocket-propelled grenade).

Ajax held the makeup bag to his face. He inhaled the perfume, the first time he'd done it sober in years, and the scent evaporated all those shame-filled nights when he'd tried to use it to awaken his pickled manhood. Now the scent inflamed his senses, sent a zing of electricity up his spine, caressed his old wound into silence and turned the handle on a rusted faucet he could not bear opened. Not now, not here alone with only the last object left in the drawer.

He fingered the outline of the perfume bottle, set the makeup bag down, and lifted out the fourth object: the bottle of Flor de Caña, extra seco. Only foreigners drank the honey-gold dark rum. Like all Nicaraguans, Ajax preferred the water-clear extra dry. He ran his fingers over the unbroken seal. He'd written out the date of his last drink, June 28, 1986. What he hoped, prayed, wished to be the last. His turning, his redemption, his rescue.

He wrapped his hand around the neck of the bottle. Wanted more than anything to wring its neck. Break the seal. Let go. He'd had a taste of letting go when he'd opened fire with the soldier's AK. If had felt good. Very good. He'd even killed three crows—one of them in flight.

Gimme! Gimme! Gimme! Gimme! Gimme just the one drink!

Burning off those rounds, he now realized, were the only moments when the thirsty voice had been quiet these past days. It seemed as if all the rum he would now not drink was rioting in his head. He fished out a Marlboro, stuck it into his lips, and flipped the Zippo into fire. It was almost lit when he saw the bloody stain running right down the seam of the cigarette paper.

He wasn't done killing, was he, you clever-stupid hero?

"Situational awareness" was what the Cuban Special Forces colonel who had trained him outside Moscow had called it. When the sum of all you knew was greater than what the five senses could take in. Ajax had once been so famous for his situational awareness that his old commander, Horacio, had christened him, "Spooky." But Fortunado Gavilan was not done killing, and Ajax had missed that situation. He seemed to miss a lot these days. Maybe the drink *had* rotted his once watertight instincts.

Suddenly he was tired—exhausted and sleepy. He swept the icons of his life off the desk and back into the darkened drawer, lit the bloodstained cigarette, and dragged his ass to bed. On the way he picked up the thesaurus, just in case.

2.

Gladys Darío parked her Lada between two broken streetlamps, in a closet-sized pool of darkness, got out, and hung her heavy purse over her left shoulder. She checked the street—traffic in front of the Metro Centro was light for a Saturday night, but then the Soviet oil tanker had still not arrived. She stepped to the curb and walked unhurriedly, as if she had no real destination. The new cowboy boots, a gift from her sister in Miami, were just a little too snug, and she had to mind her step on the accordioned sidewalk, which the avocado trees lining the street had broken and buckled with their iron root system bull-dozing like tectonic plates just below her feet.

She passed a few sets of lovers at the bus stop, half asleep in exhausted embraces like warmed candles melting into each other. At the corner where the Carretera Sur began its run south to Masaya, she saw only two vendors selling ice cream and carnitas, but not doing much trade. She didn't cross to the west side of the street where the Disco Vaquero actually sat—all gussied up in twinkling lights shaped like bull's horns and a horse head. Between the blinking livestock, the words LADIES' NITE were also lit up. Mexican norteño music escaped each time the door opened. She took up her usual observation post next to the Optica Nicaraguense at the edge of the Metro Centro directly across from the club. A trio of girls no more than ten passed her, chattering and carrying wide aluminum baskets filled with cheap hard candy, pens, loose cigarettes, matches, combs, and key rings. Where they were selling their odds and ends at this time of night, Gladys could not guess. She turned and watched them hold hands and dash across the street, first setting the baskets on their heads, which they balanced as easily as Gladys wore her cowboy hat.

She had a discreet look at herself in the darkened store window. The tight Levi's and white western shirt with blue stitching and real brass snap buttons made her feel as sexy as she hoped she looked. But the words "Made in the USA" in her sister's mocking voice came to her mind. After the Revo, her younger sister had followed their parents to Miami. The first few years of letters and phone calls had eased the loneliness. But then Gladys had graduated university and chosen the police academy over Miami. She was thrilled to her marrow that she'd been born in time to actually *live* the revolution generations of her people had dreamed of. Even her father had dreamed of it—just not one run by the Marxist children of fruit sellers and teachers. That was why he'd given up his lucrative medical practice and moved the family to Miami, where they'd spent much of their time anyway. She'd had his blessing to remain, but her training in Havana—the belly of the beast, as if Castro would personally demonstrate how to tie the garrote around the neck of Baby Freedom in its crib—was more than her father could accept, or excuse. The silences got longer and cooler. Her sister knew better than to talk politics with her, so the regular packages of clothes and makeup, jellies, soaps, and candies often arrived with no note at all—but always with the price tags still on.

Gladys adjusted the new cowboy hat on her head and checked her front in the window; from breasts to hips, she found no conspicuous flaws. She looked into her eyes in the blackened glass and felt her inner predator purr. The only disappointment was the heavy purse. Her sister had not sent a matching one. Gladys hated purses anyway, but the jeans were too tight to pack the Makarov, even in an ankle holster. She never chambered a round when out of uniform, because the pistol could double as a good bludgeon, which she had employed it as more than once. Despite the Revo she'd sworn her life to, Nicaragua was still a backward nation of Catholic machos, and she was a young, pretty dyke. She had learned the hard way that sometimes all the consciousness-raising permitted was a smack in the mouth.

"Good evening, Lieutenant."

The visitor's face hove into view in the glass and froze Gladys like a cobra's swaying head. He'd introduced himself at the graduation ceremony in Havana. He'd seemed to know everyone and everyone certainly knew him. Gladys had earned top honors, so his offer to partner her with someone like Ajax Montoya had seemed another prize. But he'd quickly made it clear she was not only to learn *from* Ajax, but about him. And report back.

"Good evening, Comandante," she said.

"Compañero."

"Compañero."

The visitor looked her up and down; his gaze seemed to linger on her purse. Then he looked across the street at the disco. "I don't like norteño music myself. Too Mexican, if that's not ungrateful of me. The Mexicans are, after all, great friends of the revolution."

"Yes, I mean, no, I don't like norteño either. It's just . . ."

He reached out and tapped her purse once, sharply, with the tip of his finger. "You go armed even when off duty?"

"Sometimes, yes. It's not loaded—I mean there's no round chambered."

"Do I make you nervous, Lieutenant?"

"No."

"Well I should. After all, I am asking you to report on Captain Montoya. He is your partner, your teacher, really. And a hero of the revolution. Doesn't that make you feel the least disloyal?"

"Um . . ." She slid the purse off one shoulder, then rehung it on the other. She regretted wearing the goddamned cowboy hat.

"And you are ready to make a report, aren't you?"

"Sí, Comandante."

"Compañero."

"Compañero."

"And you're not writing any of this down."

"No."

"And how is Montoya?"

"Fine. Well, we had a tough day. A suspect got killed . . ."

"We know. The bishop is already making a hysterical fuss about the priest, blaming it on us as if we'd crucified the poor bastard in the Plaza. *La Prensa* will have morgue photographs splashed over the front page. What happened?"

"The priest was dead when we got there."

"I mean with Montoya."

"Ajax, Captain Montoya talked the soldier out. He seemed compliant. Then he pulled a gun. We had to shoot. The guy *was* crazy."

"The soldier?"

"Yes."

The visitor moved so he could see both their reflections in the store window. "Tell me about Montoya. Was he sober?"

"Sober?"

"Sober, meaning not drunk."

"Yes, he was sober."

"Is he stable?"

"Stable?"

"Lieutenant, you keep answering questions with questions. I chose you in the hope you could observe and report, now do so."

"Yes, compañero. He was stable, rational. He's just . . ."

"What?"

Gladys moved the purse back to the other shoulder. "He's kind of an asshole."

The visitor threw his head back and laughed, showing all of his very white teeth. She could tell from the state of those teeth how high up in the government he was. You didn't get that kind of dental care unless you were.

The visitor studied her face a while. "It seems I have chosen well. Did you read his file?"

"I wasn't given it."

"Not Montoya's. The soldier's."

"Yes. I did. Hard to believe what they put him through."

"Do you know why the Contra are that way? Give me your purse."

Gladys handed it over. She rocked back and forth in her boots, relieved now that she was in them. Had she high heels on, she might have toppled to the ground.

"The Contra are that way because they don't fight *for* anything. An ideal. A goal." The visitor unzipped the purse. "Only against something. Us. This actor-president Reagan came to power with a movie-script foreign policy that he will fight communism like the cowboys he played in B-films fought Indians."

He took her pistol out.

"But the Soviets are Indians with nukes. Reagan can't attack them. So he makes this Contra army to attack us. In this way he is like the old US cavalry—if they couldn't get at the braves, the warriors, they attacked the women and children in the villages. Wiped them out. We, unfortunately, Lieutenant, are the women and children in the village. Do you understand?"

She had no idea what this was about. "Yes, compañero."

"We are too weak to defend ourselves, so we take the brunt of the battle, but there are no warriors coming to defend us, nor revenge us. In America's eyes Nicaragua's role, the Revo's role, is to suffer, to bleed, to starve. The Contra exist only to impoverish us, to sow dissension. That's why they are so dangerous. The Contra are nihilists capable of murder and suicide."

Gladys understood that. "Yes, compañero."

"That's why there can be no half measures. No half commitment. That soldier knew. It is why he submitted to torture but did not break. Did not betray his *trust*."

The visitor jacked the slide on the pistol, chambered a round, set the hammer down, put the safety on, and returned the loaded gun to her butt first—all in one fluid movement, his hands moving like a magician's.

"This is not the time or place to carry an unloaded weapon. We don't have even a second to assess the danger. We are all always on the point of being murdered. Do you understand that, Lieutenant Darío?"

"Yes, compañero."

"Good. Enjoy Ladies Nite. But don't be out too late. You've got important work in the morning."

3.

Ajax awoke with a deep shiver in the pitch dark. The shiver came from a thought ringing through his head like the report of a pistol fired from close by. The bullet was his own name. *Ajax.*

Ajax. I know why you're here. I know what I did, the soldier had said.

The kid knew my name. He knew my name!

He'd not noticed it before, but now he heard it and the sound of his own name stunned him.

He knew my name!

Then another realization cracked in his mind: he was cold, and dry. It was July and he was cold. He was awake and bone dry. His skin, the sheets, dry. So maybe he wasn't awake, he never was unless he'd sweated through to the mattress. But he didn't dream, not like this. And then he felt it, felt it in his hand. The Needle. Unmistakably, The Needle was in his hand. But now it was unwrapped from its oil rags. The leather sheath felt warm. The steel handle, too. The Needle was a wicked stiletto—long and thin with a point like a knitting needle for sticking, but with four edges honed for slicing soft tissue. It was a specialty blade he'd specialized in. He'd carried it in the mountains for years, until that last time he'd used it, and then had put it away. Forever, he'd thought. Yet here it was—so familiar in his palm. Here he was—in the dark. Bone dry. The Needle in his hand. The kid's voice saying his name.

And he knew was not alone.

He could see through the bedroom window into his garden—a blackness stood out against the blackness. A sheen reflecting moonlight—like a freshly painted board. But it moved and swayed, like a curtain hanging in the garden. Had he left a towel dangling from a branch? It moved again, fluttered like a wet black flag in a breeze. Gleaming. But more than that, too. A silhouette? It seemed to have no shape but he felt it was facing him. It couldn't be looking at him, but he felt watched. Who could it be? He wasn't in the mountains; he didn't dream like this.

And now The Needle was in his hand. And the shimmering shadow in the window was waiting. Watching. Rippling like a shroud in a draft. Ajax silently sucked air, making his chest rise and fall, exhaling for longer than he inhaled. He counted to ten breathing in, to fifteen out.

He thought he heard his front door scrape open. He turned his head toward the sound. *There's more than one!* When he looked back, the silhouette was gone. It seemed like flight, and his hunter's instinct kicked in, as it did with any predator when the prey showed its back. In a spring like a jaguar, he was off the bed, through the window, and prone, naked upon the garden ground. The Needle, too, was naked, now, shucked from its sheath. The smell of the oil on the blade. His heart thumping against the earth, his muscles flexing, coiled, his ears attuned to every sound. And then he heard it, again, his name.

"Ajax?"

In the dream, the soldier had said his name. Was that it? Had the kid's ghost followed him home? Ajax opened his mouth wide to keep silent his heavy breathing. No. This had begun before he'd met the soldier.

Again his name.

"Ajax!"

This time followed by a low whistle. Just a two-note whistle so quiet most people would not hear it. It had been the universal password up in the mountains. Only one person still hailed him that way. Horacio. Ajax rolled onto his back. What the fuck was happening?

"Ajax!"

It didn't matter just then. He could not be found crawling around naked in his garden with a knife in his hands, and especially not The Needle. He went back through his bedroom window as silently as he'd gone out, and stashed The Needle under the bed.

"Ajax?"

It would be like the old fucker to barge into his bedroom. Horacio claimed that his sense of privacy had been twisted by the communal living of the mountains, but Ajax knew he was just nosey. For once he was glad Horacio was almost lame.

"*Viejo!*" Ajax yelled through his door. "*Momentito!* Sit down."

"Where's the bottle?"

The what? The bottle. Shit! In the drawer where The Needle should be.

"I'll get it! Just grab some glasses!"

"How about some light?"

"It's Wednesday. Light the candle."

Ajax could hear him shuffling around, the cane tip tapping in the dark. His hands shook as he fumbled for his police khakis. What the fuck was happening? What had he just seen? Seen again, he remembered. It didn't matter just then. He had to pull himself together. He had to be squared away in front of Horacio. His only friend, shit, his only visitor for the last two years. Horacio was not in the government, per se, had no portfolio to speak of, yet he was rumored to be everywhere and to know everything.

Some simply called him *El Viejo*. The Old Man. His admirers called him *El Poeta*, for the poetry he'd published since he was a guerrillero. His detractors called him *The Jesuit*, for his allegedly Machiavellian ways. But to Ajax he was always *El Maestro*.

Ajax had been a teenager in Los Angeles when he'd first met Horacio. It was Horacio who had got him buying guns for "*los muchachos*," then smuggling them south, and finally it was Horacio who'd convinced Ajax to "come home" to Nicaragua. Had recruited him to the Sandinistas, and been his first commander in the mountains. Horacio had taught him how to fight. How to kill. How to survive. Then Horacio had been badly wounded and evacuated to Havana, and later to Moscow for treatment. Two years later, when they met again in Managua, Ajax was leading Horacio's old command, had become "the great hero." And the vigorous graybeard—now poking around his kitchen in the dark—had become the fragile, gentle man with black beret, mahogany cane, and all-seeing yet always smiling eyes who was determined to save Ajax from drink, from himself.

Ajax would never say it out loud, but he felt loved by that old man. And Ajax was devoted to him in return.

Ajax opened his mouth wide to quiet his breath, and then gave his body over to panic, knowing the trembling, the shaking, the spasms would soon stop. As they always had.

4.

Horacio de la Vega Cárdenas felt his way into Ajax's kitchen and found two glasses. Knowing his protégé, he sniffed them for cleanliness. Satisfied, he made his way to the garden, sat in his chair, and arranged the glasses and candles on the table with the two pistols. He heard Ajax's approach.

"Captain Montoya."

"Maestro."

"Am I too late for that drink?"

"No, no. Just in time."

"You were sleeping?"

"No. Reading."

Ajax set the bottle of rum between them and Horacio saw the slight tremor in his hand.

"Reading in the dark?"

"No, no. By flashlight. The batteries died and I must have, I dunno, drifted off."

Ajax thought he was a complicated man, but Horacio knew how simple he really was. That's why he preferred it when Ajax lied.

"So you were sleeping?"

"I guess."

Horacio picked up the bottle. "It's just I'd hate to intrude on your sleep. You get so little. How's the thesaurus?"

"Good. I'm on the Ms—makeshift: improvised, provisional, temporary."

Horacio knocked his cane over, and as Ajax bent to retrieve it the old man checked a tiny mark he'd left on the bottle to ensure it was indeed the one he'd presented to Ajax, with no small ceremony, to mark the end and the beginning.

"My new book of poems is coming out."

Ajax handed him his cane. "Yes, I've still got the manuscript in the bedroom. Just don't have the concentration for it yet."

"Gioconda's got a new one coming out soon."

Ajax snatched up a glass and wiped it with his shirttail. Horacio felt the need to update him about her. Ajax carefully set the glass down. A little too carefully, Horacio thought.

"Really?" Ajax wiped the other glass off with his shirttail. "Anyone in this country not publishing a book of poetry? Not penning a volume of verse? Not crushing out a little canto?" He slammed the glass down. "You can't swing an iguana by the tail nowadays without hitting either a foreigner or a poet."

He checked the glasses, both now cloudy from the cleaning on his soiled shirt. Horacio smiled. Poking Ajax in the old wound was one way to check his overall well-being. Sarcasm in connection with his ex-wife's name was a good sign.

"Well, that we are a country of poets is the one national vanity we can actually afford." Horacio tapped the two pistols on the table with his cane. "Lots of weaponry lying about this evening."

Ajax picked up the rum bottle and turned it in his hands. "That one," he said of the Makarov, "belonged to the soldier who got killed today."

"Fortunado Gavilan. I heard. I'm very sorry." Horacio lifted the Makarov, held it, weighed it as he was weighing Ajax for the deepest truth he could discern. For the Makarov it was easy: "Was it unloaded then, too?"

Horacio watched the lips turn in just slightly as Ajax's teeth bit at their insides. "Yeah. He charged Gladys with an empty piece."

"In America, they call that suicide-by-cop."

Ajax dropped his head into his hands and seemed to Horacio to try to wipe something away. "Who cares what the goddamned gringos call anything."

Horacio regarded Ajax for a moment. "You used to like Americans."

Ajax looked up. Horacio watched a wry smile wrestle with a deep fatigue.

"I knew some good ones. Once. In L.A."

"You almost were one, when I found you there. American teenager English. Perfect Nicaraguan Spanish."

Ajax sat back, turned his face to the cloudless night sky. "I don't know who that kid is anymore. He's like someone I read about. I swear, Maestro, I have no memories before that day we marched into camp and you put that .22 peashooter into my hands."

Horacio studied Ajax's face. He seemed to drift back to that long-ago arrival at a pitiful camp of half-starved dreamers. But he needed him in the here and now. He used his cane to sharply rap the Python's chrome.

"And the snake? Still just the one bullet?"

Ajax pulled his gaze from the stars. "The *Python*. Yeah."

"The *same* bullet?"

"So what?"

"You didn't used to court danger unnecessarily."

"Danger?" Ajax snatched up the Python. "Horacio, what is my job? Ninety-nine percent of the perps are piss-poor mestizos ground down by misery, hopelessness, until they snap one night while on a bender and kill whoever is at hand. Wives, children, drinking buddies. Then they get sober and are so full of self-hatred they sit at home and wait for me to arrest them. I don't need bullets. I hardly even need a mind. I'm a street sweeper. That's one thing the Revo hasn't changed. The debris in this country has always been the dark-skinned, the morenos."

"Jesus said, 'The poor will always be with us.'"

"That was easy for Jesus. I don't have omniscient patience." Ajax spun the Python's chamber, pointed it in the air, and pulled the trigger. *Click.* "Eighty-seven. I need that drink *now*."

Horacio was not alarmed by the Russian roulette. Ajax had always appeared crazier than he was. It was how he'd handled the boredom and the bloodletting of their long insurgency.

Horacio upended the unopened bottle and pretended to pour Ajax a large glass of rum. Then did the same for himself.

Ajax lifted his empty glass. "To all those who have died."

"And all those who will."

Ajax tipped his glass. Held the imaginary liquor in his mouth. Seemed to savor it. He "swallowed" and let loose a deep, sensual sigh.

"Ohhhh. I can feel it Horacio. That deep, wonderful burn, the blaze, the glow of the first one of the day."

"Have another?"

"No thank ya sin-your. I prumised a good ameego of mine to watch mah drankin'."

Horacio smiled, gave a little bow, laid his cane across his lap the way the soldier had his AK. "This Gladys you spoke of. Lieutenant . . . Darío? What do you make of her?"

Ajax answered without hesitation, "She's green. But she's a shot-caller. Not a sandbag."

Horacio nodded. It was an old and cruel distinction he'd taught Ajax in the mountains. You divided your troops into two types, the sandbags who were expendable, and the shot-callers you needed to lead. Ajax had found the delineation barbarous, until he'd taken command. Then it had become indispensable.

"I'm actually glad she brought those robots from State Security."

"Robots?"

"Sharpshooters."

Horacio needed another measurement. "Is State Security really so different from the Policía?"

"You ask *me* that!"

"Well, you've been both . . ."

"Is there a difference between cops-and-robbers and spies-and-assassins? I thought we were clear on this subject!"

Ajax slammed his empty glass down. Horacio pretended to pour another, and Ajax knocked it back.

Horacio felt some slight guilt, poking his son in another wound, for the more he'd put Ajax in harm's way, the more he'd thought of him as a son. "Of course we are clear on the subject. I apologize."

"Anyway. If Gladys hadn't brought the robots, she'd've had to shoot the kid. That's no way to start a career."

Horacio could see that Ajax was still shaky, but there was no time for rest. There never had been. He had to move Ajax to the business at hand. "Yes. There's been a lot of dying lately."

Ajax sat up straight, his face golden in the candlelight. Horacio saw the recognition. Ajax knew it was not El Maestro who'd come to comfort him. Nor El Poeta. But The Jesuit.

"Who? Who Horacio? Who else has died?"

Horacio almost laughed at his hooting. Then he remembered that the owl was a night predator—with talons that slay and a beak to shred.

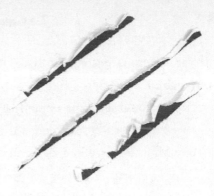

3

"Mira, Harri! *Harri Sucio*! *No dispare Dirtee Harri!*"

Ajax stopped rolling the Python's chamber over his palm and holstered it, to the groans of disappointment from the clutch of children who thought the .357 was a .44. They were the front ranks of the scrum around his crime scene. Or what was left of it. There wasn't a single television in a thousand homes in the poor barrios. So a corpse in a sewage ditch drew everyone from a mile around and provided conversation for a week. Ajax had had a good long look at the body before he'd covered it with some trash bags. He was fairly certain it hadn't been poked and prodded before he'd arrived.

The barrio was just off the Carretera Norte, the Northern Highway that ran past the airport on the way to the mountains. Seven years ago, Ajax had ridden down that very road through cheering throngs, past this very barrio, in a triumphal procession. The barrio wasn't as big then. Now a vast, dense maze of dusty, trash-strewn tracks was lined, cheek-by-jowl, with shacks. Most of them were jigsaw puzzles of discarded pieces of who knew what. The lucky residents had "acquired" a gargantuan packing crate or two—in which a tractor or crane had arrived—and cut windows and doors into it. The Russian, Bulgarian, or Romanian letters stenciled on the sides were still visible, like very neat graffiti. Those with hustle or connections had prized zinc roofs. The adversary of the poor in Nicaragua was not the cold to be kept out, but the torrential rains. Part of Ajax cringed with an ulcerous despair at so much life revolving monotonously around so much scarcity, like a cold planet endlessly circling a weak sun. There would never be enough. He hadn't grown up poor in Los Angeles, but North Hollywood was close enough to it to see it, go to school with it. Poverty in a rich country, though, was a different universe from poverty in a poor country. *The poor will always be with us,* Horacio had reminded him. Bullshit. Only someone whose Daddy was the Creator of heaven and earth could be so blithe about a broke-ass existence in a broke-ass country.

It made Ajax want to slap Jesus.

But the other part of him marveled at the tireless ingenuity, the valiant innovation of making something from nothing. After all, each family here had constructed a home; an impossible tangle of jerry-rigged wires ran from utility poles to each shack where lights kept out the night and radios brought in the world. Impossible vehicles with no glass, doors, or springs, just five-gallon gas jugs sporting a hose plugged directly into carburetors patrolled the streets as "People's Taxis."

It was an ingenuity born of necessity which never overcame the scarcity—like harvesting water from fog. You'd get enough to drink, but only just.

Ajax stood in the shade of a chilamate tree and studied the children. Few things happened in the barrios populares to break the routine, so this corpse, "their corpse," would give them bragging rights in the ramshackle school they would eventually return to. But they were all out of school today. Three days of national mourning had been declared for the death of Joaquin "El Mejicano" Tinoco. And like all the barrios of the capitol, this one was already draped in black flags. Flags as black as the trash bags that covered the corpse at his feet.

"Been a lot of dying lately." Ajax had been shocked to learn from Horacio last night that the news of Joaquin's death would be made public today.

Joaquin Tinoco had been one of the nine comandantes of the National Directorate that actually ran the country—the men behind the president. Ajax had not even known he was sick. But he'd been dropped from the need-to-know list when he'd stopped going to Frente meetings. Still, it would've been nice, it would have been proper, to have visited Joaquin before the cancer ate him up. Joaquin wasn't really Mexican. But the old noms de guerre stuck to you like grafted skin. Joaquin had been born in Mexico and moved to Nicaragua as a child—a mirror image of Ajax, who'd been conceived in Nicaragua and born in the States. Joaquin was one of the oldest living founders of the Sandinista Front. In 1969, Joaquin had marched in with a squad of men to give the oath when Horacio had put Ajax up for full membership. Ajax smiled to remember how solemnly he had taken the vow—"Patria Libre o Morir!"—Free country or death. He'd even memorized a little verse from Nicaragua's national saint, the poet Rubén Darío, to consecrate the moment. But before he'd opened his mouth to recite, Joaquin had cuffed him upside the head. "Don't fuck up, chico. I don't want to have walked all this way for nothing." And the veterans had gone off laughing to scrape together a meal. Por nada, for nothing, had instantly become Ajax's nickname.

That was the first time he'd seen El Mejicano. The last time was two years ago when Ajax had awoken in a hospital bed after wrapping his Lada around a palm tree. Like most drunks, he had an uncanny ability to survive wrecks less damaged than his car. El Mejicano had been in his room—the old comandante still looked after his boys. Ajax had pretended to be out, and watched him a while. Joaquin's face had seemed blank, eyes half-closed, the stupefied look all the old veterans had developed whiling away countless hours of waiting—for food, ammunition, battle, victory, death.

When Ajax had finally "come to" though, so had Joaquin. He'd pitched Ajax's things around the room, the bloody uniform, his battered shoes. When he'd found the Python, Joaquin pulled it from its holster, shucked five bullets out, spun the chamber with the sixth still in, and stuck the pistol into Ajax's hand. *You wanna gamble with your life, Spooky, play for real. Stop wrecking the Revo's cars!*

That one bullet was still in the Python.

A breeze off Lake Managua snaked through the warren of the barrio, rustled the black flags hung for a hero, and lifted the black trash bags covering the corpse at Ajax's feet. It was "his" corpse now.

Ajax watched the crowd. Girls held hands to their mouths and whispered to each other. Boys talked excitedly and pushed each other toward the body, inciting the usual dares.

But Ajax ignored the children. At least the excited ones. He was looking for the quiet kid. The one standing apart, observing, watching with interested eyes. The cadaver was still fresh, no decomposition but just enough stiffness in the joints to make Ajax think it was maybe twelve hours dead. If the perp was local, he'd not be hanging around. But if something bad had gone down at home last night, if an adult had brought guilt into the house, then one of these kids might be wearing a worried look. It took a few minutes, but Ajax spotted him. A skinny, gangly boy with a shaved head, hanging back behind the adults. The only one watching Ajax more than the corpse. Ajax signaled to one of the traffic cops who'd called it in.

"Compa," he said to the man, turning his back to the kid. "Look over my shoulder. You see the boy at the back of the crowd with the shaved head? I need to talk to him. Go up to the road and circle around behind. Bring him here."

The traffic cop walked off, just as Gladys emerged from the crowd.

"Any luck?"

"No one knows him. No one reports anyone missing."

"Didn't think they would. He's not local."

"But you wanted me to ask anyway?"

"Canvassing's always a good idea. Show the flag. Let 'em know we're on the job, that we care. Come on, time to see."

He walked her down to the corpse. The body lay facedown in the muck, still dressed in jeans and a white T-shirt, shoeless, beltless, one limp black sock half off the right foot.

"What do you see?"

Ajax noticed that Gladys clasped her hands behind her back in order not to touch the body, and peered down rather than knelt.

"Well, he's late fifties or early sixties, from the gray hair and bald spot. He's got no shoes. There was no wallet or money or jewelry. They cleaned that out."

"Good, Lieutenant. What does he have?"

"Clothes?"

Ajax knelt next to the body. "Get closer and look closer. What does he have? Look. He's wearing Levi's. Real ones. Look around. See anyone else wearing blue jeans?"

"Right."

"Now turn back the T-shirt. See the tag? 'One hundred percent cotton.' Only cheap polyesters around here. Ring finger?"

"Indention of a ring . . ."

"Wedding ring. But no ring. Same on his head. He's got an indention from a hat, but what kind of hat?"

"You gonna tell me that, Ajax?"

"No. But he will."

The traffic cop, breathing hard, pushed through the crowd with the boy in a headlock. The crowd let out some whistles and calls.

"This little fucker can run, compa."

The kid was squirming like he had a live wire up his ass.

"And you'd've never caught me you pig fucker except—"

"Except for what, mijo?" Ajax rubbed the boy's shaved bristles. "Except for what?"

"Except I tripped."

"Tripped over them new shoes?" Ajax nodded at the ill-fitting cowboy boots on the kid's feet.

"Fuck you!"

"'Fuck you, *compañero* Captain Montoya.'"

"Fuck you, pig fucker."

"Shameless. Lieutenant Darío, we got a bad boy here, a tough guy, a real hard case."

Ajax nodded to the traffic cop who tightened his headlock until the boy squirmed in pain. But the kid uttered not a word of protest, even as his eyes filled with tears. Ajax drew his revolver and held it to the boy's face. "You see this? This is the most powerful handgun in the whole world. . . ."

"Bullshit. That's not a forty-four. It's a three-fifty-seven Python."

"You're good kid. How'd you know that?"

"It's written on the barrel, asshole."

At Ajax's signal the cop eased the headlock.

"So you can read. But let's agree that if you run I will shoot you with it, so you will walk over here to the shade and we will chat, converse, talk."

"Fuck you!"

"That's an affirmative." Ajax signaled the traffic cop to release the boy. The kid was halfway up the sewage ditch before Ajax could blink. But Gladys was faster and wrestled him down into the muck of the ditch. He punched her once, and she would've head-butted him into submission, but Ajax grabbed the kid by the foot and dragged him through the ditch to the shade. The crowd hooted with delight, as a police pickup arrived to retrieve the body.

"How's your head, Gladys?"

"Not bad, but look at my uniform. That little shit-eater."

"Yeah, it's a dirty business."

He told the traffic cop to sit on the kid and met the compas from the pickup. They'd brought only an old army stretcher to collect the remains. Ajax had not disturbed the body, but he wanted a better look at it. He helped them roll it onto the stretcher. Felt the familiar heaviness of the dead that he remembered from burial detail in the mountains. Then he gave the corpse a going-over. The stiff's eyes were open.

There was no bloating. The skin was not dark. Whoever he was, he was a ladino—more European blood than Indian. Blood had clotted at his neck and chest. Whatever had killed him had gone right through the heart. Ajax went through the front pants pockets as he had the back. Empty. Then wiped away some of the muck from the forehead to have a look. No bruising. No signs someone had bashed him in the head.

"Where you taking him?"

The pickup driver shrugged. "Tomas Betulia." As if there was more than the one morgue to take him to.

Every building of any significance in Nicaragua was named for a hero of the nation. The national baseball stadium was named after Rigoberto López, the pistol-packing poet who had dispatched the first Somoza in 1957. Ajax couldn't recall who Tomas Betulia was. But he knew the medical examiner there from a long time back. Doctor Marta Jimenez was a full-lipped, leggy Colombian widow who'd joined the Frente years ago.

"You know Doctora Marta over there? Tell her Captain Montoya said to keep all the corpse's clothes. I've inventoried them." Ajax waved a notebook. He had inventoried nothing. But a pair of genuine Levi's, even freshly scrubbed of death, would fetch many sacks of beans or rice in the Oriental. Even a carton of Marlboros. "Tell her to keep the body on ice, but not to wash it until I get there. Me entiendes?"

"Sí, compa. I understand, but there ain't no ice, not even juice."

"Then whatever. But not to throw away the clothes."

They left, and Ajax looked at the scene again. What a pain in the ass. A morgue with no ice and no backup generator? There'd been talk about it after a big bus crash had coincided with a power outage, and the outrage at sixteen bodies gone bad. Instead of taking care of it, the government had farmed it out to a foreign aid group. Busybodies Without Borders, if Ajax remembered correctly. Either they had no one on the ground in Managua or lacked the sense God gave a stone.

So instead of a generator, they delivered a state-of-the-art industrial ice maker, which worked out very well. Until the next power outage. Ajax had to work fast.

"Gladys, we need this kid's cooperation. You know the old 'good cop, bad cop' routine? We'll do bad cop, worse cop. I'm bad, you're worse."

Ajax thought she smiled a little too readily.

The traffic cop had the kid facedown in an arm lock to keep him from rabbiting again. Ajax admired his tenacity. "All right tough guy, what's your name?"

"Rambo."

"That's a shitty name."

"Why?"

"Rambo's an over-muscled, empty-headed gringo hijueputa. The Contra use that name. You need a better nom de guerre."

"What's that?"

"Your warrior name."

"What's yours? Dick Sucker?"

Gladys unsnapped her holster. "You need a good beating you little barrio rat."

"And your name must be Pussy-Licker, you dyke!"

Gladys backhanded the kid a good one, which raised more hoots, whistles, and calls from the onlookers.

"Lieutenant, would you disperse the crowd for us? Nice and easy, please?"

The kid spat a little blood.

"What's your name?"

The boy paused. Ajax gave a small smile. He'd rid the kid of Rambo, anyway.

"Dirty Harry."

"Christ, kid, another gringo. Don't you know any Nicaraguan heroes?"

"Nicaraguan?"

"Yeah, like the Güegüense."

"The way who?"

"The Güegüense." Ajax trolled out the pronunciation. "The 'way-when-say.' Shit, what school do you go to?"

By the way the kid bent his head, Ajax knew he didn't go anymore.

"The Güegüense always gets out of trouble, and always gets what he wants because he never lies."

"He sounds like an idiot."

"But he also never tells the truth."

"So he does lie."

"No. He doesn't ever lie or ever tell the truth. And that is how he always gets out of trouble."

The kid processed this. His eyes roved, looking for an advantage.

"Did you kill that guy?"

"No!"

Ajax poked at the kid's boots with the toe of his own. "Did you steal his boots?"

"The boots are his, but I didn't steal them."

Ajax lifted the kid's shirt. "Did you steal his belt?"

"The belt is his, but I didn't steal it."

"What time was it when you didn't steal the boots and the belt?"

"Like I have a fucking watch!"

Ajax pulled a cigarette and fished inside the pack with a finger. Two left. He had to get to the smugglers. He smoked a while as the crowd melted away except for two old crazies and a huddle of three small shoeless children—two boys of maybe eight, and a girl around six holding a doll. They hugged each other and eyed Ajax fearfully. His tough guy pointedly did not look at the three kids.

"They your family?"

The kid said nothing.

"That's a yes. Got any parents? Grandparents?"

He shook his head. Ajax waved the three little ones over. "Vengan niños." The kids came as called.

"This your brother?"

The two boys dutifully muttered, "No."

The little girl began to cry. "What do I say, Ernesto?"

"That's a yes," Ajax said. He knelt before Ernesto. "If you don't tell me what you know, I'm gonna take you to a holding cell. What are they gonna do tonight with you gone?"

All fight went out of the kid.

"What time did you find the body?"

"I don't know, man. It was late. The train had passed." The kid motioned to the tracks running down the middle of an adjacent boulevard.

"The train from Estelí. That gives me a time. What else did you see?"

"Nothing, I was out . . . looking around. I saw him there. His pockets were empty. I only took his boots."

Ajax slapped the kid a good one. "Get up, Ernesto." He whipped out his handcuffs, fastened them on too tight and turned on the little ones. "You three get fucking lost!"

"Okay, okay. All right! I'm sorry."

"Last chance or they're on their own."

"I took his ring."

"His wallet?"

"He didn't have one. I swear!"

"His hat?"

"I sold it."

"Baseball or cowboy hat?"

"Cowboy."

"Straw?"

"No, not straw, something else. Gray colored."

With his index finger, Ajax lifted the boy's face. "What'd you do with his keys?"

"Keys?"

"His car keys!"

"No keys, señor. Just the ring."

"And the shoes and the hat and the belt."

"Yeah, and the doll."

Ajax looked at Ernesto's little sister. She dropped her head and held out the doll. Ajax looked it over—one of those colorful Mayan Quiche dolls with an embroidered red top with a blue skirt. Hair of yarn and face drawn in dark pencil. Handmade, Ajax thought. And well made.

"This was on the corpse?"

"Next to it."

"Where's the ring, Ernesto?"

The boy looked at his little sister, who lifted her grimy shirt to reveal a pouch tied around her waist. She handed it to Ajax, who examined the contents: about ten thousand Cordobas in old, dirty bills. Not even a dollar's worth, even at the black market rate. Some weather-beaten photos of the children with a smiling woman in a folkloric outfit at what looked to be a festival. Not more than a year old, from the look of the kids now. And a dull, gold wedding ring. Its history written in every ding and scratch.

Ajax held it up to the children.

"This goes to the man's wife, or family. I'll find them. I promise you that." He unlocked the cuffs. "You keep the stuff you didn't steal, but let me examine the shoes. C'mere."

Ajax led them to his Lada where Gladys waited in a soiled uniform. Ajax reached inside the car, took out a pad, and scribbled something. Then he bent over the boy. "Lemme see those boots, the bottoms. Now the belt, Ernesto."

Ajax scribbled in his notepad. "You know where the Cine Cabrera is, where they show the films?"

"You sending us to the movies?"

"From the Cine Cabrera you walk two blocks toward the lake

and three toward sunset. There's a white house with four palm trees in front. You hear? It's run by foreigners. They help orphans."

Ernesto stood in front of his three siblings like a mother rat, ready for all comers. "We're not orphans!"

"No? Then where's your father?"

"I don't fucking know."

"Your mother?"

"Where is mama, Nesty?" The little girl tugged on Ernesto's T-shirt.

"You know where she is, Claribel." He shot Ajax a look. "She went north and when she's got a job she'll send for us and we'll all go live in Texas."

"That's right," Ajax said, echoing the boy's story. "But until then"—he thrust the paper into Ernesto's pocket—"you go to this house. It's not an orphanage. They won't separate you. It's run by foreigners." Ajax rubbed his thumb and forefinger together. "They got resources. You ask for a Nicaraguan named Marlene. Give her this note. Tell her I sent you. Ajax Montoya. They'll help you out."

Ernesto eyed Ajax like he was a dirty old man with a bag of candy.

"Just trust me on this kid, right?"

"Maybe."

Ajax gave the doll to the little girl and shook Ernesto's hand. His little siblings lined up to do the same. Ajax watched them file off like ducklings into the maze of ramshackle homes. Ernesto turned back. "You didn't say what yours is."

"My what?"

"Your noom de whatever."

"Nom de guerre."

"Yeah."

"In the mountains, fighting Somoza, they called me Ernesto. Everyone wanted to be called Ernesto."

The boy looked like he might actually smile.

Ajax watched the little shipwrecked family drift down the crowded alley, which suddenly felt like a vast and empty shore. He let out a long breath. "'We do not simply manufacture orphans, or raise crows as children.'"

"What does that mean?" Gladys said.

"Cuadra."

"Who?"

"The poet Pablo Antonio Cuadra. 'Third Class Country.' 'We do not fold paper boats to sail puddles, or, inadvertently, raise crows as children.'"

Gladys looked at him like she was waiting for the punch line.

Ajax smiled. It had been an excellent morning. "It means, Gladys, that you must broaden your horizons and embrace the mystery."

"Of what? The stiff? In this barrio? They killed him for his wallet."

"Wrong, Lieutenant Of False Suppositions. Our stiff had knife wounds but no blunt trauma. And 'in this barrio,' you kill someone for his possessions, you bash his fucking head in. But maybe someone wanted to make it look like robbery. I'm not sure yet. The good news is his keys are missing. Whatever vehicle he was driving is still out there. We'll be looking for someone selling a stolen pickup."

"Why a pickup?"

Ajax leaned against his Lada, drew the Python, rolled the chamber over his palm and closed his eyes. "The kid said he took a cowboy hat. Farm workers wear baseball caps, landowners wear cowboy hats. Farm workers with money dress up in straw cowboy hats. You know the kind I mean?"

"Yeah, sure, I've seen them."

Ajax closed his eyes again. "Kid said the stiff's hat was gray, so it was maybe felt, not straw. The ring and the jeans show he's got money. A landowner with money drives a pickup. But he's wearing boots. Landowner with money and a felt cowboy hat doesn't wear cowboy boots on the farm. The boots mean he was driving his pickup to Managua on business, so maybe he's got family here."

Ajax holstered the Python. "If he's got family here, they'll look for him when he doesn't show. Eventually they'll go to the morgue." He opened his eyes. "I hope you're taking notes."

She fished for her notebook. "No, sorry, I mean . . ."

"Just kidding, Gladys. What do you think?"

"It's a lot of ideas, but why not robbery?"

"Why, because of the method of murder. Come here."

Before Gladys could react Ajax had seized her, pressed her back against his belly, and pulled her head back with his left hand, exposing her throat.

"Ever killed anyone with a knife?"

Her body stiffened. "No, Captain."

"Our stiff has stab wounds to the throat and the chest."

He held up his right hand with the thumb skyward like a Roman emperor about to decide someone's fate.

"To get someone in the throat like this"—he brought the thumb slowly in until it pressed lightly against her larynx—"is not so hard, if he's still, like you are now. But if he fights, fights at all, not so easy. You might even miss and get yourself."

He pulled his hand back, and thrust in again, thumb poised between her breasts. "To hit the heart, or at least a lung, is easier, again, if the victim doesn't struggle. But if you get him in the heart, why then go for the throat at all?"

Gladys managed to nod. "I don't know."

"Now if it was a knife fight"—he spun her around and brought quick blows with his hand—"a blow to your throat, what do you do? Bend over, fall down; same with the chest. If you're not dead, you wave your arms. Instinct says, do anything to live. But there were no defensive wounds on the hands or arms. No other blows but those two, one to the chest, one at least to the throat. So he never fought back. And like you said, he looks middle-aged. From his clothes, he wasn't poor. From the calluses on his hands, I'd guess he worked for a living, but not too hard, thus a landowner. So there was no knife fight. Gimme your hand."

Gladys looked at her hands, then reluctantly held out the left one. In one deft movement, Ajax bent her arm over her head, tripped her, gently dropped her onto her back and straddled her.

"But if you put the victim on his back"—with his left hand on her chin, he pushed her head back—"then you can come down clean." He brought his hand down on her throat, raised it over his head to demonstrate the blow to the heart, but then he froze as if turned to salt. His eyes went to the hand holding the imaginary knife and the world seemed to melt away. The harsh sunlight of a city without trees dimmed. The hot urban jungle cooled.

Ajax was surrounded by forest, touched by dappled sunlight, chilled by mountain air putrid with death. The woman beneath him was not Gladys in her dusty uniform, but a middle-aged lady caked in the dark earth of the selva. Ajax had brushed the soil from her ashen, bloated face. Their faces. There had been four of them: two health workers, a teacher, and a local militiaman. All had the same wounds, stabbed once in the throat and twice through the heart. He'd found out later that the Contra had made them dig their common grave. Lie in it and fold their arms over their chests. Then a Contra had straddled each and delivered the fatal blows. This was March or April 1982. It was the first of many such graves unearthed in the mountains during the early days of the counterrevolution. But he re-membered that one woman most. She'd had a hole in her sneaker and her big toe had poked out. The toenail painted red. The little piggy that went to market had gotten all prettied up for it. But the toe had been very white, not discolored like the rest of her. He couldn't stop looking at that toe and had finally pulled the shoe off to solve the mystery of its whiteness. It was a prosthesis. She'd lost her foot just above the ankle and wore a wooden one on which someone had painstakingly—lovingly—carved the separate toes. Not etched on a block, but sculpted, each toe separate from the others, just like a real foot, with toenails and everything. Then she'd painted them red, just like her real ones.

That had stayed with him. That little red toenail in that immense green jungle.

Later, when they'd taken the bodies back to the base in Wiwilí, he'd removed the foot and given it to a French group that made prosthetics for the victims of Contra land mines. For all he knew, someone was stumping around on it right now.

"Ajax?" Gladys' voice cut through the memory.

"Kill the vampire."

"What?"

"Once in the throat, twice through the heart. That's what they called it. 'Killing the vampire.'"

"Who?"

Ajax saw that he still had his hand in the air. He jumped up and helped Gladys to her feet. "Sorry."

"Why are you talking about vampires?"

He shook his head. He didn't trust her yet. "I don't know. Spacing out. Anyway, that's how it happened. They got him on his back and delivered the blows."

He spun her around and brushed the dirt from her back. His mind whirling—could it be?

"Well, that was a sweet dance! Go on, kiss her!"

Ajax hated to be surprised, so he already hated the intruder. He knew what to expect when he turned around. If it was civilians, the tone would have been a more democratic teasing rather than the cold, authoritarian mocking he had just heard. He faced the voice. The mocker was a uniform. Two uniforms. What surprised him was to see the uniforms leaning against a car marked DGSE. Dirección General de

Seguridad del Estado. It was one of the quirks of the Sandinista revolution that State Security, the secret police, traveled the country in clearly marked cars. And the two cocky hijos de puta leaning against it had Seguridad plastered all over their smirking mustachioed faces.

While he gave them the once over, Ajax carefully finished dusting off Gladys's uniform. One man was a major, the other a captain.

"Stonewall these fucks, Gladys," he whispered.

The major sauntered over. "You're Ajax Montoya."

"That why you came here?"

"What?"

"To tell me my name—is that why you came here?"

"I'm Major Pissarro; this is Captain Cortez."

Ajax snorted with delight. "I get it. The *conquistadores.* We've been invaded, Gladys."

The intruders exchanged a brief glance.

"Cortez and Pissarro, the *conquistadores.* You know, Aztecs, Incas. Guess that makes us the Indians." Ajax tried to suppress the laugh he felt welling up, but for some reason failed to muster the will power. Gladys, on the other hand, looked ready to crawl out of her skin.

"We're here about the murder, compañero."

Ajax cut his chuckle. "What murder?"

Captain Cortez stepped forward like he didn't know he was being fucked with. "You just had a body hauled away. That murder."

"Wait, which one are you again? Doesn't matter, but yeah we had a corpse taken to the morgue. We don't know if it's murder. Do you? And if so, how do you know that?"

"Look compa." Pissarro stepped in front of the other, his hands out in reconciliation. "State Security has an interest in this . . . death. We got it from here. Thank you."

"If it is murder, it's Policía, *compa.* That's me and my young lieutenant here. We do cops and robbers. You do spies and assassins. We don't need your help."

Cortez moved like he was waiting for that. "Yeah, well maybe if you'd had our help yesterday that soldier would be alive."

Ajax knew from experience that he could get people to do what he wanted, when he wanted. Not by force of will but more by a kind of telepathy, by telegraphing certain information. He thought of it as creating a vacuum that others unconsciously rushed in to fill. So at Cortez's rebuke he'd taken a step backward as if struck, dropped his eyes to the ground as if shamed, and slumped his shoulders as if defeated.

Cortez took two steps forward. Said almost kindly, "It's okay, compa. You get to take the day off." He sympathetically patted Ajax's shoulder, as Ajax had wanted him to do. Ajax snatched his hand, put Cortez in a shoulder roll, his feet swinging high in the air, then slammed him into the ground, face down in the dirt, arm twisted to the breaking point, and all in what gringos called a New York minute.

"We did have your help yesterday," Ajax hissed in his ear. "You fucking shot him."

He felt Cortez go limp from the pain of his arm halfway pulled off. Ajax was kind of enjoying it, it stirred nearly the same feeling as shooting that crow had. The feeling was cut short by the blow he took behind the ear from Pissarro. Damn! He should've known Gladys wouldn't have his back.

Ajax rolled with the punch, blinking away the stars that swam in his head, flipped onto his back in time to catch the charging Pissarro in the nut bag with his boot heel. Ajax leapt up as the conqueror of the Incas landed in a heap on the destroyer of the Aztecs.

Ajax straightened his uniform. "Someone wants to take my stiff they have to send higher-ranking assholes than you two. Let's go, Lieutenant."

Gladys looked ready to die, mouth wide open, big eyed. Ajax felt that he ought to reassure her, but the pain behind his ear reminded him that she'd failed to jump in. Then, for some reason, he remembered a delightful idea from long ago. He was making a beeline for the DGSE car when he heard the slide on a Makarov.

"Halt!"

Pissarro moaned pitifully and cradled his bruised manhood, but Cortez had his Makarov out. Right off, Ajax saw the tremor in his hand. Shit, more like an earthquake. He smiled and shook his head. "Halt? *Halt?* Where do you assholes do your training?" He made a few quick steps toward Cortez, who retreated the same few steps. "See? You escalated too quickly. What you want from me is cooperation, but you said 'halt.' If I don't 'Halt!' what are you going to do? Shoot me?"

"You want out of your misery, Montoya? I'll do it."

"I'm not miserable, but I dare you. Shit-eating puto." Ajax opened the door of the DGSE car, rolled up the windows, locked the doors and snatched the keys from the ignition.

"Stop!" Cortez waved the pistol at him. The hammer was cocked and there was a finger on the trigger. Ajax realized he might just get him to do it. He saw that Gladys had finally snapped out if it and held her pistol at her side. He wasn't sure she'd fire, or at whom, but at least her eyes were on Cortez.

Ajax waved the keys at him. "Come on. How much provocation can you stand!" He pocketed the keys. Turned his back and took his time getting behind his own wheel. Just as he cranked the engine, Gladys climbed in, shaky and shaken. His only regret was that the Lada didn't have the juice to sow a whirlwind of dust in his wake.

4

1.

The Tomas Betulia Central Morgue was an ugly, low-slung building that had been erected piecemeal amid the ruins of the original morgue, flattened, like so much else, in the '72 earthquake. Inside it was dim. Three windows had been carelessly knocked out of the cinder block walls when power outages had become a regular feature of the Revo. The morgue was as dank and unadorned as death itself. Three beat-up metal trolleys bearing corpses that emitted the nause-ating sweet smell of early putrefaction were backed up like traffic. Plastic temporary caskets lined the walls like indolent orderlies. The air stank of formaldehyde—the poor man's embalming fluid. In a country with only four funeral homes, used almost exclusively by the rich or connected, the dead got buried quickly or pumped full of formaldehyde—which smelled like embalming fluid, only more so. The colossal ice machine stood by the back door leaking tepid water. Ajax's old friend Marta had let him and Gladys sneak through that door after they had spotted the DGSE car parked out front and the two guards posted there. Marta had assured the guards would not interrupt by inviting them to help wash the corpse and witness the autopsy.

Now a clandestine school was in session.

Ajax whispered it: "Touch his penis, Lieutenant."

"What?" she had to whisper back.

"You heard me, Gladys, touch the stiff's dick."

"That's not right, Captain."

"Lift his dick and check under it for clues."

"With what?"

"I told you to have a look at him in the ditch and you tucked your arms behind your back like you're studying a pile of fresh shit. Corpses are our playground. Once you can touch a corpse's genitalia, you can examine the whole thing with ease. Right, Marta?"

"Don't involve me in your initiation rituals, Montoya. You were always a freak around death."

Marta Jimenez was a compa from the old days. An ex-pat from Colombia, still lithe and long haired in handsome middle age, she'd joined the Sandinistas fresh out of medical school in the mid '60s when their cause made tilting at windmills seem the sport of sages. She'd spent years making miracles in the mountains. And not just with bullet wounds and amputations. She'd saved more limbs than she'd sawed, conjuring penicillin out of moldy bread; kept the compas' blood strong with iron supplements alchemized from nails in jugs of water. The compas had sometimes called her Doctora Higado Mono—Doctor Monkey Liver—because she made them hunt and eat it for the vitamin A. But her nom de guerre had been Mami. She'd picked lice from their hair, hovered over their nasty feet fighting jungle rot, and wiped asses when dysentery was killing them. Hers was the last face many a compa had seen. She was now the chief pathologist in Managua—meaning the only one in the whole country.

"But you agree, Marta, that a corpse must become a thing if it is to be studied?"

In reply, Marta handed Ajax a pair of gloves—not surgical gloves, but the kind the maids of the rich wore while doing dishes.

"Why don't you show her, Ajax?"

Ajax pulled the gloves on.

"He uses these when he plays with himself, you know."

"Not this actual pair, Gladys; I keep some at home."

Ajax ran his hand expertly over the corpse. Stiffness had crept into the limbs, but he lifted them, running his fingers over the skin, looking closely.

"Some long scratches here on the right forearm."

Marta nodded. "Yeah. Mostly healed. Looks like a cat."

Ajax rolled the body to look at the back, ran his fingers through its hair.

"How long he's been dead, Mami?"

"Rectal thermometer's ready to come out."

"You have one of those?"

"Used to hang on the wall over there."

Ajax looked archly at Gladys. "Lieutenant?"

"No fucking way."

Ajax slid it out and handed it to Marta.

"Fifty-six Fahrenheit."

He finished his examination. Then, because he had to, he lifted the penis and looked under it. He pointed the head at Gladys and wiggled it. "Don't be afraid of me, Lieutenant!"

Gladys turned her face away. Ajax saw she was truly embarrassed.

"Ajax, have some goddamn respect," Marta said.

"Sorry, Marta. Sorry, Gladys. We've got to objectify the corpse. It's just ground to be searched for clues." He ran his fingers through its hair again. "And I do feel a bump on the back of the head."

Gladys perked up, suddenly interested. "Maybe someone did bash his head in?"

Marta ran her fingers over the same spot. "I don't think so."

Ajax pulled his glove off. "Tell me his story, Marta."

Marta pulled her gloves off, crossed her arms, and looked at the corpse like a sculptor at uncut stone. "He's a ladino. Mid-fifties. Got calluses on his hands, but not enough to be a laborer. With his good clothes and body fat I'd guess a farmer or rancher, but a landowner, not a worker. You saw the discoloration on the back of the left knee?"

Ajax nodded, lifted the leg to show Gladys.

"It's pre-mortem. By the color, a bruise from a blow delivered just before death. Maybe a kick. I found some loose hairs on the back of his head, so I'd say he was struck on the back of the leg. That brought him to his knees, then his hair was yanked to put him on the ground. That's when he got the bump on the head. The killer then straddled his chest and delivered the blows with a knife."

Ajax smiled, more self-satisfied than self-righteous. "We went over that very scenario at the crime scene."

Marta shrugged. "The blade was about three inches wide."

Ajax grunted. "Three inches across is a big knife."

"Doubled-edged, too. Straight down and in. Ninety degrees to the neck and chest. See?" Marta took a pen and slid it into the chest wound. "You should notice this, Lieutenant."

Gladys grimaced, took the pen, and slid it up and down into the wound. Ajax did the same.

"How many wounds, Marta?" Ajax asked, but he'd already counted them. He was hoping he was wrong.

Marta waited before answering. "Three. Once in the neck and twice through the heart." She looked into Ajax's eyes as if she wanted him to speak next. Instead they both just stood in silence.

Gladys looked from one to the other. "That important?"

"No." Ajax realized he'd spoken too fast, but he wanted to cut off Marta's response. If he was right, he wasn't yet ready to share the info with Gladys. He had a hunch she'd been assigned his partner to keep an eye on him. "No, no, it's not important." He realized he'd said too many no's. "Well, thank you, Dr. Jimenez." Ajax felt his heart beat faster in a familiar way; his thoughts spun like a chance wheel at a carnival. *This is how the Contra execute people.*

A sudden commotion in the outer office brought him out of himself. The three of them froze. Marta pointed at the connecting door, mouthed, *It's locked.*

She and Ajax slipped to the door. Marta showed him a place

where the mortar in the cinder block had cracked. He had a long look through it. A tall, blond gringo was haranguing one of the State Security guards. With him was a campesino with the hawk nose and high cheekbones of a mountain peasant. He was dressed in his Sunday whites, looking at the floor.

"He is the man's cousin." The gringo spoke slowly to the State Security guard as if to a child, the way they all did when not getting their way. As if his being denied something could only come from a misunderstanding. "The man is missing. Do you understand 'missing person'? We just want to know if there are unclaimed bodies here. We want to speak to someone."

The guard wiggled his index finger. "No bodies here, señor."

"There are no bodies in *the morgue*?"

Then the gringo turned and seemed to look right into the spy hole. Ajax recognized him. He took a half step backward as if pushed by a memory. He glanced back at the corpse—back at the crime scene his instincts had told him this murder might need some stones overturned to solve. The Conquistadores showing up had confirmed that notion. Now he wondered if an avalanche was in the offing.

"*Puta madre.*"

He let Marta have a look, then drew her away from the door.

"You know him, Mami?"

"Do you?"

"Es periodista. A gringo journalist. He hooked up with us when we were clearing out Matagalpa. Must've been spring '79. You don't remember?"

"I wouldn't unless he got shot."

"Not enough of them did." Ajax had another look. "What's his name? Marcus. Mateo, maybe. Matthew something. He was a pain in the ass like all of them, eating our food, drinking our water." Ajax turned the memory over in his mind like old compost. "But he had lots of cigarettes. I taxed him heavy on those."

Ajax smiled.

"What is it?" Marta asked.

"I sent him through the lines one night to get more. Figured either the Guardia would kill him or he'd take refuge in the nearest hotel."

Ajax looked through the crack again. "Son of a bitch was back the next day with every pack of cigarettes in the city. We smoked 'em all the way to Managua."

"He had balls."

Ajax dismissed the idea with a wave. "He just wanted a story."

"Did he get it?"

Ajax smiled again.

"Don't know. The next day we left him under a tree. Told him we'd be right back." Ajax peeked through the crack. "Ain't seen him since."

"Now here he is. Looking for your guy?"

"Gotta be. The campesino with him is country, not a refugee. You said my corpse is from the countryside."

The voices rose on the other side of the wall. The gringo threatening the guard with all the big shots he would report him to if he did not get his way. The guard was unmoved, however, and the two men left. Ajax fished out his keys and tossed them to Gladys.

"There's a tall gringo headed for the parking lot. Got a campesino with him in his Sunday whites. Take the Lada, don't approach. Just follow him."

"For how long?"

"Until he gets home."

"Should I question him?"

"No, just tail him."

"Why?"

"Why what?"

"Why am I just going to follow a gringo reporter?"

"You're not just following a gringo reporter. You're following orders. Now get going, Lieutenant. When you make his house, come back and get me."

Ajax turned back to the corpse. As Gladys exited, sunshine flooded through the door into the dark morgue and the dead man briefly flared a ghostly white.

Ajax shook his head in wonder. *"A la gran puta."*

"What is it?"

"You first."

"What?"

"You know."

"You want me to say it?" Marta touched the corpse's wounds. "Okay. I led some medical brigades up north back in '81 . . ."

"And?"

"And I've seen it before, up in Pantasma and El Cua. Once in the throat, twice in the heart. This is a Contra execution."

"Could it be an accident? Just lucky?"

"No. Not just *lucky*. The heart wounds are clean. You tilt the blade so it's vertical, it'll hit bone, gets deflected, especially by the breast bone. Tilt it horizontally and it'll slide right between the ribs, which is what your killer did." She looked down at the corpse. "Whoever wielded the knife knew what he was doing."

"Hijueputa."

"So someone read about it or . . ."

"No, Marta. We never told anyone. Kept it real quiet. The National Directorate was sending thousands up north—literacy, immunization, the coffee harvest. Shit, who would've answered the call up knowing *that* fate awaited them in a shallow grave?"

Ajax laid his hand on the corpse's chest. "I'm sorry señor. I misjudged you. I saw you in the ditch and thought 'this could be interesting.' But now . . . " Ajax lightly touched the telltale wounds. "This is *interesting*, exciting, fascinating."

He drew a clean but sadly stained sheet over the body. "Or not. Depending."

"On?"

"On whether this is murder or war."

"Don't make me point out the thin line between those two."

"Thin *and* porous. You know . . ."

"Look, if you're gonna stick around, fine. I gotta get this guy ready before he turns."

Marta went to a stainless steel sink surrounded by open cupboards crowded with unmarked bottles. She mixed chemicals from several smaller bottles into a gallon jug and shook the concoction vigorously. The motion jiggled her hips and breasts and brought a smile to Ajax.

"Can I help you with anything?"

"Grab that pump up there." She nodded at a high shelf over the sink.

Ajax got it down.

"We have to pump this guy dry and fill him with that," she said.

"Which is what?"

"My witch's brew—two parts formaldehyde to one part urine. The poor man's embalming fluid."

"Puta!" Ajax held the jug away from his body as if its nastiness might seep through the glass.

"You want the real stuff, go to Miami. Embalming is not even in my job description. Besides, the enzymes in urine have almost miraculous properties, you might remember."

"I remember you had us pissing on ourselves almost as much as in the woods."

"Cured your jungle rot."

She laid out the pump, her jug of brew, and a scalpel. "You pump out his blood and I'll listen." Marta inserted a needle almost as large as her pinky into the rubbery blood vessel. She connected it to a translucent tube attached to a device that looked to Ajax like it was made to siphon gas from a car. "By the way, you should cut Gladys some slack. She's all right. Now pump, slow and steady."

Ajax did as told, and on the third stroke blood drained into a bucket on the floor.

"Good," she said. "Keep pumping. You were saying: murder or war?"

"If this is a simple murder, why was it done? Despair. Passion. Power. Money. I'll figure that out."

"Very modest of you."

Ajax ignored or hadn't heard the barb. "But what if it *is* war, a military tactic? What's the Contra's great weakness?"

"They're the hired thugs of the yanqui sons of bitches?"

Ajax chuckled. "Well said. And mostly true. But their problem, their embarrassment, is that they're stuck on the margins, near the borders, sneaking up from Costa Rica"—he pulled the plunger up— "and down from Honduras"—he pushed the plunger down. "In our day, when we were so few, all we needed was one volunteer in every city to fire one bullet into the air every night. The Guardia had to oc-cupy the whole country. The Contra have no presence in the cities, but only the countryside, which is mostly empty. You gotta drive twelve hours to find them, if you're lucky."

"How's the bucket?"

"Not even half full."

"Go on," she said.

"Okay. So the Contra can't open an urban front. They're getting pressure from the paymaster in Washington to expand the war to the cities, but they can't. What's the cheap way to do that? Smuggle in a murder squad, start killing civilians like our friend here, your morgue starts to fill, the civilian population gets real nervous. Serial killer? Ritual murder? A cult? You can see the headlines. Is he deflating?"

The corpse's cheeks had puckered so its lips pouted.

Marta patted the corpse's cheek. "Pretty much. Means you've

emptied the veins close to the skin, a good sign. He'll refill once we pump him back up. Let's switch."

Marta removed the needle. Taped the corpse's scrotum and penis to his belly and opened his groin to reveal the artery. "What's your point, Ajax?"

"My point, Mami, is—what's the point?" He shook his head like a baseball coach watching the opposing team take the infield. "It's too labor intensive. If you infiltrate troops, open an urban front, why cut throats? Why not throw grenades in the market? That'd cause a panic. If this is not simple murder but a message, who's the message for?"

Marta plucked a newspaper from her lab coat pocket, laid it on the corpse, and unfolded a copy of the government's hot-headed newspaper, *Barricada*. "What about this?" She inserted the pinky-needle into the groin artery. "Keep pumping."

The banner headline yelled, "Yanqui Senators Arrive To 'Find Facts.'" Underneath it, "Senator Teal Leads Imperialism's Delegation."

"You suggest the Contra are putting on a show for these gringo senators?"

"I only deal in dead certainties, Ajax. It's why I like my job." She checked the tube running into the bucket. "I think we're ready to fill him back up. So what's your point?"

"It does not add up. The M.O. doesn't coincide with robbery-homicide. The anonymity of the act does not coincide with a military strike for propaganda purposes."

"And so?"

"I don't know. I don't know. I just got a feeling."

"One of Spooky's feelings? They never steered you wrong in the mountains." She laid her hand on his arm. "You never steered us wrong."

"That's because none of us knew what the fuck we were doing. How hard was it to look good? Bunch of blind blundering bastards."

"Blundered all the way to Managua."

"Yeah, how about that? Got the two things we never expected—to win, and live to see it." Suddenly Ajax was tired. His chest seemed to fill with exhaustion. He set down the pump, rubbed his face, felt the still-tender bump behind his ear where Pissarro had hit him.

"What is it, Spooky?"

Only the old veterans used that name. No one else knew it, or dared if they did.

"Been a lot of dying lately, Mami. That soldier yesterday in Jorge Dimitriov."

She tapped the paper on the corpse's belly. "I read about that."

"Now this guy shows up here bearing Contra wounds that make no sense." He nodded at the black banner surrounding *Barricada*'s masthead. "El Mejicano."

"Poor Joaquin. That was a long time coming."

"You knew he was dying?"

"Hey, I'm still in the loop."

He ignored the gentle barb.

"Ajax, there'll be a gathering of the old veterans after the funeral. At Gioconda's."

Ajax winced like she had picked a painful scab. "Why her house? She's not one of us."

"Who cares? The old guard will be there. You should come."

Ajax shook his head no, but said, "Yeah. I should go."

Marta tapped him gently on the shoulder. When he turned, she cupped her hands around his face, something she'd done when tending the wounded in the mountains. "She's your ex now. Move on."

"It's not that. I don't know what it is. Been a lot of dying. . . ."

"No." She poked him three times in the forehead. "That's all up here. What's down here?" And she poked three times on the chest.

"Vos sos gitana, Marta." You're a gypsy.

"I don't need a crystal ball to see into you, Montoya." She took the pump from his hands, looked into his eyes, awaiting a revelation he could not offer.

"I don't know Marta. I really don't know what's going on."

She leaned her nose in close to his lips. "You look good, Ajax. Real good. Your eyes aren't bloodshot"—she sniffed at his lips—"and your breath doesn't smell of that swill you used to cover up the booze. How many days?"

"Six."

"How're you sleeping?"

"A bad night's sleep would be a good night's sleep."

"Here." She went over to the far wall, to a cabinet streaked with rust where the roof had leaked on it. "What made you go cold turkey?"

"Only way to silence Horacio, quiet him, make him shut up."

She took out a vial of pills. "That man loves you."

"That would explain the not shutting up."

She held up the vial. "Valium. Take two before bed each night for the next five nights. Your system should settle after that."

"Many of your patients need Valium?"

"Sometimes I go through their belongings. Just for the meds."

Ajax took the pills. Kissed her cheek. "Take care of my corpse, Marta. He's a VIP."

Marta spread her hands, taking in her dingy domain. "It's an exclusive club."

2.

Sub-comandante Vladimir Malhora was Commander of the Directorate General for State Security, Chief Protector of the Revolution, and Guardian of the People's Will.

The J. Edgar Hoover of Nicaragua.

Secretly, he liked that one best. He admired Hoover, even if he was an anti-Communist hijo de puta. Malhora had read up on him. On Beria, too. Joe Stalin's head of state security had had even more power than Hoover—the absolute power of life or death. But the first order of business after Stalin's demise had been to execute Beria. It was the only thing Papa Joe's inheritors had agreed on. Hoover, however, had survived seven presidents. Fifty years in power! Republican or Democrat, liberal or conservative, no one had dared to mess with Hoover. That was power! Even if he was a fag.

Of course, Hoover had built himself a palace for a headquarters and Malhora only had the humble Casa Cincuenta, House Fifty, tucked up behind the InterContinental Hotel as his. And Hoover perhaps had not had so many incompetents to carry out his will. Malhora lit a lovely Cuban cigar as he listened with mixed emotions to the report from Cortez and Pissarro. He took his time firing the end and then blew a long trail of smoke while he considered the portrait of Sandino hanging on his wood-paneled wall.

Augusto César Sandino was the idol of the Revo who'd given his name to the Sandinista Front for National Liberation. The diminutive freedom fighter, two parts George Washington to one part Joan of Arc, had done the unimaginable when he'd fought ten thousand US Marines to a standstill after they'd invaded Nicaragua in the 1920s to make the country safe for banana lovers everywhere. The Marines, like the US Cavalry before them hunting Crazy Horse, couldn't beat Sandino, so they invited him to a peace conference where the very first Somoza had him assassinated.

The portrait, now bathed in Malhora's cigar smoke, depicted Sandino as he was—a pint-size man in a ten-gallon hat. But that hat had become an icon around the world.

Malhora liked the portrait because it reminded him that Sandino had been short, too. Like Hoover. Like himself.

Malhora didn't want this corpse to call attention to itself. He didn't like what he was hearing from the Conquistadores (he had borrowed the quip from Montoya). Nor did he like the frown of disapproval that spread over the visitor's face as they unfolded their tale. He didn't like the visitor still presuming to judge him at all. He didn't even like hearing the name "Ajax Montoya." He had first heard and read the name in Mexico during the final months of the insurrection.

Glowing accounts of Montoya's column rolling over Somoza's National Guard as he swept down from the northern mountains, leaving peace in his wake. The press had dubbed him *El Príncipe de la Paz*—The Prince of Peace. Newspapers and television, with their need to weave naïve narratives with crude heroes spun from simpleton soldiers! None of them knew of the secret work Malhora had done for years all over the world. And continued to do now. The clandestine meetings, shape-shifting bank accounts, ghostly merchant ships, and magical manifests that had nurtured and nourished an insurrection weren't "sexy" in the way a bearded grunt with a chrome-plated pistol was. As if this month's centerfold had no bones and gristle holding up her tits!

It had begun as envy, Malhora knew it. But it had transformed into something else that May Day party at the Cuban embassy when he'd felt compelled not only to lie about knowing Montoya, but to regale one and all with tales of their friendship. And he *had* pursued a friendship with the ungrateful son of a bitch—had teamed up with him in State Security in the early days of the Revo, only to discover the "great man" was a wild-eyed dreamer, the worst kind of romantic bourgeois. And then that night. That fateful night in Los Nubes when Malhora had killed for the first time. Montoya had come running out of the darkness and struck him! Not even a manly blow but backhanded him like a servant who'd broken a family heirloom. Malhora's feeling had hardened into cold hate, and he had filled a file with Montoya's drunken fall since. And who was the great man now?

Malhora's cigar had gone out. He regarded the dead ash the same way he studied the Conquistadores, wondering again if he had chosen his instruments well. "So this notorious drunken fool beat the crap out of both of you for everyone to see and left you stranded in some barrio where you had to beg help to get your car back, a car marked DGSE just to make sure everyone knew you two donkeys belonged to me."

The Conquistadores silently consulted each other for some way

to improve their boss's summary, but could find none. "Sí, Comandante."

Malhora knocked the dead cinders from his cigar but missed the
porcelain ashtray, a personal gift from his Chinese counterpart.

"And so you were late getting to the morgue, which is why you
did not prevent him from entering and questioning the doctor."

"Sí, Comandante."

"Neither did you arrive in time to question the gringo journalist."

"No, Comandante."

Malhora fired up his sterling silver Zippo lighter—a personal
gift from the Soviet foreign minister Andrei Gromyko. He leaned
over and lit the visitor's cigar. The visitor seemed bemused by the
shameful tale, which only further annoyed Malhora.

He snapped the lighter closed. "Compañeros, you two have
shit yourselves pretty well on this. I am closely watching your per-
formance. Put someone on the gringo journalist and milk his phones.
Find out who the peasant is. Follow the dyke. You two personally
record everything Montoya does."

"Sí, Comandante!"

"By the way, Captain Cortez . . ." The visitor spoke as if he'd remembered an unimportant detail. "You drew your weapon on a hero
of the revolution. He might be debased now, but had you killed him,
all his sins would've been forgiven. Imagine how it would've reflected
on your *Comandante* had two of *his agents* done such a thing."

Malhora had reveled in that part of the tale, had briefly wished
Cortez had done just that. Now he saw the horror of it. Goddamn
Montoya would win even by dying.

"That's right you shit brains. He ever attacks you again, let him.
Do not fight back unless he kills one of you. In fact, let him kill both
of you. Now get out!"

Their faces never changed, never quavered. They did not smile
when he complimented them, nor frown when he browbeat them.
Malhora actually rather liked them. He hoped he had chosen them

well. He sat back, smoked, and regarded the visitor. He didn't like him, found his presence an unnerving reminder of the past when Malhora had been the junior partner. Still, he was a deep thinker.

"Comandante," the visitor began, "about this corpse."

"We'll make it go away. Have no fear."

"Oh, I am utterly confident. But if the corpse is to be seen as a simple homicide, mightn't this gringo reporter ask why State Security is involved in it?"

Malhora blew smoke at the portrait of Che Guevara on the other paneled wall, next to the window overlooking the lake. "Well, maybe the Contra *did* kill him."

"Yes. But the timing is . . . delicate. The yanqui senators arrive tomorrow. Nothing inflammatory should occur during that visit, or before they vote."

"Their minds are already made up."

"True. The $100 million will get to the Contra. But the visit *here* is as much about those who *oppose* them in the gringo Congress. The enemies, or at least, the opponents of our enemies, as it were. Nothing should occur to undermine *them*. Not even the appearance of controversy. The National Directorate is very clear on that."

With that one comment, the visitor touched Malhora's soul. He stroked his Stalin mustache vigorously, as he always did when the wheels of his ambition turned. Above all else he had to be seen as serving the National Directorate. He did not care a monkey's ass about what the yanqui Congress and their retard-actor president did. They could vote whatever monies they wanted to the Contra. The more war there was, the more his domain grew. But the eight remaining Comandantes of the Directorate would soon have to replace Joaquin Tinoco. Malhora was a breath away from that prize. Only one of the nine could become president.

It had once seemed impossible. Joaquin Tinoco had detested Vladimir Malhora. Unfairly, true, but openly detested him. He was just like Montoya. As if a man's abilities or loyalties could be measured only in how many years he spent creeping around the mountains with little more than bows and arrows. Vladimir Malhora had spent the war in Mexico, true, but in Mexico he cultivated the contacts with the Soviets and Cubans, the Bulgarians and Romanians that had paid off so handsomely in weapons and training. And now El Mejicano was dead. Malhora felt his stars continue to align just as the hairs on his mustache did under the careful grooming of his heavy fingers. Align as they had since the night at Los Nubes when he'd killed that fool Salazar. He had followed the visitor's advice that night, too.

"So . . ." Malhora trimmed the ash from his cigar.

"So if Captain Montoya is as unstable as he appears to be, then his failure—which we *all* so adamantly hope for—his failure in this matter will just be bad policing by a bad policeman. Not politics. Whereas everything State Security does is political."

"So who better than Ajax Montoya to fuck up the investigation?"

"If you think so, Comandante."

Yes, he did. He was sure of it.

5

Matthew Connelly—freelance journalist extraordinaire—stood in his bathroom looking at himself in the mirror. The afternoon heat beaded sweat on his forehead while he practiced an acceptance speech for an award he had not yet been nominated for.

He was certain that journalists and writers all over the world began their mornings the same way. But he felt close, so close now. If his full-time war reportage from the mountains didn't put him up for a Pulitzer, then the book he was closing in on must.

"This award is not for me, but for the people of Nicaragua."

Yeah, that would do it.

Then the doorbell rang.

"Shit."

"Matthew, le buscan!" That was his housekeeper, Graciela.

"Momento, Graciela. Momento!"

Someone's looking for you! At this or any time of day—post-siesta—the doorbell could mean bill collectors, panhandlers, vendors of almost anything—last time it had been his errand boy, Jerónimo, with an ocelot cub on a rope. Still, a quiet caller who simply knocked was a blessing compared to the daily street vendors below his window—usually while the sun was still cruelly low—crying, "Mangooooooos! Fruuuuuuuutas! Banaaaaaaanos! Tomates! Ce-booooooooooooyas" in that distinctive, ear-splitting, high nasal screech of the street merchant. In fact, it was a kind of extortion. They might as well be screaming, "Buy my pathetic fruit or I will stand here and drive you mad with my screeeeeeeeching." As often as not, he did.

But whoever it was now would have to wait. He was late sending copy and the afternoon deadline raced toward him. He'd even left Epimenio parked downstairs under the care of Graciela, whose roots in the countryside put Epimenio at his ease. He looked back into the mirror. *What a trip this place is.* He'd gone to bed last night ready to wake up this morning and send copy or tape to every one of his seven major strings. Instead, even before he'd coffeed up, Graciela had called *Matthew, le buscan!* And he'd found Epimenio perched downstairs on the edge of a rattan chair in his Sunday whites like some great egret. Matthew knew Epimenio well from his many visits to Enrique Cuadra's coffee farm, and Epimenio's arrival *sans* Enrique had seemed strange. But nothing could have prepared Matthew for the bombshell Epimenio had dropped: *Don Enrique asks that you help find his murderer.*

What the fuck was he supposed to do with a line like that?

"Matthew, le buscan!"

"Momento, Graciela. Momento!"

Matthew turned to the mirror to scrutinize his reflection. He didn't look bad. Blond hair, not prematurely gray; deep blue eyes, neither lined with bags nor bloodshot; white teeth un-rotted; and a pink tongue uncoated with bad news. Even his long nose was still straight, despite having been broken twice diving for cover.

But he felt *tired*.

"I am bushed from all that bush."

It was a cutesy line he'd coined for dinner parties and cocktails with friends when they inquired after his health.

But that wasn't it either. He was scared.

Matthew Connelly was the only truly full-time war correspondent in a country whose war was a major headline around the world. He had remade himself from an adventure-seeking tourist from Boston Catholic into a freelance journalist whose byline was read in every

capitol from Washington to Moscow. Matthew was the only inde-
pendent witness to the hottest proxy battle between the Cold War
superpowers. In Managua, he was a downright luminary: visiting
journalists and broadcasters, dignitaries, celebrities, the Managua-
based diplomats, and especially the military attachés all wanted brief-
ings from him. It was lucrative, too, kept a staff of four working in a
house grander than any he'd known back in Boston, nor was likely
ever to know. It was his future, too. If he could gather enough material
to finish his book on the war, it would open doors to any newspaper or
magazine back home.

All he had to do to remain a big fish in a small pond was to not
get killed delivering the goods.

He locked back onto his own eyes in the mirror. That last trip
north. He had tape and photos from the biggest firefight yet. An actual *battle* between Contras and the battalion of government troops
he was writing a biography on. But six more of the original one
hundred and sixty boys he'd been writing about were dead. A total of
thirty-one KIA in a year. His editors *should* love it. But the phone
messages last night were all about Senator Teal and the death of
Joaquin Tinoco. It was a fucking parlor game to them—a game played
in Washington, Miami, and Managua. He had to fight every time to
get space for the war in the countryside.

Then his white phone rang.

Then his blue phone rang.

He drew himself up in the mirror. He shook off the funk. Matthew Connelly liked this part of the job.

"Showtime!"

By the time he crossed from the bathroom to his desk, he had
done his dispatches in his head. He snatched up the blue phone, NBC
radio: "Sheila? I'm ready. One second."

He snatched up the white phone, the *Miami Herald*, "Paul? Pass
me to the tone. I'm sending now. Six hundred words on the senators,
and four hundred on who'll replace Joaquin Tinoco."

What a world! Matthew had stayed long enough to see the journalism biz rocket into a new age. For years he'd had to laboriously dictate his stories over the phone and have them read back to him, or, worse, to go down to the international exchange and bang them out on the old Teletype and then hand feed the tape into the machines. But now, these new RadioShack computers let you store 1,200 words and then send over the phone to any newspaper office in the world. (As long as the international operator didn't mistakenly cut in, or the wind wasn't blowing the telephone wires too hard.) Soon they'd be coming out with a model that could store 2,000 words!

He stuck the white phone's handset into the rubber cups and sent his copy to the *Herald*. Then he went back to the blue phone—NBC radio—closed his eyes a moment and composed.

"Sheila? Okay, recording in three, two, one: Nicaragua's ruling Sandinista Front is engaged in their biggest internal crisis in years as different factions fight to place one of their own on the National Directorate, which makes all policy for the beleaguered country. The Nine, as they are known, became eight with the death of Joaquin Tinoco, known as *El Mejicano*. Tinoco was one of the last original founders of the Front to serve on the Directorate, and his replacement represents a generational turnover. The only candidate openly talked about for the position is Vladimir Malhora, the current head of State Security, who is known as a hardliner. The skirmish takes place against the backdrop of tomorrow's arrival of a fact finding mission from the US Senate whose verdict will sway the pending vote in Congress on a one-hundred-million-dollar aid package for the Contra rebels, which will likely pass and instigate a huge escalation of the war. For NBC radio, this is Matthew Connelly in Managua. Three, two, one. Out. How was that?"

Sheila would have a supercilious comment or two, or three, to make. Every editor he'd ever had believed reporters were simpletons sent to the field because they didn't have the brains to be editors.

"I used 'known' twice? Okay, I'll do another one for another fifty bucks, but then I just used 'another' twice, too . . . What? Great. I'll send the profile of Malhora to the mainframe for the commuter rotation."

He hung up, checked his copy had gone to the *Herald*, and walked to the bathroom, running the abacus in his head. Between Tinoco's departure and the senator's arrival, the radio pieces alone would cover expenses for two months. The newspapers would surely cover his R&R to Belize in September. He flipped open the medicine cabinet and ran his finger along the rows of pills. He chose a Praziquantel for his Olympian battle with intestinal parasites. It would turn his stools rock hard. He hadn't had a satisfying bowel movement since 1984.

He closed the medicine cabinet, had a good look at himself in the mirror, and dry chewed the Praz.

"*Matthew! Le buscan!*"

He did not hurry downstairs, but as he went, he picked up the faint murmur of Spanish from his sala. To his surprise, he saw two uniforms, a captain and a lieutenant, seated around his matching rattan rockers and table. Graciela, he noticed, had laid out the good cups and served up the good coffee in the French press. Epimenio sat with them, ramrod straight, his face the stoic blankness of the campesino in the presence of power. And for a campesino, that was pretty much everybody. Matthew's left foot had just touched the marble tile of the sala floor when he recognized the captain's face. For a split second, he was amazed. *Son of a bitch, that's Ajax Montoya!* But then the full memory flooded back. *Ajax Montoya, that son of a bitch!* For a very long moment he stood staring at the captain, who kindly returned the stare.

"Got a cigarette?"

Montoya patted his pockets. "No."

"Do I know you?"

"I don't think so."

"And you don't have a *cigarette*?"

Montoya held his hands up. "I don't smoke."

"You don't smoke."

Neither of the uniforms had risen, so Matthew looked at the short-haired lieutenant with the crisp uniform. "How about you?"

"She doesn't smoke either."

"Does she have a *name*?"

She stood up smartly. "Lieutenant Gladys Darío."

He shook her hand.

"Nice to meet you, compañera. I'm Matthew Connelly. This is my house."

"Yes, compañero, we know."

"Do you? How?"

Matthew was sure he saw a flicker of a smile on Montoya's face. But Epimenio remained stock-still, not knowing what part was his in the game. Matthew released Gladys's hand and turned back to the son of a bitch who, seven years ago, had abandoned him under a tree after he'd risked his life to bring back a bag of cigarettes meant to secure his passage all the way to Managua in the company of the most renowned guerrilla leader of the day. It would have been a hell of a story, and now here he was sitting in Matthew's chair, drinking his coffee and pretending not to remember him.

"I'm sure we know each other. Ajax Montoya right?"

Montoya stood and held out his hand. Matthew took it and pumped in a friendly way, but he was sure he detected recognition in Montoya's eyes and felt he was being fucked with.

"I didn't think the Policía Sandinista were of interest to you big-shot international journalists."

"Well, you weren't always Policía." Matthew scrutinized his insignia. "Captain now, is it? You used to work State Security, didn't you? As a colonel?"

Montoya's grip seemed to lessen. Matthew gave in to the affront of being fucked with and decided to fuck back: "Weren't you involved in the killing of Jorge Salazar?"

The iron went back into Montoya's grip before he broke the handshake and sat down. The lieutenant sat up straight and almost turned the French press over trying to pour more coffee.

"Lieutenant, you look kind of young, do you remember *l'affaire Salazar*? Cotton grower back in '81 got caught up in a CIA plot to turn the army high command against the National Directorate, staged a coup d'état." Matthew took the French press from her fumbling hands and poured for her. "Salazar was shot by State Security agents, some say executed, at a gas station up in Los Nubes. They found some weapons in his trunk." He turned to Montoya: "Or maybe you found the weapons, Colonel. I mean Captain. More coffee?" He overfilled Montoya's cup.

"I only bring it up, Lieutenant, as it was one of my first front-page stories. Graciela!" Graciela hurried into the sala from the kitchen. The look on her face showed Matthew she'd heard every word and disapproved of every one.

"Sí, don Matthew?"

"Bring the Oreos from the Diplo store. Would you like a cookie, Captain Montoya?"

A rueful smile had come over the captain's face. It didn't connect to the look in his eye.

"Lieutenant, cookies?"

She shook her head. "No."

Matthew was pretty sure she wasn't talking about the cookies.

"So." He leaned closer to the lieutenant, as if catching her up on old-school stories he and Montoya shared. "After the killing, the MINT put the weapons on display and a photographer friend took close-ups of them, close enough to get the serial numbers, which I was able to track back to an East German weapons shipment that State Security received the previous year. Bingo! Front page!"

Matthew turned to Montoya for help to close their mutual trip down Memory Lane. "And do I remember right? It was never really explained how Salazar got hold of weapons shipped to State Security, assuming, as the government had assured us, the weapons weren't planted there after the fact to justify Salazar's killing."

Graciela hurried back in and handed off a plate of cookies to Matthew, who held them out in the cold, dead silence he had woven.

"Now, how can I help you, Captain?"

"Enrique Cuadra is dead."

Matthew was lifted out of his chair by a cold shiver down his spine. He turned to Epimenio, who'd brought the news Matthew had dismissed as foolery. He didn't realize he'd dropped the plate of cookies until it broke at his feet.

"Dead?"

Montoya set his coffee down. "Dead. Deceased. Murdered. Last night. Maybe early this morning. It seems a robbery."

Matthew cut his eyes surreptitiously at Epimenio. But the campesino was staring at the tiled floor.

"Murdered? But we went to the morgue. They said there weren't any unclaimed bodies."

"Why did you go to the morgue?"

Matthew shook his head. No matter how long he was in Nicaragua, how much he felt he knew it, the country always made him feel like a child bewildered by the adults.

"Epimenio brought me a message from Enrique's wife, she . . ." Matthew couldn't finish. How could he without implicating Epimenio?

Epimenio looked briefly into Montoya's eyes, Matthew knew, to signal he was addressing the captain, and then back down at his shoes. It was the manner of the campesinos Matthew often saw. The revolution had changed many things, but not the humble farmer's view of where he stood in relation to the world. Epimenio had not once referred to his dead cousin as anything but *don Enrique.*

"La señora woke me up. She was very upset. . . ."

"Enrique's wife, you mean?"

"Yes, Captain. Doña Gloria. She said she saw her husband in a dream." Epimenio spread his hands as if the dream unfolded between them. "Don Enrique said he was lost, that he needed help. That she should ask don Mateo in Managua to help find him."

Montoya briefly touched Epimenio's knee. "When was this dream?"

Epimenio counted on his fingers. "Night before last? Yes."

Montoya and his lieutenant, who'd been taking notes, exchanged a look, like a tag, and the lieutenant jumped in. "Enrique Cuadra wasn't dead the night before last."

Epimenio spread his hands again, as if reviewing the film of his story. "Doña Gloria came to me as soon as she woke up. She was so frightened she didn't even want to wait until dawn to send me, and the roads are full of soldiers at night. She paid a man, a neighbor, to drive me here."

"That's true, Lieutenant," Matthew jumped in. "Epimenio called me from Matagalpa yesterday saying he was coming and asking directions to my house. I'd had a message from Enrique, too."

"When?" Montoya deigned to speak but didn't take his eyes off Epimenio.

"Two nights ago. Said he was coming to Managua and we should talk."

Montoya's eyes now fell on Matthew, and he was relieved to be the center of attention again. He felt a need to protect Epimenio.

"Talk about what?"

"He didn't say. Enrique and I exchanged hospitality. He stayed with me and I with him. We're friends. I report a lot from the war zone; he was a source. His coffee finca's in El Tuma. Lots of Contra and army around. He kept tabs on a lot of things through a store on his farm. Man knew what was what up there."

"And what was what?"

"Battles, troop movements. Comings and goings. The price of coffee. Local gossip. Everything. We just talked, mostly. He had no secret knowledge of anything."

"You ever discuss it on the phone with him?"

"What?"

"Whatever information he was giving you? Did you talk on the phone?"

"There's no phones up there. You know that. The nearest town only got electricity two years ago. Enrique ran a generator for what he needed. He'd call when he got to the Hotel Ideal in Matagalpa. But only to say when he was arriving. And he didn't give me information, per se. He gave me perspective, like how the revolution's going for the average Nica."

"And how is it going, our revolution, for the 'average Nica'?"

Matthew leaned forward. "It's a mixed bag, Ajax. Prices for goods are up, but for coffee down. No one's got money and the córdoba ain't worth the price of the toilet paper it's printed on."

Matthew hoped to prick Ajax's nationalist feelings with that one. "Then there's the war you may've heard of."

"A lot of Contra up there?"

Matthew smiled. "What're you kidding? You're gonna tell me *you* don't know? The Contra are all over up there. It's the base for the *Jorge Salazar Command*. Your little gas station caper gave them their first patron saint."

Ajax didn't skip a beat. "Enrique got along with these Contra?"

"You asking me if he was one?"

"No, Connelly, I asked what I asked."

"Enrique got along with everyone. Frente, Contra, neighbors, workers."

Ajax turned to Epimenio. "How did don Enrique get to Managua."

"He drove his pickup."

"What kind?"

"Toyota."

"Color?"

"White."

"What year?"

"Señor?"

"Old or new? In good shape or bad?"

"Not so new, but in good shape. Don Enrique loves that truck."

Epimenio bowed his head until his chin brushed his chest, as if the burden of the past tense weighed him down.

"He loved it."

For the second time Montoya patted Epimenio's arm.

"Thank you, señor. I am sorry for your loss. Go back to the morgue today. His body is there. But you might have to wait a day or two until you can take him home."

Matthew felt his heart beat hot, the old fucking runaround. "We were there yesterday. State Security wouldn't let us in."

"Thank you for the coffee." Ajax stood, then his lieutenant. "Epimenio should not take the body home unless he informs me first. Understood?"

Matthew followed Montoya outside.

"Compañero. Ajax."

"*Captain* Montoya, remember?"

"Okay, sorry about all that. I didn't know why you were here."

"Now you do."

"Captain, please. Enrique was a friend of mine. Is there is anything I can do, any help I can give?"

"Help? Are you looking for another front page story? A scoop? An exclusive? The man was killed in a robbery. How are you going to squeeze scandal out of that?"

Montoya turned on his heel and left, but before he had, Matthew had noticed a look on the lieutenant's face when Montoya said robbery.

6

1.

The Mercado Oriental—Managua's Eastern Market—was a vast, crowded, smelly chaos of low-rent free-enterprise and black marketeering. Hundreds of women in various states of obesity presided over it. Their flabby arms flouncing in blue, red, yellow, or green rayon blouses. Their skirts hidden behind identical frilled aprons with bulging pockets that served as cash registers. *Bizneras* they were, and *bizness* was their life. They were the backbone of Nicaragua's emaciated economy. Tough as an alligator's back, as volatile as boiling gasoline, these pitiless businesswomen were the bearers of a cutthroat capitalism that would have terrified Adam Smith and left a whimpering J. P. Morgan bleeding out of every orifice.

Ajax loved the place. He coasted his Lada to a stop, fearful of wearing down the last of his brakes—no telling when Moscow would send *that* freighter. He parked behind a chile mate tree, which afforded the view he wanted. If Enrique Cuadra's pickup was not a smoking hulk or sinking into the muck of Lake Managua, then all or part of it was for sale here in the Oriental. Ajax smiled for the first time that day, maybe all week. The sheer dynamism of the place never failed to cheer him.

He needed cheering from the black mood that had settled after Connelly had rubbed his nose in *L'Affaire Salazar*. Rubbed his nose in it like a puppy's in its own piss.

"I hate this fucking place." Gladys peered through the window like a cat studying Dogville.

"Why?" Ajax drew the Python and rolled its cylinder over his palm.

She pointed out the window. "They hate us here."

"Who's 'us,' white man?"

"What?"

"Nothing. American joke. How can you hate a place as lively as this? Look at it—thousands of citizens selling, buying, shopping, swapping. This is good energy."

Gladys pointed her chin out the windshield. "They're all Contra here."

"Oh shut up, you big baby. Listen to yourself. 'They hate us here.'" Ajax flipped open the Python's cylinder and spun it, looking at the Mercado through the five empty chambers, then slapped it closed and holstered it. "Lieutenant, the contra-revolución and the contra-revoluciónarios are an armed insurgency raised and paid for by the imperialist yanqui putos. They are on both our borders *killing* people." He tapped her playfully in her temple. "I have to explain this to you?"

"Okay, fine, but *these* people *are* anti-Sandinista, and this place is a fucking cesspool of criminality and counterrevolutionary feeling." She gave the entire market the finger.

"Counterrevolutionary *feeling*? People have to like you? The Revo is a popularity contest? These bizneras hate rules and regulations, not Gladys Darío! Can you blame them? You ever read the government wage and price controls? Have you?"

Gladys just flattened her lips into a long thin line, which meant *no*. Probably no one had, ever.

"Everything you can think of, from a bag of frijoles or an entire crop of coffee to the dingleberries clinging to your butt cheeks has an official price. And out of whose ass did they pull that bright idea? Jesus had a hard-on, Gladys, that's not the revolution, that's an import from the goddamn Soviets as surely as this Lada is, and it works just as well."

"That's right, Ajax, without the Soviets we wouldn't have this Lada. So how about some gratitude for that?"

"For what? The Soviets came here telling us what to do like we were the inmates taking over the asylum and they had our medication. Look out there. *There* is an energy, a vigor, a spirit that the Revo should've freed, not caged."

Ajax hid the Python under his seat. "Little countries like ours are threatened by a two-headed monster, my dear lieutenant. One head's an eagle, the other a bear, but know what? No matter which mouth chews you up, they shit out the same asshole, comprendes?"

"Whatever."

"I'm not grateful for anything but a good night's sleep and a decent cigarette. You, on the other hand, should be grateful, 'cause without this Lada you're the burro I'd be riding."

She looked out the window—he hoped, to hide a smile.

"Donkeys kick. And bite."

"Not if you beat 'em regular. Come on. Let's go walk amongst the people."

"Unarmed?"

"Scared?"

No sooner had they plunged into the market than Ajax felt its inner order alter slightly. At the sight of their uniforms, a flabby arm waved and a whistle tweeted. It started up close and rippled two hundred yards away. The monkeys passed the word: jaguars on the prowl.

In a nation that lacked everything, the Oriental was chock-full of goods as only a black market can be. Foodstuffs, hardware, dry goods, textiles, American cigarettes, French perfumes, Mexican porn, Chinese watches, live iguanas, dead monkeys, old pistols, and love potions were for sale. Anything that came within a hundred miles of Nicaragua's coast could be found here—or anything that went missing inside its borders.

They walked under the high zinc roofs and among the tin shacks of the official section of the market, past the greens, reds, and yellows of the fruit and vegetable vendors. Discards made a slimy skin on the concrete. The screechy symphony of voices calling prices and enticements in this grubby market was the same energy that had built the temples of the Maya, the pyramids of the Aztecs, stacked the monoliths at Stonehenge. And if women had not built those wonders? Well, the men who did had had mothers like these women.

Ajax stopped to look over some guavas at a stall lorded over by three women with identical fat rolls and mischievous, quick eyes who were so homely in late middle-age they reminded Ajax of the Weird Sisters who ruined Macbeth.

Gladys sidled up close and whispered, "What did you make of that dream Epimenio went on about—the widow seeing her dead husband?"

"What do *you* make of it?"

"He seemed to tell the truth, but who knows with that type? Superstitious bullshit is as much an opiate of the masses as the church."

Ajax repressed a need to smile and shake his head disapprovingly. "Ah, Lieutenant, there are more things in Matagalpa than are dreamed of in your Marxist philosophy."

"Meaning?"

"First of all, never judge any information. Just study it." He picked up two guavas, weighed them, and set the lighter one down. "Either Epimenio told the truth or he did not. If he did, then the question is, why would the widow tell him such a thing? Either she had the dream or she did not. If she did, then she did. But if she did not, why would she tell Epimenio she did? If you wanted to get a campesino moving, but couldn't tell him the truth, you'd make up such a story."

Ajax thumped one guava with his forefinger to check its ripeness.

"So, she either had the dream or made it up to hasten the messenger. The more interesting scenario is that there was no dream. So what did the wife know about her husband's business that she would send his cousin to look for him under such a pretense?"

"She comes down to collect the body we can question her."

"I suppose . . . maybe . . ." Ajax uttered the words softly, let the words hang there, like butterflies amid the raucous cawing of the bizneras. They finally alighted on Gladys's mind. She snatched the guava from his hands.

"You can't fucking seriously be thinking of us going to Cuadra's farm. *In the mountains!*"

"No, not *us*." He took the guava back.

"Hey, Comandante, you gonna buy that guava or just play with it?" The larger of the three snatched it from his hands and wiped it down. "You should, you know. Guava puts iron in your pole!"

A second laughed and held up another guava. "Two for the price of one—twice the iron, twice the pole!"

Ajax held his hands up. "Señora, please. Don't embarrass me in front of my girlfriend."

The sisters eyed Gladys up and down. "That cat don't eat sausage."

Gladys flushed red, and Ajax hurried her away as the sisters' laughter followed them like flies.

They walked on in silence until the pavement ran out. They were on the dusty tracks of the unofficial section of the market, now. It was filled with stalls run by those without a government permit, only need. The sounds and sights were the same, but the vendors' eyes were harder, narrower. There were more men than women. Not only were the stalls technically illegal, but they sold only what had been smuggled or stolen.

Ajax spotted the two young guys he was looking for, lounging in front of a stall. A dirty curtain veiled the action behind it. They wore the latest tough-guy styles—T-shirts rolled up their chests to show off their flat stomachs and olive-colored nipples. In the States, they'd have been called "guidos." They spotted Ajax and ducked behind the curtain.

"Come on!" He sprinted down the alley with Gladys behind him and heard a car engine fire up. He got to the stall, ripped the curtain back, and got his hand on the pickup truck's hood just as the driver clutched it into gear.

"Don't do it!"

The truck engine raced, nosed forward, pushing Ajax, flat-footed, on the dirt. Gladys crashed in behind him with a .38 snub-nose in her hand.

"Shut it off!" she yelled.

The driver killed the engine.

"Get out of the vehicle!" She turned on the nipple men. "Hands up!"

Ajax was amazed. "You carry a backup?"

"And aren't you grateful."

He pushed her gun hand down, went to the driver's window, and greeted the smuggler fuming behind the wheel. He was a wiry bantam cock of man with a spine so twisted he always appeared to be leaning away.

"Qué pasa, Hunchback?"

"Captain Montoya."

"You were gonna run me over?"

"Accelerator got stuck."

"That hurts, Hunchback."

Gladys stuck the snub-nose in his face. "Get out of the goddamn vehicle!"

Ajax went to the truck bed, laid his hands on the unopened boxes there. "I thought we were friends, compadres."

"Why, 'cause you clip me for product every month?" The Hunchback climbed out the cab. "I would break my own blood's legs for shit like that. And you ain't family."

"I'm not here for cigarettes, Quasimodo." Ajax drummed his fingers on the boxes. "Just some information."

The Hunchback looked him over. "Take your Marlboros and fuck your 'information.'"

Gladys grabbed his shirt collar, kicked him in the knee, and the moment he dropped to the ground she slapped the snub-nose's barrel into his temple.

"Watch your mouth!"

"He's half your size and a hunchback, Gladys. Let him up."

Ajax pulled the Hunchback up and dusted off his dirty blue jeans. "You okay?"

"*Viva la revolución.*"

"Holster it, Gladys. Wait outside and take the nipple boys with you."

She walked out ahead of the Nicaraguan guidos, and Ajax pulled the dirty curtain closed.

"Sorry about that."

"You ain't sorry about shit. Why me, Montoya?"

"'Cause you sell the good stuff." Ajax tore open a box in the truck bed and peeled out one of the many red-and-white cartons of Marlboros. He ran his finger along one side. "See? Says right there. 'Made in Winston Salem, North Carolina.' Rest of your compañeros sell cheap Mexican knockoffs. These are quality. You sell quality, you get quality customers."

"Lucky me. You gonna pay for them today?"

"I can't afford these on *my* salary. Besides, I'm not here for the cigarettes, but thanks for offering." He tucked a carton under his arm, considered for a moment, and helped himself to a second. "I need to know where to buy car parts. Fresh ones, not something been sitting out in the sun and rain for weeks."

"You steal my merchandise *and* want a favor?"

"Let us agree we have marveled at that irony. And I'm not stealing. I'm taking a small bribe for not arresting you."

"Then how about some help with the others?"

"The economic police? I've got no influence with them. I'm homicide, so if you ever kill someone . . ."

"Don't think I haven't thought about it."

Ajax looked the Hunchback up and down while he peeled open a carton. He could tell the little man *had* thought about it.

"Hunchback, we've all thought about killing. Some have done it, and others not. And of those who've done it, some of us got good at it and others not."

He fished out a pack and opened it.

"So you go about what you're good at, smuggling these smokes in. It earns you some hard currency, eh? *The yanqui dollar.* You got this truck, a house with a concrete floor I bet, electricity, and kids that don't know hunger and go to school, don't they?"

The Hunchback squinted, but nodded yes.

"Your customers are foreigners, big shots in government, the rich, so you pass on the cost from me tapping you to them, and you go on while you still can. This black market won't last forever. The government's gonna wake up to the inevitability of *market forces* and eventually all this"—Ajax swept his arm around the dirty little stall with its dirty little truck while he pulled at a butt in the pack—"will go away and be given back to the rich who had it all in the first place. And you'll be back selling mangos in the street, which is where you started, wasn't it?"

He held a pristine tobacco cylinder in front of the Hunchback's face. "Got a light?"

The Hunchback flipped open a Zippo embossed with a Budweiser logo.

Ajax blew a long trail of smoke into his face, smacked his lips. "Now *that* is a good smoke."

The Hunchback smiled. "Other than to break my balls and talk me to death, what do you fucking want?"

"I want to know who I would see if I had a stolen pickup to get rid of. Cigarette?"

The Hunchback shook one loose and fired it up, took a long drag and let the smoke drift into Ajax's face. To the Hunchback, Ajax knew, it felt like defiance. But it really signaled capitulation.

"Don Augustino."

"He got a stall here?"

The Hunchback snorted like a pig at the trough. "He sells here, the parts after they're chopped. But he don't come here. He's got an office. At the Inter."

"The InterContinental Hotel?" The Hotel Inter was the one true landmark in Managua. Its claim to fame was that it survived the '72 earthquake when Howard Hughes was slowly decomposing on its top floor. The crazed billionaire had decamped right afterward, taking, local lore later suggested, the last of the Ogre's luck with him. "He buys stolen cars out of the Inter?"

"No, sells them. To your friends in the government. Foreigners. Everything that comes across the borders, mostly from Costa Rica. He's the stolen car king."

"What if it's stolen locally?"

"Chopped for parts. That stall's down toward the fence. Look for the blind gypsy. If they don't know you, he'll have to read your palm before they'll sell to you. But everything either side of him has been chopped."

Ajax patted the man's shoulder. "You know, Hunchback, I could grow to love you."

"Then my damnation will be complete."

Ajax left Gladys with the blind gypsy who, Ajax was sure, was neither. He went on alone, to stroll among the jumble of car parts trying to assemble a jigsaw. He'd liked doing jigsaw puzzles as a kid. They had been a part of the "Nicaraguan education" his father had furiously built, like a dam against assimilation, while dreaming of going home.

In the Los Angeles of his youth, Ajax recalled, if you weren't

Anglo or Black, you were Mexican. No one thought or cared about shades in the Latino crowds. Not even the Mexicans. It had driven his father crazy—the food, the holidays celebrated in schools, the ethnic slurs, all Mexican. His father had been shocked by the prejudice he'd encountered when they first fled to California after he and his coconspirators had bought their way out of the Ogre's prison. "Even the Mexicans hate us!" he would shout and thump the table. But the Anglos could not care less, and the Mexicans all looked down their noses at Nicaragua the same way that the gringos did Mexico.

So his father had determined to make Ajax and his siblings as Nicaraguan as possible. History and geography lessons were mandatory over the summer. Dessert was a reward for reciting poems by Rubén Darío.

And then the puzzles.

His father gathered topographical maps of Nicaragua, old newspapers from Managua, or portraits of the heroes like President Zelaya and Sandino. Ajax's mother would painstakingly glue them onto old cardboard, and then cut them up into jigsaws. Doing one such puzzle Ajax read an article in an old *La Prensa* about a group of bandits who'd robbed a bank in Matagalpa. It was the first time he'd seen the word *Sandinista*.

So Ajax had learned early to like puzzles, and the quarters his father handed out with squeezes to the neck for the first to finish. Not that his father's puzzles had been that difficult to solve. It took Ajax a few years to realize that the puzzles were only a prelude to his father lecturing on geography, biography, history, poetry. He had been one of the youngest-ever professors in Managua before "my blindness," as he called it, led him to his failed rebellion which he'd mourned first as tragedy, but later as folly. His daily humiliation as a gardener and pool cleaner made his exile, and heart, bitter. He hated the Mexicans who daily dismissed him as an overeducated bourgeois. And he despised the Americans who would not believe their gardener had a PhD.

He had died while Ajax was in the mountains.

Ajax walked the alley, an automotive abattoir, until he spotted a pickup's radiator grill with TOYOTA on it.

"*Cuanto e'?*" he asked. How much? He asked the same of the green seats Epimenio had mentioned. Two doors, a hood he was sure of, and even maybe a transmission on down the line. Each "*cuanto e'?*" was answered in dollars, not córdobas. In less than twenty minutes, he'd completed the jigsaw to know Enrique's Toyota had been chopped and brought to the Oriental. To reassemble it piecemeal would've cost him over $2,000. So he calculated that whoever had sold it got maybe $600. Ajax earned $800 a year as a police captain. Not quite a year's salary, but enough to make someone sloppy. What might be burned or disappeared beyond help as evidence in another country, had to be recycled in Nicaragua. The thought made him happy.

He strolled back to Gladys and the gypsy, stopping to trade a pack of Reds for a headlight for his Lada.

He found her looking decidedly uncomfortable. "Has your future been revealed?"

"She is reluctant to let the art read that part of her life." The gypsy, his eyes hidden behind oversize sunglasses, held up a tarot card. "But she pulled the ace of cups. Hers will be a rich life."

Ajax thrust his hand out. "Read mine, viejo."

"You see, señorita," he said to Gladys. "He thrusts his hand into mine. You were hesitant, like you have something to hide. But you, señor, you have no secrets so you present your palm."

"I'm an open book."

"I haven't seen a book since I was a boy." The gypsy studied Ajax's palm with his fingers. "But I remember if you couldn't read, an open book wasn't really open to you."

"You are a philosopher."

"And you once had a difficult job. A hard life. These calluses are old, but will never go away. And this." He pressed hard on the fleshy mass beneath Ajax's thumb. "This is the Mound of Venus. Yours is too full of blood."

"Do I need more exercise, Doctor?"

"No. Different circulation. Your blood does not live in all of your body. Some of what's left over hides in the Mound of Venus. Your heart is sick. Pull a card."

Ajax fiddled in the deck, digging for the least obvious one. He flipped it over with a snap.

The old man felt it with his fingers. "King of Swords." He nodded, ran his fingers over Ajax's palm again.

"King of Swords means something, viejo?"

"Most definitely, señor. He is the black king. The cards have spoken."

"Should I buy a Lotería?"

"Not about luck, señor. Your palm points to a sick heart. The card speaks of friendship, loyalty."

"I'm to be blessed with both?"

"No, señor. Neither."

2.

Matthew Connelly liked puzzles, too. He held the phone to his ear and sat in his office in the deepening darkness surveying a well-orchestrated chaos of old news clippings and spilled file folders, thinking just that thought, *I like puzzles*. It was why he kept his files detailed and cross-referenced. They were the pieces of the life-size puzzle of Nicaragua he could never quite get right. Of course it helped that he could pay someone to do all the clipping and the filing and the cross-referencing for him. Like he paid to have so much done— cooking, cleaning, shopping, standing in lines for gas or bread or bureaucracies. He paid Lydia, the money changer, to come to him, but not as much as he paid Patricia from the phone company, but less than Marco, the car mechanic who made house calls, as did Silvio, the Italian doctor all the journalists used—as much for his skill as the cachet that he was a fugitive Red Brigades terrorist wanted by Interpol.

At times he thought his life was obscene, really. He lived in neo-colonial splendor on not quite twenty-five thousand a year. (And a full one-third of that earned from double or even triple-billing his many strings.) In a country where even the locally grown rice and beans were in short supply, entire supermarkets could be full of nothing but light bulbs, depending what Soviet freighter had docked. Yet his biggest worry was if the Dollar store was out of pesto. In a country at war with itself, the only policy all combatants agreed upon was never to kill a journalist, and particularly not an American. Beyond the war there was very little violent crime.

Indeed not much crime at all except for the ubiquitous thievery. And even that had its charms. Once, when a pair of favorite pants had gone missing off the clothesline, he'd confronted his washerwoman, Lola, who'd sworn it was the work of trained crows that flew them directly to the Mercado Oriental. Three days later, Lola's father showed up for work as Matthew's night watchman proudly wearing his new khakis. Who could get angry at such lack of guile?

He also knew he was a bit player, a member of the chorus—a very well paid member of the chorus. Well paid and well protected—always a mourner, never a corpse. So he had appointed himself the private archivist of the Nicaraguan revolution and the American counterrevolution. If it was on paper, Matthew had a copy of it in his exhaustive files—newspaper clippings in Spanish and English represented the bulk of them, but also every press handout, white paper, and brochure ever produced in Managua, Miami, or Washington. Stacks of reports—official, unofficial, and downright dubious. And cartons of notes he'd scribbled on cocktail napkins (and even a few his colleagues had scribbled and he'd filched). Pages copied or simply yanked out of books, and folders full of typed transcripts from his own notebooks (which he also paid someone else to do). And boxes of the tapes he'd recorded over seven years.

It was all organized by the major events since he had arrived in 1978, and the people involved in them. When someone's name was mentioned in association with an event, that person got a file; and if that person's biography included some event, that event got a file, and so on. He'd laid the files out for tonight's dispatches and sidebars so he could peruse the life of tonight's topic, the rising star of Vladimir Malhora—before the war, during, and after. Malhora was, Matthew thought with no little envy, one of the few people who had more extensive files than he did.

New York was making him wait on the phone. When he got the green light, Matthew would give them a thumb-sucker on what it all means for the folks back home. *What does it all mean for the folks back home, Matthew? For Mom and Pop Main Street?* His editor, Sheila, loved to issue orders like that. She thought of them as a challenge, but they were orders. Her way to let him know that his job out there in the field, witnessing firsthand the agonies of the world, was nothing compared to her job in midtown Manhattan as gatekeeper for all that news, as if the purpose of building highways was to hang traffic lights.

On the other end of the line, he could hear the wire service Teletypes clacking away, bringing photos and new stories from all over the world. He could hear electric typewriters tapping, each keystroke like a single bee in a humming swarm. He could hear a television reporting news. Maybe that new cable channel everyone was talking about.

A twenty-four-hour news station! Matthew liked the sound of that. Trying to reduce Nicaragua into a sixty-second news report or an eight-hundred-word story was like asking a novelist to write a haiku. This twenty-four-hour news channel would revolutionize news reporting. The only way to fill that big a news hole would be with in-depth reporting. No longer just twenty-two minutes for world news, but twenty-two minutes just on Nicaragua. Even if he got on once a week, it would be like making a documentary! A brave new world was coming in which television news would make the world a global village.

Still, he had to plug Shelia and Mom and Pop Main Street into his world now.

So little of what actually happened in Nicaragua was of any use to the average American. How could Matthew pull the files and link the pieces together to make a picture for the folks back home? He could barely connect the pieces himself.

His spilled Ajax's file on the table.

Fucking Montoya. Treating me like a tourist.

The Montoya file was thin—clippings from the early days about his exploits as a guerrilla commander. *And fucking cigarette thief.* Sidebars highlighting his American upbringing, a couple of bits about his foreign travels with his then-wife Gio. A few clippings about his role in Salazar's execution. The foreign and local press pegged him as at the scene with Salazar, but not in charge. That had been Malhora.

Then nothing at all until Montoya showed up making a splash as a cop, busting a serial rapist and murderer who'd preyed on prostitutes. Matthew remembered that one. *El Gordo Sangroso.* The Bloody Fat Man. That had been in April 1984. Salazar had been killed in June 1981. So Montoya must've left State Security and gone over to the policía shortly after the Salazar affair. But had he been fired and farmed out, or resigned and stormed out?

Matthew retrieved the Salazar file, fatter than the other two combined, and spilled it on the burgeoning pile of headlines, stories, and photos. All puzzle pieces.

And then he saw it. Flitting and quickly buried in the pile. A photo. A piece of a photo. One face in one piece of one photo. He flicked clippings to the floor until he uncovered it. A photo from *Barricada* taken at the gas station where Salazar had been killed. It was dated June 23, two days after the killing. The caption explained

Malhora and other government officials were reenacting the incident. Specifically the moment Salazar had "gone for his gun."

In the background, wearing a gray felt cowboy hat, was the face. The face of Enrique Cuadra.

It was then Matthew Connelly heard his own name being sounded over the phone. He hung up.

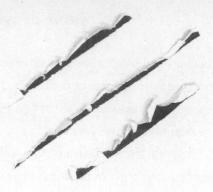

7

1.

The moment the plane door opened, Amelia Peck gazed upon the Nicaraguan delegation through the lugubrious heat waves rising snake-like from the tarmac. She could feel her mutinous, bright red hair begin to defy the bands in which she'd trapped it. She was going to have a bad hair day. The humidity was like a clammy pillow forced over her face, and rivulets of sweat flowed instantly down the freckled skin under the ridiculous business suit she'd had to wear. But her senator had wanted her in uniform, as if dressing without regard to local conditions would convey some moral message to the people he'd come to save from communism.

Amelia stepped off the plane to the sounds of cameras whirring and light applause from the opposition leaders gathered at the bottom of the stairs. It wasn't for her, specifically, but it filled her belly with delightful stirrings. She scanned the assembly like a raptor and immediately noted the presence of a print journalist on the ground, the first violation of protocol. It had been agreed that no journalists would be on the tarmac, only photographers. All others would wait for the press conference in the terminal. She doubted it was an innocent oversight. The Sandinistas, like all Communists, were devious bastards who did their homework. They certainly knew her senator was a fountain of malapropisms, faux pas, and Freudian slips. Anthony Teal styled himself in the folksy manner of the Fearless Leader of the Free

World. But Ronald Reagan sailed on a genuine sea of charm honed from years of navigating the most treacherous waters in the world: the shark tanks of Hollywood. President Reagan might be acting, but he'd long ago lost himself in the role he played, and so exuded a disarming sincerity in his cluelessness, which utterly escaped her senator. Tony Teal was precisely what he appeared to be: a moneyed frat boy with movie star looks too indolent and dim to take up anything more challenging than politics.

But the junior senator from Ohio was her ticket out of her father's mill town and into the towers of power. Tony's last minute, fill-in appointment to the Foreign Relations Committee had blissfully coincided with Reagan's equating the Contras to freedom fighters descended from the Founding Fathers. The trope had rocketed a backwater like Nicaragua both to the vanguard in the fight against Worldwide Communism, and the front page. Now Amelia Peck was lunching with the staff of senators whose names were legendary—at least among the wonks of the poli-sci club she'd been president of at Ohio State.

She'd already shaken Reagan's hand twice, and the second time he'd been on the verge of remembering her name when the protocol officer had filled in the blank. Now she stepped off a plane to meet head-on the newest legion of the Evil Empire, and all she needed, other than a change of clothes, was to get Tony to the embassy without embarrassing himself.

Last week's committee meeting in Washington with the Contra civilian leadership about this trip had been a worrying precursor. Tony had been keen to deploy the one Spanish phrase she'd drilled into his head to lavish on the freedom fighters. But he'd tongue-twisted the key word for courage and so:

The whole world admires your courage.

became:

The whole world admires I shit myself.

Spanish could be like that.

Not one of the Contras had batted an eye. They seemed wearily accomplished at not noticing such things.

She watched Tony shake hands with the Sandinista foreign minister, a wily rogue priest whose profile reminded her of Alfred Hitchcock. Then, with a courtliness he'd truly mastered, he kissed the hand of doña Violeta, elegant grand dame of the opposition. Tony had killer charm, no doubt. So long as you hadn't seen it too often. Amelia had not only met doña Violeta in D.C., but had gone shopping with her. She was wearing the faux pearl rope necklace Violeta had given her. She also spotted the vice foreign minister, her true adversary: Gioconda Targa was the perfect mouthpiece for a Communist revolution. Beautiful, with a tangle of chestnut curls that should have been impossible to maintain in this climate, she was elegant in a way that Amelia could only describe as Gallic. She spoke flawless English and was absolutely a diva in her native Spanish, trilling her Rrrrrrrrrrrrr's in an operatic fashion that set even Republican hearts atwitter. And the TV cameras loved her. Amelia secretly wanted to splash her with acid. Not that she'd admit that to anyone. The few times Amelia had been on the news, glimpsed momentarily handing Tony some briefing paper, she'd not looked bad at all. Amelia Peck just looked like what she was: a freckled twenty-seven-year-old Scotch-Irish daughter of steelworkers with a PhD and more interest in policy than in fashion. Her wild carrot-orange hair made her look like she'd stuck her tongue in a wall socket. Amelia had also met Gioconda on the cocktail party circuit in D.C. She was still alarmed by a certain timbre she'd heard in Tony's laugh when Targa poured on her Medusa charms.

"Amelia!"

The delegations were finally making their way inside to what Amelia prayed was an air-conditioned terminal. Five minutes on the ground and she was at the melting point. Targa looped her arm through Amelia's like they were sorority sisters.

"Your Excellency."

"Oh please, Amelia, this is Nicaragua. Call me Gio. I was thinking of you this morning and I brought you a gift. I made it myself."

She slipped something into Amelia's hand. Instinctively, Amelia checked to see if they were being photographed. They'd been warned in their CIA briefing: "You are nothing but a propaganda opportunity to the Communists. Thus the first commandment is: thou shalt assume you are being recorded and photographed at all times, except in the embassy itself. Thus the second commandment: accept no items, gifts, nothing, from a Nicaraguan national that you take into the embassy. Their holy grail is to penetrate our walls with listening devices."

And while Amelia would rule out nothing, she was surprised to see a spritzer of hair spray in her hand.

"Brazil-nut oil in seltzer water. All the women with hair like ours use it down here."

2.

Ajax twirled the handcuffs on his index finger like an asymmetrical propeller. The smooth, repetitive twirling stirred the only breeze in the otherwise darkened terminal of Augusto César Sandino International Airport. The monotony of it soothed him as he watched the lean Aeronica DC-10 touch down. It gently hopped three times, each feathery bounce detonating a puff of white like a spray of water. Ajax admired that something so massive could appear so nimble. He most definitely did not admire the man who would soon get off the plane.

A man he'd given up hope of ever seeing again.

He still keenly felt the shock when Horacio had called to tip him off.

"The Costa Ricans are sending him back. You'll pick him up at the airport."

Horacio hadn't said who, hadn't needed to.

And now his plane has just touched down. Almost right on time. A nervous-looking official had informed Ajax a half hour ago that the plane would have to circle while the tubby TWA 737 carrying the

American senator landed first. Ajax had watched the half-dozen gringo busybodies disgorge from the plane in their absurd business suits and ties in the grinding Managua heat. The sight had made his trigger finger itch. Then a sudden poetic wind had gusted in, blowing their ties straight up over their heads, like God might hang them right then and there.

A welcoming committee of professionally blank-faced government officials and childishly enraptured opposition leaders had waited on the tarmac. He'd scanned the assembly on the ground for signs of his ex-wife's russet ringlets. He'd spotted the elegant white hair of doña Violeta, publisher of *La Prensa*. That was easy, she stood a dancer's head and shoulders above the dwarves in her cabal, several of whom were so unable to contain their glee that Goliath might shit corn kernels for them to peck that they almost seemed to flap their hands like chickens.

The Buddha-like rotundity of the foreign minister had been unmistakable. But this Buddha was a Dominican priest, which Ajax always thought appropriate. The Dominicans had been invented by the pope to fire up the Inquisition, and the dinner parties at the father's house had been about as much fun as dining with Torquemada. But that was a lifetime ago, when Ajax had moved in those circles.

Then he'd spotted his ex—dashing out to the plane, late, as usual. Trailed, like pearls slipping from a broken necklace, by journalists and TV cameras. *As usual.* Still, his traitor's heart had skipped and the handcuffs had gone flying like a small moon ricocheting out of orbit. He caught them, barely.

"Ajax."

Gladys pointed her chin through the window. The DC-10 taxied to a stop. A couple of workers languidly pushed a set of stairs out to meet it.

"We going out?"

"No. Let them come in. Technically, they're not on Nicaraguan soil until they're in the terminal."

"Big day for you, huh? El Gordo Sangroso. Man, I remember

reading about this case at school. Even *La Prensa* gave you good coverage. 'The Sherlock . . .'"

"Shut up."

Her mouth dropped open, and then dutifully snapped shut. "Yes, *Captain*," she hissed.

Damn, she could milk that word for every bit of meaning short of his rank. He let the handcuffs fly up and off his finger with just enough spin that they twirled in perfect symmetry, and he caught them easily in his cupped hands. Gladys took no notice.

She was right, that case had been his greatest moment since the Triumph. Real police work—interrogations, forensics, and stakeouts. The first time he'd laid eyes on El Gordo, he knew he had his man, and the six days it took to break him were as great a battle as any he'd ever fought. And then, the fat fuck had escaped! Inexplicably to Ajax, as Gordo had no friends or money to buy his way out with. He'd gotten as far as the Costa Rican border, where they'd picked him up and plopped him in jail for the last three years.

He eyed the long black baton hung at her hip and slipped it out from the leather loop and handed it to her.

"He gets uppity, you go for his balls, his throat, or his kneecaps. Don't bother wailing on all that blubber."

"Yes, Captain."

She was going to shut him out all day. Maybe Marta was right, maybe Gladys was okay. He took a breath.

"Gladys, when you upend the world the way we did in '79, things, people, and all kinds of shit gets shaken loose. Even if by turning the world upside down you were setting it back aright like the Revo did, when you do it, people get knocked loose, fly out of their orbits."

He smacked the baton into his palm, then pointed it at the plane.

"The ones he killed were like that. They'd been the girlfriends and concubines of the Guardia, living it up right to the very end, even while their boyfriends were dropping bombs on the barrios. When the Guard fled, they got kicked to the curb, became streetwalkers.

Maybe that was justice." He hung the cuffs on his belt. "That's where *he* found them. Walking the streets."

"You pitied them?"

Ajax frowned, trying to remember if he had felt much at all back then, the early days of his drunken fall. It had been El Gordo Sangroso's escape which had pushed him over the edge, right into the bottle.

"*Humo de leña,*" he muttered.

"Huh?"

"*Humo de leña.* Wood smoke. They smelled of wood smoke. The three I saw in the morgue, his last three, their hair smelled of wood smoke. I don't know why. . . ."

"That him?"

Ajax smiled for the first time that day. El Gordo Sangroso, The Bloody Fat Man, put the O in obese. From a distance he looked like a mammoth sack of sorghum with a little melon stuck on top—his too-small head with its too-small eyes. If he'd weighed a hundred-fifty pounds his head would fit his body, but even then his eyes would be too small. The moment Ajax had looked into those little gray eyes he'd known he had his man.

"He's lost some weight."

Six uniformed Costa Rican cops led the handcuffed prisoner down the stairs, which, Ajax noted, the fugitive walked like they led to a gallows. And they might as well. Twenty-five years was the longest stretch the worst scumbag could pull in Nicaragua. But the prisons here were like most prisons everywhere, and rapists were the lowest of the low, the outcasts. Fair game. Each day of each year would be a torment for this evil fuck.

"I never understood how he got away." Gladys put her baton back on her hip.

"Me neither, really. Three compas took him in a van from the prison. The court is ten minutes away. The next we heard the Ticos had caught him crossing the border."

"He's back now. He'll get his due."

"Don't think this is justice either, Gladys." Ajax spoke but never took his eyes off El Gordo. "This is all politics."

"What politics?"

Ajax made a gun out of his right hand, pointed it at the senator's entourage filing into the terminal, and pulled the trigger. As he did, he noticed Gio walking next to a gringa with the orangest hair he'd ever seen on someone not dressed as a clown.

"The Ticos are honoring the extradition treaty today as a signal. This is all timed to coincide with the gringos and their fact-fucking mission."

"I don't get it."

"The Ticos are a timid bunch, but they know the senator is only here for a look around before he goes back and votes another hundred million to the Contra. They send El Gordo back the same day to signal they'd prefer normalizing relations to escalating the war to a new level."

"How do you know that?"

"I read the papers?"

"That wasn't in the papers."

"Newspapers are clues, Gladys, and only one set of clues. You find them like ones and twos and then you add them up, or subtract. That's what makes a good detective, knowing when to multiply or divide the data you've collected. You got to do the math, constantly."

The Tico cops walked El Gordo into the terminal.

"Listen, Gladys. We sign the paperwork. They sign the paperwork. They take their cuffs off, we put ours on." He took his truncheon out. "Remember . . ."

"Balls, knees, or neck. Think he'll remember you?"

Ajax smiled.

3.

"Please, Captain Montoya, I need my medication. You remember, don't you?"

Ajax remembered nothing about The Bloody Fat Man except the

pictures filed in his head: the color "before" photos El Gordo took and the black-and-white "after" ones Marta snapped at the morgue. But he was pleased that the shit-eater remembered him after three years. The exchange with the Tico cops had been quick and efficient. He and Gladys had had to use both sets of cuffs to get the fugitive's hands behind his colossal girth—Ajax reckoned that he must be topping out at three hundred pounds. All of it packed into a two-hundred-fifty-pound gray prison jumpsuit quickly going dark with sweat. Ajax remembered that. El Gordo sweated more than some clouds rained.

"Captain, you remember about my medications, don't you? They wouldn't give it to me on the plane."

"There's a team of physicians at the prison who'll sort you out. Shut up and walk."

He and Gladys took El Gordo, still muttering about his meds, the long way out, to steer clear of the crowd of journalists and photographers now surrounding the senator on a small podium behind a sprawling bouquet of microphones. Ajax hesitated only briefly when he spotted Gioconda in the back, smiling and waving girlishly to reporters between questions. The pretty gringa with that crazy orange hair was pointing at a reporter. Ajax stopped when Matthew Connelly rose to speak.

"Senator Teal," Connelly began, "in a couple of weeks the Senate will vote on a hundred-million-dollar arms package for the Contra, twice as much as the Reagan Administration has given them so far, and it will spin the war up to a new level; given that you're known as a rising star in the Republican party, is it fair to ask if you are really here to 'fact find' or have you already made up your mind about the Contra?"

Ajax wasn't sure, but it seemed that the senator glanced at Carrot Head, who gave him a signal before he spoke, like a pitcher checking the sign from his catcher.

"Well, let me just stop you right there and talk about this word *Contra*."

Teal smiled a quick sly smile, but it seemed to Ajax Carrot Head did a double take, as if the pitcher had shaken off her sign for a curve ball.

"You use the word 'Contra' as if it was a bad word, but what does it mean? Contra-rebolushonaireo in Spanish is counterrevolutionary in English. But what is a revolution? Revolution means to go all the way around and finish where you start, like on a clock you start at twelve and when you finish you're right back at twelve, right?"

Connelly consulted his watch. "Even if you started at midnight and end up at noon?"

Teal seemed not to notice that Connelly had hit one up the middle, and he shook off another sign from Carrot Head. "So Nicaragua started with the Somoza dictatorship and the *revolution* brought it all the way around and now it's back at a Communist dictatorship. See? Twelve to twelve. The counterrevolutionaries just want to turn the clock back."

"To what time, Senator?"

Teal blinked, Ajax thought, the way a pitcher might when he watches the ball sail deep into the bleachers. Teal seemed to check the sign from Carrot Head, and nodded agreement.

"You may not realize this, my friend, but San José, Costa Rica is closer to Washington, D.C., than San Jose, California."

Ajax joined in the brief, puzzled pause.

"Not sure I take your point, Senator."

"The internal affairs of Nicaragua are a matter of grave concern to US national security. We don't want another Cuban missile crisis, for example, and, with all due respect to our hosts, if the Sandinista army decided to invade us, there is only Mexico between them and Brownsville, Texas."

"You mean, sir, with the exception of Honduras, Guatemala, and possibly El Salvador if they hooked left a little?"

The senator seemed not to get the correction.

"Senator, you're saying the US is in danger of being invaded by

Nicaragua? A country in which there are only five elevators and one escalator. And the escalator doesn't work."

Ajax noticed a sudden stiffness in Carrot Head's spine. What he didn't notice was that El Gordo had stopped murmuring about his meds.

Teal checked the sign again, and seemed to wind up to his fastball. "The Sandinista government has chosen to align itself with the Communist International. Nicaragua is a beachhead for the Comintern on the Central American Land Bridge. A threat to our national security is a threat. It doesn't matter the *size*. After all, great packages can come in small presents."

A self-satisfied titter flitted through the journalists, and when Carrot Head made her move for the microphones, El Gordo Sangroso made his.

"A . . ." was all Ajax heard from Gladys before the fat fuck flattened her against the wall and barreled over him. It was unlike any sensation Ajax had ever had. He'd been knocked down plenty. But this sweaty, swollen man running him over was like God's tortilla maker dropping a gob of batter on him. He was flattened, but it was all gooey and sticky.

"HELP!!! Help me, America! Help me! Communists want to kill me! I am kidnap!! HELP!!!"

Son of a bitch! Ajax had a millisecond to notice the cocksucker could run like the water buffalo that had birthed him, before he chose Gladys's baton instead of the Python. Amazingly, by then El Gordo had legged it halfway to the podium.

"Help me, America. I want free from kidnap! Help me, America!"

El Gordo slammed into the cameramen at the back of the crowd, bowling over their gear. Video cameras smashed to the floor, lights toppled and popped like pistol shots.

"He's got a gun!"

Ajax would never know who shouted that, but it was like a pop heard 'round the world.

Panic was unleashed like a pack of dogs, like a flood. Like an attack of diarrhea. People fled blindly, ran over each other, and hurled others in the way of imagined gunfire. Bodyguards from both delegations pulled their service revolvers. But Ajax stayed focused. He launched himself on El Gordo, knowing immediately he'd gone too high, would only be carried along like an alley cat attacking an ox. He let himself slip down and with a prayer on his lips tripped Gordo and actually felt the vibrations as he bounced like the DC-10 that'd brought him home for retribution.

His peripheral vision took in the terror of the stampeded crowd. Wild-eyed like steers, they scrambled out of the way. He saw the backside of Gio and her foreign minister being hustled away. Journalists lunged onto the small stage and toppled dignitaries in an undignified heap. Carrot Head, Ajax noticed, held onto her senator, so at least he didn't go down until his bodyguards hustled him off as well. Yet she remained. Ajax saw her mouth working, something like, "Help that man!"

Camera flashes popped the whole time. Still photographers, like bodyguards, were trained to turn toward the sound of gunfire and "shoot back."

Ajax flailed with the baton looking for an opening in the balls or throat. But his prisoner crawled toward the stage on his knees, hands still manacled behind him, shouting, screaming. Ajax slowed him with a hard smash to the back of his head, but when El Gordo tried to get up he knew there was only one way to go. He reached for the Python—that one bullet was all he needed. But then his mind flashed on the corpse he'd helped Marta pump out—the carotid artery. "It'll drain the brain." He laid the baton against El Gordo's neck, where he'd seen Marta slice the other open. Then he pulled with all his might to choke off whatever heated, infected blood flowed to that sick mind. Ajax conjured the morgue pictures of the dead girls and with all the strength he could muster he tried to choke the life out of Nicaragua's only serial killer. As the evil fuck slowed and gasped, Ajax laid his mouth against his sweaty little ear and whispered, mantra-like—"*Humo de leña. Humo de leña.*"—as he choked him into unconsciousness.

The body went limp, Ajax let it go and the fleshy face smacked the floor. He stood one end of the baton on the bluberous back, and rested his chin on the other, panting for breath. Blood pounded in his ears, but he was certain he heard Gladys calling, "*Policía Sandinista! Holster your weapons! Policía.*"

Ajax caught his breath and surveyed the wreckage of the international press conference he'd toppled like Jericho. Some of the dignitaries had slowed their retreat, others still loped away. He was surrounded by a scrum of bodyguards and photographers. But, small miracle, only the photographers were "shooting." He looked at the stage into the green eyes of Carrot Head, her mouth hanging open and body frozen like a wax figure. As he pushed himself to his feet, her eyes followed him, but nothing else moved.

He couldn't resist. "Welcome to Nicaragua!"

Then she slapped him.

4.

Ajax looked at it.

And it looked back.

He was sure of that now. There were no eyes in the silhouette beyond his darkened window, no face to hold eyes. But he knew when he was being watched. He realized now that this was where these visitations—hallucinations?—were going.

Growing, evolving from a sheet rustling in the breeze, like the other night, to this: a presence watching him. Either he was sleepwalking and hallucinating, or . . . What?

The Needle was in his hand again, too. He could feel its heft—not brawny like a boxer, but lean like a ballerina. This time he wasn't thinking about how it got there, nor chasing the *why*. It was in his right hand, blocked by his body from the watcher's gaze. He slid the blade out and curled his fingers loosely around it. He hadn't thrown it in years, but hoped he remembered how.

If he could hit it, then maybe he wasn't crazy, because he'd know there was an "it" to be hit. If he missed, well, he was tired of being stared at. He tightened his fingers on the blade when the night was shattered by a shrill scream. In the millisecond it took to realize it was his phone ringing, he knew he'd missed his chance but launched the blade through the window anyway. And himself after it.

His garden was empty, as he'd known it would be. There was no solace in finding the blade buried in one of the posts that bore his hammock up.

And still the goddamn phone rang. He answered the one in his sala.

"What."

"Ajax."

"Marta?"

"Everything all right?"

He could feel his naked feet on the cool floor, sweat rose on his temples and back in the hot night.

"All right?" He could feel the ache in his arms from choking out El Gordo. "Have you been in a cave all day?"

"No, I heard about it, it's all everyone is talking about."

Ajax actually managed a kind of strangled chuckle. "Then my damnation is complete."

"I need to see you, now."

"Please don't. I don't need comforting."

"This won't comfort you."

Ajax and Marta were in his garden. He studied the black-and-white photographs she'd brought. *It's like death has set up a waiting room in my life.*

"What's this?"

He looked over to see Marta trying to wiggle The Needle free of the post where he'd sunk it.

"Nothing."

"Nothing? This is The Needle; I haven't seen this in years. You kept it?"

Ajax held up one of the morgue photos. "Was he blind?"

"Which one?" She walked over and took a seat at the small table in his garden. Spread out before Ajax were six photographs of two dead men; he touched one.

"This one?"

"No."

"I didn't think so. He styled himself a blind gypsy fortune-teller."

"You knew him?"

"Both of them." Ajax touched another photo. "That's the Hunchback."

"He wasn't a hunchback. He had spinal encephalitis, a crooked spine. Painful, too, I'll bet."

"Maybe that's why he was always mad."

"At you?"

"Marta, you're sure?"

She looked down at her photos. "Both of them. Once in the throat, twice in the heart. Just like the first one."

The first one. Damn, he hadn't expected that. Enrique Cuadra, okay. But now these two, and the same MO? He traced a finger around the Hunchback's head. "When and where?"

"Both found today. Crooked Spine floating in the lake, the not-blind gypsy in a garbage heap at the Oriental." She studied his face a moment. "How did you know these two?"

"I might be the last one to have seen them alive."

Marta lay down in his hammock, used her ass to swing it gently. "You can't be your own suspect."

"No. Maybe just suspect."

She rocked for a while. "Joaquin's funeral is tomorrow," she said.

"I know."

"You're going."

"Am I? After the spectacle I put on at the airport? Can you imagine what the papers will make of that?"

"Don't have to. *La Prensa* put out a special edition already. You made the front page. But you have to attend, Ajax. All the old comrades will be there. Friends."

"Not the burial, too many grandees. But afterward, maybe. I don't know."

"Come on." She got out of the hammock. "Let's go see what detritus you've got in the kitchen. We'll make a camp mash out of it."

"You gonna cook for me?"

"Hell no. But I'll slice some mangos."

They stood around Ajax's stove and slowly made a serviceable meal out of whatever was at hand. They ate together, sitting on stools in the kitchen, trading remembrances of Joaquin and the old days.

In the garden, the black-and-white photos curled in the humid night.

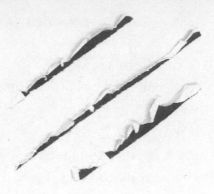

8

Ajax and Horacio silently drove south out of Managua on the Inter-American Highway. Ajax daydreamed of not stopping until he awoke drowning in the Panama Canal. Strangely, the seasonal torrential rain had skipped a day yesterday. He slalomed easily around the potholes on the dry road under the burning sun on his way to Gioconda's house to mourn the passing of Joaquin Tinoco. The Soviet tanker had finally brought the gas, so the carretera was again busy with over-stuffed Bulgarian buses, big Russian IFA trucks, Lada taxis, Toyotas, Jeeps, hawkers, and walkers.

As the sprawl of the city thinned out, Ajax took in smaller de-tails. He passed the city's first and only McDonald's, which gamely limped on even though it'd been excommunicated from the parent company for serving tacos and yucca instead of burgers and fries. The foreign aid groups and UN missions had offices here, flags flying over them. Long stretches of ugly concrete walls enclosing military bar-racks were covered in the graffiti of Sandinista and opposition youth groups trading insults. A long stretch of revolutionary murals and slogans was painted just north of his destination. He grunted his approval as they drove by his favorite—Que se rinda tu madre! Your mama surrenders. It was the kind of slogan Ajax like best: street-wise and not fit for polite company.

"What?"

Horacio was watching with a sly smile, which meant he'd been watching for some time. He had a habit of watching, which made Ajax feel both esteemed and spied on.

Ajax nodded at the slogan-covered walls: "Leonel."

Leonel Rugama had been a young poet and guerrillero when he'd been caught in a safe house right here in Managua in 1970. Surrounded by two hundred National Guardsmen, he'd held them off with one Thompson submachine gun and a few grenades. The Ogre had been so thrilled to have caught an actual Sandinista he'd ordered the siege broadcast live on TV and radio. Leonel had held them off for hours as the entire nation watched, transfixed. No one, literally, had ever seen such a thing!

Leonel would pop up in one window, fire a burst, and then weather a shit storm of lead from the Ogre's best troops. Then the rascally bastard would pop up in another window and toss a grenade. It was during this siege that an officer had broadcast a demand for his surrender, and Leonel had shouted for the entire world to hear live on TV, *"Que se rinda tu madre!"*

The Guard finally had had to call up a tank to blast the house. Still, the country watched the Guard hesitate for an hour before making the final assault. And when they did, a broken, bloody Leonel got off one final burst before dying.

"Que se rinda tu madre." Horacio smiled. "That brother was more than a compa. I think he was a nuclear physicist. Or an alchemist!"

Ajax cut his eyes at the old man, wondering how he would bring *that* together.

"Do you know what $E = mc^2$ means?"

Ajax paused to light a Marlboro. "Ah, it's Latin for 'your mama surrenders'?"

"Always the vulgarian. It means that from a small thing comes a great energy. Leonel understood that. He understood in his revolutionary consciousness that holding the Guard off like that he was the smallest grain of plutonium, but he would unleash a firestorm that would make him immortal."

Ajax exhaled a cloud of doubt. "You think he died knowing that?"

"None of us die knowing the good we did. But the real tragedy is that he died not knowing that as a poet he gets to be remembered for his shortest verse. It was the beginning of the end for Somoza."

"You think?"

"Of course. No amount of Somoza propaganda or intimidation could ever overcome the unifying, collective grief—the sigh heard 'round the world!—when they dragged Leonel's body from the rubble. *Your mamma surrenders* instantly became a cultural touchstone. College students graffitied the country with it. Children shouted it at rivals in the schoolyard. Workers whispered it behind their bosses' backs. Henpecked husbands and neglected wives prayed it into their pillows. Farmers spelled it out in their cornfields. And all of them, every one of them, muttered it under their breath as they passed the Guardia."

They arrived at a windbreak of trees, and Ajax turned off the carretera into Las Colinas and Gio's house.

After a long pause, Horacio simply said, "It was a slogan worth fighting for."

And that it had been, Ajax agreed. But it was no longer the slogan they fought for.

He had joined the war, and so he had done what the logic of war dictated. Ajax had learned early on that he had a facility for night fighting, and yes, for throat cutting. And he'd told himself, believed, that every life he took with The Needle—whether of a sleepy sentry or a lost soldier—had needed taking. He had never complained. And when it had begun to feel that each time he stuck The Needle into a man's neck he was shaving off a bit of his own soul, he'd accepted the price. He'd had faith that if his motives were pure, then his soul would be restored, either in victory or in death. That faith had been slowly replaced with rum. Now that the rum had ceased to flow, he was waking in his bed with The Needle in his hand, and something staring in his window. It only just now occurred to Ajax that the specter outside his window might be connected to The Needle's well-worn blade.

Been a lot of dying lately. Horacio's words again floated through his mind, but as past or prologue he was no longer sure.

At least all this death would get one good funeral.

He drove on, turning left or right without thinking, to Gio's house. *Our house.* There were no ugly gray walls here. No graffiti, no slogans. *No compañero.* Las Colinas was an upscale barrio of about twenty acres, full of diplomats, foreigners, and the upper-middle-classes of the Sandinista "nomenklatura"—a term imported from the Soviets as surely as the Lada he was driving. It was an old saw that there were three social classes in Latin America: dirt floor, concrete floor, and tiled floor. The Revo could no more change that than Christ could've declined crucifixion. Las Colinas was nothing but tiled floors as far as the eye could see, which was maybe why it was stashed behind the trees.

He turned down Gioconda's street and found it lined with vehicles. He parked at the end of the line. Their rides informed him how his old comrades had fared over the years. Some were Ladas, like Ajax's, only in better shape and none marked POLICÍA. But most were Jeep Cherokees and Toyota pickups from various ministries: health, land reform, education, defense, State Security, the army. A dozen drivers milled around, the mark of the truly "in."

He pulled to a stop, but could not yet will himself to go in and join old compañeros in mourning the death of one of their greatest. He'd skipped the burial service, as he'd told Marta he would. The morning newspapers, lying on Horacio's lap, had featured his exploits at the airport. *Barricada* and *El Nuevo Diario* had played up the government line about a desperate escape attempt by the notorious killer of young girls. But *La Prensa* had run an enormous headline,

"Bienvenidos a Nicaragua," above a half-page photo spread of a crazed-looking Ajax murdering the fat fuck, accompanied by one of that gringa in mid-slap. Connelly, all wide-eyed, was in the background of that one. Worse, they'd run two full pages inside—a sequence of shots from dignified VIP press conference to bedlam. The last one featured El Gordo in the choke hold, almost unconscious, Ajax's mouth pressed to his ear, a sadistic scowl twisting his face. Carrot Head was in that one, too. Strange, but she didn't look panicked. The worst, however, was a photo in dead center capturing Gioconda and the portly Foreign Minister running for their lives. For those not familiar with their ample backsides, the paper kindly identified them in a caption in type as large as a bullet.

How could he face anyone, even at this more private memorial service? Especially Gio. She was so vain about her ass. What could he say? "Photos never lie, but liars publish photos?"

He lit a Marlboro and smoked without pleasure, thinking that the Hunchback was not a hunchback, but had always been in pain.

The sounds of a mariachi band playing a funereal "La Vida No Vale Nada" floated out from the gathering. Ajax silently cursed himself for feeling so nervous.

"Ready, Ajax?"

"Do me one favor?"

"Of course."

"Feed me what looks like rum and cokes, so I don't have to explain, you know. . . ."

"Your sobriety." Horacio patted his leg. "Of course."

"Horacio, *amorrrrrrrr*!" Gio trilled her R's at him. "Come on, come in."

Gioconda glided toward them. Barefooted. Her face unmade. Dressed in a simple black shift. Her hair tied back in a bandana—the red and black of the Sandinista Front. That hair. It was an unimaginable tangle of curls no woman ever believed was natural. The one time in his life Ajax had waxed lyrical, he'd compared her locks to vines in the Garden of Eden. How long had it been between that sober night and the drunken one he'd stood over her with scissors determined to denude the Gorgon?

"I see you brought the saboteur with you."

He and Horacio climbed from the Lada. She hugged the old man's neck. Ajax noticed that she'd resumed shaving her armpits. Funny, she'd gotten all hairy back in '79 when the fashion was guerrilla chic.

She kissed Horacio on the mouth, and turned to her ex-husband.

"Why does it seem whenever I see you there is some disaster? The last time you were here"—she swept her arm over the house—"you started a fight with that American film director and pushed Bianca Jagger into the pool."

"Did I?"

"She slapped you for it."

"Her, too?"

Gio put her arm through Horacio's and led him inside, but turned back to Ajax.

"It is my honor to host this memorial. A truce for today. Come inside, everyone is waiting for you."

Ajax followed a few steps behind. As they entered, Ajax slowed to let Horacio enjoy his greetings. But also to reconnoiter the walls of the entryway. They were covered in a gallery of photos of Gioconda in various places with a menagerie of the big shots she entertained as vice foreign minister—not of a nation, but of everyone's favorite *Revolución!* Ajax recognized the Vietnamese general. He'd been on that trip, the furthest from home he'd ever been. He also recognized a few of the Cubans. The others were a mélange of European, Russian, and Latin American dignitaries. Pride of place, he noticed, was given to the writers and artists who came to soak up the revolutionary milieu. He'd been around for a few of those assemblages. Gio had given him Graham Greene and Gabriel García Marquez to read before their

visits. That photo was dead center on the wall, showing those two li-
ons and a laughing Gio at a table littered with food and drink. He
had sat somewhere to her left, not really following the literary shop
talk that had droned on for hours. Maybe the scowl on his face had
got him cropped out of the trophy shot. But he spotted his pack of
Reds on the table at her elbow—which, as he recalled, the other two
sons of bitches had helped themselves to all night while skewering
yanqui imperialism with their wit.

It was after that visit he'd realized that all the novels and plays
were not meant to enlighten him, but to make him presentable.

He searched the wall and was heartened to see himself in one
photo—a copy of the one he kept in his drawer with her makeup bag.
If the gallery was a map of her life, his photo had once been closer to
the equator, but had since drifted to the far northwest. Any further
and it would fall off the edge of the world.

The lawn in back of the house was filled with people in various states
of mourning and sobriety. The crowd spilled around the tasteful
flower beds, and around her small, crystal-clear pool. Ajax was met
by a chorus of hearty voices.

"Ajax! Look at you, fucker, I thought you were dead!"

"Until we saw you in the paper! You fucked that fat shit up!"

"And scared them gringos back on the plane, man. I heard they
went home!"

"You don't get out much, bro, but when you do, you know how to
make some noise, compa!"

"Give up them Marl-burros, Spooky!"

Ajax handed around one of the extra packs he'd brought. He divided the mourners into two types, as he did the world, those he
knew by their nom de guerre, and all the rest. El Chino was there. As
were Flaco, Blondie, Isadora, Gordo, Negro, three different Gatos, El
Matador, Rhino, Nora, Esteben, Cuqui, and Blue Eyes. Marta was
there, too, huddled with her boys, and looking fine in jet black. These

veterans—all of them the shot-callers of the Northern Front who'd survived at the expense of so many sandbags—all stood together, drunker and noisier than the other guests.

Ajax joined them, and amid their too-loud, backslapping, ball-busting camaraderie he felt the walls of his solitude become porous enough so that he could pass through. He wondered how they dealt with their ghosts, or if they had any. He guessed that some threw themselves into the work of the Revo, some obviously drank too much, and some lost themselves in the rhetoric that had sustained them as kids, The New this or the Socialist that, down with the yan-qui something, up with the Soviet something else, or long live the Internationalist whatever.

He felt a drink pressed into his hand. Horacio slipped him a glass of teetotal Coke with lime that all but the most discerning eye would think was the standard Cuba Libre. Ajax sipped and felt a warmth spread across his middle, which once would've been the li-quor. He realized it must be pleasure. He was happy to be among the old comrades.

"Be careful, Captain," Horacio whispered. "You're smiling."

"Been a while since we were all together."

"It's been a while since you were together with all of them."

Horacio turned to the assembled mourners. "Compañeros."

He said it softly, but in the tone with which he'd called them into formation in the mountains. All the veterans immediately came to order, and shushed those who had not been trained to pay attention, so they fell silent, too.

"Compañeros. Our old friend Death has harvested yet another of us. It is his manner and so we do not begrudge him. We have come to bid 'Saludos' to our comrade commander, Joaquin 'El Mejicano' Ti-noco. And we do so by quoting that ancient proverb, whose still-ringing wisdom reminds us: It is a far, far better thing to have died under the care of a pretty French nurse than with any of you ugly shit-caters!"

The old compas let loose a roar of approval that Ajax thought loud enough to reach El Mejicano on the other side.

Horacio raised his glass: "To Joaquin, and to Victory. *Patria Libre!*"

"*O MORIR!*"

Ajax tossed back his drink along with the others, and in that moment he meant it—*Free country, or Death!*

It was a fight to the death. Or it had been. Someone, maybe Horacio, maybe Joaquin, had explained it to them years ago. The guerrilla fought so he could live, so that he could die in the fight to be free. And if he did not die that day, he fought to live to die another day. Fighting to live, living to die, it had been so simple.

"*Compañeros! Compañeros!*" Gio tapped a knife to her glass. "We must mourn our friend Joaquin, but we must also celebrate him. *Música!*"

The musicians broke into a Mexican norteño, one of Joaquin's favorites. A paroxysm of Yips! And Ye-Haw's! rolled out as one and all put on their best Mexican accents and stormed the dance floor around the pool like it was the Bastille.

Ajax watched the dancing, and held down a flank of the bar. The uniformed waiter was from the InterContinental Hotel. It reminded Ajax that the Hunchback had steered him to a don Augustino there; it was his next stop after the funeral. He'd already sent Gladys to stake out his home.

"Ajax! My brother!"

Rhino assaulted him with a sloppy, smelly hug.

"I love you man. I love you!"

Rhino was a few years younger than Ajax, shorter and squatter, a light-skinned pure-bred barrio boy from León. Rhino had joined them in the mountains later in the war, and so always felt like the little brother who had to catch up. Ajax and he had worked State Security in the early days of the Revo. Rhino was another one who adjusted to peace with too much drink.

"Rhino, you smell like a drunken Rhinoceros."

"Yeah, man, 'cause I drink like one. Hey you! Give us some more here." Rhino grabbed two glasses from the waiter.

"I'm good, just filled up."

Rhino drained half the glass. "So, Captain Ajax Montoya, Policía Sandinista. How's that going, man? You working anything good?"

"No, man. It ain't like you cowboys in State Security. Working homicide in a country at war is like selling flip-flops to fish."

Rhino smiled the way drunks did, out of camaraderie more than comprehension.

"Listen, Rhino. You know two Seguridad compas, Major Pissarro and Captain Cortez?"

"I love what you did to El Gordo Sangroso, man, you fucked him up."

"Couldn't let him escape twice."

"Fuck no, bro." Rhino checked over his shoulder, although Ajax doubted he could see if anyone had been eavesdropping.

"I used to go with one of the girls he killed, you know."

"I didn't know."

"Not regular or anything." Rhino looked into Ajax's eyes and smiled. "She charged me Nica prices!"

Ajax had learned in chasing down El Gordo Sangroso that Managua's whores always charged in dollars. It was a true mark of favor to accept the inflation-ravaged córdoba as payment.

"She must've liked you, Rhino."

"She did man, she did."

"So, you don't know Cortez or Pissarro?"

Rhino seemed to sober infinitesimally. "You fucked them up, Spooky!"

"Yeah, they rubbed me the wrong way."

"Fucking Spooky, man. You don't give a shit about *anything*!"

Rhino swayed for a moment, his body, like his mind, leaning toward something. "You shouldn't do that man. Them two . . ."

"What?"

"These newer guys, man, they ain't like us. It's like . . . they're like . . ."

"Squares."

"Yeah man! Back in the old days they woulda been goin' to catechism class while we were out gettin' high! Remember?" Then Rhino did remember. "Well, you were in the States. Boomboomboom. But León in them days, man. Shit. We partied."

Rhino staggered through his memories of the good old days. "You been to Russia, right? Man, I fucking love Russians! They're all into the black market, drink more than I do. And sing! I mean who knows what they're singin' about but they are some singing motherfuckers! Am I right?"

Rhino shook his head at some inner marvel, and then threw an arm around Ajax's neck. "Pissarro and Cortez, they're more like East Germans, man. Boomboomboom!"

"Yeah, I hear you, Rhino. But what do they *do*?"

Rhino waved his glass around. "Whatta they do? They get fucked up by you!"

He grabbed Ajax in a sloppy hug. Rhino loved him in the way the old veterans were all devoted to each other. But Ajax had seen him pause and decide not to answer the question, reveal more than orders allowed. Not even Rhino ever got *that* drunk.

"Ajax, my brother. *Mi jefe*, right? The 'Prince of Peace,' wherever we went we made peace, didn't we? Huh? We did something, didn't we?"

"Freed the nation."

"That's what I'm talkin' about! We freed the fucking nation!" He drained his glass so deeply he almost toppled backward off his heels. Ajax grabbed his arm and Rhino lurched forward, his head pounding into Ajax's chest. He left it there, rotated it against one of Ajax's shirt buttons, as if drilling a hole.

"It ain't like it used to be." He spoke into Ajax's chest. "We ain't like we used to be."

"We're not the rebels anymore."

"We are not the fucking *rebels* anymore, man."

Ajax patted Rhino's back. Knowing the drunken sobs would follow.

"The shit we do now, man. The shit we do now."

But Rhino pulled himself back from tears and bear-hugged Ajax, lifted him off the ground, kissed him on the cheek, and whispered fiercely, "Don't fuck them up anymore, them two. They watching you, Spooky. I don't know why. You gotta be cool, man, them two ain't *compas*."

Ajax almost didn't hear the last part. Gio had caught his eye with a smile that meant she would deign to recognize him now.

"What is it about you boys and homoeroticism?"

"We ain't homos!" Rhino was the clown again. "We fucking love each other!"

Rhino was still sober enough to know he should move on and went pinballing away. Ajax watched him—Rhino had more to tell him, he was sure. But the news that he was under surveillance brought the Hunchback's face to his mind.

Gio touched his arm. "How are you Ajax?"

She was flushed from dancing. The beads of sweat on her forehead looked to be made of crystal with the tiniest drops of nectar locked inside. Ajax's tongue should twitch with the desire to lick them off. But did it?

"This is a great party," he said. "Joaquin would've liked it. Did you see him, before . . ."

She nodded. "The day before. He'd been in a lot of pain. Very doped up. But near the end he made the doctors stop everything. I think he went back to the mountains, in his mind. He kept asking for powdered milk."

That made Ajax smile. "Our only luxury all those years."

"I bet you still keep some in the house."

"Who's gonna replace him?"

"He was one of a kind."

"On the National Directorate, Gio. Who's gonna take Joaquin's place?"

"So you do still think politically."

"I'm not dead, Gio. Just busy. And of the 'Nine' on the Directorate, Joaquin was the tiebreaker. So who'll replace him?"

The band swung seamlessly into a slow song, "El Cantante." It had been one of *their* songs.

He was about to ask, or not ask, just take her arm and lead her to the dance floor, when her eyes bolted over his shoulder and she grabbed him by his wrists.

"Ajax, please behave."

"Hey! I was just gonna ask, you know, request, invite you to . . ."

But then he saw that she was not speaking of the music, nor the gathering, nor them. There was a snatch of panic in her eyes, or worry. Fear? She took his wrists even more firmly before he could see what she saw.

"You owe me for yesterday so control yourself."

"What . . ."

"Please."

"I will."

He turned to look, and it felt as if his body did a somersault. At least on the insides. Whereas the moment before his blood had been headed south to the groin region where dancing with his still-sexy ex had held the possibility of a polite boner; now all that same blood reversed and rushed to his head where it already pounded at his temples until the colors of the sky and earth darkened.

Malhora. Sub-comandante Vladimir Malhora swept into the house, with an entourage of bodyguards.

Ajax put his lips to her ear. "You invited that shit-eater *here*?"

"Ajax, he's head of State Security, he doesn't have to be *invited* anywhere."

"But here? Joaquin hated him!"

"You're such a boy! Who cares who liked who?"

Ajax looked over her shoulder. Many of the dancers stopped to greet Malhora, who had swept his entourage onto the middle of the dance floor to make sure that they did.

"He's still playing games, the low-life piece of shit. If Joaquin were alive he'd never show up here."

"Joaquin is dead, and that is all history. I've got to live in the present and deal with his type. *That's* politics."

Ajax felt a sneer cut so deep on his face it might lop his cheeks off. "Politics, all right. He's here to show he's the next one, the one to replace Joaquin. Cocksucker."

"Just let it be."

His eyes went back to hers. Maybe she was right. He would have reconsidered further, but Malhora's voice dragged his eyes from hers. Malhora had dragged poor Rhino—too drunk to notice his boss had arrived—sopping wet from the pool he'd gone into since leaving Ajax. Malhora was dressing him down to maximum humiliation.

"You are a goddamned disgrace! You come to the funeral of one of the Revolution's heroes and act like a fucking clown while in the same uniform I wear!"

Without a word or a glance at Gio, Ajax sprang to Rhino's defense as if to the sound of gunfire. He strode across the lawn, easily avoiding Horacio's move to intercept him. Rhino's mind seemed to have sobered considerably from shame, but his body was still too drunk to right itself from the onslaught of Malhora's words.

"You don't have enough respect to keep sober? Is this how you honor *El Mejicano!*" Malhora was reaching for Rhino's soaked shirt when Ajax caught his wrist, and held him in a grip one millimeter away from pain.

"Who? Who are you talking about?"

The bodyguards moved in, but Malhora flicked them away with his other hand, like whisking flies.

"What are you doing, Ajax?"

There was a timbre in Malhora's voice, like a stage actor projecting to the balcony.

"I asked who you're talking about, 'cause I get confused, see? You say *'El Mejicano'* and I don't know who you're talking about 'cause we used to call *you* El Mejicano. Did you know that?"

"Ajax, it's okay, compa." Rhino was sober now in mind and body. "He's right. It's okay."

"No, it's not, Rhino." Ajax released Malhora's wrist, the better to get into his face. "We called Joaquin *Mejicano* because he was born in Mexico. We called *you Mejicano* because while we were dying in the mountains you spent the whole fucking war sitting *in Mexico* sucking down Russian vodka and Cuban rum and . . . well, you know we were never sure what it was you were sucking on up there, *comrade*."

Ajax had experienced moments in battle when time slowed down and a second seemed to allow him minutes to reflect on his action. But few times had seemed to slow as much as this moment when he looked around Gio's crowded lawn and saw that not a single face turned toward him. Not one pair of eyes would meet his, openly or clandestinely. Least of all Rhino's. Men and women who'd taken on an entire army with only twenty compañeros and eighteen shotguns were subdued by one bureaucrat in a uniform. Ajax felt the walls through which he had so recently passed become impermeable again. And he realized that Gio was right: the joyous camaraderie of only a moment ago was not their present. It was the past, shaken out like old flags, dusted off like the trophies of youth, and borne awkwardly to send off a fallen compañero.

They all lived in the present and Malhora owned that present, which was why in the seconds after Ajax's insult no one breathed, awaiting their *padron's* leave to do so. Malhora stared unflinching into Ajax's eyes, reveling in the triumph. It was, Ajax knew, why he'd come.

Malhora finally looked away from Ajax. "I think we need another toast to Joaquin."

Gio took Ajax's elbow and held him in check as the waiters frantically recharged glasses.

Malhora turned on Rhino. "Get out of my sight, you buffoon." Rhino slunk away, eyes on the ground. He left unseen, like an exorcised ghost. The guests played busy getting their glasses filled. Ajax looked around; only Horacio and Marta returned his gaze. Gio was right, he knew it. He only owned the past. He gently broke Gio's grip on his arm and followed Rhino's wake out the door.

Malhora's voice trailed him like an ill wind.

"To Joaquin Tinoco. Commander of the Northern Front. Member of the National Directorate. Hero of the revolution. Our beloved *El Mejicano. Patria Libre!*"

"*O Morir!*"

As he passed through the entryway, never, he knew, to return, Ajax stopped to look over the map of what had been their lives but was now only hers. He lifted his photo off the wall, the clean white square behind it like a sail that took him over the edge.

Outside the sun had tilted over enough to spill red over the western horizon. He watched Rhino drive away in his Toyota Land Cruiser.

"Ajax."

Gladys was waiting by his car.

"Gladys."

She nodded to the house. "How was it?"

Ajax followed her gaze. "Sad."

"I'll bet. I went by his house."

"Who?"

"Stolen Car King."

Ajax looked at the photo, and then tossed it into his car onto the pile of newspapers. "Anyone home?"

"No one. What now?"

Ajax looked at the young lieutenant; she was worried.

"What is it, Gladys?"

"Bodies piling up."

Ajax looked back at Gio's house. "That they are."

"Were we the last ones to see the Hunchback and Gypsy alive?"

"It could be said so. But we've got to stay on Enrique. His truck. Let's try for an audience with His Highness the Thief of Automobiles."

9

1.

The outdoor dining lawn of Managua's InterContinental Hotel was, Amelia Peck observed, supposed to be a refuge of first-world finery in this most third world of cities. Its high, whitewashed walls were supposed to white-out what its customers wanted an evening's respite from. Its tables were supposed to be like flowers cast around the pool, which itself was supposed to be an oasis. The waiters in maroon livery with green trim were supposed to move quickly and quietly, like a rumor among the boisterous guests.

But Amelia also noticed that the tables were wobbly, the cloths spread over them—bleached to within an inch of their lives—still held the ghostly contours of stains; even the white of the whitewashed walls seemed to run off into the grass beneath, as if they sweated milk. The pool, if Amelia could guess by the last red-eyed bather to emerge, was over-chlorinated. And the waiters, Amelia noticed from the face of the man setting another round of mojitos down at her table, seemed mostly terrified of making the mistake that would land them back in the street.

The American ambassador, George Lackley—a balding sixtyish academic as frumpy and rumpled on the outside as he was razor witted and hard boiled on the inside—had insisted she and Tony join him for a very public dinner at the Inter. "Let's take you out and show the flag," he'd said. "You're the only non-covert asset to ever actually lay hands on these sons of bitches."

Lackley raised his sweating glass: "To the slap heard 'round the world."

Amelia sipped from her half-finished first drink, but Tony gulped his down without taking his eyes off the lithe woman fronting a trio of musicians set up next to the pool.

"It wasn't as loud as that fat bastard doing all the screaming." Tony laughed to himself and Amelia recognized the signs—she'd known she should have put some food in him before they'd left the embassy. She stole a glance at the ambassador, who'd noticed, too.

"I don't know, Senator." Lackley lifted his glass to Amelia. "It was loud enough to make the front page of the Cleveland *Plain Dealer*."

That turned Tony's head—the largest daily in his home state. "The *Dealer* ran it?"

"Above the fold. *The Post*, too."

"*The Washington Post?*" Tony downed the rest of his mojito.

"On page nine, but nevertheless your fact-finding mission has taken on a new meaning. I heard high praise from State this morning."

"The secretary called you?"

Amelia and Lackley took identical sips to hide their smiles. "No, Senator, the head of the Central American desk, but he always lets me know what's on the Secretary of State's mind."

Tony's gaze wandered around the grassy dining area, stopped briefly on the costeña woman crooning a Caribbean love song, and then rode what Amelia knew was a stairway of ambition up to the night sky.

"Well, if the secretary is aware, then the White House must be."

Amelia chewed her lower lip. Lackley passed an amused eye over Tony—they'd decided not to tell him that only Amelia was in both photos.

"Well, Senator." Lackley raised his glass again. "There's only two years to the election and the vice-president will need a viable running mate."

Tony swallowed what was left in his glass and waved too enthusiastically for the waiter.

Lackley raised his glass to Amelia and murmured, "And Ohio might need a new senator."

Tony grabbed Amelia's untouched drink. "And all because of that awful fat man and that stupid cop. I don't know which one was scarier!"

That cop, Amelia thought. That strange cop bent over that enormous man, as if he might choke the life out of him, and whispering in his ear, "*Humo de leña.*" Wood smoke? Even in the midst of the chaos at the airport, Amelia thought the words sounded like a chant, or a prayer, maybe even an exorcism.

Then he'd stood up. "Welcome to Nicaragua." As if teasing her. That's why she'd slapped him, if she was honest. She hadn't been scared or angry. The way he'd looked directly into her eyes, unapologetic, as if the carefully choreographed diplomatic moment he'd imploded was less important than whatever a lowly cop was doing. She'd felt put in her place. That's why she'd slapped him.

She'd really belted him, too. The kind of smack she'd used on a Saturday night with the boys back home to transmit through their alcohol haze the knowledge that, no matter how tight her jeans, her ass belonged to her.

Amelia looked down at the palm she'd used on him. She smiled without meaning to, and so quickly looked away.

Ajax Montoya. She'd gone through the embassy's files and pulled the original clippings. The obese man was a serial killer and the cop had cracked the case. The killer had escaped and just been returned yesterday after three years. So it hadn't been a provocation. She'd tried to brief Tony on it, but stopped after he asked why someone would name their child after a cleaning product.

Then she saw him. As if her thinking made it so. Ajax. Not a cleaning product, but the Greek hero. He sauntered into the dining area trailed by a woman, also in uniform. A pretty young woman with close-cropped hair. Kind of butch, Amelia thought. She tried to discern their relationship from their body language.

The two of them bent their heads in conversation, he handed her some keys, and the young woman left. Ajax gave the diners the once over, and before Amelia could react he was looking right at her. He seemed to need a moment to recognize her, as if he'd been looking for a particular someone else. But when he did, she was sure he smiled, or at least his eyes did. He rubbed his left hand over the cheek she'd smacked.

Then she realized Ambassador Lackley was making kissing noises at her.

"It's how you call your waiter in Latin America," he explained. And sure enough, a smiling—semi-terrified?—waiter appeared.

"That policeman by the door," Lackley said. "Ask him to join us."

"That's a bad idea." The words went right from mind to mouth without passing through Amelia's finely meshed editor. "I mean, Mr. Ambassador, maybe it would not be appropriate."

"Nonsense. What do you say, Senator, shall we dine with the enemy?"

"Of course!"

Amelia studied her senator again. Tony had inherited that patrician's gene which allowed old money to suppress the glassy-eyed look of the inebriate. Amelia hoped the heat on her face was the night air and not a blush. The waiter returned with Ajax. Lackley rose.

"Ambassador Lackley." He held out his hand.

"I know you from your photos. Captain Ajax Montoya."

"And I know you from yours. This is Senator Anthony Teal."

Tony took his hand, Amelia thought, like he was glad-handing a beat cop in Columbus. "Glad to meet you, Captain. Join us, please."

"I'd enjoy that, Senator, but I'm afraid duty calls."

Lackley turned to her. "You know Miss Amelia Peck, of course, the senator's senior advisor for foreign affairs."

Amelia hoped she had carefully calculated her expression—

amused but not too much, friendly but not joking. She stuck out her hand and spoke the lines she'd prepared.

"Yes, we *have* met."

And the son of a bitch left her hand hanging there! His eyes were smiling, again. *Damn it!* She could feel her expression slipping. He leaned his head back, as if to get his face out of range, and then took her hand.

"A memorable meeting."

He shook her hand beyond the usual three-pumps-and-release, until she really was not sure of her expression. *Now the son of a bitch won't let go!*

"Señorita, my apologies for ruining your press conference."

"Well, it was really my press conference," Tony piped in.

"And my apologies to you as well, Senator. It was unforgivable, but things got out of hand. Literally."

"And I'm sorry my aide slapped you. Amelia's from the rough part of Cleveland."

Now she was sure her cheeks burned. Tony was oblivious to the slight, of course. Lackley noticed; so did this captain.

"She shouldn't be." He turned those smiling eyes on her again. "You shouldn't be, Miss Peck."

"Why not?" Lackley was leaning his doughy chin on his suety hands, but Amelia could see the fire in his eyes.

"Because I'm sure that slap is playing pretty well at home, isn't it Mr. Ambassador? In fact, Miss Peck, I'm sure the ambassador has already told you, you are likely to be the only American to *ever* lay hands on a Sandinista official."

"That's exactly what he said!" Tony was delighted by Ajax's deduction, and he was the only one not to register the incredible faux pas of saying so.

"Well, I must be going, I'll leave you to your dinner. Enjoy it, Miss Peck, you are at the Hotel Inter, the Rick's Café Américain of Managua. Everyone comes to the Inter. And everyone who does is either a spy, a refugee, or a crook. And by refugee I include all journalists, tourists, aid workers, and the like."

"Which one am I, then?" She spoke before she'd really decided to.

"While here, you and the senator are diplomats, and diplomats are by definition spies. Isn't that right, Mister Ambassador?"

Lackley bowed his head.

"Then what are you?" She'd spoken again without deciding to.

"Me? I'm a crook."

Amelia laughed, like a burp escaping her esophagus, and threw a hand over her mouth. He leaned so close to her that she could smell him. He stage-whispered, "I come here to buy black market cigarettes from the bartender."

"Really?"

"Really. I used to extort them from a hunchback, but no more."

"What happened?"

"He died."

He was joking, Amelia was sure, yet there was something in those eyes again.

"A hunchback?" Tony finished the latest mojito, and despite his genes his glassy eyes began to show. "What a character you are! Sit down here. I want to pick your brain!"

Amelia flinched inwardly as Tony grabbed Ajax's wrist with too much frat boy bonhomie and tried to pull him into a chair. "The politics in this country is complicated and I want to discuss it with a local, for once."

She wasn't sure how, but with a move so fast and strong, yet so deft that Tony didn't notice, Ajax slipped his grip and turned it into a cordial handshake. Ajax leaned over Tony as if to whisper in his ear. Amelia pretended to reach for her drink so she could listen.

"Senator, politics here is very simple. The world is divided into two hostile camps and the weak must choose."

"Us or the Russians."

"Yes. Two giants that stride the world, and if we don't choose correctly they will grind our bones."

"To make our bread."

"To make your bread, Senator."

Amelia took a sip, dumbfounded that Tony actually followed the allusion.

Ajax let go of Tony's hand. "So for us, Senator, the formulation is simple: politics is the art of choosing which dick to suck so we don't get fucked twice."

Lackley threw his head back and laughed. So did Tony. So did Amelia. But she'd just taken a drink and the mojito in her mouth exploded out just as Ajax turned away from Tony. He took most of it in the face.

She'd slapped him again.

2.

The Stolen Car King didn't live very far from the hotel. Barrio Bolonia was full of foreigners, mostly journalists who liked the convenience of being close to Government House and its press conferences, and the Inter and its mojitos. But a few well-off Nicas lived among them. Ajax felt sure the King lived here to be close to his client base.

He and Gladys walked down the middle of the street, dressed in civvies. The sidewalks were too crumpled and treacherous to use at night. Curbside was no safer, as the iron grates covering the city's gutter drains had all been pilfered for their metal, and many a pedestrian had disappeared down those dark holes, feeding, it was widely believed, the Ogre's many exotic pet reptiles he'd fed into the sewers as his last "Fuck you" before fleeing. So, the middle of the street was the safest place to be.

They stopped in front of don Augustino's house—a pretty two-story place with two tall jacaranda trees out front with twin tire swings dangling in the dark. A long, high-walled patio lined the upper floor. Big "buena vista" windows downstairs faced the street. The house was in complete darkness. The King was clearly not home.

"Too not home, don't you think, Gladys?"

She stepped away, relieved, he was sure, to get his arm off her after he'd insisted they pretend to be strolling lovers. But it had been that goddamned gringa he'd been thinking of. *Son of a bitch.* She'd slapped him *and* spit her drink on him. But instead of being outraged, he felt his face smile. *Pobrecita.* She'd looked so mortified, he'd been a bit charmed; the scarlet flushing her face had highlighted all those freckles and made her green eyes just pop. *What color do you call that kind of green anyway? Emerald? Jade?*

Then he realized Gladys was talking to him. "What?"

"I said, I'd never go out without leaving some lights on. There's two swings. He's got kids, where's the nanny? The maids? They'd leave lights on."

He smiled in the dark. She was getting the hang of it. "And no cuidador."

Cuidadores were the ubiquitous night watchmen who, in some parts of Central America, were organized gangs of thieves paid protection not to rob you. In Nicaragua they were often the brothers or uncles of your maids, paid to hang around out front from lights-out till dawn. He'd seen cuidadores up and down the street. Don Augustino, a well-to-do thief and racketeer, had none?

Gladys checked the street. "Should we just try knocking?"

The door wasn't open, but neither was it bolted. Ajax was pleased at how quickly Gladys popped the spring lock. She went in first. They stood in what felt in the pitch black to be a foyer. He took Gladys's arm and guided her into a crouch while he counted to ten to let their eyes adjust. When he could make out the inner door, he put his lips to her ear.

"Find the light switch, but don't turn it on."

Ajax could hear her hands searching the walls while he went

through the inner door. After two steps, the smell of blood stopped him dead.

It was not as heavy as it had been at the morgue emptying out Enrique Cuadra, but it was unmistakable.

Suddenly Gladys was at his side. He knew she'd drawn the Makarov from her purse the moment before he heard the hammer click. Maybe he could trust her, and should have all along.

She handed him a penlight.

It took only a few seconds to find don Augustino. The Lord of Car Thieves was sprawled in a chair in the middle of his sala, his head thrown back, mouth and eyes wide open, a stream of blood from each slit wrist ran down his legs, spread across the floor, and merged into one, like streams feeding a lake. A hunting knife lay at his feet.

"Turn the lights on Gladys. Check the house."

Even with the lights on, he used the penlight to get the best view of Augustino's wounds. By the time Gladys got back he knew what was to be done.

"Look close at his wounds."

She did. He was reassured to see her carefully but thoroughly examine the wrists, even touching a hand to pull it back and reveal more. "Damn, he really sliced himself, these are deep."

"What do you see?"

If she got this right, he knew he would tell her everything. She looked over the wounds again, the knife, the streams and pools of blood. Then the lightbulb went off in her head.

"The blade is long enough to cut that deep. But the wounds are almost identical. He couldn't have made the second one as deep as the first."

"So it's murder made to look like suicide. Like Enrique Cuadra was murder made to look like robbery and/or the Contra."

Her head snapped up. "The Contra?"

"Yeah. Once to the throat, twice to the heart. Their MO. Marta recognized it, too."

"You didn't mention that before."

"Just did."

Gladys stood up from the corpse. "How are they connected?"

"The Hunchback and Gypsy from the Oriental are both dead. We talked to two of them and were looking for the third, and now they're all dead."

"Who the fuck is doing this?" Gladys looked around the room as if the murderer might materialize.

"Not *who*, Gladys. *Why*. Who killed these three is hidden now with them dead—which is *why* they are dead. But they were killed because we were looking for Enrique's pickup, I'm sure of that. So, why was Cuadra killed? Find out why he was killed and we'll find who killed him. Whoever killed Cuadra, killed these three."

"I follow that."

"So the question is: Where do we find the answer to the *why* of Cuadra's murder."

It took a moment for her to do the math; when she had, she took a step in as if she might grab his shirt. "You can't go up *there*. It's the hottest front in the war. You *can't* go there! No one goes in less than battalion strength."

"Captain Ajax Montoya can't. You're right." Ajax looked at the bled-out white of Augustino's face. "But if I've got this right—I know how I can get to where the answer to the *why* is. And that will lead me to who."

"How do you get there without joining the dead?"

Ajax looked around for a telephone. "Journalists can go anywhere in our country. Connelly wants to stick his nose in our business? Good. He'll be my cover, hide me in plain sight all the way to Cuadra's farm."

"And me?"

Ajax scanned her face, like a tracker cutting for sign. But what does trust look like?

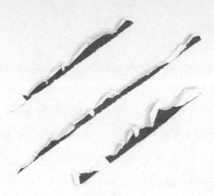

10

1.

The Carretera Norte up to Matagalpa split the Sébaco Valley, which, this rainy time of year, stretched away in such a luxuriant green it challenged even Ajax's thesaurus reading. The valley, in the foothills of the northern mountains, stippled in the sharply angled light just after dawn, like now, drew an almost hallucinatory response from Ajax's eyes, so long accustomed to the flat dull colors of the city. He combed his mind for some synonyms but couldn't find them. In his haste to leave he hadn't packed the thesaurus.

He stole a glance at Connelly, who had blessedly dropped off to sleep almost before they'd cleared Managua. Ajax was relieved to have time to enjoy the view, and even the driving. Connelly's pickup was a dream—power steering, power brakes, power windows, the air-conditioning whispering coolness in his face and the radio softly playing music with a static-less clarity he'd forgotten was possible. The truck seemed to run the gauntlet of the highway's potholes of its own accord. He felt at one with the machine in a way he only did when rolling the Python's cylinder over his palm. Through the steering wheel he could feel the miles falling away as he fled the raucous capitol, as if the alien city pushed him away from it, while the mountains in the distance drew him to them.

He picked up the wallet with his new identity, which was his disguise. Connelly, Ajax almost hated to admit, had come through in a short time. An ID from the Foreign Press Association identified him as "Martin Garcia, translator and fixer." And, for this trip, driver.

He and Connelly would be safe as far as Matagalpa, the last stop before the war zone. After that it was wide-open country in one of the least populated regions in all of Central America. His disguise should get him through any Sandinista checkpoints on the way to Enrique's farm. But if they were stopped by the Contra? Cuadra's farm sat right in the middle of a free-fire zone often occupied by the Contra's Jorge Salazar Command—the singularly most effective combat unit in an otherwise ineffectual army. Most Contra units and their commanders would leave their bases over the border in Honduras, make a raid or quick strike, usually against soft targets, and bolt back over the border. But the Jorge Salazar Command was run by a scrappy and wily veteran called Krill, a former sergeant in the Ogre's National Guard who, while maybe not the best military mind, was widely known as the Contra who most liked to fight. It was his men who most often went after the Sandinista army rather than school-teachers or health workers.

It wouldn't be hard answering their questions, he knew, as most of the Contra were campesinos who wouldn't know how to question someone. His survival would hang on that first impression. He'd sell the disguise in an instant or die right there on the roadside. The thought made him check the rearview mirror—in the truck bed, where he'd tied it down, was Enrique's casket. That, he knew, was the best "beard" he could have. No one really wanted to mess with a corpse bound for the boneyard.

That's when he saw the little girl in the road dead ahead.

The pickup was just rounding a curve and the girl was just, suddenly, there, like a ghost.

Ajax stomped on the brake pedal, trying to drive it through the floor. He kept his eyes on the girl. She was dressed all in white, in her first Holy Communion dress. He could see the tin can in her hands and the rope stretched across the road behind her. Ajax tried to stand up on the brake, but he could feel the road sliding away under the locked-up tires. He ripped the hand brake up and slewed the pickup sideways, the girl seeming to move from the windshield into his side window. "Goddamn STOP!!!"

"What the fuck!" Connelly awoke to find not the road in front of him but the countryside, and braced his arms on the dashboard.

And then the world did come to a stop. The pickup rocked back and forth as if it, too, was confused. The world inside the truck was silent. Somehow the radio was off.

"What the fuck?" Connelly was still straight-arming the dashboard.

Ajax looked the little girl in the eye, peeled his hands off the steering wheel, and lowered his window. She was close enough for him to reach out and pat her head. So he did.

"Para la Santa Madre." She held up her can for a donation as cool as if the Holy Mother had stood between her and hurtling death.

In a country like Nicaragua, charity was rare enough in the city where red lights at least held up traffic long enough to beg. But in the countryside people made their own stoplights: dress a few kids in their Sunday best, give them a can, and stretch a rope across the asphalt. A charity roadblock.

"What just happened?" Connelly almost whispered.

"Charity roadblock. Give me some money."

Connelly seemed to finally notice the girl in white, and reached into his pants for some bills. Ajax spotted the old woman sitting near the handful of huts that comprised the nameless village. There was always an abuela somewhere nearby keeping an eye on the kids, and her cut.

"Abuela!"

She waddled over while Connelly counted out a million córdobas in hundred-thousand cord notes. The bills themselves were laughable. They were older thousand-córdoba notes that had become so ravaged by inflation that the government simply had recalled them, stamped the three extra zeroes on, and reissued them. The makeover was so poorly done the bills screamed their uselessness even to counterfeiters.

"Only in Nicaragua can you make someone a millionaire every day." Matthew handed the bills to Ajax. "Even if it is only twenty bucks."

Ajax grunted, but took the wad and stuffed it into the girl's can. The smile she gave him was a mixture of gratitude and relief. Ajax reckoned she'd probably just made her monthly quota and could now go home.

Connelly reached into the backseat and took a bar of soap out of a boxfull he'd loaded back in Managua. He leaned across Ajax and gave it to the girl. She took it, pressed it to her nose, and inhaled until her eyes practically rolled up into her head as if in ecstasy.

"Gracias, señores."

She took off running, handing off the can to the abuela. The old woman called another little girl over, gave her the can, and set her at her post on the road. Ajax, who had for a moment just before the near fatal accident shed his cop's skin, slid it quickly back on.

"Abuela, you move this rope and these kids either a hundred meters in front of the curve or a hundred meters back that way."

"Yes, señor."

"Granny, I'm policía, don't let me come back here later and find these kids in the same place."

"Yes, compañero."

He felt a tap and found Connelly passing another bar of soap. Ajax handed it over. Like the little girl, the old woman inhaled it as if she might snort it right up her hairy nostril. Then she smiled with genuine, toothless cheer, and ordered the kids to relocate up the road.

The horn blast of an IFA truck clambering up behind them made Ajax pull off the road while a convoy of six laden trucks passed. They were full of soldiers.

Ajax gave a sideways look at Connelly.

"What is it, *Martin*?"

"I was wondering what all that soap was for."

"Let me guess, you thought I brought them because I'm a dirty gringo journalist."

"Something like that."

"Or just a dirty gringo?"

"Something like that, too."

"Soap's for charity roadblocks; soap's even gotten me through military roadblocks. Usually after I interview some campesino or a family in the war zone. My little rule, 'Take someone's time, leave a bar of soap behind.'"

"Why not money?"

"That, my dear Martin, would be paying for information. A mortal sin in journalism. The soap's more of a treat."

Ajax had noticed several cartons of Reds in the back with the soap. He'd helped himself to a pack.

"Why not Marlboros?"

"You're a fucking addict. Cigarettes are for soldiers. For dirt farmers, perfumed soap is a gen-u-ine luxury."

The last IFA truck passed. Ajax started the pickup, rolled up the windows, and waved at the old woman and kids as they rolled by. As he turned on the AC it occurred to Ajax that this gringo might not be a complete asshole.

The idea died a quick death thirty minutes later at an abandoned gas station just inside the hamlet of Los Nubes. Back in Managua, while Ajax had waited for Connelly to ready his disguise, he'd studied the map of their route. His attention had lingered over Los Nubes, and the gas station he'd known would be there. It had been the one stop Ajax did not want to make—too many ghosts.

"Look!" Connelly pointed to the soldiers' convoy that had stopped in the ruins of the gas station. "Pull in. Pull in!"

"Why?"

"Pull over when I tell you to!"

When Ajax didn't slow, Connelly reached for the hand brake.

"All right!" Ajax distressed the brakes again but missed the gas station. He reversed fast and slid the pickup to a halt. "You think this is funny?"

"Jesus, *Martin,* not everything is about you!" Connelly scrounged in the crew cab and came up with a carton of Marlboros. He hung a Canon 180 camera around his neck and loaded a micro tape recorder with a tape. "It's a military convoy pulled over. I'm a war reporter."

"They're not going to tell you anything."

"Of course they're not going to tell me anything. They've been trained not to talk to reporters and certainly not some foreigner on the side of the road. We all agree they're not going to reveal mission information, so that lets me spread some smokes around and find out what I do need to know."

Ajax felt the ghosts crowding around him in this place. Still, he was curious about Connelly's interrogation method. "Like what?"

Connelly stuck the tape recorder in his shirt pocket. "Questions like, are they conscripts or volunteers. See that last truck? The flap's closed, so it's full of gear. A convoy of conscripts is most likely militia, but volunteers might mean a hunter-killer unit. And five trucks of specialized troops and one of gear could signal a fight in progress or one to come. If they complain about riding the trucks all day, they might be coming up from the south, so reinforcements. If they're not ass-sore they might be from the base in Pantasma moving to a new post, in which case if I ever run into them later they'll remember me for the smokes I hand out now."

Ajax had to admit he was impressed by Connelly's interrogation style.

"Impressed, *Martin?*"

"No. Pressed for time."

Connelly smiled and got out, slamming the door with as much pique as he could muster. He took two steps and opened the door.

"And, yes, Captain Montoya, I notice where we are, and why you wouldn't want to stop here. So sit and ruminate with your ghosts or get out and help."

As he watched Connelly walk away he pulled out the Reds he'd caged. Ajax read the side: MADE IN MEXICO. The tight-assed gringo. He lit one anyway. He watched Connelly approach the trucks and pass out cigarettes. He had to admit the closed, blank faces of the soldiers cheered and opened. Ajax lowered the power windows so he could overhear them. He rolled the tawny-colored filter between his thumb and forefinger and studied the sky; fat black clouds were rushing in from the west to match Ajax's mood.

Connelly was right, he thought. This ruined gas station held more ghosts than Ajax cared to wrestle with—more than just Jorge Salazar died here. He climbed out to retie Cuadra's coffin against the fast approaching storm; but really, he wanted to eavesdrop on the reporter.

"I know you wish these were pillows," Connelly said, handing out butts to the soldiers in the closest truck. "Ass sore as you must be coming all this way."

The soldiers made no definite reply, but it was clear to Ajax that they had come far, as Connelly wanted to know.

Fat drops of rain the size of small tortillas slapped onto Cuadra's coffin. The first splash took Ajax in the eye and he retreated to the truck cab.

Matthew climbed in after the rain burst drove the soldiers back under their tarps.

"I love this rain, man. You ever come up here in March or April? This whole valley is like a desert; two months of rain later, it's as lush as the Garden of Eden."

Ajax stared out the window, recalling, as he often did when safe inside from the rain, all those years in the mountains when a deluge like this would catch him and his men far from their base, from any shelter at all.

"Tree stumps."

"What?"

"Tree stumps!"

"I heard you." A long, low rumble of thunder whooshed in on the wind. "It wasn't the volume I queried after but the enigmatic nature of the comment."

"When we were in the mountains, we'd get caught in this kind of rain, there was no shelter, no ponchos, and we'd just have to sit in it until it was over. Endure it. It could drive you insane, a rain like this. We sat like tree stumps. No mind, no awareness. A tree stump. You could see it in their eyes, how far away into themselves they went, the compas, to endure it. Not easy to come back all the way after that."

"Well, if it was as a coping mechanism, it seems a good tactic."

"No." Ajax cracked his own window a bit so the tormenta's wind song drowned out the radio, which he shut off. "It was a dangerous time. The compas were shut down, not paying attention to their surroundings, if the Guardia had had more balls, they'd have caught us out every time."

"You, too? A tree stump?"

"Somebody had to keep watch."

"The privilege of command."

"Or the price."

Matthew put away his camera and tape recorder.

"You know, I always assumed that you weren't in command that night here."

Ajax blew a cloud of smoke into the reporter's face, but Matthew just lolled his head back and the smoke was sucked out the window.

"The papers said you were."

Ajax smiled. "You say that, 'the papers said you were,' like you were saying, 'God wrote on a tablet.'"

"Do I?"

"You ever wipe your ass on *The New York Times*?"

"It's my absolute favorite. There's something about the texture that . . ."

"Shut up about it. Okay."

"Look, Ajax. I'm not judging you here. I think it could've been a beautiful operation."

"What?"

Matthew spread his hands to encompass the ruined gas station, invisible behind the curtain of rain that beat on the roof like hands demanding shelter. "The Salazar Operation."

Ajax turned on Matthew, and for once his innate hatred of all that was gringo gave way to an actual curiosity.

"What the fuck, exactly, could some fucking clown like you know about *any* of that?"

"More than you might think. It's about mid-1981, the Revo's not even eighteen months old, but America's got a new president and Reagan wants to cowboy-up something bad. He's called out the Russians, the Evil Empire, and he needs to beat up on them a little, but not head on, and here is a nice little country, just down the road, piss-poor in everything but Marxist-Leninist rhetoric."

Matthew paused for confirmation of his accuracy. "Tablet or toilet paper?"

Ajax smiled. "So far, tablet."

"So all the black-ops guys have hard-ons like no tomorrow and they come up with Jorge Salazar. I knew him. Before the Revo he was a nothing cotton farmer under Somoza. Afterward, he sets up his own cotton-growers union and he's a big cheese."

Matthew paused.

"Tablet." Ajax said.

"Then someone gets word he's sniffing around the Americans for backing and that same someone gets the idea to feed Salazar some rope to see if he'd not only hang himself, but the CIA, too."

"Tablet."

"So someone from the Revo, they get the word to ole Jorge, or, better, he overhears a 'private' conversation about discontent in the Estado Mayor. Rumors of mutiny in the Army High Command! Salazar thinks it's a thread he can pull to unravel the Revo, but I think it was the first inch of that hangman's rope someone was feeding him."

Ajax took a drag on his butt. Matthew tilted his head back to let the smoke cloud escape out his window. Instead, Ajax blew it out his own window and rolled it up so that the storm outside receded. "Tablet."

Matthew smiled, actually pleased to receive the man's approval.

"But it's a misinformation campaign, so no one feeds Salazar any more info. They make him go sniffing around. Make him pull the next thread. He reports it back to his CIA contacts and they, duped by their own propaganda about the Evil Empire, think they're onto something and give him the green light to spread some cash around, lots of cash to what they think are a bunch of unhappy colonels ready to stage a coup."

"Tablet. Very tablet."

"You were a colonel in State Security then, and I think you were in charge of that operation."

"Toilet paper."

"Toilet paper? Or no comment?"

"Okay. No comment."

"Okay. But then it must have gotten tricky. Salazar is pulling in that hangman's rope as fast as he can. But, what to do? What should Salazar's puppet masters do with him? How would the lesson best be learned? Catch him, try him, convict him, and let the whole world see the CIA had been duped, suckered like country bumpkins right off the bus in the big city, or . . ."

"Or?"

"Kill him and be done with it."

Ajax looked out the window. The storm was weakening, some

light in the western sky forecast its end. "Rain's going, we should get going." He turned the engine over.

"I think you were in charge of that first operation, the capture one." Matthew reached over and turned the engine off. "But someone changed the orders, they made it an execution. And they didn't tell you. Which means they knew you would not carry out such orders. And it means they knew that before you did."

Ajax had his fingers on the keys; the lightest pressure would turn the engine over. Put it in gear and drive, he thought. *Drive, push, propel!* But Matthew had so touched the needle, had counted every angel squatting on the rusted pinhead of Ajax's life.

"How do you figure that?"

"Files, my friend. I keep files on everyone. Before *l'affaire Salazar* you were popular, you show up in my files regularly—hero of the Revo, travels with your beautiful wife, on the American news shows, the *Gringo Sandinista* they called you. Then, that night here, at this gas station in Los Nubes. After that you disappear from my files for three years, when you turn up a lowly police *captain*. Admittedly, you had caught El Gordo Sangroso, so you were back to the hero stage."

The rain had stopped and Matthew rolled the window down.

"I meant it when I spoke of your ghosts. I think that night here haunted . . ."

Ajax turned the engine over, gestured to the army trucks just doing the same.

"Let's follow them, in case the road's washed out."

"Okay. They'll go as far as Pantasma. That's the Seventeenth Light Hunter Battalion."

Ajax turned off the engine. The Seventeenth was the suicide soldier's unit. He grabbed a pack of Marlboros and dashed to catch the trucks.

"Oyen! Compañeros!" He held up the Marlboro pack and jogged after one of the trucks. "Any of you know Fortunado Gavilan? Fortunado Gavilan!"

One soldier leaned forward when he heard Ajax call the name of the boy Ajax could not save.

"Did you know him?"

The soldier leaned out the back of the truck; Ajax broke into a run to hand off the smokes to him.

"Did you know Fortunado Gavilan?"

The soldier stared at Ajax a moment, stared hard, and then shook his head, no. He crumpled the pack and lobbed it at Ajax's feet like a grenade. The trucks growled in low gear as they climbed the foothills into the mountains from which more than a few of them would not return.

Ajax studied the crushed smokes. He kicked them just in case they might go off. The road to Matagalpa was proving a strange one.

It would only get weirder.

They hadn't gone more than ten miles, Ajax flooring it like he might catch something, when they rounded another curve and had to swerve to avoid a white Toyota half sunk into a pothole the size of a moon crater. There was already a yoke of oxen trying to drag the broken vehicle out. Ajax slowed as he swerved but pushed the pedal to the metal as soon as he was clear of it. But watching the wreck in his rearview as they sped away, he noticed a very familiar head of carrot-colored hair appear, and a milky white arm signal the oxen to pull.

11

1.

Ajax didn't notice Amelia Peck until it was too late. He should have seen her right off because he'd stationed himself in the patio restaurant of Matagalpa's Hotel Ideal to do just that. He'd spent no little time thinking about her the night before as he tossed and turned in a bed in the casita Connelly kept near the center of town. What the hell would someone like her be doing so far from Managua, and without handlers? At least the visible kind, which would mean she either was trained to elude handlers, or, worse, had unseen handlers tracking her, which could mean agents from State Security who might recognize Ajax.

But she didn't seem the spook type, so he'd come to the one place someone traveling in the open would come to in Matagalpa—the Ideal's restaurant.

But he'd been distracted by the Hula Hoop Queen doing her morning workout on the patio.

He and Connelly had passed the one-ring Soviet circus tent set up in Matagalpa's main park yesterday as they'd cruised into town just before sunset. Indeed, the vision now before him, with her implausible white gold hair, and cobalt eyes, was prominently depicted on the socialist-realist mural advertising the show. *The Hula Hoop Queen!* He and Connelly had wondered what kind of main event that was. But Ajax could see now that every male over thirteen and every female under thirteen would line up to see this wonder. More than once.

He counted again the hula hoops spinning before him like so many hypnotists' pendants. Six on each arm, eight around her waist, and three around her neck, all on a figure clothed in a form-fitting second skin like a gymnast might wear. The hoops spun harmoniously, the left side clockwise, the right side counterclockwise. All of them kept in perfect, perpetual motion by the most subtle flick of her hips. The energy from that undulation flowed through her torso and limbs like the tremors of some benign earthquake, which, rather than topple buildings and kill people, turns down your bed linens, or picks the mangoes from your trees.

This was the kind of fraternal socialist exchange his country needed.

The Hula Hoop Queen slowly stripped the hoops off, one at a time, until there was just the one left, dizzyingly spinning around her waist. Her rhythm changed, morphed, and she moved that one hoop up and down her body like a snake slithering over her skin. Ajax thought what he had been watching was the kiddy matinee, but this was a belly dance for the grownups.

"The greatest show on earth."

Amelia stood over him dressed in hiking boots, khaki pants, and a floral print T-shirt under the kind of many-pocketed safari vest photographers often wore to hold rolls of film. She held a wide-brimmed sun hat in her freckled hand, and had her mad tangle of orange hair tied down like the sails of a schooner. Her freckles seemed to climb up out of her shirt like tiny footprints, track along her white neck, across her ears, and disappear in her scalp.

Ajax thought she seemed dressed for gardening, or a lion hunt. He chose gardening. It made him smile.

She sat down opposite him, pointed at a waiter, then at Ajax's coffee.

"Café con leche, por favor."

She gave the Hula Hoop Queen the once-over, and smiled into Ajax's face.

"Breakfast and a floor show, quite a hotel."

"Circus is in town."

"So I saw. You seemed engrossed."

"Engrossed?"

"It means to be held in the grip of . . ."

"I know what it means. I espeaky Englishy berry goodee."

She nodded to the doorway. "I was standing there watching you watch her. You seemed held in a grip of . . ."

The waiter set a menu in front of Amelia.

Ajax looked over at the Hula Hoop Queen, who let the ring fall to her feet, grasped it with the toes of her left foot, flipped it into the air, and caught it with her right index finger. Ajax applauded quietly and she rewarded him with a bow before sashaying off to her room, chamber, boudoir.

The waiter set Amelia's coffee down.

"To eat, señorita?"

"What do you recommend, *Martin*?"

Ajax snapped his head around. No, he realized, it was a lion hunt.

Amelia leaned over the table, whispered like a conspirator. "I met Matthew outside, he said his 'driver Martin' was in here. I'd thought I'd play along."

Fucking Connelly, Ajax thought. Stupid goddamn gringo. Ajax could've covered Captain Montoya's presence in Matagalpa with the thinnest of lies. But not the subterfuge of Martin Garcia. Ajax shot the waiter a look.

"Okay, I come back." The waiter disappeared.

"Where is Connelly?" he asked her.

"He went to the gas station to see if he could get them to expedite repairs on my Toyota. I hit a pothole. . . ."

"I saw."

"You saw? Thanks for the lift."

"You seemed to be doing fine with the oxen. You asked me what I recommend. I recommend you get back to Managua unless you have valid, written permission to be outside the capital."

"Permission? I don't need permission. There are no restrictions on my visa."

"But there are. You can't go traipsing around our country dressed in your safari outfit like you're on the Serengeti. You're an agent for an enemy state."

As he'd hoped, the color rose in her face, darkening it like a cloud over the sun.

"Our countries are not at war."

"Really? We have been at war for years, and once Senator Teal makes his report and you vote another hundred million to the Contra, we will still be, only more so."

The fire in her face cooled, her skin went from red to white. The freckles now looked more like rose petals on white marble, or maybe alabaster.

"When Senator Teal's mission is complete, he will make a report . . . ."

"Miss Peck, spare me your fact-finding mission bullshit. You're here to air the senator out, get him some experience in the field; maybe he'll bag a lion for the newspapers back home, that's why you dress like you're on safari isn't it?"

He'd hoped she'd take the bait. He needed to distract her from *his* mission in Matagalpa and why he was traveling incognito. But she didn't. Ajax watched her spoon hover between two bowls on the table. She dipped it into one and dropped two dollops of white granules into her coffee. Ajax waited as she stirred thoroughly and sipped it. The bitterness made her spit it back out, but she seemed aware of his gaze, so she tried to reverse the action, like a batter's checked swing. Some of it dribbled down her chin.

Ajax smiled. "Well, at least you didn't spit it on me."

Amelia dabbed a napkin to her chin. "Or slap you."

Ajax pointed at the two bowls. "Here's some fact-finding for you—in the wilds of Nicaragua, the salt is white, the sugar is brown. Now get in a taxi and go home!"

He said it more violently than he'd meant to. He'd got up faster than he'd meant to. He'd embarrassed her more than he'd meant to. And as he stormed out he felt worse about it than he'd meant to.

2.

The Conquistadores enjoyed Matagalpa. Their Toyota Land Cruiser had working AC, a new radio, and smoked-black windows. But mostly they enjoyed the abundance of the town. Managua was far from the fecund mountains, and often the best of the harvest never made it to the capital, or at least not to the government-approved markets, where even they were sometimes forced to shop. (The definition of a black market economy was many a slip between cup and lip. So it was no secret that most landowners had perfected a sleight-of-hand by which they sold some of their harvest to the government buyers and the rest to the highest bidder.) Matagalpa sat at the foot of the mountains, so by a kind of economic gravity it collected the abundance of meats and grains, fruits and vegetables that filled its shop stalls and restaurants. And the Conquistadores' bellies. The black market was driven by dollars, which few in the countryside had, so Nicaraguans mostly bartered. Imported manufactured goods were also in greater abundance here, to be traded for the scarce foodstuffs. The Conquistadores already had stocked up on four cartons of Mexican cigarettes, a case of Russian vodka, a pound of Cuban sweets, three Romanian wristwatches, and they even split a sack of potatoes they'd bought from a house just around the block from the American's casita. Potatoes! It was the biggest luxury of all and cost them dollars. But why not?

The only drawback was that in order to enjoy the abundance of Matagalpa you had to live here as well. But they were only visiting.

And as soon as their orders came to kill someone, they'd be heading home.

3.

Amelia Peck went back to her room in the Ideal, grabbed a fresh bottle of water, and wrung the cap off like it was the neck of that smug, Communist, son of a bitch. Damned if she had grown up with five brothers, the only girl, in the testosterone tempest of East Cleveland to be bullied by the likes of him. She'd carried a wire cord up her sleeve all four years of high school and had used it more than once on boys who'd tried to paint a bull's-eye on her ass.

She used the bottle of water to rinse her toothbrush over the plastic basin that served as a sink, and gave her teeth a quick wash. She looked into her own eyes in the mirror and practiced: "A la mierda hijo de puta!"

Her hair seemed to spring out angrily in response to her mood. She grabbed the spritzer bottle Targa had given her and sprayed some on. It was like Jesus calming the seas. She had to shake it to mix the seltzer and oil and apply it instantly, but her hair obeyed and there was little or no greasy residue. It was an ingenious innovation. She applied it and felt again the pang of guilt for not having turned it over to the embassy security staff. She didn't believe you could bug a bottle of liquid, but she'd failed to report it. It had not been her only violation of protocol. She brushed her hair out. The concoction put it under control and left a fine shine.

She finished combing and pulled the loose red strands from the brush. "'Enemy agent on safari,' you smug son of a bitch."

Arrogance and machismo made him speak that way to her, play games with the salt and sugar. Well, she would show him exactly what she was *hunting* on safari. Amelia smiled, and her reflection smiled back in approval of the plan she'd made weeks ago that now would be all the sweeter once that shit-heel Ajax Montoya realized what she had been up to all along.

Sweat trickled down from her temples and under her arms. She pulled her shirt off and tugged at her bra. Why was the damn thing so tight? She allowed herself a brief paranoid trip of Sandinista agent-provocateur baggage handlers going through her luggage and exchanging her bras for identical but smaller ones. Just to mess with her. She slipped out of the bra, pulled on a T-shirt from Ohio State, and debated whether or not to use the last of her water for an in-room bath.

She set the hotel's bath towel on the floor so the word "Ideal" was right side up. It was pronounced "Ih-de-al" in Spanish, and the hotel seemed anything but. The rooms smelled of mildew and the sheets were a bit sour. She had been warned about drinking the local water. *Sandino's revenge* seemed to preoccupy her briefers at the embassy as much as Marxism-Leninism's hold on the country did. She'd brought her own water for the trip, but had wrongly assumed she could buy more on the road. She had about two liters left for drinking before she'd have to go native, or ask the hotel staff to boil some for her. That would be rude, she feared, and she didn't want to appear the Ugly American no matter what Montoya thought of her.

So she'd have to pass on the birdbath. Instead, she retrieved her folder on the family she'd come to take out, and flipped through the pages once more before her contact arrived. Henri Rodriguez and his fifteen-year-old son had arrived in Cleveland, Ohio, in 1983 from Nicaragua, and moved into where all new immigrants moved into—a tough neighborhood. A few months ago the son had been killed in one of those random acts of violence that was making war zones of many inner cities. It was the street sale of cocaine, and a new witches' brew known as "crack," fueling the carnage. But once the Nicaragua trip was on Tony's schedule, Amelia had conceived the plan to locate Henri's remaining immediate family in Nicaragua, and have Tony "bring them out." The Catholic Church had been most helpful in the finding, and the Sandinista government wanted very little in exchange for what Amelia knew would be a great humanitarian gesture and even better photo op.

The whole plan was so high level she couldn't wait to rub Montoya's nose in it.

Someone knocked lightly at her door, and she leapt off the bed, fearing it was Ajax and he might barge in on her. The bastard! "Just you wait a minute!"

"Señorita Peck?"

"Espera momentito!" She pulled her T-shirt down, checked her reflection in the mirror, and went to the door, heart pounding. "Who is it?"

"Father Jerome."

Her contact had arrived.

She pulled on fresh jeans and opened the door. The American priest standing there was so tall the top of his head was hidden above the doorjamb. They had corresponded for several weeks, and for some reason she'd created an image of a roly-poly priest in a brown cassock. Sort of a Sancho Panza or Friar Tuck. Father Jerome wore jeans and a blue cotton shirt. He must've stood six foot eight, was rail thin, sallow skinned, sad-eyed, and looked tired beyond what she knew were his fifty-plus years. He hardly seemed to blink at all. The first word that came to Amelia's mind was "Lurch." She stuck out her hand.

"How do you do, Father, I'm Amelia Peck. Sorry to make you wait, I was cleaning up. Please come in."

She moved aside to let him pass, but Father Jerome took a step backward. Amelia got a look at the top of his head and was surprised to see that his hair, which must have been dyed jet black, was combed in what could only be called a pompadour straight out of the early 1950s.

"Perhaps we could talk in the restaurant, Miss Peck."

"Oh. Okay. I thought we would have more privacy here. There's a journalist in town. . . ." She opened the door wider.

Father Jerome took another half step backward. "If you mean Matthew Connelly, he and I are acquainted. He is trustworthy. And I don't think the appearance of deliberate secrecy will help, Miss

Peck. Few actual secrets are kept in Nicaragua, and after all, you have assured me this is all on the up and up."

"Absolutely, Father. The senator insisted as well. May I buy you a meal?"

"That would be generous of you. The hotel does very nice frijoles con crema."

Father Jerome led the way, Amelia fell in behind him. She noticed that his arms—which dangled to his knees—moved almost not at all. She thought this might be because his huge hands, only one of which could cover her entire skull, acted as weights to hold the arms in place. She felt her heart beat a little faster. Her special assignment had begun. She walked with an extra bounce in her step.

It was the bounce that made her realize she'd not put her bra back on.

4.

Connelly's little blue house sat at the top of a hill on the north side of Matagalpa, its back to the mountains that crowded, shoulder to shoulder, as far as the eye could see. Ajax was in the dirt driveway bent over the gringo's yellow motorcycle fixing the gas line back to the carburetor. He'd been tinkering with the bike all afternoon, both to avoid talking to Matthew about breaking confidence with Amelia, and to avoid thinking about her. He stopped when the sunlight bent toward dusk. He looked west toward the far ocean beyond the curve of the earth. The sky was layered in clouds tinged a rosy purple where the last of the sun's rays touched their bottoms. But they seemed to lack the density to make rain. Now was a good time to take the bike for a ride. He put the Suzuki 500 into neutral, hopped on and off the kick start, and stepped back as it came to life.

"Fuckin' gringo."

Last night, when Ajax had commented on the bike tucked into a corner, Connelly had claimed it was unfixable. Ajax had correctly assumed Connelly meant there were no spare parts, which in Nicaragua

did not mean unfixable, but in need of immediate repair or your whole
family walks. Ajax squatted, closed his eyes, and laid his hands on the
gas tank. The vibration was regular and smooth. He straddled the
bike and gently popped it into first gear. He'd done some riding before in Managua, so he knew what to expect in the narrow streets of
the darkening neighborhoods—dogs. But he didn't mind. Despite
his run-in with Amelia, Ajax felt, somehow, free these past hours
in Matagalpa. The confusion of Managua seemed far behind to the
south, the very real dangers of the war still lay ahead to the north. For
a few hours he was free of both, and something stirred in him—
something animal. But purr or growl he wasn't sure, yet.

5.

Matthew heard his Suzuki get fired up and fade away down the street.

"Son of a bitch. He fixed it to spite me."

He peeked out the window and saw the red taillight disappear
around a corner. A Toyota Land Cruiser with smoke-blacked windows rolled down the street behind Ajax, and Matthew wondered
which of his neighbors could now afford such a luxury.

He went back to his desk and finished the plate of pico de gallo
doña Estrella had left him. He kept the house here as a place to rest
between tours in the mountains. Here he could rejuvenate without
making the trip all the way home to Managua.

Home. It was a little word, but to Matthew a big idea. He felt at
home in Managua, but knew it was not home, or at least would not
always be. Like all the journos, he'd move on one day—a stateside
newspaper, graduate school, a book contract. Hell, he was already
working on the book. *The Boys in the BLI: Life and Death Among the
Davids.* It was his first-hand account of traveling with the BLIs—the
Batallónes de Luchar Irregular, or specialized warfare troops. They
were the counterinsurgency troops the former insurgents had trained
to fight the current insurgents. All that irony had first attracted him
to the idea. How would an army led by revolutionaries who were all

ex-guerrillas fight a guerrilla army led by counterrevolutionaries? It had seemed so clever. Mostly what he had learned was that war sucked. Big time. It was either backbreakingly strenuous, mind-numbingly tedious, or nightmarishly terrifying. And all any of the soldiers ever wanted was to go the fuck home. But he rarely wrote that story. No one wanted to read or know that story. The Sandinista revolution had lit a fuse, and everyone wanted to know if it was gonna blow. Nicaragua was a proxy battle in the Great Game between the Superpowers. And every battle between America and the Soviet Union bore the whiff of nuclear war. Their proxy fights menaced the very survival of the planet. Nicaragua was, as his editor never tired of telling him, *the great existential conflict of the last decades of the twentieth century!* It was, in a word, sexy.

Matthew's editors did not want to read about tedium, scarcity, or boredom. But terror? That sold newspapers. And books. How it would all end, Matthew was not sure. But he did know that one day it would end, and when it did he and his kind would pack up and move on—taking a lifetime's worth of war stories with them. And what would Nicaragua be then? Just another dull banana republic full to the treetops with poor bastards' ghosts.

What would he have given for all he had taken? Maybe that's why he was so keen to play detective with Enrique's killing. He spread out the file he'd made for the Salazar killing and looked it over. He kept going back to that photograph—the one with Malhora at the gas station and Enrique just behind him. The gas station where they'd done in Salazar. The gas station where he and Ajax had stopped to talk to the troops. The gas station the caption said Enrique had owned. Owned? How was it that Matthew did not know this? Or better, how was it that in all the nights Matthew had sat up talking with Enrique he had never mentioned it? All journalists worth their salt knew that what someone least wanted to talk about was the one thing you most had to hear about.

Sure, the Salazar killing had been overshadowed by the widening war. But never to have mentioned it? That was more than peculiar. Ajax clearly had not wanted to stop at the gas station, even seemed spooked by it. Nor had he mentioned that the body in the truck bed had been the owner of the gas station. He acted like he didn't know who Enrique was, so Matthew hadn't mentioned it either.

12

1.

Ajax cruised through Matagalpa's dark streets, the motorcycle humming between his legs. He was on his fourth circuit of the town, going downhill toward the Ideal, when he saw Amelia Peck emerge into a pool of light and shake hands with some gringo giant. The giant headed uphill toward Ajax. Amelia Peck strolled toward Morazán Park, where the Soviet circus had set up. Ajax waited for the giant to pass by him. As he did, he drew out of his belt, like a sword, a three-foot-long switch he'd cut. On his first circuit around the town in the gathering dark he'd been ambushed by a pack of scrawny, vicious dogs—the poor man's burglar alarm. They were a necessity to the poor, but a dangerous plague to someone on a bike. The dogs seemed frenzied by the whine of the Suzuki's engine. At first he'd just wanted to drive them off. But then he'd sought them out and made a game out of it, staying just enough ahead of their snarling teeth to keep them charging, and occasionally counting coup on their heads with a light blow from the switch.

The gringo giant ambled by and Ajax pretended to study the switch. But he got enough of a look to determine that the giant must be a longtime resident. No one arrived in Nicaragua with a pallor as sickly as his, and no one who'd been in-country a while kept a pallor as glowing as Amelia's.

His cop's intuition told him to delve deeper. Or, at least that's what he told himself. He slid the switch back into his belt, revved the engine, raced up behind her, and slewed the bike to a noisy stop.

"Hey, jugo."

She spun around and Ajax pretended not to notice the two shimmies it took her breasts to come to a complete stop.

"I'm not Hugo."

"No, not Hu-go, Who-go."

"What?"

"Like jugo de naranja."

"Isn't that . . ."

"Orange juice."

"You are such a goodwill ambassador."

"Who's Lurch?"

"What?"

"The giant gringo you just said good-bye to. *The Addams Family*? Didn't you watch TV as a kid? Lurch, their giant butler."

"You grew up in America."

"*The Addams Family* was as much an American export as the Marines."

"I'm not asking, I'm telling you. You grew up in Los Angeles."

Usually at this point in an interrogation, he'd lay his hand on the butt of the Python to signal authority. He wasn't wearing it, so he laid his hand on the switch.

"How would you know where I grew up?"

"I suppose you're off to the circus to drool over your Hula Hoop Queen?"

"No, I caught the matinee. You?"

"I had wanted a quiet stroll, but seems not."

"Why are you here?"

Ajax turned off the bike. When he looked down to set the kickstand, Amelia grabbed the switch, and before he could stop her she'd drawn it and held it over her head, like Arthur had Excalibur from the stone.

"What're you playing? Knights in shining armor? I bet you'd like that Russian as your damsel." She laid her hand over her forehead. "Oh, sir knight, please save me, the dragon has melted all my hula hoops!"

She put a hand over her mouth and laughed, either at him or her own hamminess, Ajax wasn't sure. He didn't like being teased. Nor did he really dislike it. He did like looking at her neck as she bent her head back.

"I use that stick to hunt wolves."

That, he noted gladly, stopped her.

"Wolves? There are wolves in Nicaragua?"

"There are wolves everywhere. These are urban wolves. They come down from the mountains at night. Root around in the garbage."

She ran the switch over the palm of her hand. "And you use *this* to hunt them?"

"I don't kill them. Kind of like your American Indians, I use it to count coup. It's a national pastime in Nicaragua."

Amelia turned her head to the side, pressed her lips into a flat line, and made a skeptical noise in the back of her throat. "Yes, I'm sure you do."

"You calling me a liar?"

She looked directly into his eyes, and even in moonlight they shone emerald green.

"I don't think the delusional are liars."

Ajax stood the bike up and kicked it to life.

"Get on."

"I'm not . . ."

"You're one of those gringos who come down here with fixed ideas who won't be shown otherwise no matter how *wrong* you are?"

"No! I'm not. I mean . . ." She looked at the bike. "I've never been on one."

Ajax reached back with his foot and flipped down the passenger footpad. "I'll drive slow, at least until we find the wolves."

Amelia Peck swung her leg over the seat. She seemed to adjust herself as far back on it as possible to avoid actual contact with his body. But he felt her knees touch his hips.

"How do I hang on?" she asked.

"There's a handhold just under your leg. Grab it."

She waved the switch. "What do I do with this?"

"It's your coup stick. Slide it in your belt, like a sword."

"Go slow."

"Of course."

Ajax popped the clutch and the bike lurched forward. Amelia squealed. To save herself from tumbling backward she threw an arm around his neck.

As they rode off into the darkness, the Conquistadores' Land Cruiser trailed slowly after them. Captain Pissarro was behind the wheel; Major Cortez was next to him, an AK between his legs.

"You think he's fucking her? The Boss would love to hear that."

Major Cortez looked at his partner. "Don't be a dumbass. Don't you get it?"

Pissarro studied his partner—he didn't.

"Montoya's with the gringa, she's with the priest, they may all be with the reporter, and they've got Cuadra's body in the gringo's truck. Where do you think they're *going*?"

Pissarro watched the motorcycle's single taillight disappear around a corner. "Cuadra's farm?"

"Goddamn right. El Tuma. Fucking bandit country. Krill operates in the whole area and what the Boss expects to *hear* is that we followed them there."

"Oh."

"Oh." Cortez laid the rifle in the backseat. "I say we lost him."

"But the Boss . . ."

"Ain't nothing compared to Krill."

2.

Matthew was into his third rum and OJ when he answered the knock at his door.

"Father Jerome."

"Matthew. I'm sorry if it's late."

"No. Come in."

The priest ducked his head and took the seat Matthew offered, folding himself like a paper doll with well-worn creases.

"Can I get you something? Coffee? *Trago* of rum."

"A rum and coffee would be welcome."

Matthew knew Jerome was a "whiskey priest." So were most of the priests he'd grown up around in Boston. It was no sin among the campesinos who made up most of Jerome's flock. Matthew also knew Jerome, while a drinker, was celibate—unlike many country priests whose "housekeepers" produced children known locally as *milagritos*: little miracles. Celibacy counted more than sobriety in the mountains, and explained the high regard in which Jerome had been held for the twenty years he'd ministered to a parish a hundred miles in diameter, much of it accessible only by horse.

Matthew set down the drink. "You know about Enrique. I was with Gloria."

"Yes. Epimenio told us what he knew when he returned."

Gloria and Enrique had been married some twenty years. She was his second wife and was fifteen years his junior.

"How's she taking it?"

Jerome spread his enormous hands. "Devastated. She lost her sister recently. And now Enrique. All those years farming amid all that war, and he is killed in Managua. Was it robbery? Epimenio said they killed him for his car."

"I don't know. Maybe."

For reasons he wouldn't understand until later, Matthew pulled the old newspaper photograph from his desk and handed it to Jerome. The priest took a long drink of his rummed coffee and read the caption.

"Do you know about this? Enrique's connection to this gas station?"

"He owned it, of course."

"I was there just yesterday. What happened to it? When did he sell it?"

"He didn't. Sell it. It was confiscated by the government."

"When?"

"After Enrique was released from jail."

"Jail?"

"El Chipote."

"Chipote!" Matthew drained his drink. El Chipote had been Somoza's most infamous prison during the dictatorship. It was now the Sandinistas' most infamous prison, and was the private reserve of Sub-comandante Vladimir Malhora, head of State Security, the man who had certainly executed Jorge Salazar and who was front and center in the photograph.

"Why would they put Enrique in El Chipote?"

"You had better ask Gloria that."

3.

Ajax cruised the side streets of Matagalpa looking for wolves.

Amelia balanced her discomfort at their closeness on the bike with a need to stay on by placing one hand on Ajax's shoulder. The other clutched the bar beneath the seat, the coup stick in her belt.

"This is silly."

"Shhh." Ajax braked to a stop at the bottom of a darkened side street. One hand held in the clutch, the other revved the accelerator. He'd done battle already up this street, and now the engine sound was priming their foes somewhere up ahead in the dark.

"Do you hear that?"

"No."

"Hold the coup stick in your right hand. Hang on with your left."

Amelia's giggle seemed to Ajax more delighted than doubtful.

"Anything else, Captain Crazy Horse?"

"Yeah. *Confías en mí.*"

"Trust you?"

Ajax's left foot pressed down on the shift pedal, the bike popped into first gear, and he launched them into the Valley of Wolves. They hadn't gone more than ten yards when the headlight picked them out of the gloom: six genuine curs, lining both sides of the street in squads of three. Crouched in full-on ambush mode. Scrawny little things, none over two foot tall, but they packed eighty pounds of meanness into forty pounds of lean.

"There they are!"

"But they're . . ."

"Get the stick out!"

"Don't go up there!"

"Patria Libre . . ."

"No!"

Then the dogs attacked. Launched themselves, ears flat, hackles raised, teeth bared, snarling, growling creatures whose ferocity, Ajax knew, would pierce some ancient part of Amelia's brain, set off some primal alarm. As it did his own.

"Get me out of here!" One arm locked around his waist, the other around his throat, choking him. He had to let go the accelerator to free his larynx. The move slowed the bike and the curs gained, inches from Amelia's freckled ankle.

Her squeals of fright were more roller-coaster panic than Grim Reaper terror. Ajax sped up, keeping just enough ahead of the snarling teeth to ensure both Amelia's safety and maximum alarm.

"Get me out of here!"

"Use the stick, use the stick!"

"No! Just go!"

She'd freed one hand, the better to pound him on the back, but the other was wound tightly around his waist.

"Count coup. You've got to count coup."

"*Nooooo!*"

Ajax slowed so the mutts could gain a few inches. Amelia screamed again, but stopped pounding his back. A moment later, Ajax heard a pain-filled, "*Yip!*" In his side mirror he saw one of the dogs fall off from the chase.

"Coup!" He laughed so hard the bike wobbled for a horrible moment.

"Now go, you fucking maniac!"

Amelia pounded his back, but her laughter made her clutch him tighter with the other hand. Ajax hit the gas and sped them to the top of the hill. As they had before, the dogs broke off the attack at some invisible boundary where honor was secured.

"You're such a bastard! You are a lunatic!"

She kept hitting him, but each blow was softer than the one before, gentler, a little more helpless. She reached around his body, pressed both hands into his chest, and leaned into him, exhausted with terror and laughter.

"You are an insane person. Who *does* something like that?"

"Hey, you got one. You counted coup."

She giggled into his back. "The poor thing, I really nailed him, too." With her forehead she banged his back. "I can't believe you made me do that."

Ajax let himself relax into her, and for a moment they quietly held each other up.

"The good news is, you're now halfway to membership in the '*Cazador de Lobos Urbanos.*'"

"Dad will be so proud." She lifted her head, and Ajax felt her breath on his neck. "What do you mean 'halfway'?"

He revved the engine, downshifted into first, and started back down the hill. Amelia's shriek could be heard for blocks, but Ajax saw the coup stick rise over her head.

4.

"Oh yeah. *Oh yeah*. Oh yeah. *Oh yeah*."

Ajax's head was locked between Amelia's thighs as she rocked them both in the twisted sheets of her bed. His mouth was wrapped around as much of her sex as he could get hold of, his tongue frantically working that button her fingers had guided him to. Her orange pussy hair was scratching his face. Her hands kneaded his head, then pulled at his hair as she ripped his face up from between her legs.

"We've got to put it in now!"

She handed him the round, slippery diaphragm, a thing Ajax had never touched before. Earlier, in the midst of shredding each other's clothes, she'd paused—agonizingly—to smear the diaphragm in spermicide, and had told him she liked her men to slip it into place when the time came.

It had come.

Ajax took hold of it, but when he tried to bend it in half like she'd shown him it popped out of his fingers like a spring, flopped open, and landed on her belly with a plop. They both laughed, and Ajax was amazed at how it thrilled him, fired him, to look into her eyes while she laughed. Amelia grabbed hold of his neck and lifted her hips while her other hand dexterously folded the barrier and slid in into place. She moaned a little when it entered her.

"I hope that's all the help you need, Captain Crazy Horse."

Ajax lifted her left leg and used it to turn her onto her belly. She obeyed and her fingers grabbed a handful of sheets as Ajax entered her from behind.

"Oh yeah. *Oh yeah*. Oh yeah."

He slid his cock only halfway into her, and then most of the way out. It opened her up and made her flow. He counted silently each time until he reached nine, and on the tenth thrust he rammed himself into her as far as he could, and then more until Amelia's head smacked into the headboard.

"OH YEAH! *OH YEAH!*"

Each time he thrust in, she pushed back. Putting her hand on the headboard for leverage she slammed her ass back as hard as he slammed his hips forward. Ajax laid his hands on her ass and was moved by the contrast of his brown skin on her milky-white butt cheeks. Even they were freckled! A wicked feeling he'd never known before, or even imagined, made him raise a hand and smack her on the ass.

Only once.

But hard.

"Oh. My. *God!*"

Suddenly Amelia flipped herself over; her nails dug into his arms as she pulled him on top of her.

"Give me your tongue and I'll suck it out of your head."

Ajax complied. Amelia seemed to be trying to do just that. He slid an arm under each of her legs and set them over his shoulders. He pinched a nipple in each hand and slid into her again. Only halfway in and out again, like before. But when he reached ten he let her have it.

She let go his tongue. Her eyes rolled into her head. Ajax arched his back and lifted his head to the ceiling, to the sky, to the heavens.

"Ajax, yeah. Ajax, yeah. Ajax, yeah."

Damn, this gringa was a talker. And damn how he liked it!

She grabbed the back of his neck and bent him down to her, the look on her face half pleading, half exalted.

"Make me come, Ajax. Come in me and make me come."

"Yes, *amor*, I will, I am."

"Look at me, Ajax. Look in my eyes."

Ajax bent himself so their noses touched, almost eyeball to eyeball. Every time he slammed his cock into her he went deeper into her eyes. And she into his. A strangled cry gathered in her throat. She gritted her teeth, it seemed to him, in order to keep her eyes unblinkingly open. This was a new thrill. He'd never looked so directly, so openly into a lover's eyes. And he'd never heard tell of it either.

"You want me to fuck you in the eyes, too, gringa? Huh?"

"Yes! Come in my eyes, too!"

As if one detonator for twin grenades had been pushed, their orgasms exploded with such force Ajax was almost thrust out of her, but she pulled him back in, and they both finally had to shut their eyes and lock each other in an embrace, while their bodies were rocked, wracked, with spasms of such shuddering power Ajax felt as if huge ice sheets from some vast inner glacier were toppling into an emerald green sea sending tsunamis of pleasure rolling through his body, his eyes, his fingers, washing over Amelia and back over him again.

There followed a wonderful silence. Punctured only by small moans shaken from one, or the other, or both of them as delicious aftershocks dazed them.

"Oh, my good God. Ajax Montoya. Ajax Montoya. Ajax Montoya."

"Amelia Peck. Amelia Peck. Amelia Peck."

"That was fucking amazing."

"And amazing fucking."

She giggled in a way he'd not heard before. It made him open his eyes and look again into hers. She stared unblinkingly back. No fear, no discomfort, no postcoital shyness. He thought: *This gringa's got some sand.*

"What was that? You were like halfway in and then mostly out and . . ."

"Yeah, till the count of ten and then . . ."

"Blast off!"

She bit his neck, not quite as hard as he'd smacked her ass, but close enough.

"That was a good trick."

"Well, I been around you know. *Don Juan* was my nom de guerre."

"I didn't read *that* in your file."

Ajax saw a drop of sweat slip down her neck into that little hollow at the base of the throat. He licked the salty pool dry. Maybe it was hers, or his, or both of theirs. Then his head snapped up.

"My *file*?"

Amelia giggled again. "Uh oh. Spilling secrets like it was jism."

Ajax made a face. "Ewww."

"That was gross. Sorry."

Ajax sat up, and even though he was concerned by her revelation he still had to admire her body, sweat-soaked and glowing in the single candle she'd lit.

"Really, Amelia. My file. You had a CIA briefing on me?"

Amelia sat up, too. Her back against the headboard, she bent her legs and laid a hand on each knee. Damn! Ajax marveled. He would've never guessed she would lack inhibition like this. Amelia Peck seemed completely comfortable in her skin. Her naked, flawless, delicious skin. He sat back on his haunches, and although he was concerned by her slip, he still could not keep his eyes from roving over her body and down her legs to her carroty sex.

"Goddamn, you are a beautiful sexy woman."

"And you are a beautiful man." She ran her fingertips over his shoulders and chest, lingering on an old pucker of skin. "Complete with a manly scar or two. And you make love like a lion, or whatever big cat is appropriate."

"Jaguar."

"Yeah, a jaguar."

"Didn't say that in my file. Least I hope not."

"Ajax, it's not a 'file' as in a CIA file. They keep newspaper clippings and radio transcripts from all sorts of media. I was just curious."

"About what?"

"*About what*, asks the guy who brought my carefully laid plans within an inch of carnage, gunfire, and death? About what?"

"Look, I didn't plan it to happen like that."

Amelia rubbed her hand through his hair. "There was a lot of talk at the embassy about it being a provocation—your, you know, 'show.' So I read up on El Gordo Sangroso. He was a serial killer. Preyed on *señoritas de la noche*."

"Whores."

Amelia gently took hold of Ajax's ears and turned him around until his back leaned against her boobs and belly. She wrapped her arms around him. "Such a hard man with your bad language."

"Hard man?"

"It's a colloquialism for tough guy, such a tough guy with your bad language." She ran her hands down to his sex. "And a hard man, too."

"Well, give me a minute."

She fondled his sagging dick and gently stretched it out. "There's always a pause between eruptions; this volcano's not spent yet."

"You know, for all your prim and proper language, you're hardly the wilting lily."

"And for all your cursing and rudeness, you're kind of shy, aren't you?"

"Me?"

"Yeah, talk all you want. But in all those newspaper articles about the murders there were no direct quotes, like you didn't talk to the press even though they were writing glowing articles, even *La Prensa*. And the photos of you, they either looked like stock ones from some other time, or there was just one where you looked like you were dashing from a car into a building, like you didn't care if your fifteen minutes had arrived. So, yeah. Maybe you're shy, but disguise it with foul language and rudeness. The whole tough guy thing."

"A la gran puta, Jugo. You'd make a good detective."

She nibbled his ear. "Or a spy?"

"Don't. You'll make the volcano go cold."

"By nibbling?"

"By saying 'spy.' Our nations are technically at war; more than technically. More like literally at war."

"Okay, no jokes. Just nibbling. In your file there's a bio sheet. It said you grew up in Los Angeles. Hollywood. How American is that?"

"North Hollywood."

"Is that close to Hollywood?"

"Not the way you mean."

"And what way do I *mean*?"

"You mean Hollywood and movie stars. Swimming pools. That's Bel Air. I left Hollywood in '69 when it was skanky. Junkies, runaways, drifters, and hippies."

"Were you a child of the sixties?"

"Jesus fucked a goat. No! 'Child of the sixties'? You had to be white to be that. Or at least American."

"What do you mean?"

"The hippies were white, the Black Power brothers black, the Chicano Movement Mexican. We Nicas just did our thing."

"And what thing was that?"

Ajax smiled and shook his head at the memory. Or, rather, he shook the cobwebs off the memory. It seemed to him that Amelia sensed this and began kneading his scalp with fingers whose strength he'd already admired.

"My father liked to quote the favorite line of the Mexican guys he worked with: *En America trabajamos como negroes, a vivir como blancos.*"

"We work like blacks to live like whites?"

"That's good, gringa. But more like: We slave like blacks to live like whites."

"What'd he do, your father?"

"He was a professor. Of history. At least down here he was. When he got to *El Norte* all he could get was gardening. Pool cleaning. Laborer at first. He ran the crews later. Didn't my *file* cover that?"

She stopped kneading and gave him a playful slap on the temple. "You think your embassy in Washington doesn't keep files?"

Ajax turned his head to look at her. "Do you know why there's never been a coup d'état in the United States?"

"Checks and balances. It keeps the branches of government from . . ."

"No, Jugo. It's a joke. Like a knock-knock joke."

"Oh. Sorry. Go ahead."

"Do you know why there's never been a coup d'état in the United States?"

"Who's there?"

"Cabrona!"

"Okay. Why has there never been a coup d'état in the United States?"

"Because there's no American embassy in Washington."

"I don't get it."

"You would if you were Nicaraguense."

"Oh, here it comes. We're the big bad wolf. Blame everything under the sun on *los Estados Unidos*."

"And here you come with all that 'land of the free, home of the brave' crap."

"It's not crap, if by crap you mean untrue."

"By crap I mean bullshit, which it is unless you live *inside* the United States."

"Which is why so many come to our shores, to be free."

"You think the Statue of Liberty lights the way for the huddled masses. . . ."

"Yearning to be free, that's right!"

Ajax turned his face from her, looked up at the ceiling and re-cited: "Lady Liberty lights the way to conquest."

"What?"

"Rubén Darío. Everything we're going to argue about he put into a poem to Teddy Roosevelt. 'You think the future is wherever your bullet strikes . . . while Lady Liberty, lighting the path of easy con-quest, raises her torch in New York.'" He rubbed his hand along her thigh, perhaps in farewell, but he really hoped not. "No matter what you Americans see when you look in the mirror, Jugo, the rest of the world does not see that."

"The emperor has no clothes?"

He patted her naked leg. "You have no clothes. You are a gorgeously naked gringa. I'm talking about perspective. You gringos stand behind the Statue of Liberty and see the ships coming into the dock full of huddled, yearning masses. Latin America stands in front of the statue and all we see are the huddled masses of Marines leaving the dock for our shores."

"Now I'm a gringa again. Is the moment lost?"

"Magma cooling rapidly."

She rolled Ajax onto his back, pinioned his arms, straddled him, and settled her orange-maned pussy right on his belly button.

"Didn't you say you left the states in '69?"

"I did."

"That's my favorite number."

Her green eyes lit with a feline hunger. Ajax rocked his hips side to side until he felt his belly button grow moist from her. "Magma warming quickly."

The soft knock at the door put an end to it all. Ajax laid his hand over her mouth, then took it away and nodded for her to answer.

"Quién es?"

"Señorita Peck? Llamada."

She looked back at Ajax. He mouthed, *phone call.*

"Quién me llama?"

"Dice es 'Tony.'"

"Tony! Oh my God." She leapt out of bed and covered her breasts and sex with her hands. "What time is it?" She shouted through the door, "Qué hora es?"

"Casi media noche."

"Midnight! That figures. Okay señor, thank you! Ya vengo!"

Ajax laughed. "Not '*vengo,*' '*voy.*'"

"What?"

"In Spanish *ya vengo* means *I'm coming,* but as in the kind of coming we both already did. *Ya voy* means literally *I go,* but as in *I'll be right there.* So while you did already come, you are now just going because you'll be right there."

Amelia dropped her hands, cocked her hips. "Strangely, I understand that."

"Amelia." Ajax kissed her palm. "Your jefe calls you in the middle of the night. Why are you here? Really."

She pulled on a T-shirt, sat on the edge of the bed, took a deep breath and held it a moment. When she exhaled she seemed to expel her doubts.

"It's all on the up-and-up, but very quiet. Tony has a deal with the foreign minister to take three people with him, when we leave, to reunite with their family in Ohio. A 'humanitarian gesture.' They live in Father Jerome's parish. I'm here to pick them up."

"That's why you're traveling without an escort."

"Yes."

She stood up and Ajax watched her do a little circle dance, sliding on the jeans he had so enjoyed sliding off.

"You'll wait for me?"

"No way. Truce is over." He smiled as he said it, but it was true. "I don't need to warn you, if anyone finds out you're sleeping with the enemy your job is gone, right? Fucking Republicans got no sense of romance."

"No worries there. No one knows I'm here but Tony. The name is Amelia D. Peck, and the D is for Discretion. And you could probably be shot. Freaking Communists got no sense of romance."

"Not me. My job's probably lost anyway, but I'm still a bona fide hero of the revolution. You're just a carrot-headed gringa from Podunk, Ohio."

She grabbed him and poured her tongue down his throat. He pinched her nipples through the T-shirt.

"When I saw you near the park and realized you weren't wearing a bra, I knew I had to fuck you. I contemplated taking you by force."

She pushed him back on the bed. "Hold that thought."

She kissed him and slipped out the door. Ajax meant to dress and slip away, but a delicious sleep overcame him. There was nothing as peaceful as sleep after sex.

5.

Ajax awoke from the dream. Or, as sometimes happened, told himself he was dreaming in order to rush back to consciousness. As he crossed back into his waking life, it seemed he had time to lament that it all had been a dream—that he had not left Managua, had not hunted wolves, and had not made wild love with Amelia. The thought floated in his mind, *I will awaken in my dark room, on my dry sheets. I will have The Needle in my hand and I will not be alone.*

The fear of that shining black shadow, that ghost's shadow, was, in the moment before waking, not as big as the regret that Amelia Peck had not given her body to him, nor he to her. And it had been good goddamn sex. Gio, while they'd been married, had always seemed to be trying to teach him how to be a good lover; like she was comparing their lovemaking to something she had learned or read. But Amelia had seemed mostly concerned with her own pleasure, or rather so lost in it she seemed not to worry about Ajax. The feeling that he had to take from her as she took from him—frantically, greedily—was more arousing than anything he had ever known.

But it had all been a dream.

Then he awoke, in the pitch dark. The sheets were dry. The Needle was in his hand. He sat up in bed.

"What? What do you want?"

In a corner there was movement. The hairs stood up on his arms and the back of his neck. Ajax sucked in a deep breath, fear flooded his veins and brain. He swung his legs off the bed, and made himself concentrate on the coolness of the tiles beneath his feet. But then he thought, *I don't have tiles in my bedroom.*

"What do you want?"

The black shape moved toward him. But now it was clearly a human form, a man's form. Ajax stood, shucked the blade from its sheath.

The silhouette seemed to jump at him. A coldness moved through him, not over him but through him. The physical sensation pushed him back, he put his hand on the bed to steady himself and felt the bed depress as if someone had lain in it. He heard mattress springs creak with the additional weight. He had read of Old Testament prophets who had wrestled with angels. He'd see if he could kill a ghost.

Ajax pounced. Grabbed the ghost by what he hoped was its throat.

"Now, motherfucker, one of us is going to die!"

Then the ghost struck back. Hammered him in face and he pinwheeled off the bed onto the floor cracking his skull on the tile; The Needle clattered across the floor. A light blinded him.

"Ajax what are you doing!"

Amelia Peck sat up in bed, one hand on her throat, the other on the bedside lamp, which wobbled and fell to the floor. The lightbulb popped like a pistol shot and everything went dark.

13

1.

"What happened to you?" Connelly asked, handing Ajax a cup of coffee over the back of his pickup.

"Let's leave, we're late."

"Isn't that like a classic cop's rule?"

Ajax finished packing Matthew's truck with Enrique's coffin, which reeked of decay despite being double wrapped in a tarp. The sun was just over the eastern mountains, and Ajax had quietly prepped the pickup for the journey north while listening to Connelly puttering around inside his casita.

"What 'cop's rule'?" Ajax slammed the tailgate closed.

"That a suspect is hiding something when they pretend they've not been asked a direct question. You're standing there with a shiner on your face. I ask what happened and you say, 'we're late.'"

"We are late. Can't you smell your friend's stink pouring out of that box? What happened to me is not the direct question, the direct question is, don't you think we ought to get him in a fucking hole?"

Connelly sipped his coffee. Ajax lit a Marlboro, and realized he'd not had one nor craved one all the time he'd been with Amelia. Even better, he'd not felt the thirsty bastard begging for a drink since he'd cleared Managua.

"We should go."

Matthew nodded at the coffin. "What do you know about Enrique?"

"Know?"

"Yes, know about him. His background. History. Did you even check?"

"Yeah. There was nothing in the Policía files, if that's what you mean. No criminal record or court records. I know he had sons in the Frente during the insurgency and one of them was killed by the Contra in '82."

"I told you some of that."

"And I told you this investigation is none of your fucking business. You *got an interest* in this case, who goddamn cares? So does his family. The State. Me. You're here to get his body home. I'm here to investigate a crime. Agreed?"

Matthew went about checking the knots Ajax had already checked. "Answer me, Connelly."

"How'd you get the shiner?"

Ajax waved the keys at him. "I'm leaving."

"You won't get anywhere without an escort, *Martin*."

"But you'll just wave your American passport and magical things will happen."

"No. Father Jerome Sanderson will be here shortly. He flies the Vatican flags on his Jeep and has both sides' permission to travel anywhere in his parish, which includes the Cuadra finca. We're supposed to meet him at eight thirty just north of town. I would've told you that last night—if you'd made it back."

Ajax climbed into the truck and fired it up. He had it in reverse when Matthew jumped in. Ajax made a squealing-tire U-turn and headed down the hill and out of town. As they rolled past the center of town, Ajax scanned the front of the Hotel Ideal—he flushed at the body memory of fucking Amelia, and for a second he could smell her sex again and he regretted having washed so thoroughly. But his mind recoiled at the memory of the fear on her face after she'd awoken with his hands on her neck. He'd fled the room barely dressed, and so he didn't know if she'd even realized there had been a knife blade against her throat.

They reached the end of the paved road just outside of Matagalpa. From here on, there would be only graded dirt roads, if even those, all the way to the Honduran border and beyond. North and east of this point was bandit country, always had been, all the way back to General Sandino's shellacking of the US Marines in the 1920s and '30s.

"Where the paved road ends, the war begins," Matthew said, staring straight ahead at the road. He lit himself a Marlboro.

"Haven't seen you smoke."

"Don't really." Matthew didn't take his unblinking eyes off the road. "Just a little ritual. I always stop here and have one before heading out."

"What're you nervous?"

Matthew blinked. "You know who's out there, right?"

"You mean Krill?"

"Yeah."

Matthew lowered the window and flicked the unfinished butt away. "Those are nasty. You know I quit back in '79 after some Sandinista cocksucker stole all my cigarettes."

"So he did you a favor, yet you've got a chip on your shoulder."

"Speaking of chips on shoulders."

"I don't have a chip on my shoulder. I just don't like pushy, know-it-all, nosy gringos, which is to say every gringo I've ever met."

"That's a little reductionist, isn't it?"

"Oh really?" Ajax turned to look at Matthew for the first time since they'd left his house. "Why are you here?"

"We're going to Enrique's. . . ."

"No, no, no, no, no. In the country? I'll tell you why. . . ."

"I'd rather . . ."

"You are here for precisely the same reason as that carrot-headed gringa and her *Senator Tony* with his fact-fucking mission are here. Wanna know what that reason is?"

"Can I say 'no'?"

"Because we can't keep you out, that's why you're here. We are too weak a nation to keep you meddling sons of bitches out. You come down here and live in neocolonial splendor because your goddamned democratically elected government has elected to impoverish and murder us. And whether you support or oppose that policy makes not one scintilla of difference to us. So Jesus Christ yes, I have a chip on my fucking shoulder."

Matthew let out a long breath. "Well, Professor Garcia, may I ask one question?"

"Sure."

"How do you know she calls him Tony?"

"What?"

"How do you know Amelia Peck calls Senator Teal, *Tony*."

"What?"

Matthew spoke slowly. "You said you'd never met her before yesterday at the hotel, other than that show at the airport, so how do you know she calls him *Tony*?"

Ajax pulled a long face to show his disappointment at the question, but he was thinking fast. When you were caught in a lie by someone unlikely to use physical force, obfuscation was often the best tactic.

"Why does she call him Tony? You're asking me?"

"No, I asked how *do you know* she calls him Tony?"

"I don't know why she calls him Tony. Ask her."

Matthew pointed into the sideview mirror. "Let's."

The squeal of worn brakes sounded. A beat up old Jeep flying yellow Vatican flags rolled to a stop. Lurch sat behind the wheel, next to him a shock of orange hair and freckles.

Ajax muttered a curse, but his heart did a drumroll. He climbed out of the pickup and hoped he could maintain his most severe look while the drumroll in his chest beat on. He pulled her door open. But didn't look her in the face.

"Miss Peck, you cannot make this trip. Please get out."

"No, Captain." She didn't look at him either, but drew an envelope from her bag. "Sorry, but I have a letter from the Interior Ministry giving me permission to travel anywhere in Matagalpa province."

Ajax pointed up the road. "That's Contra country up there."

She revealed a second envelope. "And I have a letter from the Contra leadership requiring their forces to let me pass peacefully."

"May I see them?"

"And what are the chances of me getting them back if you do?" She put them away, and then looked at him. "It seems, Martin, I am better protected than you. If you and Matthew won't lead the way, we're going on alone. Aren't we, Father?"

Ajax returned to the pickup thinking, *This* was precisely why enforced celibacy had been the rule in the mountains during his guerrilla days.

2.

They arrived at Enrique Cuadra's coffee finca at sunset. Father Jerome's Jeep had broken down a few hours out and they'd had to tow it with the pickup the rest of the way. Enrique's house was a low-slung bungalow raised a foot off the ground on concrete blocks. Most unusual, it had a tile roof in a part of the country where all but the richest would've had zinc. It meant the house was either pre-revolution or exceptionally well cared for.

The sun was down beyond the western mountains, but enough of it still shone to smudge the high nimbus clouds a prophetic scarlet. Ajax got out and stretched. He immediately picked up the scent of jasmine from the shrubbery surrounding the house and the smell of coffee ripening in the fields. It was an indelible smell, hundreds of acres of coffee beans.

Epimenio appeared first. Ajax could tell from the look on his face that he was stunned to see the police captain here. Ajax went straight to him and in greeting whispered, "I'm Martin Garcia, I work for don Mateo. Keep my secret, hombre."

Epimenio nodded. He began to slowly ring a bell on the house's deep porch. Workers began to arrive in ones and twos and gathered around the pickup with what Ajax could only describe as reverence. Then Enrique's widow appeared. Doña Gloria was a strikingly lovely woman, tall for a Nicaraguan, with the jet-black hair and eyes of an Indian, but the white skin of a Ladino. Ajax reckoned she had to be fifteen years Enrique's junior. A beautiful young widow immediately raised his cop's suspicion. But they were temporarily allayed when she took one look at the coffin and collapsed to the ground.

3.

"Can we speak in English?"

Dinner was a subdued event with the mystery of Enrique's death made all the more real by the evidence of his life—family photos, a rack of shotguns on the wall, his spare cowboy hat on a side table as if he had just taken it off after a day in his fields. And of course, his widow, whom Ajax was now fairly certain was unlikely to be hiding any knowledge of the truth of her husband's murder.

But the fare was better than Ajax ate at home or in the comidores populares he could afford back in Managua—tamales with pork, gallo pinto laced with cilantro from Gloria's garden, and black beans in a heavy cream that might have been warming in a cow's udder that very morning.

"Yes, mine is not so good, but okay." Gloria was a gracious hostess. Once revived from her faint in the yard, she had immediately set about seeing to her guests, who would have to be fed and put up for the night. And the faint had been real. He had checked. Ajax had learned from Marta that if he wanted to make sure someone was truly unconscious he had to lift an arm and let it fall directly on the face. Someone who was faking would instinctively correct to make it a glancing blow. Connelly had looked at him like he was crazy, but to hell with the gringo. Ajax was here to solve a murder.

"I speak Spanish as well, señora." Amelia shot Ajax a look. "We don't have to speak English for me."

"Please, Amelia, call me Gloria."

"Gloria."

"We're not speaking English for you." He didn't want to explain himself, but English gave them privacy. He turned to Gloria, but paused as her cook set down another steaming bowl of frijoles. "Gloria, I know your family and employees are close to you. But I have to keep my identity secret while I make inquiries. I trust Epimenio to do that." He gave the others at the table a sharp look, "And everyone here as well."

"Of course, Martin. But what do you expect to find here?"

"Perhaps it's what I don't expect to find here. Can I speak plainly about your husband?"

"I've had several days to, to adjust to his death."

"Your husband's wounds suggest he might have been killed by the Contra."

"What wounds?"

"Señora, I . . ."

"Tell me."

Ajax looked at Connelly, who nodded his agreement with the widow.

"He was stabbed once in the throat and twice through the heart. It's a common type of Contra execution."

"That's true, Gloria." Connelly, seated on her left patted her hand. "I've seen it, too."

Gloria's hand went to her throat, and then slid down to her breastbone. "The Contra? But why would they . . . ?"

"I don't think they did." Ajax was thinking he should've had this conversation in private. "But that puts me in the minority. I don't believe the people who killed him are here. But the reason he was killed might be here."

"But what reason could there be?" Her composure broke and she wept into her napkin. Ajax was unsure what to do. To his surprise, Amelia was out of her chair and by Gloria's side in a heartbeat. She said nothing to the widow, just gave her a literal shoulder to cry on.

The next moment, Epimenio slipped into the room, splattered in soil from the grave he'd dug. He watched Gloria cry. It seemed to Ajax that his eyes filled with more pain than Ajax would credit a man capable of. Epimenio looked away from Gloria, then nodded to Father Jerome, who pushed himself from the table.

"I'll get my vestments."

Ajax stood on the Cuadra porch and peered around the corner of the house, back toward the small fenced-in plot where, under a half full moon, he counted eight other headstones. One, he noticed, stood over a recent grave, if the earthen mound, which had not yet gone flat, was anything to go by. He wondered who else Gloria had lost.

He felt as if he was spying on the huddle around Enrique's grave, but he had wanted to see without being seen. He'd told himself he might learn something from watching the mourners' body language. But now he thought not. How many funerals had he been to in his life? These very hills were dotted with the graves of many old compas whose remains had never been recovered after the Triumph and removed to Heroes and Martyrs cemeteries. So, too, he supposed, were all the bodies of the Guardia he'd killed—after all, who would have come looking for them? These hills were strewn with the fallen going all the way back to Sandino's fight against the Marines. And before that to the Independentistas who fell fighting the Spanish. The Indians who fought the Spaniards, even the Spaniards who'd fought the Indians, and on and on all over the world to the last Neanderthal who'd fought the first Cro-Magnon. The land was full to the treetops with ghosts. It occurred to Ajax that maybe he was lucky to be haunted by only one. Because he was sure now that's what it was. He just wasn't sure whose ghost.

She came up on him like a specter, too. She didn't speak, just leaned around the corner of the house with him, and watched in silence as he did. But close enough to make him suddenly feel deeply the loss of Enrique Cuadra to his family, his finca, his land. He turned his head enough to see her freckled nose, and could not contain a flood of feeling, which brought tiny diamonds of pain to his eyes.

They spoke each other's name at once so it came out as "Amelajax" or "Ajamel." It brought smiles to their faces so that they could face each other, chests lightly touching without embarrassment, or regret.

"I'm sorry, Ajax, I should've told you I meant to come here. Or, maybe not come at all."

"It's different for me and Connelly. We . . ."

"I know. I'm a tourist."

"I don't want you to get hurt. I . . ."

"I know. Me, too."

"I almost . . ."

"Shhh." She pressed her fingertips to his lips. "My father was like that, too."

"Like what?"

"He was in the Korean War. My mother said they didn't spend a whole night together for the first two years they were married."

"What're you talking about?"

"It's called post-traumatic stress. Even when I was a kid, Mom told us to never, ever wake Daddy if he was asleep. And never touch him if he was having a nightmare. He still has them."

"I don't . . ." Ajax was dumbfounded. *Post-traumatic stress?* That was something rich people got, gringos with money and too much time on their hands. But then he remembered Fortunado Gavilan, so haunted by crows he'd killed *his* lover and then forced his own death.

"Amelia, I almost . . ."

"But you didn't. You scared me, scared the crap out of me. But you didn't hurt me. I'm okay. I'm not the feeble little gringa you think I am."

"I don't . . ."

"And Matthew is not the annoying, nosy gringo you think he is. Okay?"

Ajax was staggered. He looked into her eyes, which were green even in the dark, and for the first time in years he was empty inside. Empty of noise. He didn't want a drink, he didn't want a smoke, and he didn't want to yell at anyone. He didn't want to speak at all. He was empty of anger. He wasn't angry at anyone about anything. Not even himself. He realized that the emptiness was stillness. A stillness Amelia had brought to his mind. And in that stillness all he wanted— God help him, even more than to prove them all wrong about Enrique Cuadra—all he wanted was her mouth on his. Her body against his.

"You should visit Granada before you go."

Those green eyes smiled at him.

"Should I?"

"It's the jewel of our country. A little colonial town, down on the big lake. Like something preserved inside one of those snow globes."

"Are you asking me on a date, Ajax Montoya?"

Stupidly, foolishly even, moreover, unwisely in the extreme—he realized—he was. Or wanted to. He wanted to want something, frankly, a little silly.

"We could 'make the clock.'"

"Is it me or is there a double meaning in that?"

"In colonial times, Granada was a wealthy town with a clock tower on the main plaza. The children of the rich couldn't court each other because of the Honor Code. Marriage was business. So they'd 'make the clock.' One lover would send an anonymous note with a clock face and a time drawn on it. The recipient would go the plaza at that time, but also stand in the plaza aligned with that time. *At* three o'clock *on* the three o'clock position. Whoever was directly opposite you was pitching woo."

"You didn't just say 'woo.'"

"It sounds better in Spanish. Then the couple would promenade around the plaza. . . ."

"Clockwise naturally."

". . . but always keeping the other exactly opposite. Family, chaperones, friends, would be clueless. The lovers would never even glance at each other, yet be utterly focused only on each other."

Amelia's patella brushed like a whisper against his inner thigh. "You want to make the clock with me?"

"I do."

Then Gloria Cuadra's weeping came to them from the graveyard. Ajax peered back around the corner to see the widow being held up between Father Jerome and Connelly as they and the other mourners processed back to the house. He felt Amelia slip away, but said nothing.

He watched the graveyard and listened to the sounds of the mourners in the house. He was about to join them when a lone figure returned to the grave, carrying something. A sack? It looked like Epimenio. Whoever it was laid the sack on the ground, lifted a shovel, and brought it down violently. The figure tossed the sack into the grave and shoveled the freshly turned earth into it. Ajax's cop sense set off a silent alarm which pushed him off the porch. The sounds of the shovel covered the sound of his light steps.

"Epimenio."

It was just a whisper but the campesino jumped out of his skin.

"Captain, you scared me to death."

"Martin."

"Yes, don Martin."

"Just Martin."

"Yes, señor."

Ajax watched his silhouette in the darkness. He could not see Epimenio's face, but he could almost smell the fear. That nervous fear of someone caught in the act. Ajax let several seconds tick by, and then he gently took the spade by its long handle.

"I'll finish."

"No. No, señor, it is the last thing I can do for don Enrique."

"What did you put in there?"

Epimenio stuck his left index finger into his ear and rattled it around like he'd not heard right.

"Señor?"

"What did you put in there with Enrique?"

Epimenio knelt and used his hands to scoop earth into the dark hole. It was the blackest black Ajax had ever seen. He gave the spade back.

"Answer me."

Epimenio put the shovel back to work.

"A jaguar."

"What? A real one?"

"A cub."

Ajax rubbed his fingers along his right forearm. Enrique had had scratches there, he'd seen them in the morgue. "Why did you kill it?"

"I couldn't bury it alive."

"No, I mean why put it in there at all?"

"Doña Gloria said it was evil."

Ajax looked back at the house and wondered what the pretty young widow was literally trying to bury.

"Why?"

Epimenio sighed in a manner Ajax had heard before—it was usually followed by a confession.

"Its mother killed one of our cows, our best milk cow. Enrique and I tracked her for a few days. We didn't find her, but then we were hurrying home and we came across her very near here. Don Enrique thought she was coming back for another cow. He got one shot off. We tracked the blood for a while, but lost her. A neighbor found the carcass and the cub the next day."

"When was this?"

Epimenio stopped for a moment. "The last full moon."

Ajax looked up to the half moon. "Three weeks ago."

"I suppose."

Ajax watched him shovel earth for a few moments. "Why were you hurrying?"

"What?"

"You said you and Enrique 'were hurrying home.' Why?"

Epimenio had the spade in the small mound of earth, and had only to lift it and toss the dirt in. Instead, he left it there a good long while. Ajax knew from many interrogations that it was vital not to speak next, because whoever did would lose. He took out the Reds Connelly had given him, lit two, and passed one over.

4.

"Are you insane?"

It was precisely the reaction Ajax expected from Connelly, which was why he hadn't revealed his plan to him before they left Managua. The dawn was breaking rosy as the four of them drank coffee on the porch. The morning sky was more beautiful than the sunset's scarlet, but it was still red. A cock crowed and Ajax smiled.

"Define insane."

"You go hunting the Contra and they kill you."

"But we've got a get-out-of-the-grave-free card."

"What?"

"My letter," Amelia said. "From the Contra leadership." She handed it to Matthew, who tried to give it back.

"Amelia, please don't encourage this."

She held her hands up and refused to take it back. "It says '*the bearer* is an aide to Anthony Teal of the United States Senate, a great friend to our movement.' I won't be going, so you'll be bearing it."

"I am not going!" Matthew read the letter, and shook his head no. It seemed to Ajax he was disagreeing, rather than refusing.

"Ajax, what makes you even think we can find them?"

"Epimenio knows where to start looking. We use that point as an anchor, and hike a circle around it. If we make enough noise, they'll find us."

Epimenio seemed to study the grain in the floorboards. Connelly was unconvinced.

"Epimenio?"

"There was a place, planes came and went."

"An airstrip?"

"Sí, don Mateo."

"You know where it is?"

Ajax switched to English. "He and Enrique found it. Stumbled on it while hunting a jaguar."

Ajax could sense the wheels turning in Connelly's mind.

"You mean maybe the Contra did kill him?"

"Or the CIA."

"What?"

Ajax switched back to Spanish. "Epimenio says he and Enrique heard the men at the airstrip talking. Enrique identified their accents as Cuban. And you know Miami Cubans are the CIA's favorites for black-bag jobs."

Matthew studied Epimenio for a moment. "Is that true?"

"Sí, don Mateo. Don Enrique was very upset. Angry. He made me swear to tell no one, which was strange."

"Why?"

"He had never made me swear to keep anything from doña Gloria."

Ajax watched Matthew take it in, slowly buying it. "Look, Connelly, do you think the Contra run their war without air supply? Do you know how long it takes to pack ammo in from Honduras?"

"I'm not arguing that, I've heard planes when on patrol with the army. There have been reports out of Washington about air resupply, a reporter in Miami even identified the airline, an old CIA front. Which would also explain the Cubans out here. But you're suggesting

Enrique found an airstrip and the CIA killed him for it? CIA assassins operating in Managua?"

"Those putos in Washington deny the CIA is involved *at all*. But let's say a good citizen stumbles on an *illegal* clandestine airstrip, brings proof to Managua just before the senators arrive where they are met with proof of their lies, in whose interest would it be to prevent that?"

Matthew looked to Amelia for help. "You buying this?"

She waved her hands at them both. "He ran this down to me already. I certainly don't believe my government is killing 'good citizens,' but if I was a cop I'd follow the lead if only to *disprove it.*"

Matthew raised an eyebrow. "What do you mean he ran this down to you already?"

"I explained it to her earlier when I asked for the letter."

"When earlier? It's dawn."

"Earlier! Stay focused."

"Fine. Good. So then why didn't they kill Enrique here?"

"Maybe they missed him, maybe he left for Managua before they could get him."

"So, what? A hit squad the CIA keeps on retainer killed him?"

"I don't know, but the CIA just joined the list of suspects and we are going to find the local Contra commander and we are going to . . ."

"What, interrogate him?"

"Interview him. I'll give you the questions. You ask them. I'll watch to see if he's telling the truth. You said you wanted to help solve this didn't you? Well, this is how it's done. Now you're either in or out."

Connelly shook his head no, but Ajax was sure he meant yes. The journalist could not resist.

"How will we explain your being with me?"

"I'm the sherpa. Pack your rucksack with unnecessary things, the

Reds and soap, but your coffee and toiletries especially. I'll carry it, make me look like your pack mule when we find them."

"When they find us."

"Fine, when they find us. But it'll make me look like a servant, set up the right dynamic. I can roll my eyes and make comments behind your back. The Contras are mostly campesinos, they respond to that. Throw suspicion off me."

Matthew turned on Amelia.

"What're you going to do?"

"What I'm here for. Father Jerome will get his Jeep fixed. We'll go meet the family Tony's going to take home with him. I'll wait two days. If you're not back I'll see you in Managua."

"Why would you help us like this?" Matthew waved at Ajax. "Why help him? He hates gringos, you know."

"I don't care what Captain Montoya likes. I sat up with Gloria a long time last night. Her husband was a good man. Maybe it's a girl thing, I don't know. Or maybe I'm just the kind of gringa idiot who believes in truth and justice as the American way."

Goddamn, Ajax thought, *this chica is good!* She'd said it just as they'd rehearsed it. He'd find the Contra all right, and he'd get his answers. And he'd get back in time to spend one more night with her.

14

Lieutenant Gladys Darío softly tapped her cowboy boots like a metronome on the dark tiled floor. *Left right left right left right left*. They'd done marching drill at the academy and she'd always enjoyed it. *Left right left right left right left*.

Somehow the pleasing monotony of it helped clear her mind, focused it as she took inventory of what she was prepared to defend, and what to surrender. For that had to be why she was here.

Comandante Malhora sat in a leather swivel chair the color of blood. He held a stout cigar in the chubby fingers of one hand as he flipped through the file on his desk with the other. The file sat in a small pool of bright light, like a suspect being interrogated in an old movie. At one edge of that pool of light sat the visitor, staring at a worn book with a marbled cover in his lap. Neither had looked at her since she came into the room. *Escorted in*, she corrected. The Conquistadores—now crowding the narrow straight-backed chair she'd been led to at the outer reaches of the light—had come into the Disco Vaquero as if on a whim. Uniformed and armed. They had strolled around the room, crisscrossed the dance floor like they didn't know what Ladies Nite meant. They had come upon her as if by accident, all smiles and *Compañera!*

Then they'd invited her to a chat with *the Boss*. They'd even tried to wedge her between them in the Land Cruiser, but she'd made a deft move and hopped in the back. *Damned if I'll ride the bitch seat between you two.*

She'd never been to Casa Cincuenta before, but she knew this windowless, underground box was not the Comandante's office, but a room with another purpose.

But what purpose?

Through the gloom, she peered at the title in the visitor's lap, *Antigone.*

"I'm trying to read it in the original Greek." The visitor seemed almost apologetic about it. "Do you know the story, Lieutenant?"

"Yes . . ."

"Poor girl. Caught between the rock and the hard place the Greeks did so well. Her brothers led opposing sides in a civil war in Thebes. The one who lost was declared an enemy of the state and denied proper burial rites, so that his soul would have to wander forever. Antigone had to choose between her duty to the state, her king, and her duty to her brother."

The visitor looked down at his book, which, Gladys was pretty sure, was not in any kind of Greek at all.

"I'm sure she chose duty to her king," Malhora said. He had finally deigned to look up. "Aren't you, Lieutenant?"

"Actually, Comandante"—the visitor adopted an air of fascination, as if he'd just discovered a new star—"she snuck outside the city walls one night and sprinkled some dirt on her brother's body, just a handful of dust to complete the rites so his soul could rest in peace."

"Then she was a traitor."

"And she paid with her life."

"Good. But we're not here to discuss the Greeks, are we, Lieutenant?"

Why she was there was still obscure, like the corners of the room itself.

"No, Comandante."

"Compañero."

"Compañero."

"Why do the Contra leaders all live in Miami, do you suppose?"

Malhora had seemed to ask no one in particular, so Gladys stayed silent. He took a long drag on his cigar and let the smoke drift gently into the space between them. It took an interminable time to encircle her face.

"Do you think the weather reminds them of home, Lieutenant?"

"I don't know."

"I know Miami. We used to smuggle guns through there."

He addressed the last part to the visitor, who nodded without committing to an answer.

"It did remind me of home, of Managua," Malhora said. "Just the weather, though. And just enough to remind me how much I missed home. I suppose exile is a lonely thing. Even for traitors."

The Comandante was silent for a while. The others, the small room, maybe the entire city had gone silent. It was not lost on Gladys that of the words spoken so far, *traitor* had come up twice, illuminating, if not the room, at least the corners of the conversation.

"Have *you* been to Miami, Lieutenant?"

"When I was a child, with my family."

"But not since the Triumph?"

"No."

"But your family all live there?"

"Yes."

"They don't ever come home? Don't ever get lonely for the patria?"

"My sister has visited."

Malhora went casually back to the file. "Yes, three times since 1979, but not for two years now. She brought you gifts, this sister . . ." He looked back at the file. "Teresa? Presents?" Malhora gestured to Gladys's outfit. "Clothes?"

"Yes, Comandante." He didn't correct her that time. Gladys understood now the direction of the interrogation, if not the final destination: *Bring the rich girl in, the bourgeois, sweat her, scare her, crack her.*

Malhora took his time rolling the ash off his cigar. "Well, you might have gone to Miami with them, so the revolution is lucky to have you, compañera." He looked at the file again. "Graduated the American Nicaraguan School, very fancy. *Prestigious.* Joined the Sandinista Youth in 1979. July the 20th." He looked up at her. "The day *after* the Triumph, very good!" He went back to his file. "A degree in political science from the UCA. Joined the Frente in 1985. Volunteered for the policía. First in your class at the academy in Havana."

"Yes."

"And then an assignment in homicide, with Ajax Montoya."

"I went where assigned, Comandante."

"Compañero."

"Compañero."

"Where *is* Captain Montoya?"

"I don't know."

Malhora closed Gladys's file. She steadied herself for an on-slaught, sure Ajax's location was what Malhora most wanted. She was glad she didn't know, not really. But instead, Malhora only nodded, then drew three photographs from under her file and spread them out for her to see—morgue shots of the Hunchback, the Gypsy, and the Stolen Car King.

"It is true Captain Montoya was the last person to see these three men alive?"

Puta.

There it is, she thought. *The last person to see these three men alive* could only break one way.

It was all part of the investigation, Gladys almost blurted. But another voice cut her off: *Shut up, idiota. This is not a conversation. It's an ambush.* Her feet went still. The room was so small. So full of these men. They filled it with their bodies, their cigar smoke, with their authority. The Conquistadores pressed so close their hips touched her shoulders.

"No," she said, and in more ways than one.

"'No'?"

"The last person to see these men alive was their killer—or killers." She rocked side to side so her shoulders bumped the Conquistadores. "You're crowding me." They shuffled a half step away—it was all the space she needed.

"So you're saying . . ." Malhora began.

"No, you're saying. And it's absurd, outrageous to imply Ajax has anything to do with these murders other than investigate them." She stood up so fast Malhora almost flinched. "I would like our conversation to be finished now."

Malhora gestured to the visitor: "And I think you'd better consider the fate of our friend's little Greek girl, *compañera*."

"*Lieutenant.* She dies. But the King's son was in love with her, so he kills himself, which causes his mother, the King's wife, to go mad and kill herself. The people turn their backs on him, as do the gods. And because the King wouldn't bend, he broke."

She brushed past whichever Conquistador was between her and the door, but at a total loss what she'd do if that door was locked. It wasn't.

The four men sat in silence a moment, some stunned, at least one awed.

"Well," the visitor finally said. "She seems more learned than we thought."

15

1.

If the world run by men was based on the size of their dicks, Ajax thought, then Ronald Reagan had an enormous hard-on for Nicaragua. A vast, colossal, gargantuan boner he wanted to ram into every orifice of the young revolution's body.

The man did not walk softly, and the Contra were his big stick.

And Ajax Montoya, *comandante guerrillero, héroe de la revolución y capitán de la policía Sandinista* was looking right at one of Reagan's biggest sticks.

Krill.

He and Connelly had hiked fourteen hours, breaking brush the whole way, avoiding any roads or even well-worn paths, winding their way up unnamed streams or along tracks so slim they often lost the way. And all through a selva so dense, so choked with life it lost all beauty and became almost satanic in its impenetrability. They'd camped on a hilltop not as densely woven with trees as others, made a fire, and waited. Ajax had heard, no, sensed, the Contra in the night, but they'd waited until a few minutes ago to show themselves.

A patrol of twenty-two men in jungle fatigues had materialized out of the trees, encircling the two intruders. Then they'd just stood there, heavily armed but not pointing any weapons at Ajax and Matthew. Ajax inventoried their hardware—mostly M16s, a few Belgian FALs, one M60 machine gun, and two 40mm grenade launchers.

One radio man. Their equipment was well-worn, but not worn out. Each man had a machete strapped to his back.

Then Krill had appeared—two of his men stepping aside like a gate swinging open to let him in, and the circle grew tighter until they were only a machete stroke away.

Krill.

Krill was as famous among the counterrevolutionaries as Ajax had been among the revolutionaries. A sergeant in the Ogre's National Guard and an original founder of the Contra who actually did the fighting, Krill had been at the top of the Sandinista kill list even when Ajax was working State Security. Krill's exploits in battle were famous, his treatment of prisoners infamous—especially women. The government liked to portray the Contra as ignorant dupes or psychotic hillbillies—gap-toothed and cross-eyed. But Krill was recruiting-poster handsome—early thirties, with high cheekbones, small eyes, and closely trimmed beard and mustache. He was short, in the Nicaraguan way, but a bantam-cock from a poor barrio whose penchant for violence and prowess with a gun had lifted him out of generations of poverty and made him a leader of men.

So, like Reagan, Krill had a titanic woody.

But, Ajax reminded himself as Krill pawed through his wallet, it wasn't the size of your dick that mattered. It was the heft of your balls. Unfortunately for Ajax, and maybe Matthew, too, Krill seemed to have big ones. He had the aura of authority Ajax recognized. One that comes from commanding men who obey without question.

"Martin Garcia," Krill said. "You of the Garcia family?"

Ajax laughed and snapped his fingers in appreciation of the joke. He noticed that Matthew did, too, and wondered if he found it as easy to fake a laugh as Ajax did. In Spanish "the CIA" was pronounced "La See-ah," and in rhyming slang is known as "la familia Garcia."

Krill, however, was not laughing at his own joke. He went through Matthew's wallet, too.

"And Matthew Connelly. North American journalist. We know you, Connelly. You're the gringo who loves them fucking *piricuacos* so much."

"No, Comandante, forgive me, I do not *love* the *piris*."

Piricuaco was the Contras' favored term for Sandinistas, it meant *rabid dog,* for which there was only one solution. Ajax was glad Connelly knew the right lingo to use.

"A journalist writes the stories his editors tell him to." Connelly shrugged his shoulders like a laborer ordered to dig a hole in a swamp. "My bosses tell me to write about the army, I write about the army. I am like a soldier following orders. We have that in common."

"No, gringo, we don't. I am the only one who gives the orders here."

Krill's men smiled and murmured their agreement. Ajax smiled, too; even Krill didn't like gringos!

"True, Comandante," Connelly bowed his head, as he, too, seemed to feel these soldiers' disdain. "But I am here now because I told my bosses I had to write about you as well. That's why I arranged this letter and came all the way here looking for you."

Connelly handed over Amelia's letter from the Contra leadership. Krill read it.

"You and your mule." Krill nodded to one of his men, a bearish man with one eye almost closed by scar tissue. One-eye quickly stripped Ajax of the heavy pack he'd been toting since Epimenio had led them into the bush. "I know nothing of this letter. No one told me you were coming."

"Son of a bitch, Krill look at this!" One-eye keened like a kid in a candy store and dumped Ajax's pack on the ground.

The rest of Krill's patrol stared gape-mouthed at the cartons of Marlboros, bars of soap, and packets of instant coffee piled like a Christmas miracle. Greedy hands reached out. Ajax kept his eyes on Krill, whose gaze never wavered from Amelia's letter. But one short, sharp hiss from their leader froze his men's hands just short of the pile of goodies. Krill finished reading the letter with silent, slow-moving lips. Then he deigned to look down at the goodies, then back at Matthew.

"This is all for me?"

"Of course, Comandante. A good guest always brings gifts to his host."

Krill signaled One-eye again, who quickly broke open one pack and handed the Reds around. Soon all were smoking.

"You are not my guest yet, gringo. I think you might be spies." One-eye handed Krill a lit butt. Krill inhaled deeply. "We will see."

Krill turned and walked off. His men hoisted their gear and fell in behind him. Ajax thought first contact had gone well. Then One-eye ordered two men to tie "the spies' hands" and bring them along.

They walked for six hours. Almost due north by Ajax's reckoning. He and Matthew had crossed one river, where Epimenio had left them, looking glum and guilty. He and Matthew had wandered north-by-northwest. They'd made as much noise as they could without being too obvious. Left tracks and made a big fire that night. They'd met no one, yet still, in this isolated vastness, they had come across two huts of such desperate poverty the word hovel was too grand to describe them. They'd left soap behind at each one and kept on.

If things went badly now, they might not be able to flee the way they'd come, Ajax knew that. So he kept a map in his head anyway. If they had to run for their lives, he at least needed to know the way home.

They were in Krill's camp before he or Matthew had realized it. In the darkening dusk it was eerily familiar to Ajax. Fires banked so low the flame tips barely peeked over the mound of earth piled to snuff them out instantly. They gave off little light, but enough to reflect the eyes of each Contra as they led Ajax and Matthew deep into the camp. There were more than three dozen in all, plus the twenty-two Krill had with him on patrol. Krill and One-eye bivouacked at the center, with the others in three concentric circles. There was very little talk, but what there was grew louder and more relaxed when Krill arrived, as if the return of their leader signaled all was well. In any event, they seemed not a troop of men expecting imminent attack.

One-eye led them to Krill's fire, pushed them to the ground, and slit their bonds. He dumped half of Matthew's goodies on the ground and went off, Ajax assumed, to distribute the rest. In a few moments, whispered cries of joy confirmed it. Matthew collapsed onto the ground. He had been blowing hard for hours on the long slog. Ajax had found the pace exhausting, too, but his body still remembered how to handle it, and, in truth, he welcomed the thirst and pain of a grueling march—it sweated you down to your core.

"I am fucking dying, really." Matthew flopped onto his back. "I died before the sun went down and I would kill for some water!"

"Keep your voice down, Connelly." Ajax was surprised at how raspy his voice had become.

"Yessir, Martin. Martin the mule. Oof!"

Matthew sat up as a full canteen was dropped onto his soft belly. Ajax caught with one hand the canteen tossed at his face. Matthew gulped mouthfuls, while Ajax took one long pull and swirled it inside his mouth until the parch was gone, then quietly gargled and swallowed the rest.

"You're going to get a bellyache from drinking so fast, gringo." Krill sat down, stoked his little fire, and set a canteen cup of water on it. "You ought to drink like your mule here, nice and slow." He emptied two packets of the instant coffee into the water and stirred the contents with the tip of a skinning knife. He gave Ajax a good looking over. "You don't seem too tired, Martin."

Ajax shrugged. "We're Nicas, Comandante. Stoical on the outside, exhausted on the inside."

Krill smiled. "Yeah, the gringos are a soft people. I had some other reporters with me. *The New York Times* and *The Washington Post*, they almost died just from the walking. You know them, Martin?"

"I know Mary Lantigua, but I don't think it was her; *The Post* has many reporters."

"No, they were men. But even ignorant, simple Krill has heard of those papers." Krill took out the ID cards he'd confiscated earlier. "But Matt-hew Con-no-lee? You don't work for the big gringo newspapers?"

"Comandante, I work for many newspapers and even though they are not so famous, my reports reach more people than *The Times* or *The Post*."

"Like who?"

"*The Christian Science Monitor, Financial Times, Toronto Globe and Mail, The San Francisco Examiner.*"

Krill stuck the tip of his knife into the coffee, then tested it on his tongue. Satisfied, he sheathed the blade and sipped his brew. As he did, One-eye joined them at the fire. Ajax could see now that he was younger than Krill, heavier, with a wolfish cut to his face when he smiled. And smile he did as he sat down and locked his eye on Ajax.

Krill looked into his coffee and swirled it in the cup, as if, Ajax thought, he was consulting a Rolodex. "I never heard of these newspapers."

"Well, the story I will write about Comandante Krill will be read by people in the United States, Canada, and Britain."

"Any Nicaraguan people read it?"

Krill gulped his coffee and looked over the cup at Ajax. It was then Ajax was sure of what he'd suspected: Krill was fucking with Matthew, maybe with them both. But Matthew didn't get it, yet.

"Sure, some people in Managua, maybe. But the Foreign Ministry reads it and your leadership in Miami and Honduras."

"Leadership?" Krill tapped One-eye. "You heard that? Leadership? In Miami? Honduras? What are these places?"

"Miami is a faggot town where the faggots live," One-eye said. "Krill is the leader."

A murmur went through the camp echoing One-eye's words, and Ajax realized Krill had been performing for his men, not Matthew.

"Of course, Comandante, here you are . . ."

Krill threw the dregs of his drink on the fire. "It was nice of you to bring Enrique Cuadra's body home for burial. Was doña Gloria grateful?"

"Doña Gloria," One-eye repeated, and that, too, passed like a murmur through the camp.

One-eye was watching for a reaction, and Ajax knew it had to be the right reaction. So he laughed. It took Matthew a half second to catch on but then he did, too. Ajax picked up Krill's cup and began to make his own coffee. "You are like God, Comandante: all seeing and all knowing."

"Yes, yes, right." Matthew tried to catch up. "Omniscient."

"Enrique was your friend, Con-no-lee?"

"A good friend, Comandante. And a good man. Did you know him?"

Krill shrugged as Ajax had earlier. "We took provisions from him when we needed them. He complained less than the others do. How did he die?"

"He was murdered." Ajax tried to make it sound nonchalant, timing his words with setting the cup to the fire.

"Murdered, for real?" Krill, Ajax assessed, was genuinely surprised to hear it. "What a fucking country. Did the piris do it?"

"Ah, well, I don't think so." Matthew took a long pull on the canteen. "Some say maybe a robbery."

Ajax emptied a packet of instant into the cup. "Some say you did it."

"Me?"

"The Contra."

Krill drew out his knife again and stirred Ajax's cup for him. "Listen, Martin, Gar-CIA. We are not 'Contra,' understand? Because to be 'en contra' is to be opposed. We, in fact, are 'in favor' . . ."

One-eye leaned forward. "In favor of killing piricuacos!" A mirthful murmur passed through his men as the joke was repeated outward in the dark to the edge of camp.

Ajax laughed, too. Then he set his hand on Krill's knife. "Can I borrow this?" Krill smiled, but nodded. Ajax took the blade. "The papers in Managua say it was you because—" Ajax touched the blade tip to his throat once and over his heart twice. "He was killed like that: once to the throat, twice to the heart."

"No? For real?" Krill held out his hand. Ajax stirred the coffee with the knife and then returned it, handle first. "I invented that, you know." Krill touched the blade tip to throat and heart. "'To kill the vampire.' But no. We did not kill Cuadra. If I wanted him dead, he would be dead here!" Krill drove the knife into the ground. "Who Krill says dies, dies."

Ajax expected that to go round in murmur as well. Instead, Krill's men suddenly appeared out of the dark and formed a silent circle. Krill looked first to Ajax, then to Matthew, and back again, and again.

"Is this why you came here? To ask me if I killed Enrique Cuadra?"

"No, Comandante," Connelly said. "I told my editors I wanted to write about the famous Krill."

"And my men."

"And your men."

"Then go and talk to them." Krill waved at the soldiers whose circle had grown tighter. "Ask them anything. They will tell you why we fight." Krill turned to look at his men. "Answer the gringo's questions. Teach him what he needs to know." Then he waved his leave for Connelly to go.

"Thank you, Comandante. Martin, bring the tape recorder."

"No." Krill jerked his knife out of the ground, wiped the blade on a pant leg, and sheathed it. "You go, gringo. Martin Gar-CIA stays."

Ajax could feel Connelly's eyes on him. He passed the micro tape recorder to him and tried to avoid the gringo's gaze, which Ajax knew would flash some concern for his safety.

When they'd gone, One-eye lit himself and Krill a cigarette. He tossed one to Ajax, who made a show of leaning down over the small fire to light it, thus exposing his neck and back to them. Prey who have no fear don't hesitate to show their bellies to a predator.

"So, Martin, how old are you?"

"Thirty-six."

"Really?"

"Yes, but I fuck like a teenager."

Krill and One-eye guffawed. Krill emptied out Ajax's cup and made himself more coffee. "So you must've fought for the revolution, huh, when you were a kid?"

"Not me, I grew up in the States. Los Angeles."

"For real? Grew up there?"

"For real. My mother and father immigrated when I was a baby."

For the first time, Krill seemed actually impressed. "I lived in El Norte, too."

"Yeah? For real?"

"Why do you say it like that? You think I can't live there?"

"No, but Connelly said you were one who stayed."

"Yeah, I did. But they brought me to Miami in 1980. I was supposed to get some 'training' from la cia."

One-eye laughed and mumbled, "Krill gives the training, he doesn't receive it."

"That's what I told them, but they never gave me shit anyway. That faggot-lipped Carter was still president, so I get to Miami and all they want to do is talk. Talk to me!"

"So you didn't stay long?" Ajax flicked his cigarette ash into the fire where it burned a second time.

"A few weeks. In Miami. You ever been to a mall?"

"Oh sure, L.A. has lots of them."

Krill looked into his newly brewed cup of instant coffee and smiled at the memory of it.

"The first time I went into a mall, it seemed to me to be one of mi General's palaces." Krill shook his head in disbelief, but Ajax doubted he'd ever set foot in one of Somoza's mansions. The Ogre had been as much a light-skinned, upper-class snob as any rich Nica was likely to be. "It was amazing. Huge, like nothing I had ever seen. Air-conditioning everywhere, it was like winter inside. And clean?" Krill made a snapping gesture with his fingers, which in Nicaraguan meant a thing was incalculable. "But you know what? Fucking gringos let *anyone* go inside! Not just whites and Cubans, but the blacks, too! And not just the black gringos, but the Jamaicans and even the Haitians." Krill shook his head at what Ajax was sure was the still-lingering disbelief at the stupidity of gringos to hoard so much wealth, but then invite everyone to come in and gawk at it.

One-eye shook his head in disbelief, too, but not, it seemed to Ajax, because he had been there. Krill was repeating a story he had heard many times before. "Fucking Cubans think they're white, too."

"They do, too!" Krill laughed. "Fucking Cubans are more annoying than the gringos!"

Ajax laughed a real laugh for the first time.

"What is so funny, Martin?"

"You sound like my father. He said in Los Angeles the Mexicans treated Nicas worse than the whites did."

"*Así es.* There you go. Your father was a wise man. Fucking Cubans are more arrogant than the gringos!"

The three of them laughed and smoked their Mexican Marlboros. In the silence that followed, they all seemed to marvel at the foolishness of Gringolandia.

"So, Martin, I remind you of your father?"

"Comandante, you certainly joke like he did. Like a true Nica."

"And how is that?"

"Nicas make fun of everyone, but ourselves most of all."

"Why is that? You think we are ashamed of ourselves?"

"No, Comandante. My father used to say, Nicaraguans are proud in the 'I' but humble in the 'We.'"

"Proud in the 'I' humble in the 'We.'" One-eye repeated it as he had Krill's words before.

Ajax thought he might be making some progress. He tossed his butt onto the embers, and watched it ignite its own flame and be consumed by it.

"So, Comandante, why didn't you stay in Miami?"

"Stay?" Krill seemed to drift away from the moment, as if he were looking back over his decision. He closed his eyes and Ajax imagined Krill was feeling that air-conditioning flowing over his body. "No. If I stayed there I would've been a peasant watching those malletes and Cubans buying their things. Here I am a king. A poor king. But better a poor king than a rich peasant."

"You are very wise, Comandante."

Ajax meant it as a compliment, but Krill didn't seem to take it that way.

"What are you doing here, *Martin*?"

"Me? I'm taking the gringo for all the money I can get!"

"God bless this cocksucker for a brother!" Krill smacked Ajax on the shoulder. "We try to do the same thing, although I think our fearless leaders do it better in Miami. Does the gringo want to solve who murdered Enrique Cuadra?"

"I think he thinks he does. He feels like he owes a debt, you know, to the country and that might be one way to repay it."

"Does he think I killed him?"

"I don't think so."

"Do you think I killed him?"

"I don't see why you would. Like you said, if you wanted him dead he'd be dead up here. Why would you follow him all the way to Managua to do it?"

"Yes, when I go to Managua it will only be to kill shit-eating Sandinistas, which you know Cuadra probably was."

"You think so?"

"In his heart not his boots. He was a civilian, but his sons were piris going way back. But that old man's finca gave us coffee, rice, beans, and more. If his widow goes back to the city we lose our best store."

"So you wouldn't want him dead?"

"Not him, Martin. Not him."

Ajax felt the air rush out of the moment just before he heard the hammer go back on One-eye's .45.

"Comandante, I am just . . ."

"Yes, yes. A mule. Martin Garcia, translator and fixer." Krill hoisted his cup, almost as if to toast something, and then emptied it onto the ground. "But we watched you before we let you find us. Out there," Krill waved at the impervious jungle, the implacable blackness, "out there you led and the gringo followed."

"The mule led the friar," One-eye chanted.

"We saw that. Only when you 'found' us did you become the mule and Connolly the friar."

"I am not CIA. . . ."

"No. You're Frente Sandinista."

"*Piricuaco.*" One-eye drew out each syllable in a deadly whisper, *piri–kwa–koooo.*

Only then did the hair stand up on Ajax's neck and arms. Only then did he realize that Connolly was likely already dead.

"Don't worry, Martin, we are not going to kill you."

"Not in the dark," One-eye chanted.

"Not in the dark."

"Comandante . . ."

"No!" Krill unsheathed the knife and touched its tip to Ajax's chin, and then slowly drew lines around his face as if making a map. "No. You have not made me angry yet by talking too much. Of course, talking too little also can make me angry." Krill sat back and studied the blade as if it held the story he wanted to tell. "We had one little piri like you. He talked too little. Have you heard of the Seventeenth Light Hunter Battalion?"

"Not really."

"Do you know what they call themselves?"

"No."

"'The Whales.' Do you know why?"

Ajax nodded his head, as much as at Krill as at what fate had decreed. "Because whales eat krill," he said.

Krill smiled and slapped his knee. "Yes! This is an educated man! Very good! Because whales eat krill, they want to eat me. But we captured a few of them. One boy was the radio man. He had all the frequencies. You can imagine how much I wanted those numbers?"

"I suppose they would be good for you to know."

"Good for me to know. So I tell this boy, 'Look I am not going to hurt you. Instead I will show you on your friends' bodies what I *could* do to you but won't.' Wasn't that fair?"

Several short bursts of gunfire rang out from the dark, followed by panicked commands Ajax could not quite make out. For a moment, Ajax thought he might be saved by an ambush. But neither Krill nor One-eye moved. He assumed it was Matthew's firing squad. Krill looked over his shoulder, then back at Ajax."

"Now we are alone."

"You kill an American. . . ."

"Do not make me angry, hijo de puta! I want to finish my story. So I showed this boy what I could do to him on his friends, and after some time when they were begging for death, I told the boy, do you want them to suffer or die? But he still wouldn't talk. So I let him kill his friends. One by one." Krill made a stabbing motion over his throat and heart. "Just like that. Like your friend poor Enrique."

"Poor Enrique," One-eye added.

"But still," Krill went on, "still he would not talk. And he knew what was coming for him. Do you know how we do it?"

"Torture."

"Of course, but how?" Krill leaned in closer as he warmed to his tale. Ajax studied the sticks burning in the fire. "I was sent to Argentina for training, back in the early days before the fucking gringos took over everything. And let me tell you, those Argentines are *men*." Krill clasped three fingers together and drew a straight line from his head to his navel, indicating these Argentine torturers were *estrechos*—proper gentlemen. "They have balls. They are proud of what they do. Do you know why I hate the gringos so much? They think everything Krill does is dirty, they are afraid they have to *clean up my mess*. Clean up? All this—" Krill spread his arm to take in not only Nicaragua's green mountain selva, but the entire world and its whorish allegiances and Cold War alliances. "All this is a dirty game to them. But to me, to Krill, it is my glory. My destiny! And those shit-eating gringos think I am dirty. *Dirty*."

One-eye didn't repeat the word. Instead he laughed, low and deep in his chest. "Krill will clean the world."

"Yes, hombre." Krill patted One-eye's shoulder as he might his best hunting dog who was his only companion. "We will clean them all. Piricuacos, Soviets, Cubans, all those faggots and then those arrogant gringo sons of bitches."

"And then we will own the malls!" One-eye spoke it like a punch line. Ajax realized One-eye was playing his part—the chorus in an oft-told tale.

Krill leaned over the fire to light another cigarette. Ajax studied his eyes, but didn't see a psychopath, only a man for whom killing is a way of life.

"What the Argentines taught me," Krill sat back. "And this is something they learned from *history*, what they taught me is that when you are questioning a guest you tie him upside down. You know why?"

"No sleeping," One-eye intoned.

"That's right. The blood flows to the head and the guest stays awake through all kinds of shit, like the shit we put this piri's friends through, okay? For two days he watched his friends suffer, bleed, plead. Still he didn't talk. Do you know why, Martin?"

"He had balls."

"Enormous fucking balls! And I respect that, Communist, non-Communist, I don't care. And you know what happened when we tied him upside down?"

"Nothing. He escaped first."

Krill's mouth dropped open; for the first time he was surprised. "A la gran puta!" He tapped One-eye's arm. "How does he know this?" Krill leaned in to study Ajax even closer. "You are not his brother. Not his father. But you know him, yes? So, Martin, you are military. Army?"

"No."

"State Security?"

"Fuck them."

Krill laughed out loud, a real laugh that sprayed the campfire like spittle. "Fuck them? Fuck them! You sound like me. But why? You know this boy? Did he survive his escape?"

"He's dead."

"Ah, so you have come to revenge him?"

"No."

"How did he die, our big-balled guest?"

"He killed his girlfriend, then a priest."

"Really? Well, at least the priest was not his girlfriend."

Krill slapped One-eye, but he didn't laugh, just kept his .45 pointed at Ajax.

"So, Martin, how did he die?"

"He killed himself."

"Really?" Krill made a finger gun and pointed it at his own head. "Shot himself?"

"No. It's called 'suicide by cop.'"

"Ah, he killed the others then made the police kill him. I have seen that in soldiers." Krill leaned over the fire and laid a hand on Ajax's knee. "Now I see. You are the police of *suicide by police*."

"Yes."

"So you *have* come to revenge him?"

"No."

"Then why?"

"I want to know who murdered Enrique Cuadra."

"Wait, *you* want to solve the murder. Not the gringo?"

"It's my job."

"You have to come to Krill's camp, a place, my friend, from which you now *know* you will not leave, to solve one murder?"

"Yes."

"And you think I killed him. Why?"

"Enrique found your airstrip."

Krill and One-eye exchanged a look. To Ajax's cop eye, they didn't seem to be readying a lie.

"We know of an airstrip, more than one. But they aren't ours. What we get by air is dropped to us. So you don't think I killed Cuadra?"

"I have to eliminate suspects."

Ajax had deliberately given Krill the word "eliminate" to play with, but he didn't. Krill didn't laugh. He didn't smile or look triumphant. He seemed to Ajax to be genuinely curious. "This whole country is a great pile of maggots." Krill turned his knife as if lifting one wiggly worm. "And you want to pick up one maggot and say, 'This worm offends me.' You are confused my friend. Deeply confused."

"I have been told that before."

"Have you ever been told you are going to die?"

"Yes."

"Good. Because you are, Martin the mule. That is why you have come to Krill's camp. To die. Maybe we can call this 'suicide by Krill.' Tie him to a tree."

Krill rose and One-eye produced rope and reached for Ajax's

hand. Ajax had been studying the fire for some time, so he knew just which burning stick to use. It had, he reckoned, worked for Ulysses, why not him?

But One-eye was too fast. As the embers flew when Ajax ripped the stick from the fire, One-eye turned his head just enough so that the burning coal hit not the fleshy grape of the one good eye, but the rough scar tissue of the other. The burly bastard seized Ajax and leapt on top of him, roaring in pain and surging with the power of it. *Son of a bitch!* While he fought with One-eye, Ajax noticed that Krill did not come to his dog's defense. He just stood there, smiling, while his men appeared out of the dark like demons. Demons with fists like rocks and feet like logs. Ajax hoped the beating would put him out quickly, because he knew once he was upside down he would never lose consciousness.

2.

There is a certain release in pain. Pain that is not mere discomfort. Ajax had learned in the mountains that men could be driven mad by too much rain, too little food, or too much illness. But he had never seen a severely wounded man lose his sanity. In those cases you simply gave in to the pain, surrendered to it. Like a drowning man who capitulates to the water—you would live or die, but not go insane.

Ajax was like that now. He had not lost consciousness during the beating, but he'd been able to protect himself. His balls were not swollen and his teeth still felt all in place. But the pain was everywhere else. Like a heat rising from his feet, up each leg, in all the muscles and joints and bones all the way up to his face. He could taste blood in his mouth. He let it pool there and then slowly spat it out. Sitting against the tree they'd finally bound him to was perhaps the worse discomfort. The shrapnel in his coccyx felt as if it had been driven deep into the bone and sitting on it drove a slow stream of pain up his spinal cord into his brain. Once there, Ajax pretended to suck the pain out of his head through the cuts inside his mouth. As the blood filled it, he imagined himself spitting out the pain.

It actually helped. The spurting noise was the only sound in the dark camp. So he didn't fight the pain, didn't fight the knots. He just rested his head against the tree, looked at the half moon risen over his head, and spit blood. At first he'd just wanted to keep it off himself. Then he'd noticed the flat top of a buried stone between his legs and he'd aimed for that. He was hitting it pretty good when a memory floated home to him. Years ago, during the final offensive, his column had been halted outside of Matagalpa. Rhino had joined them by then, and one quiet afternoon he had stumbled out of the bushes, fumbling with his fly, practically screaming, *"A la cachimba!"*—the Nicaraguan version of "Eureka!"

"Compas, I have just figured out the warlike nature of our people and indeed all men," he'd called out. Rhino's clownish goodwill had made him an instant hit with the veterans, even those like Ajax who'd seen right off it was Rhino's way of dealing with fear.

"I was taking a piss and it hit me like a bolt from the blue—men are naturally warlike because we piss standing up!"

That had provoked no small amount of mirth and a few suggestions that Rhino maybe pissed with his hat off, rather than his fly down. But Rhino had not been deterred.

"No, listen. What do we all do when we piss? See a little leaf over here or a stick over there or a stone further on and what do we do? We aim for it, right? How many of us pass the time while passing water aiming at something? Well, what's the difference between aiming a stream of piss at a rock and throwing a rock at a target? It's the same, right? It's the same geometry to aim a stream of piss, a rock, a spear, an arrow, or a bullet! It works the same. So from our earliest age while we piss standing up we are learning the geometry of war."

Rhino had never been a serious person, but his "pissing and the geometry of war" was widely discussed for days afterward.

Ajax felt his mouth fill again with blood and he aimed carefully for the stone. Then a sentry approached. A bored sentry could be a dangerous thing late at night when all others were sound asleep. The strange way this one moved injected a dose of fear into the streams of hurt flowing through him. But that, Ajax thought, was another benefit to sustained pain. It made you not give a fuck.

"Come on, boy, play with me." He sucked blood into his torn mouth and readied a gob for the sentry's face.

There was no doubt the sentry was moving toward him, coming for him. But even in the quiet of the camp this one moved silently, as if floating just off the ground. The sentry seemed in no hurry, stopping by little piles of what might be rags or forest detritus, but Ajax knew each one was a sleeping Contra. When the sentry was a few yards off he stopped and seemed to look right at Ajax. But in the moonlight he could see it had no eyes to see with.

The apparition was back.

The silhouette stood off a ways, staring sightlessly. Maybe this was a good thing, Ajax thought. Maybe if he lost his mind before they hoisted him upside down, he would not feel what they meant to do. Still, he tugged uselessly at his bonds. No matter what or who, he did not believe he should go down without fighting. He spat out more blood and filled his lungs to cry out when the apparition began to change. Ajax wasn't sure what was happening, but the silhouette seemed to spasm as if jerked by invisible wires. Then it seemed to shimmer, as if stirred by a breeze. But there was no breeze, nothing, only the moonlight falling silently.

And then, there they were—two eyes looking at him. Unmistakably eyes, whose wetness was the only living thing in the camp that could reflect moonlight as these eyes now did. Only then, Ajax realized, when it had finally taken full human form, did the shining apparition approach. Slowly, but close enough for Ajax to see, to know, to recognize not only what this was, but who.

But first he understood its look. That first night in Managua when he'd watched it watching him through the garden window, it had shimmered as if covered in a shining veneer like black paint. But now, as the ghost closed in on him, he realized to his horror it was not paint, but gore. There was a single, long slash across the apparition's throat from ear to ear; the wound hung loosely open, the severed flesh like two lips. The ghost's chest was soaked in still-wet, gleaming blood as if every drop had poured out of the wicked gash and saturated its front. Not its chest, Ajax saw, but its shirt. Its uniform, for the apparition was dressed in army fatigues.

Ajax pulled furiously at the ropes. Krill might have him in the morning, but he would wrestle this demon right now. As if reading his thoughts, the apparition moved in very close, inches from Ajax's face. And then, quite deliberately it seemed, the apparition tilted its head just so to find a spot where the moon leaked through the canopy, like a weak spotlight illuminating a lone actor about to deliver a soliloquy to an empty theater. Ajax could not take his eyes off the horrible gash, which moved like a mouth when the apparition moved.

Again, as if reading Ajax's thoughts, the ghost moved its head as if to show Ajax its eyes. No, not the eyes, but the eyelashes—impossibly long, utterly girlish, and completely alluring, at least in life. He had thought the same thing when he'd first seen the boy with the long eyelashes. They were a feature rarely seen on men, such sensual eyelashes. Ajax remembered they had given the boy a doe-eyed look of utter vulnerability in life that he had taken with him into death.

He'd noticed them even as he'd held the boy's mouth closed after he'd slashed his throat and his life pumped out. It was the boy from whom he'd taken the Python all those years ago. The boy whose throat he'd cut for that gun. Not because he'd needed it, but because he'd wanted it.

The boy with the long eyelashes.

The only time in all those years of killing that Ajax Montoya had murdered someone.

His heart beat faster now than when he'd realized Krill had

found him out. They were almost nose-to-nose. They hadn't touched, but he was sure the boy was a physical thing in front of him.

"Son of a bitch," he muttered. "You pick the one night I don't have the fucking thing." For he was sure the ghost had come to reclaim the pistol. And he was as sure it was safely hidden in Matthew's pickup as he was now sure that it was a ghost that stood before him. He took a small comfort from the fact that he was not insane, just haunted by someone he'd murdered. He was going to die soon, and Ajax preferred to die sane and screaming, rather than insane and laughing.

"Okay. Here I am. You going to do it yourself or hang around for the morning show?"

There was no response. At least no words. But the ghost of the boy with the long eyelashes moved closer. His lips opened and closed like a fish out of water gasps. Each time his lips moved, so did the awful gash in his throat. The ghost was so close now Ajax feared it would Judas-kiss him, and he leaned back until he was hard against the tree. The ghost moved closer still until it should have touched Ajax's face. He shut his eyes but did not feel a physical contact as the ghost leaned into him. Rather, he felt heat like a roaring fire had suddenly been lit before him, his front hot, but his back against the tree chilled in the night air.

And then he felt it.

It.

The Needle.

The ghost had put it in his hand! The steel grip as familiar to his touch as the Python's ivory handle. The very blade he'd used to kill the boy. Ajax should be frightened, but he was confused, even fascinated. Either Ajax had somehow (unconsciously? psychotically?) hidden The Needle on his person, or a ghostly apparition had passed him a physical object.

But then, as suddenly as the flame had come on, it was gone. Ajax was alone. Alone, cold, and armed in a camp full of enemies. It didn't matter where the blade had come from. He sawed slowly but surely through the ropes until he was free. He sat for a while letting tingling blood flow back to his aching limbs—the sweetest pain of all.

He turned The Needle over in his hands. A well-machined specialty blade, The Needle was actually rather delicate for a killing tool. None of the bulk and heft of a bowie knife, built like a boxer. The Needle was like a ballerina—thin, but all muscle and gristle. It was no bigger around than a fat knitting needle, and shaped like a diamond so that each angle of the diamond formed a razor's edge. That way, no matter how it was drawn out, a cutting edge could lead the way. It was of no use other than what it was designed for. You could not cut wood with it or even whittle. The point was too long and delicate to stab anything of any heft. It was made only to pierce soft tissue. The point was meant to penetrate the side of the neck, puncturing the carotid artery and then the larynx. The blade was meant to be flicked forward, away from the body, carving open blood vessels and the voice box.

That was precisely what Ajax did to the boy with the long eyelashes. It had been late in the war, and Ajax was already a renowned comandante guerrillero. But he'd still performed his own reconnaissance. He'd been outside one of the last National Guard posts still in proper order. He'd seen the boy only from afar, but had spotted the ivory-handled Python in a shoulder holster. His recon had been complete, but when he'd spotted the boy near the camp's edge, he'd waited until long after dark. Maybe it had been something in the boy's gait, something not quite soldierly, which had caught Ajax's attention—had put him on full predator alert. But he remembered now, turning The Needle in his hands in Krill's camp, that without thinking he'd gone into a crouch and drawn the blade. Something about the boy stank of prey and Ajax had moved to intercept him.

It had been an easy kill. Ajax infiltrated the camp and the boy had practically walked into his arms. He'd taken the boy down, straddled him, and clamped his mouth shut. The boy hardly resisted at all. This surprised Ajax until he'd got a look at the unlined face. The long eyelashes and full lips. The boy had been a dark-skinned campesino and could not have been more than thirteen or fourteen. But the Guardia, in the final days, had been conscripting anyone it could lay its calloused, shaking hands on. Ajax had known right off the Python did not belong to the boy. No weapon this fine would be issued to such a child-soldier, nor would he have been allowed to keep it had he taken it as a prize.

No. He carried it for another, an officer, perhaps even the colonel Ajax's sniper had been trying to pick off for two days. "Gun bearer." It was a term they'd heard, an affectation of some of the high-born officers who choose privates to carry their favorite firearm. But one look at the boy's long lashes, his delicate features, the way he'd surrendered instantly, and Ajax had known the boy had had other duties as well.

That wasn't why Ajax had killed him. All the throats he'd cut as a foot soldier. The men who'd died in his ambushes, or because of his orders. The *sandbags* sacrificed, the collaborators executed. Why should that boy have been any different? He didn't know why. It was just what he had done.

All he could remember now was that, holding the boy down, he'd seen tears flowing freely as he drove The Needle in drew it out. As he had so many times before—so often, in fact, he'd learned that a well-cut throat made a man feel, in his last moments, that he was drowning as blood poured into the lungs. Ajax had decided to spare the boy that end and so had sat him up and let him bleed out. Once the boy had ceased spasming, Ajax had almost left without the Python, took it as an afterthought. He'd stopped carrying The Needle after that. Three days later the garrison had surrendered. For the first time, Ajax broke his promise of quarter. He executed the colonel with his own pistol. It was the only time Ajax had fired the Python in battle.

And now the ghost of the boy with the long eyelashes had set

Ajax free with the same knife. Maybe the ghost meant to save Ajax so he could persecute him in his own way. Maybe the ghost thought even a pain-filled death at the hands of the Contra was too good for him. Too quick. Whatever the ghost's reasons, Ajax rolled onto his belly, determined to make his way slowly through Krill's camp. As he did, a line of poetry came to him:

And Jaguar ruled the Kingdom of Death, undiscerning and blind.

16

1.

Matthew Connelly stood in the graveyard at Enrique's finca doing the math. There were different kinds of math. There was, for example, the Mystery of Life math, like the first time he'd gone to New York City. For three days, every time he'd tried to cross a street, the very moment he'd lifted his foot off the curb, the light had changed from WALK to DON'T WALK. What was the equation to figure that message? More importantly, there was Imponderable Life Math. Like, *I should be dead but the Contra didn't kill me and now I'm sitting on a scoop that might get me killed.* Then there was simple arithmetic. Fractions. Addition and subtraction. Like, five hundred thousand dollars minus two hundred fifty thousand dollars equals two piles of one hundred and twenty-five thousand dollars. He'd found one of those piles, he was sure of it. But that kind of arithmetic led to Mystery Math, like, then where the hell is the rest of it? Or, even, should I get on a plane and get the hell out of town? But he could solve that equation: he would never leave such a story. It was too huge.

It was the scoop of a lifetime.

2.

Ajax knelt at the bank of a stream and looked at himself flowing by in the water. His face was neither as cut nor as bruised as he had expected. But his nose looked broken and he'd not realized that. He gingerly touched it and the pain awoke his whole body, which had operated on some inner power since he'd left Krill's camp. When was that? He couldn't be sure. He couldn't be sure how many men he had killed either. Some of them? All of them? Not even if he'd gotten Krill or One-eye. He had just moved from man to man on his belly, more of a slither than a crawl. He'd clapped one hand on the mouth, the other drove The Needle in through the jugular, out through the larynx. Each bloody death making no more noise than a sigh and a gurgle. Then on to the next. And the next.

There had been no sentries in the camp, just a listening post at the outer edge. That had been his last stop. One of them had been asleep. He'd killed the other so swiftly that one had not wakened. Then he'd clapped his hand over the sleeping one's mouth. His eyes had snapped open and Ajax could tell he'd thought he'd been busted for sleeping on guard duty. Ajax had waited until the reality had registered in those eyes, and then put him to sleep forever.

Then Ajax had slithered into the night.

When dawn came he'd finally stood up, and known he did not have to hurry back to Enrique's finca. There were too few left to give chase. He had faced south and started walking. He did not return the way he had come.

Now he was parched, and his ribs and tailbone ached. He stuck his head into the water to drink and soak. Then he took stock. The sun slanted late through the trees; he had maybe three hours of light left. His clothes were torn. But it was his hands that caught his eye. His hands and even his forearms were caked in blood. He soaked them in the stream, then drew The Needle and soaked it as well. He remembered the cleaning power of a stream bed and used the pebbles and soil to scrub himself and his knife.

He watched the flakes of blood re-liquefy and disappear in the flowing water.

Then he heard the footfall. He crouched low, almost snarled, and had thought to throw The Needle point-first before he saw it was Epimenio. Ajax wasn't sure what he looked like. He recognized his own reflection in the water, but that wasn't the same as knowing how he was doing. By the horrified look on Epimenio's face, he assumed he was not doing well.

"Señor Martin."

"Captain Montoya. No need to lie anymore."

Epimenio sat down hard on the ground. He sank his head in his hands, then used his hands to pull up great clumps of turf from the ground. "If I did not lie, he would not be dead."

"Connelly? Connelly's dead?"

"No, Captain. Don Enrique."

"What? Connelly's not dead?"

"He's at the house. He came yesterday."

Ajax bounded across the stream and knelt beside the tormented campesino. "Epimenio, you're sure Connelly's alive?"

"Yes, señor, he is at the house right now."

"Thank God. I did not want his death on my hands." Ajax looked at his hands, still wet from the stream, and grunted at the damnable irony. "Wait, then what lie are you talking about and whose death?"

"Don Enrique."

"The Contra didn't kill him."

"I know. I know. I know."

As he watched Epimenio's face the phrase *the wretched of the earth* floated into Ajax's mind. The campesino seemed to embody a wretchedness found only among the most powerless of the world. Still, his cop's instinct told him Epimenio had reached the point of confession.

"Explain it to me."

Epimenio sighed and seemed to relax. His fists unclenched, his shoulders sagged, and his jaw dropped a little. All signs, Ajax knew, of impending admission.

"Don Enrique told me not to tell anyone, not doña Gloria, don

Mateo, no one. He had never spoken to me that way before, like he was ordering a servant."

"What was the secret?"

"The jaguar cub you saw me bury. When we were out hunting its mother, we heard a plane in the sky."

"The airstrip—you told me about that."

"But that night, we heard men's voices. Enrique insisted we get closer. We snuck up near to them. I knew it was a bad idea. We listened for a while and then we snuck back down. Don Enrique seemed angry. He insisted we leave that night for home."

"What were they talking about? Did you hear?"

"Some. I didn't understand much, but I think it was about money. They spoke about 'fifties.' I asked don Enrique, but he told me never to ask him nor tell anyone."

"Fifties? How is that money? It's not a córdoba note. Were they talking about American money? Fifty-dollar bills?"

"I don't know, Captain. Enrique wouldn't talk about it. I didn't understand the talk. I thought it was maybe about a bank, or someone's house. All I heard was cincuenta."

"Casa Cincuenta? House Fifty?"

"I think."

There is a phrase for a certain state of mind: *reeling*. Until that moment, whenever Ajax had heard that word he pictured a person stumbling backward, arms pinwheeling from some shock. But now he had a different image: a fishing pole with a long line out in the water and an angler spooling the line in very fast. The angler feeling the weight at the end of the line, but not knowing what it would bring up. The fisherman was reeling. And what Ajax saw emerge finally from the water was not a fish, not a log, not an old boot or discarded trash.

It was a face.

The face of the man who had killed Enrique Cuadra.

Ajax tried to calm his pounding heart, tried to speak calmly. He took Epimenio's shoulders in his hands and looked at him very closely.

"Were they Nicaraguans? These men you heard?"

"I don't think so. Their accents were not Matagalpan. Don Enrique said they were Cuban."

"Cuban? You're sure?"

"That's what he said and what he made me promise not to tell. I never knew any Cubans. Not until I met your friend in Managua."

"Friend? What friend?"

"The lady doctor."

"Lady doctor? Marta? Doctor Marta Jimenez? In the morgue?"

"Yes, she has the same accent."

"Son of a bitch. Son of the great shit-eating puta of all putas."

"Captain?"

"She's not Cuban."

3.

As soon as Ajax emerged from the bush, Matthew raced from Enrique's house and lifted him right off the ground in a bear hug.

"You're alive!"

Ajax contorted in pain, every muscle and bone screeching.

"Let go of me, Connelly. We're leaving."

"What?"

"We're leaving. For Managua. Now."

"Yes, Matthew. So glad you are alive, too."

Ajax went straight to Matthew's truck and retrieved the Python.

"You have a gun? In my truck!"

Ajax checked the six rounds, and then fitted the holster to his hip. He did not think of the boy he had murdered for it. But he had an inkling that he might kill with it one more time.

"Give me your keys, Connelly, and get in."

"Ajax, listen for a second. I think I know why Enrique was killed."

"So do I. Why and by who. Give me your keys and get in."

"We can't leave without Amelia."

Amelia. Ajax had to think for a moment. It was not that the past few days were hazy. Rather, Epimenio's revelation seemed to have erased the past few years.

"Amelia," Ajax repeated. He knew that name.

"Senator Teal's aide."

"I know who she is, Connelly. Where is she?"

"With Father Jerome getting the family she's taking out. They'll be back soon."

"Too late. You wait for her. Now gimme your keys."

"You're not taking . . ."

Before Connelly said more, Ajax had him in an armlock jacked up against his truck and fished the keys from his pocket. Fished. Reeled. Ajax was going to reel it all in now.

"You stay and see Amelia gets back safe. I'll leave your truck at your house."

"You can't travel by yourself, *Martin*. What about the Contra?"

"They didn't kill Enrique." *But I know who did*. He didn't say it out loud, this was private business. *Nicaraguan* business, and Connelly was no longer a part of it.

4.

Captain Ajax Montoya stood in a bucket of water. That's what had made him look at the calendar. He'd arrived home late yesterday from the long drive with only one memory of it: stopping for gas and realizing Krill still had his wallet. If Krill was still alive. He'd bartered the last of Connelly's stash of Reds and soap for fuel. When he'd walked into his house, a rank smell had assaulted his nose. It had taken a moment for him to realize he was the source of it. He'd sat in a chair to get his boots off and woken up there twelve hours later. That was a pain in the ass, but it had been at least forty years since he'd last slept. He awoke around midday, reeking of sweat and blood, his civvies saturated in it. He'd tried to take a shower but there'd been no water. That's when he'd started to think, *No water so it must be . . .* But realized he didn't know the day or the date. So he'd checked the calendar: five days he'd been gone. Five? It wasn't possible. That was too few. Or too many.

He'd stripped and gotten into the plastic tub he kept filled for days the water was off. He'd washed slowly and carefully, spoiling the rest of the water; he wouldn't need it anymore.

He dressed in his cleanest uniform, strapped on the Python, and decided to take Matthew's truck. He considered taking Gladys as well. But Gladys was a rookie and if things went down anything like he thought they might, it was best to keep her clear of it.

He drove off, knowing both where he was going and how to get there. Managua was a warren of unnamed streets, so everyone used the same landmarks. The Hotel InterContinental. The Metro Centro. The military hospital. The Cabrera cinema.

And Casa Cincuenta.

House Fifty. Headquarters of the Dirección General de Seguridad del Estado. The DGSE. State Security. It was known as Casa Fifty because of the huge numbers painted on the outside wall. As he pulled to a stop, Ajax tried to remember why or how it had gotten the name. He couldn't, and it didn't matter. He drew the Python, half cocked it, and rolled the fully loaded cylinder over his palm to ponder his next move.

Then he stopped.

Strange, but it just didn't feel right. He'd always used the Python to help him think. But maybe, he reckoned, that was it: he didn't need to think anymore. He'd figured it out. Why it had all gone wrong. How it did. And who'd done it.

He holstered the Python and watched the two guards at the entrance as they checked cars passing through. He knew the layout and routine well from his time in DGSE. It would be easier getting in the gate on foot and still easier if he was unarmed. He had handcuffs on one side of his belt, the Python on the other, The Needle hidden in his boot, and Connelly's micro tape recorder in his shirt pocket. He hadn't decided what he would do yet, but was leaning toward the handcuffs. That night in Krill's camp still hung on him like a smell. The boy with the long eyelashes had given him his life back. No, that wasn't it. It was the *ghost* of that boy who had given him his life back. Why? To surrender it in some OK Corral shootout inside the DGSE?

"No. Cuff him and perp-walk the shit-eater right out the door."

He slid the Python under the seat and walked to the guard gate. He nodded at the two street guards and handed his police ID to the lone but heavily armed compa inside, who monitored a closed-circuit video of the street from inside a concrete booth.

"Buenos compañero. Captain Ajax Montoya to see Comandante Malhora."

He'd hardly got the words out when the black, hulking Russian phone in the guard booth rang. The compa snatched it up mid-ring. He listened for a heartbeat, then thrust the receiver through the window.

"For you."

Ajax listened: "He's expecting you." It must be one of the Conquistadores. He handed the phone back as the metal gate rolled open just enough for him to slip through. He knew the camera covered the street, but thought he'd parked in a blind spot.

The Conquistadores waited at the heavy, bombproof front door. Ajax took his time walking in and studied the interior courtyard. He spotted the Land Cruiser with smoke-blacked windows he'd noticed in Matagalpa. So he'd been followed. Heat shimmered off the hood, like they'd just gotten back. So they hadn't followed him home yesterday.

As he walked on, the pressure of The Needle in his boot reassured him.

"You donkeys enjoy your vacation in Matagalpa?"

"Not as much as you did."

So they knew about Amelia.

5.

Sub-comandante Vladimir Malhora sat behind a desk not much smaller than Connelly's truck. In his soft, clean hand he held a cigar not much shorter than the blade strapped to Ajax's leg. His uniform was immaculately pressed, the insignia on it perfectly placed. His boots shone like black mirrors. He barked orders into a phone. Ajax suspected there was no one on the other end. While he waited for Malhora's theatrics to conclude, he let himself imagine how the co-mandante would look after a week in the same cell as El Gordo Sangroso. He smiled at the thought, which was what he needed to be doing right now, smiling.

Malhora hung up the phone, took his sweet time lighting his cigar, and then dismissed the Conquistadores with a wave.

"Ajax. Would you like a cigar? Cuban."

"No."

"How about a Marlboro Red? Made in America."

"No."

"It's funny, isn't it? The Communists make the best cigars and the capitalists the best cigarettes."

"No."

"No?"

"It's not funny. The word you're looking for is ironic."

"Ironic. Yes." He rolled the cigar between his fingers. "Ajax, why have we never been friends?"

"I don't know." Ajax looked around the office, Malhora's throne room, as if it held the answer. "Maybe because you are the kind of man I despise most: you're vain, greedy, and deep down, a coward."

Malhora smiled and drew deeply on his cigar. "There are only a handful of people in this entire country who could dare speak to me that way."

"If everyone spoke to you that way you'd be a better person. And we'd have a better country."

Malhora knocked a head of ash off the cigar into a jade ashtray.

"Ajax, you have always thought you were special. *The great hero.* No one can tell you anything, but what are you really? A drunk? A killer? Hmm? That's right, we know. We've been monitoring Contra radio chatter. You scared them out of their boots. They think you are the Angel of Death. But what are you, really?"

Ajax took the handcuffs out of his pocket and hung them from his belt. "Get to your point."

"What you are, Ajax, is a child. A Boy Scout. You speak like a Nicaraguan but you think like an American. An American fool." Malhora made six-shooters with his hands. "Pow. Pow. Pow. Everything is a cowboy Western. White hats and black hats. It's always made you unreliable, *that's* why there was no place for you after the Triumph. You're a liberal bourgeois, not a comrade. Now, tell me what you think you know."

Malhora took another long pull on the cigar. Ajax wandered over to the portrait of Sandino hanging from the wall. It was an excellent oil painting done from the iconic photograph of the diminutive rebel general in his ten-gallon Stetson. Ajax saw it all clearly—as clearly as when Epimenio told him the men at the airstrip had Cuban accents, just like Marta. But she was Colombian.

"You're running drugs out of a secret airstrip in the mountains of Matagalpa. Cocaine probably. Enrique Cuadra came upon it by accident while hunting a jaguar. But the men you use for it are blowhards like you, can't keep their mouths shut, don't know about light and noise discipline. Cuadra heard them talking, recognized their accents as Colombian. He put two and two together and decided to do something about it. You found out and killed him before he could tell Matthew Connelly."

"And what if that is true? So what?"

Ajax turned from the portrait of the past to the face of the present. There was a cockiness to Malhora that hinted at a hole card.

"You murdered a citizen of the republic. A good man who gave three sons to the revolution." He slid the handcuffs off his belt. "I'm going to put these on you and take you to jail, or I will kill you where you sit. There is no third option."

Malhora smiled a serpent's smile and took his time relighting his cigar, the pride of the worldwide communist movement. "There is always a third way, Ajax. Morality is not arithmetic where this and that will always equal something else. Morality is like an industry. If you have certain resources, you make one thing. If you lack those resources, you use something else to make something else. Just like in war. You use what you have."

"If you're trying to buy time until someone comes to rescue you, don't. If that door opens, I'll have you dead before they touch me. What happens after will not matter to you." And that was true. He would carry out his threat to the letter, he was ready for that. But he sensed that Malhora had an ace facedown behind that door. What Ajax could not fathom was why Malhora had sent the Conquistadores out in the first place.

"You would kill me."

"Yes."

"I'm not asking. I'm telling you, you *would* kill me. But would you kill the enemy?"

"Define enemy."

"American Imperialism! The colossus to the north. Ronald Reagan and the entire shit-eating evil empire that sucks the life out of us, all of us! That puts its boot on our neck and pushes our face into the mud until we suffocate. That screams we are a threat to them while they kill us. Literally kill us. The enemy, goddamn you, the fucking *enemy*!"

"And the murder of Enrique Cuadra served how, exactly, to kill the enemy?"

"We cannot attack the United States from outside. Only from within. Their decadence is our greatest ally. Their love of the coca is an undefended flank we can attack. We can feed the Giant poison. Right now there are tens of thousands of Americans going to jail for drug sales. In ten or fifteen years these *narcos* will have become hardened criminals to be released back into their communities to wreak more havoc. Millions of children born to drug-addicted mothers. Their Negro inner cities are like war zones. The impact on public policy, resources, the very politics of the whole country change as we make them fight the war on drugs, which they will lose. The cocaine is a weapon, a bomb we can explode now, and again fifteen years from now! Do you see?"

"The poor man's weapon of mass destruction."

"Yes! Yes! My God, you do get it. Those shit-eating gringos never, ever have to pay for what they do. Look at Vietnam, the millions dead, the forests agent-oranged to death—and who paid for that? The Vietnamese. You know what they have done to us: Guatemala, Chile, the Dominican Republic. And El Salvador worst of all, seventy thousand dead already. Do you think we would have this Contra war were it not for them?"

Malhora ground out the cigar in the ashtray like it was Reagan's own face. "And how many thousands have we already lost? And yet every time the Americans get to walk away complaining that they could not do more. Walk away clean. And they will do that here. No one will ever pay for the misery and death—no one. Ever! They never do. But this way, this way we can infect them with a disease. 'The poor man's weapon of mass destruction' indeed! But unlike a nuclear bomb it does not kill all at once, but slowly, over time. As hatred should kill."

Ajax finally sat down, relieved that he was not the craziest son of a bitch in the country, as he'd feared. "I'll take that Marlboro now."

Malhora offered the red leather box of cigarettes and lit it for Ajax.

"And you are going to accomplish all this with one little airstrip hanging to the side of a mountain in Matagalpa?"

Malhora laughed. "Admittedly, the means of production are not yet sufficient to our purposes."

"Why not use the airports if you had to move bulk?"

"*Our* airports? Ajax, even you have heard of satellite surveillance. No. An airstrip in Contra country would have to do, and, yes, if in a few months we decided to 'raid' the airstrip, capture it with its evidence of drug smuggling, then who else would the world blame but the Contra? *Surely the government could not run an airstrip in such a place.*"

Ajax took a drag on the red. It was American-made, he had to admit. "So it was a setup against the Contra. Okay. We've done that before. But why kill Enrique Cuadra? Didn't he think it was a Contra airstrip?"

"Cuadra was not the great citizen you think. He was Contra. Did you know he was involved with Jorge Salazar? Yes, our old friend Jorge. It was Cuadra's gas station Salazar used. Why? Because he felt safe there to plan his treachery."

"There weren't any traitors. That was a setup. We lured Salazar into it."

"Yes, but Salazar chose where to meet. And that revealed his network of traitors. Salazar and Cuadra were related by marriage. Did you know that?"

Ajax did not, but he did not reveal it.

"Salazar's widow and Cuadra's wife are cousins, raised together. She is buried on Cuadra's farm."

Ajax had noticed the fresh grave, but had not thought to ask about it. And now the urgency in Connelly's voice came back to him. *I know who killed Enrique.* But Ajax had had too big a hard-on to listen. Doubt began to creep in.

"Do you begin to see the method in my madness, Captain Montoya?"

"What about the money?"

There it was, a flicker in his eye. Malhora had blinked. He'd shied. He'd flinched.

"Money?"

"There are no profits from the drugs? No one is getting paid?"

"You think I am enriching myself?"

Now Malhora had answered two questions with questions. In an interrogation, this was classic avoidance behavior. He'd learned that first in the mountains. It had been a rule among the guerrilleros: when you got to a campesino shack, you began by making small talk and then got quickly to questions about the Guardia. If three questions were answered by questions you assumed the farmers had been compromised and ran for it. Malhora shifted in the high-back leather chair that was not quite as big as a church door. He toyed with the extinguished cigar like he might put flame to it again. He shook his head as if deeply saddened by Ajax's lack of faith. Ajax did not know precisely what it meant, but he did know the money was the key to the mystery.

"Answer me. You think I am enriching myself?"

"I think I don't trust you as far as I could throw Enrique Cuadra's rotting corpse."

"There is money, of course there is. A lot of it. We use it to fund certain black operations, which you will forgive me if I don't share with you." Malhora allowed himself a chuckle as if from some private joke. "You don't think I came up with all this on my own, do you?"

"I don't think you've got the brains or the balls." Ajax drew himself up out of the chair, dropped the handcuffs on Malhora's desk, and let his hands dangle loosely at his sides. He threw the inner switch of fight-or-flight into fight. It was time to see Malhora's whole card. "What I do think is that you will now put those handcuffs on or I am likely to break a bone doing it for you."

"Interesting isn't it?" Malhora lifted the handcuffs as if he would put them on. "In Spanish our word for handcuffs is *esposos*. The same as spouse." Then he tossed the handcuffs at Ajax's face. "Come in!"

Ajax ducked the handcuffs, went over the desk, and had Malhora in a choke hold so fast he had time to relish Malhora's stiffening with fear. Yes, that was what Ajax wanted, to feel his fear. The desk was enough of an obstacle that he could get to The Needle if he needed to.

But through Malhora's door came not henchmen, but Gioconda Targa and Horacio de la Vega.

Esposos.

Or the enemy?

Ajax released Malhora, who sunk back into his chair. The looks on the faces of his best friend and ex-wife foretold what they had come to propose.

The three of them just looked at each other in silence. Ajax thought, *Here we are, the Father, Son, and Holy Ghost.*

Then he had another thought, and spoke it: "'Each Judas a friend of every Cain.'"

Horacio looked away, but Gio reacted as if struck. "What did you say?"

"'Each Judas a friend of every Cain.' It's a quote from Rubén Darío."

"I know what it is! How dare you quote that to me!"

Horacio stepped between them. "Ajax, we must talk. Comandante, would you mind?"

"If he tries to leave the room, he's a dead man."

"No, he's not, Ajax." Horacio signaled for Malhora to leave. "And it is unhelpful to even talk that way."

"It's quite all right, Horacio. I will wait right in the outer office. I believe Lieutenant Darío is there?"

Horacio nodded.

"Then I will leave myself in the 'custody' of compañera Darío. Ajax, if, after the three of you talk, you still want to arrest me, I will be waiting for you."

Malhora opened the door to show Ajax that Gladys was, indeed, there. Ajax looked at her. She nodded, but he was not sure what that meant. His eyes went to her sidearm, then back to her eyes. She shifted her right hand to the Makarov. But he did not know what that meant, either. He felt as if the boards and concrete of Casa Fifty had dropped away and he was falling through the foundation, through the dirt and rocks and bones of the Earth into an abiding void. And the fear which flopped his belly was not of his death upon hitting bottom, but that he would never stop falling.

The few seconds it took Malhora to vacate the room and click the door shut were the worst moments of Ajax's recent life. He stood looking at the shut door, the sealed portal which might have led to another world, another life.

Horacio, at last, walked around the desk and draped a hand on his shoulder. "Thank God you're safe, Ajax. Malhora told us about Krill."

"Why would you even go there?" Gio sat down, folded her arms over her bosom. "Do you have some kind of death wish?"

Ajax faced them. It was like having a blindfold removed, and, blinking in the weak dawn light, discovering that his two best friends would command his firing squad.

"Did you know about this?" he asked.

Gio shook her head. Her chestnut-brown ringlets shuddered like vines hanging from a tree, vines he had once wanted climb. But now they seemed like the vines in Paradise that shook as the snake slithered up the tree of knowledge. "Of course not."

"You, Horacio?"

"This is not about Malhora. It's not about airstrips or cocaine. And it's not about Enrique Cuadra."

"And it's not about your gringa lover either," Gio added.

"Are you jealous?"

"Don't be a child. This is politics. What I care about is Senator Teal and the deal we are trying to make with him while you are off fucking his aide de camp! Do you think we let Teal come here for *his* reasons? We have worked this out, I have worked this out so carefully. And now you . . ."

"Gio, that is also not what this is about." Horacio eased Ajax into

Malhora's chair and then sat himself down, taking a moment to massage his crippled leg. "Ajax, this is about Joaquin."

"Tinoco?"

"Yes, and his seat on the National Directorate. Since it became clear that he was dying, and dying quickly, everything has been about who would replace him. In very, *very* private meetings many things have come out. It was decided weeks ago that this ludicrous cocaine operation would cease. If anything, Cuadra probably stumbled on the last flight. It is over, the airstrip destroyed, and any connections between us and it have been erased . . ."

"Or killed off."

"Or killed off. I am sorry for the death of Enrique, but everything is at stake right now. Everything!"

"Except bringing a murderer to justice."

"Oh please." Gio sat down as if exhausted. "What is justice to you but getting your own way?"

"Gio." Horacio leaned on his cane and struggled to his feet. "I asked you to come with me to help."

"Help with what, Horacio?" Ajax rose to his feet. "Why are the two of you *here*?" He gestured to the room.

"To adjust your gaze."

"What?"

Horacio hobbled to the big picture window overlooking the city all the way down to the lake. "Our war with America . . . is not a war between civilizations. Capitalism versus Communism. North versus South. Like all wars, it is between the civilized and the uncivilized. In both countries, in all countries, there exist only those two camps. The uncivilized in each country wish to make war on the uncivilized in other countries. And the civilized in each want to make peace with the civilized in other nations. We are the same. The uncivilized in America want to invade us, crush, kill, and destroy us. We have our barbarians, too. They, too, want to war with America. They want to provoke an invasion so that Nicaragua can be another, the final, Vietnam that brings America down. They are the ones who planned and launched this drug business, 'poor man's weapon of mass destruction.' Malhora is a barbarian. My job is to keep him off the National Directorate where he will be the deciding vote in favor of all-out war."

"Then let me arrest him and your problem is solved."

Horacio smiled, but Ajax could see there was no mirth in his eyes.

"No, it is not. It will be infinitely worse. We—you and I and Gioconda—are among the civilized; we want peace and prosperity through coexistence and we have our counterparts in America. We need to make peace with them, through them. If you arrest Malhora, if one more goddamned person knows about that goddamned airstrip, it will explode! If word of this gets out, the civilized in both countries will be defeated, utterly, and the barbarians will get their war. Do you know what that will mean?"

Ajax got that falling feeling again. "Of course I know." He looked at Gio. "Better than most." He had to throw that line in, had to push back on something, someone.

Gio ignored the barb. She stood in front of Ajax. Close to him. Her hands behind her back. "Then what will you do?"

"He murdered Enrique Cuadra. Isn't that enough to keep him off the Directorate?"

"No." Horacio moved subtly so that he and Gio were now side by side facing Ajax. "He no more killed Cuadra on his own than he dug the airstrip with his own hands. He's close to the Directorate, but there is still a chance to have someone else take his place. Malhora's masters are a minority; they are reeling from the near disaster of Cuadra's death revealing the cocaine plot. Meaning they are frightened that instead of botching this case, you have uncovered the truth. You may have wanted to move away from politics, but you are now the fulcrum on which all is balanced. How it tips is up to you."

Ajax smiled; now the big picture was getting clearer. "I see. So Horacio de la Vega will finally mount the steps of destiny to the National Directorate. Or maybe Gio is to be the first woman to join the boys' club."

Gio shook her head, it seemed to Ajax, with genuine regret.

"No, Ajax, not Gio. Gio is not eligible. You have to be a comandante guerrillero to be nominated for the post."

"And you are one, Horacio."

"And so are you."

"Is that what this is? You've come to bribe me? Let Malhora go and you'll nominate me for the Directorate?"

Gio shook her head, but Ajax could not tell if it was in disgust or defeat. "I would move to Washington and become a Republican blow-job queen before *that* would ever happen."

So it was in disgust. "You don't think I'd make a good comandante?"

"No. I mean before I would *bribe* you. You will do what is right, what is necessary because you have to do it! We will not offer you anything. We are not asking for your kind consideration or indulgence. You will do it, Ajax, because it is the right thing to do, because we have come here to tell you what to do!"

"Ajax." Horacio slid his body between them. "We need to replace Joaquin with someone popular with the masses. Someone with credibility from the old days. And you *are* Spooky, el Terrorifico. The Prince of Peace. And your name *has* come up. Not everyone is . . ."

"Is?"

"Apprised of your . . . unorthodoxies. You're a long shot, Ajax, but I am not here to bribe or pander to you."

"So Malhora goes free? That piece of rotten shit will just walk, or get promoted?"

"It is not about Malhora. It's not about you. It's not about Enrique Cuadra. It's about more war or less war. And you have to decide right now. You, right this moment."

Ajax knew he had lost. The knot in his stomach told him that.

Every opposing idea he could not reconcile was tied there. How had it come to this?

"How has it come to this, Horacio? Is this what we fought for? If you kill someone, you go down for taking that life. We aren't supposed to measure lives for their value. Listen to yourselves: Knight takes Rook, Bishop takes Queen, Queen takes King."

"Yes. And you want to ask about the Pawns."

"I didn't fight all those years just to be a pawn, anyone's pawn in some Cold War chess game."

"Then what did you fight for Ajax?"

"Flu shots and flush toilets." He picked up the handcuffs. "Equality before the law."

Gio sat down again. "Well, what you got was superpower Cold War chess games. You still haven't said what you're going to do."

Ajax knew what he was going to do. Knew the moment these two had come in.

Esposos.

He turned his gaze away from the tawdry scene in Malhora's office and out the big picture window. He looked at the piss-poor, crazy ass city filled with a million pawns and knew he would not sacrifice a one of them—not to take a bishop, a queen, or even a king. But he also knew he could not win by playing defense. He could only delay the inevitable—eventually the other side would take the pawns first.

He strode across the room and threw open the door. The outer office was empty.

As he knew it would be.

He reached into his pocket and clicked off Connelly's tape recorder.

17

1.

Ajax drove the pickup to Matthew's house in Barrio Bolonia. There was a light on, but he left the keys under the seat and decided to walk home. He headed south until he passed the Ministry of Culture and reached the Pista de la Resistencia which he could follow home to barrio Bello Horizonte. He had passed the Plaza 19 de Julio when the smell of food cooking stirred his belly to life. He stopped at the China Palace for a plate of chop suey and mystery meat. As he wolfed down what tasted more like chop suet, he tried to recall the last time he'd eaten. It must've been with Krill, whom he was now certain he also hadn't managed to get rid of. When was that? It seemed ages ago now. He knew that during combat time seemed to slow down because the mind sped up, as in a movie. To create the illusion of slow motion you increased the camera speed. But now time seemed to be coming to an end. The camera of his mind was not speeding up nor slowing down. It was running out of film.

He trudged homeward, when his legs, following a body memory, turned right and stopped in front of a beer joint, Jardín Central. A beer. A cold beer. *Gimme, gimme, gimme, gimme, gimme just the one.*

"You're back." He said it out loud like he'd bumped into someone.

A cold beer. The local brew, called Victoria, was made without hops, which Nicaragua did not grow and could not import because of the American embargo. It had a shelf life of only three days before it turned to piss. Beer without hops. Bricks without straw. Victoria.

By the time he stood at his own front door the sun was going down. There were newspapers strewn in front of it, and he realized he could calculate time that way. He got three newspapers a day, so he counted them. Eighteen newspapers. He'd been gone six days, not five. He scooped them up and locked the door behind him.

He went to his office, sat in his chair, and pulled the dead drawer open. In it was the photo of him from July 20, 1979, Gio's small makeup bag, the suicide soldier's Makarov, and the bottle of Flor de Caña Extra Seco. The Needle was still strapped to his calf. He sat staring into the dead drawer until all the light crept away and night skulked in.

2.

Taking a drink was like lighting a homemade rocket. There was, Ajax thought as he lay on his back in his tiny garden looking up at the stars, that moment of anticipation when the hand holding the match hovered near the fuse. Will it go off in your face? Or burn nice and smooth before it explodes into the sky? There was no way to know but to touch flame to fuse, step back, and await the wonder, the release of detonation. When he'd finally cracked the seal on the bottle of rum, it was like pointing a rocket at the sky. Pouring himself three fingers of the liquid sulfur was like striking the match. Then tossing all of it into his mouth and holding it there for a moment was like that very first spark on the fuse. Holding it there just long enough for the taste buds to communicate to his stomach, to his body, to his entire being: Stand by for lift-off!

Ten, nine, eight . . . Then—and this had always been his favorite part—the slow burn of the fuse as the rum ran slowly, dreamily, languorously down his esophagus to his belly. Three, two one . . .

BANG!

Of course, it was not so much an explosion as an implosion. And he did not so much watch the rocket go as ride it. With the bottle in one hand and the glass in the other, Captain Ajax Montoya pushed himself off the damp earth.

"We have lift-off!"

He stumbled over the low table on which he had assembled the contents of the dead drawer and sent them and himself tumbling back to earth.

"Houston, second stage not complete."

He sorted the items he'd knocked off the table into a little pile of his heart's detritus. He had added Horacio's poetry manuscript, his thesaurus, the Python, and The Needle, its blade cleaned and oiled since its last use.

"Too much ballast, Houston."

"Copy that, Captain Montoya, lighten your load."

He tore Horacio's manuscript, *Poems from the Volcano*, apart, piled the pages into a vague cone shape, and soaked them with rum. Ripped a few pages out of the thesaurus.

"Ballast, weight, counterbalance . . ."

And added them to the pyre. Next he picked up the photo, looked at it one last time, and smashed his fist into it. He was drunk enough not to feel the glass shards go into his knuckles, but not so drunk he didn't notice the blood trickle down his fingers. He watched a few drops make their slow progress until one slid off his fingernail onto the photo, obliterating his face there.

"Bonfire, flare, beacon . . ."

He ripped the photo from the frame, flicked his Zippo to life, and set it alight. When the flames had consumed half the picture he dropped it onto the manuscript pages. They burst into flame so quickly that he had to roll away. He poured himself three more fingers of rocket fuel and knocked it back. Then he fed a little more onto the fire.

"Second stage is complete!"

He fumbled for the small makeup bag, spilled the four items onto the ground, then fed the bag into the fire. He held the hairbrush over the flames until the acrid smell of burning hair roused his dulled nostrils. Then he fed the brush to the flames. The nail file he drove into the ground like a spike, using the butt of the Python to hammer it into oblivion. The lipstick tube, he rolled open. He ripped another page from the thesaurus and smeared on it in his bloody hand. *Judas Cain.* He held the page over the fire, and as it caught, some of the lipstick melted and rolled down the paper like the blood down his fingers.

"Now the secret ingredient."

He lifted the petite, cut-glass perfume bottle, tore the top off as he had done the rum bottle, and dribbled what was left into the fire. The alcohol in it flared and singed the hair on his hand.

"A la gran puta! Gotta have the last word, don't you, bitch!"

He hurled the vial over the back wall and heard it shatter in the darkness. Ajax stirred the fire to keep the manuscript pages burning. Then he stared at the flames with the unfocused countenance of the drunkard. His mind was not blank so much as adrift, like a satellite out of orbit, drawn into the void of space. He waited—as the flames got smaller, as the fire died—for something, anything to come into his mind. Nothing did. That was when he noticed he had the Python in his hand. He rolled the cylinder back and forth across his palm.

Back.

And forth.

Then he stopped. He held the weapon in both hands. Looking at it. The last of the flames glinting off the chrome. He felt he was trying to remember something.

And then he did.

He flicked open the pistol—all six cylinders held a bullet.

"Eighty-eight. That's the lucky number."

He spun the cylinder as he had eighty-seven times before.

"Loaded dice. Yeah."

Ajax screwed his eyes shut and began to rock, back and forth. He gripped the Python in his left hand and cupped his right on the pistol butt, to steady it. His face twisted into a grimace, he grunted aloud as if in pain, and rocked, rocked back and forth. He touched the Python's barrel just beneath his chin. He rocked and grunted as he tilted it from one angle to another, tracing in his mind's eye the path of the bullet. Ninety degrees was too vertical: he saw himself alive but chinless. Forty-five degrees was too low, and he conjured an image of a quadriplegic with a diaper full of shit. About sixty-five degrees should send it through the roof of the mouth and into the brain. And all the time he rocked and grunted and grimaced.

He squatted on his haunches. "Come on! You goddamned chicken-shit little puto! Okay, okay. Gimme, gimme, gimme, gimme just one more drink."

He held the Python under his chin with one hand and poured with the other until his cup overflowed. He swallowed most of it and threw the rest into the dying fire, which flared into flame.

And in the fleeting illumination he saw eyes.

The boy with the long eyelashes crouched in the corner of his garden, watching him.

"You!"

The ghost, he saw, squatted with his hands cupped under his chin. It took Ajax a moment to realize he was posed just as Ajax was, his index finger pointed like the pistol barrel. Ajax lowered the pistol from his chin, and the ghost did the same. Ajax rolled from a squat to his knees, and the ghost did, too, like a child imitating an adult.

"Is this what you wanted? By my own hand? Is that it?"

Suddenly Ajax could see himself as the ghost must have. A wretch. A wreck, squatting upon the ground. Bestial. A gun to his head.

"Then come with me."

Ajax fired into the boy, and fired again and again as if he could kill him again. Then he leapt to his feet and lobbed the almost empty bottle at the ghost-boy and kept firing. Somewhere in the darkness he heard a crash, wood splintering. He thought he heard his name shouted.

"Fuck you! Fuck you! Fuck you!"

He put the Python to his temple and pulled the trigger. Click. And again. Click.

"No!"

Click. Click. Click. Click.

He'd emptied it into the ghost he could no longer see, blinded as he was by the muzzle flashes.

"Ajax!"

Then Ajax understood. The Needle. He scrambled on the ground until he found it.

"Is this it?" He shucked the blade from its sheath and pressed it to his neck. "You want me to die like you did?"

"Ajax!"

Gladys tackled him and they wrestled, his blood aflame again with the killer's rage.

"Ajax, stop!"

She rolled him onto his back and pinned his hands. It was the heat from the fire that brought him to his senses. The heat, as his body extinguished the last of his bonfire, brought him back to earth. He opened his hand and The Needle rolled away.

"Stop moving!" Gladys sat on his chest. "Stop!"

"What?"

"What are you doing?"

"Gladys?"

"Yes, it's Gladys. What are you doing?"

"I think I'm on fire."

She rolled him over and brushed the embers and burnt paper from his back.

"What's happening over there?" A voice as annoyed as frightened called from the other side of Ajax's wall, which now bore six holes in it.

"Everything's fine, señor," Gladys called back. "Police business. Everyone okay?"

"Except for the fucking firefight over there."

Ajax rolled onto his belly and tried to push himself upright. He got as far as his knees and stayed there, not sure if he would rise again. He heaved once and puked, the recent rocket fuel coming back up like acid. He laid his hot forehead on the cool earth.

"Puke. Hurl. Retch."

Gladys knelt next to him.

"You're drunk."

He heaved and puked again. "Deduced that, did you?" He dry heaved; the convulsion made his body feel like a bag of sand being beat with a bat.

"What the fuck are you doing?"

"'Wine is a mocker, strong drink a brawler.'"

"What?"

"Proverbs."

"What were you shooting at?"

Ajax managed to sit up. "What'd I hit?"

"The wall, on the other side of which people live, Jesus Christ."

"They all right?"

"Nice of you to care after you shot the place up!"

His dry heaves passed, but his limbs trembled and the bat being used on his body moved to his head.

"Why are you here?"

"Because you're not answering your phone."

Gladys squatted down in front of him. Put a hand on his shoulder. She gave it an imperceptible shake, as if trying to wake something very small and fragile.

"I just had to work some shit out, Gladys. Okay? Everything's fine."

"No. It's not."

She shook him again, like one of the many tiny tremblers Managua had—so slight you'd call out to someone, or no one, *Did you just feel that?*

He'd felt it.

"Ajax. I got a call. Six bodies were brought into Matagalpa. An ambush on the road from El Tuma. A bloodbath."

The bat banging his head was joined by a hammer in his heart in a race to see which could pound fastest.

"No, no. They were a few hours behind me. Can't be." He grabbed Gladys's shirt and used it like a rope to help pull himself to his feet. "She's here, she's back. She's got to be."

"Three Nicas and three foreigners."

"No! No. Call her. Call Connelly, get the phone." He let go of Gladys—the phone was . . . where? He couldn't recall the layout of his own home. The earth undulated like a full-on quake, so he had to put his hands out to steady his balance like a drunken tightrope walker. He reached for the wall to steady himself, but it was miles away and he fell, but there was no net and he hit the ground, hard.

"Ajax, I'm sorry. But the foreigners were two men and a woman. No IDs yet, but . . . I'm sorry."

"No. No it's not her. It can't be!"

"We've got an hour before the ministry informs the embassy; if we want to get there before the media circus we've got to go *now*."

"No! No. The Contra wouldn't . . ."

And then it all stopped: the earthquake under his feet, the bat against his head, and the hammer in his heart. Ajax stood up, flat footed, steady. He looked into the corner where the ghost had squatted. He counted the bullet holes, sloppily placed like slurred graffiti—six of them, so that one didn't go into his head.

"Maybe you're right, Ajax. Maybe even the Contra wouldn't dare . . . ."

"It wasn't the Contra. Get in the car."

18

1.

Gladys stood in the entrance of Saint Peter's Cathedral. There was no morgue in Matagalpa. Not even a proper hospital. Saint Peter's was the heart of the town—a whitewashed colonial church that soared above the rest of the city. Most of the town's tragedies ended up here. The church faced west, so it was still dark in the dawn light.

People buzzed around like the flies trying to settle on the six corpses laid out in the nave. She'd tried to keep them out, to give Ajax a private moment, but the church was too public and the news was too big. They'd arrived just before dawn in a Red Cross Jeep Marta had conjured up. Having the "chief medical examiner" with them had given Gladys and Ajax some control over the scene, but as the sun rose the street filled with government officials and journalists, most of whom outranked two city cops. Still, most of them held back while Marta examined the dead.

Gladys had watched Ajax for several minutes now. He stood over the covered body of the redheaded gringa as Marta examined the others. She'd never seen him stand so still, frozen. Only the fingers of his left hand flexed, like an irregular pulse. His stillness and that small twitching made Gladys think of a broken mechanical man. He'd joked often enough about the things that made his trigger finger itch. But if the guns he'd stashed in the back of Marta's Jeep were a clue, Gladys was sure he wasn't joking now.

The Jeep had been Marta's idea when she'd called her last night. From the moment Gladys had broken the news—and, she saw now, Ajax's heart—it had taken twenty minutes for the three of them to be on the road, him driving, Gladys next to him, both of them dressed in civvies, and Marta in the backseat crowded with her medical bag and the weapons.

Marta pulled a bloody sheet over the dead priest, who was so long it reached only to his calves. The three Nicas in the nave, on the other hand, were short enough so that their improvised shrouds covered them entirely. Gladys had stood over Marta while she examined them. From their ages, Gladys figured they were the middle-aged sister, her teenage son, and younger sister, or maybe daughter, of the man in Ohio Amelia had been taking them to meet. Their dark mestizo skin had taken on a gray pallor in death. All the bodies had multiple gunshots, but it seemed to her the Nicas had been dressed in their Sunday best. The women wore colorful shirts—one a deep red, the other lime green—and black skirts to their knees, which made Gladys think it more likely they were sisters than mother and daughter. The boy wore khaki pants and a T-shirt with VAN HALEN printed on the front.

Marta knelt next to Amelia. She looked at Ajax. Gladys laid a hand on his shoulder. "Do you want to see this?"

Ajax nodded and then changed his mind. "No, wait."

He knelt next to the body. Gladys was surprised when he drew a knife like a knitting needle from his boot. He clasped a sprig of red hair, sliced it off, and slid the blade back into his boot. He looked at the lock of hair for several moments, then closed it in his palm. Whatever Gladys's confused loyalties had been up to this moment, she knew now whose side she was on. Where she belonged.

"Go ahead, Marta," he said.

Gladys watched Ajax's face. When Marta drew the sheet back, he looked for the quickest of moments, then turned his head as if slapped. The gringa's body was riddled with bloody holes, like the others.

He turned away. Gladys watched him take a pack of Reds out of his pocket, slip the cellophane wrapper off the box, and place Amelia Peck's hair inside. He rolled it up and slid it into his breast pocket.

A sound of brakes and the quiet commotion of people arriving drew Gladys back to the cathedral's huge doors, big enough for a Goliath to enter. Outside she saw only small people, but the big shots had arrived. Gioconda Targa was there with Senator Teal, Cardinal Obando, and a man she was pretty certain was the American ambassador. She intercepted them on the cathedral steps.

"Senator Teal, I'm Lieutenant Darío. I'm so sorry for your loss."

"Amelia is in there?"

"Yes, sir." Gladys tried to send a discreet signal to Gioconda. "So is Dr. Marta Jimenez. If she might have one minute to finish examining the body."

"No." The ambassador stepped forward, all fight. "We want to see them now."

Gladys could see she'd get no help from Gioconda, so she led them all inside. She was surprised that Ajax was gone. A discreet nod from Marta signaled the door he'd left by.

2.

"Forty-three, forty-four, forty-five."

Gladys counted bullet holes while Ajax searched the priest's vehicle. The Jeep had been hauled in a few hours after the bodies and dropped at a gas station just outside of town. As far as they could tell, no one else had been here yet.

They had already gone through all the personal effects they could find. There seemed to be nothing left of Matthew's or Amelia's. But the Nicaraguan family's two enormous vinyl suitcases were still in the back. It was the cheap luggage normally used by black marketeers hauling goods back from Costa Rica or Miami. They proved the family did not expect to return. Gladys had already inventoried them. They held shirts, skirts, sandals, and one set of Sunday bests for each person. There were photographs, crucifixes, and three bedspreads. But they had also packed plastic cups and plates, knives and forks, a small cooking pot, stirring spoon, and even a machete, as if life in Ohio might require them. Their belongings had baffled Gladys at first. But then, how would campesinos such as they calculate traveling to the mythical El Norte? Not in time or miles. How do you prepare to travel to a place where the map in your mind was blank?

The sight of such common household goods so innocently packed had affected her more deeply than the sight of their bullet-riddled bodies. *The map in their minds was blank,* she thought, *and so is the map in mine.* She didn't know where all this was leading, but she knew she was a part of it now. The sound of Malhora's voice on the tape had changed something. Ajax had let her listen to it on the ride up. It was not so much what he had confessed to, but how he had said it. He'd had Enrique Cuadra killed, so he was the prime suspect in these killings, too. On the ride to the gas station, Ajax had told her Marta's opinion: each victim had gunshot wounds all over their body, but each also had an exit wound over the heart—they'd been shot in the back. The other wounds were all postmortem. Marta was certain: they'd all been executed, then ripped with bullets.

"I count forty-seven holes, Ajax."

He was on his knees, searching under the truck's front seat. He seemed to find something, and pulled his hand out. It was a doll. He held it up to Gladys.

"A doll?"

"Recognize it, Gladys? Your friend Ernesto at the crime scene. His little sister had one. He said he found it next to Cuadra's corpse. I saw several up at the finca. Cuadra's widow makes them."

Ajax looked the truck over.

"Okay. Other than the cheap suitcases, there's nothing left in the truck. No papers in the glove box. Amelia's purse and the backpack she brought with her are gone. No wallets or papers from the men. Connelly's bag is missing. Everything connected with those three

was taken. Everything connected with the Nica family was left behind. Yet, it's the spoons, plates, and cups the Contra would've valued
most."

"We know it wasn't the Contra."

"Do we, Lieutenant?"

He seemed to be asking not so much what they knew, but if both
of them accepted the same facts—was she with him?

"We do, Captain. The arithmetic seems to add up to two shooters."

She could tell by the look on his face he hadn't thought of that,
and she was glad.

"How?"

Gladys walked around the truck, looking at the holes. "Forty-
seven holes in the truck. All four tires are flat, so more went into
them. A few would've missed. There's thirty rounds in an AK clip,
multiply by two shooters is sixty rounds. There's that many in the
truck. Marta counted eight to ten bullet wounds to each body. That
also adds up to about sixty." Gladys held an imaginary AK-47 and
acted out the bizarre math. "They execute them, spray the bodies . . ."

Ajax turned his head away.

"Sorry."

"Go on."

"They reload, spray the truck. Call it a Contra ambush."

She watched Ajax take it all in. Strange as it seemed, she'd hoped
for a pat on the back. Instead she watched him close his eyes and re-
play her scenario in his mind.

"So the Conquistadores took everything connected with the
Americans." He opened his eyes. "Why?"

Gladys looked at the truck, but had not failed to notice it was the
first time she'd heard him use the word American and not gringo.

"Think like the murderers, Gladys."

"Okay. They were looking for something one of the Americans
had."

"But?"

"But they weren't sure what, so they took everything."

"Right. So only the doll . . ."

Ajax squeezed the doll, idly, but then seemed to find something. He lifted the doll's skirt and took out a slip of paper, which to Gladys looked haphazardly folded many times and, she assumed, hidden hurriedly against the doll's corncob body. Ajax fumbled with the paper, unfolded it like he thought it was a treasure map, or maybe, it seemed to her, a final note from Amelia. But as he looked it over, it become clear there was no X marking the spot. He showed it to her—there were only numbers:

$$\frac{500}{2}$$

$$\frac{250}{2}$$

$$125 \ \& \ 125$$

And beneath them the hastily scrawled words: *Do the math*.

"What the fuck?" she asked.

"It's Connelly's handwriting, and look, see the perforation at the top of the page? It was torn out from one of his reporter's notebooks."

"What's it mean? Five hundred over two?"

"Do the math: that's five hundred divided by two. And two-fifty divided by two."

"Then one hundred twenty-five plus one hundred twenty-five."

"No. Look, the one hundred twenty-fives are connected by an ampersand, not a plus sign. So it's not *plus*, it's one hundred twenty-five *and* one hundred twenty-five."

"That makes it clear?"

"In a way." Ajax folded the paper and put it in the same shirt pocket where he'd entombed Amelia's hair. "It makes it clear you've got to take Marta back to Managua and I've got to go back to the Cuadra finca."

"But we know who did it."

"But we still don't know why. When I left Connelly, the last thing he said was he'd figured out who killed Enrique. But I had a hard-on to come back and get Malhora and I didn't listen. Now 'do the math' is all that's left of them. I'm going back and this time I'm doing the math, all of it."

"You're not leaving me . . ."

"I am. . . ."

"You got a thing about leaving people behind. I'm sorry, Ajax, but you left Connelly and them behind and that was a mistake."

"You can't . . ."

"Just listen!"

Her voice drove him back a step. And in the small space he created, it all became clear to Gladys Darío.

"You see this?" She pointed at the ground. "This is as far north as I have ever been. I grew up in Managua, summered in Granada, *on the lake.* This part of my own country is a blank in my mind. A blank!" Tears sprang to her eyes, and their hotness enraged her. "Look at this!" She flung open one of the suitcases. "They packed plastic cups and plates to go to America!" She flung them as if angry at the owners. "Who the fuck does that? Who the fuck *were* these people? I don't even know!"

"Gladys . . ."

"No, goddamnit! They shouldn't be dead. None of them. I'm going with you. Besides, you can't drive in your disguise."

"Disguise?"

"Come and see."

Gladys led him to the Red Cross Jeep and opened the back hatch. She lifted the floorboard revealing a medical kit; inside was another marked BURN TRAUMA. "They've got these big bandages and even mittens for burn victims. You put the mittens on your hands, the bandages around your head. We lay down the backseat and put you in there. I drive. Anyone stops us, you're a burn victim I'm taking somewhere. When we put the backseat down, we can stash our pistols and AKs underneath it. Plus, I got this."

She handed Ajax an ID card from the Red Cross. Marta's name was on it.

"There's no picture."

"Marta says the Red Cross does that on purpose in case they need to slip someone an ID to get them out of somewhere dangerous. Or in this case . . ."

"Into somewhere dangerous."

Ajax smiled at her. The word *rueful* came to her mind. He kept looking at her a long time after the smile had faded. She knew he was judging her trustworthiness, and no matter what she said or did, his decision rested on his judgment alone. She looked right back at him knowing, even fearing, that much of the rest of her life hung on what he said next.

"It's not the Contra we have to worry about. Any shooting is likely to be with someone wearing the same uniform as us."

"Doesn't mean they're on our side. I understand that now."

He finally gave her a pat on the cheek. "You're a good man, sister."

19

1.

The light had gone out of the room, and out of the world. The generator was silenced. Ajax, Gladys, and Epimenio sat in the flattering candlelight over the remnants of their meal while Gloria poured coffee.

"I don't know what it means, Captain."

Ajax watched her closely. She wore a Spanish-style black shawl over her shoulders. She was handsome in the way worn women were—a beauty tempered by life. Made harder, yes, but stronger, too. Deeper.

The hush was disturbed only by the sound of wind pushing unseen clouds to who knew where. Gloria sat back down at the head of the table and studied again the doll she had given Matthew Connelly and the clue he had given Ajax Montoya. Gladys studied Gloria, too. Epimenio stared blankly at a candle flame.

"Connelly said nothing to you about math, numbers? Your husband's death?"

"Not to me."

"What do you mean 'not to you'?"

"The two of you left, and he came back two days later without you. In the afternoon. You came back the next morning. That night he and Father Jerome went to the graveyard. I thought they were paying respects to Enrique. They talked a long time, I heard them arguing. Afterward, Matthew seemed excited, agitated. Jerome, well, he seemed upset but he was very quiet. I thought it was because we all assumed you were dead."

"Did he say anything to you, Epimenio?"

"No, señor. Nothing."

"Captain, why was my husband killed?"

"I thought I knew." He studied the note Matthew had hidden in the doll. "Now I'm not sure. When your husband and Epimenio hunted that jaguar they saw something, something secret. A dangerous secret. You didn't tell her, Epimenio?"

"No, señor."

Epimenio sank his head into his hands. "I'm sorry doña Gloria, but when we got back don Enrique made me swear not to tell. He put my hand on the Bible and made me swear!"

Epimenio's voice cracked with anguish and the secrets he'd kept. Gloria reached out, and did not pat his hand, but squeezed it, held it as if transferring her strength to him. She has lost much, Ajax thought. But this woman will survive. Epimenio fled the room.

Gloria adjusted her black shawl. "He's lost without Enrique. And he's afraid I'll lose the farm." She looked around the room, Ajax, thought, like she was surveying what more might yet be lost. "So this 'secret' they found—Enrique wasn't killed for that?"

"I'd thought so, yes. I was even told so. But these other murders, Matthew, Father Jerome . . ." He could not say her name.

"Amelia." Gloria said it for him.

"And the others. None of them knew what Enrique and Epimenio had found. So their deaths make me think it must be something else." He stabbed the table with his finger. "The answer must be here."

Gloria picked up Matthew's note. Ajax could see her mind working. She shook her head, no. It was more of a tremor even than a motion.

"Just say it, Gloria."

"Could this have anything to do with the killing of Jorge Salazar?"

And there it was. Salazar's name struck Ajax like a white-hot needle shot into his brain by a howitzer pressed to his temple. He could almost smell his singed hair. Every atom of his being was screaming, *Goddamn, this is it!*

"Why would you say that?"

Gloria went to a cupboard and took out a file folder. While she did, Gladys tapped his foot and mouthed, *Salazar?* Ajax nodded, but mouthed back, *Malhora.*

"Matthew left this here, I think by accident. I looked through it, but I didn't see any connection until now. You're all in here."

Ajax took the folder. "All who?"

"You, Enrique, Salazar, and Evelyn."

Ajax looked through the folder. On top was a photo with circles around the heads of then-major Malhora and Enrique in the background. There was another photo of Ajax looking grim as he ducked into the DGSE headquarters. The rest seemed to be news clippings of the case. He scanned them. Then scanned again. None of them had been written by Matthew.

"You did kill Jorge, didn't you?"

"I had orders to arrest him. For treason. He was a traitor. But someone else," he tapped Malhora's photo, "had orders to execute him."

Gloria smiled ruefully. "And now *someone* is one of the most powerful men in the country and you are a police captain."

"Who is Evelyn?"

"Evelyn Zuniga. She's buried out there next to Enrique. She was my sister, well, my cousin but we were raised as sisters. Zuniga's her maiden name. Her married name was Salazar."

He had forgotten. "Your sister—your husband's sister-in-law—was Salazar's wife?"

"And then his widow." Gloria pulled the black shawl close around her neck.

"And Enrique owned the gas station where Salazar was killed?"

"You said murdered."

"I said executed."

"Enrique had three of them. Gas stations. He lost them all when he got out of El Chipote. One of his sons was held there by Somoza. And that son was later killed. Can you imagine what that did to him? To be held in that prison?"

"Showing the instruments of his torture."

"What?"

"Jailing him. They were showing him what silence would buy him out of, what disobedience would buy him into."

Ajax reached for a Red; Gloria nodded her acceptance.

"So after they released him?"

"The government confiscated his gas stations and we moved here."

"Did he ever speak about it, tell you why or what they did?"

"Never." She ripped the shawl from her shoulders and threw it onto the table, where it knocked over her coffee cup. A dark stain spread. "And now I sound like such a child. *No one told me this, no one told me that, no one told me anything!*"

Gladys lifted her shawl off the table and righted her cup. Then she led Gloria back to her chair. "And Evelyn?" Gladys asked.

"Came to live with us, and no, we never talked about Jorge. She and Enrique did, I think."

Gloria suddenly burst into tears, sobs exploding out of her. To Ajax's great relief, Gladys comforted the widow.

"I don't want to end up like Evelyn. It broke her, her grief, up here." She touched her temple. "During the day she was mostly all right. The dolls helped. She was the one who started making them. She showed me how. There isn't a child for miles who doesn't have one of them. But at night, at night I could hear her muttering in her room like she was arguing with someone."

"What did she say?"

"It was nonsense mostly, like a monologue. I don't want to end up like that!"

Gloria's sobs fell like a hard rain. Gladys consoled her with a tenderness Ajax found surprising in his flinty lieutenant. But then he realized he was seeing her as a woman, maybe for the first time. A line of poetry came to his mind, *All these abandoned women have wept so the king can rest in his bed.*

Ajax turned the news clips in Matthew's file. A page from *Barricada* was folded in the back. The headline leapt out. Blood burned in his face. He turned the page so Gladys could see it: "Salazar had $125,000 in CIA Money." He held Matthew's note next to it: *125,000 & 125,000. Do the math!*

"Gloria, when did Evelyn die?" he asked.

She didn't even raise her head. "In May. May twenty-sixth."

"Think carefully, please. Enrique said nothing about her? After she died. The night she died. Anything at all?"

She lifted her head and wiped her face. "The night she died, Father Jerome was here. He gave her last rites. We all left her bedside so he could hear her last confession. We buried her two days later. At the service, I don't know why I noticed this, but Father Jerome said she'd been buried with all her grief. I thought Enrique looked at him in a certain way. I don't know why it caught my eye."

But Ajax did. He did for sure.

"Gloria, I have something terrible I must ask of you."

2.

Two hours later, the moon almost at its zenith, Ajax and Gladys wiped mud from their arms, their boots—and from Evelyn Zuniga Salazar's casket. Epimenio had helped them dig it up, but Ajax had sent him away once they'd hauled it into a shack used to store coffee beans during the harvest. The shack was filled with the reek of decrepitude.

He gave Gladys a rag soaked in vinegar. "Put it on." He tied one over his own nose and slid a machete under the coffin lid. "This is gonna get worse."

To his surprise, Gladys made the sign of the cross. Then slid her machete under the lid.

They pried it off. The stench of rot hit them like a gas bomb. Ajax slid the lid over a few inches; he didn't need to see Evelyn's rotting corpse. He stood the machete up and measured the coffin's depth, then laid the machete against the outside of the box—there was a four-inch difference.

"You want to explain . . ." Gladys turned away and retched up most of the tamales Gloria had fed them. "Goddamn it."

"There's a false bottom. In it we'll find money, yanqui dollars."

"We have to take her out?"

"I don't think so. Help me pry off this side board."

It took only a minute to wedge the machetes behind the board and pry the nails out enough to see in: stacks of what had to be money.

Gladys wedged a stack free and flipped through the bills. All hundreds. "How much do you think there is?"

"Do the math: Connelly wrote there were two one-hundred-and-twenty-five-thousands, right? The headline in *Barricada* said they'd found one hundred and twenty-five thousand when they tossed Salazar's car. This has got to be the other one twenty-five."

But he was wrong. Again. By the time they'd pulled the stacks of bills and counted them, there was $250,000 laid out from Evelyn Zuniga's coffin. It stank of putrid death.

3

Ajax awoke with a deep shiver in the pitch dark.

Amelia.

It was a thought, and a word, and a feeling all at once. A whimper and moan. The milky white of her skin and the gray pallor of her corpse. It was two green eyes and a dozen bloody holes.

Every wreck and ruin of his life he could accept. Like a field he'd sown and then failed to tend. He'd watched the weeds grow and choke whatever love had been in his marriage and had not cut them back. He'd seen the weevils crawling over his commitment to the Frente, and he'd not pulled them off. It had happened gradually, fertilized with rum, and there was residual sadness but no real regrets.

But Amelia. Amelia.

He tried to say her name, tried to lift his hands to his face. But he couldn't—his hands felt like stones; he couldn't move, couldn't speak her name.

That's when he realized he was not awake, but dreaming. Dreaming of her.

He opened his eyes. It was unusually still in the little room with the two small cots he was sharing with Gladys. The moonlight illuminated his surroundings well enough, but everything was made translucent by the mosquito net shrouding him. Still, there was no mistaking the silhouette standing at the window.

Amelia? He whispered it, "Amelia?"

A head turned. But he already knew it was not her, because as soon as he'd whispered her name he felt that his hands were full—the Python's pistol grip in one, The Needle in the other.

"You just don't quit do you?"

He lifted the mosquito net and stood. As he did the ghost seemed to turn his gaze out the window. Then he passed through the wall and out of the room. Ajax stood in his bare feet. He could make out Gladys's sleeping outline in her cot. When he went to the window to have a look, he heard, distinctly in the too-quiet darkness, a small metallic click.

Then another one.

The unmistakable sounds of someone shutting a car door. Two doors.

They had come for him.

He silently leapt to Gladys's side, clamped his hand to her mouth, his lips to her ear.

"Don't move. There are armed men outside." He felt her body stiffen, but her eyes met his. "Where are the AKs?"

"In the Jeep."

"Get your boots on and grab your pistol. Go to the front door and wait for me. Don't fire unless they try to come inside."

He slipped soundlessly into Gloria's room, woke her as he had Gladys, and ordered her under her bed.

"And don't come out no matter what you hear."

He found Gladys combat-ready by the door.

"We've got to get out of here, draw them away from the buildings."

"Contra?"

"Not unless they're driving cars."

Grimly she nodded, and Ajax knew she was ready.

"We go out the back door around to the front. I go left, you right. Wait until I get to the trees. I'll fire twice so you know. You watch the return fire to see if they follow me, but don't shoot. Get to the Jeep and get those AKs. Then try to come up behind them."

"How will I know who's who?"

"I'll fire twice each time. They'll unload all over the place."

"Okay."

He put his hand on the back of her neck and squeezed gently. "We're expendable, Lieutenant. No more civilians die."

"Yes, Captain."

They went silently out of the house and to their posts. Ajax waited for more light. There was no sound, no movement. He assumed the Conquistadores were doing likewise. He belly-crawled away from the house, the dew soaking his shirt and pants. When he was about five yards from the trees that led to the coffee fields, he took up a prone firing position, and waited the longest minutes of his life. But it was long enough for the earth to turn that fraction until night was gone, but dawn had not yet come. He'd read poems about this moment, clichéd references to fingers or feathers of light. He knew it only as the moment all ambushers prized, and all defenders dreaded.

Ajax saw movement. He fired twice, and rolled for the trees.

Two AKs on full auto raked the ground where he had been. He low-crawled into the bush until he had some tree trunks for cover, then fired twice more. The return fire was too high and leaves dropped like rain. The Conquistadores had made the classic mistake of assuming that because they were standing and firing, he must be, too. He was relieved to face mere assassins and not combat veterans. On the other hand, they had rifles and he had two more shots in the Python.

He had no choice but to become part of the landscape and wait for them. This was what he'd been so good at as a guerrillero. Blending with the bush had meant not just camouflage. He had precious little of that now. It also meant slowing the heartbeat, shallowing the breath, lowering the blood pressure, emptying the mind of thought, and elevating the senses. Being less human, becoming more animal. Prey did this before flight, predators before fight.

He felt more than heard footfalls, then silence. Then two long bursts ripped the trees, followed by the metallic clacking of magazines being changed out. They were trying to flush him by blind firing. An excellent tactic—if you were hunting birds. The earth was turning quickly toward dawn, but it was still mostly night. They were scared.

"Montoya!"

That was Cortez. Ajax used the sound to locate him, and then slowly slid behind a tree. They could walk up on him now before they spotted him.

"Montoya, we're here to arrest you!"

Cortez again, which meant Pissarro was probably flanking him.

"Lieutenant Darío! We know you're with him. Montoya is wanted for murder in Managua."

Keep talking, you idiot. He had a good fix on Cortez to his front, so turned his eyes and ears to his right, Pissarro would come that way.

"Darío! You help us and all the rest is forgiven! Otherwise you go down with Monto . . ."

The last syllable was cut off by a long burst of fire from Gladys. She'd gotten to the AKs. *You're a good man, sister!* Ajax saw a jerky movement a few meters to his right, leapt to his feet and fired twice. Pissarro went down as if shot, but Ajax couldn't be sure.

"That's all six, Ajax, don't move!"

There was a millisecond to be gained in such moments, Ajax knew that. If you could act without thought, you could beat the bullet by that millisecond the shooter needed to pull the trigger. In combat, action without thought separated the dead from the living. Ajax had lost that millisecond because he'd recognized the voice.

"You got the snake in your hand and that's all six shots. Don't fucking move!"

Rhino.

Ajax turned around.

"Don't move brother, I'm begging you!"

"Rhino?"

Rhino was ten meters away, a deadline sight down his AK to Ajax's chest.

"I ain't you, Ajax. I'm sorry."

Rhino advanced until he was only a few feet away.

"Rhino."

"It's true, Ajax, I saw the warrant. They got eyewitnesses. I'm here to make sure you get back alive."

"I'm shot!"

That was Pissarro.

"Rhino."

"Don't give me that look, brother. I ain't the *Great Ajax Montoya.* I'm sorry. I can't just walk away. I've got to live in the world. I follow fucking orders. You've always been royalty. I'm just a prole."

"You didn't always have such a flair for speeches. Do you think . . ."

"Shut up, you're not distracting me, Cortez!"

"Here!"

"Move toward Pissarro and see how bad he is! Lieutenant Darío! The next shot I hear I empty my clip into Captain Montoya's chest. Tell her, Ajax. Tell her. Save her fucking life and tell her."

Ajax counted to ten. It was full dawn now. If he'd been standing on a beach facing east, he'd see the sun just peeking over the horizon. In the mountains not yet, but the light had changed and all was visible now.

"Tell her."

"Gladys! Hold your position! Don't fire unless you hear a shot, then kill anything that moves!"

Rhino shook his big head. A lock of dark hair fell onto his forehead. He was bleary-eyed. Ajax figured he'd been laying out here for hours. "Not what I said, Ajax. But it will do. Drop the snake."

"Why? You said it was empty."

"It is. But I'd like to avoid massive blunt trauma."

Ajax looked at the Python, hefted it in his hand. "You remember the night I brought this back?"

Rhino chuckled. It seemed to Ajax to be genuine mirth. But he kept his bleary eye sighted onto Ajax's chest. "Of course I remember. The night you had us sneak into the Guardia compound and steal the keys out of their trucks. Fucking genius, man. Pure genius. The newspapers called you the Prince of Peace, but to us you were always Spooky. *El Terrorífico*. It wasn't just tactics, man, you cared for our lives. If we'd've stormed that compound a lot of compas wouldn't've made it home. That's why we loved you, man. When we rolled into Managua, we would've made you king if you'd told us to."

"Yeah, well, democratic socialism and all that."

"Yeah." Rhino nodded at the AK he was holding. "See how that's worked out."

Ajax half-cocked the Python and rolled the cylinder over his palm. "The boy I killed for this, he was only maybe fourteen."

"The Guardia were all pigs for the slaughter."

"That's the thing, Rhino. I don't think he was military. I think he was his jefe's homo. The bottom to the colonel's top."

"No shit? That why you executed the colonel?"

Ajax tucked the Python in his belt, and nodded yes.

"I wondered about that. But look, hermano, you drop the snake to the ground."

"The thing is, though, that boy's ghost has been following me lately."

Rhino laughed, but his firing posture tightened up as he did.

"Spooky's gonna tell me a ghost story? Great. But my arms aren't tired and neither is my trigger finger. Gladys won't fire on me when I'm this close to you. Stall all you want. You are going back with me."

Rhino, Ajax knew, was not the brightest light in a room full of candles, but he was no idiot. Ajax *had* seen movement behind Rhino. Not a person, but there was no wind to explain the tremors the bush. Ajax *was* stalling.

"Your compas are not going to take me back alive."

"They're not my compañeros." Rhino spit to prove it. "You are. And I will take you back alive. It's why I came. I don't know what they'll do when you get there, but Rhino will take Spooky home alive."

Ajax wasn't sure Rhino could do that. But he saw the movement behind him. And if Gladys could get the drop on Rhino, he would kiss her on the mouth. Deeply. He was sure of that.

Of course, he was wrong. Again. Whatever or whoever was behind Rhino had hair on its face. He didn't lose the millisecond this time, but went straight down.

"Drop, Rhino!"

Rhino's AK followed him down, and he wasn't sure if he would fire. Nor would he ever know. Bullets ripped Rhino from buttock to neck. As he fell dead, his AK pointed skyward and he fired a long burst into the treetops. Ajax grabbed the rifle and rolled clear expecting more fire. Strangely, neither of the Conquistadores opened up on him. He low-crawled back to where he reckoned Gladys might be. Still, no bullets tried to find him.

"Marrrrrrrrtin!"

Krill.

"Marrrrrrrrrrrrrrrrrtin!"

Now this was scary. Ajax wasn't afraid, yet. But this was *scary*. He had to concentrate, not dissipate, so he took a chance and crawled, loud and fast, to where he hoped Gladys was. After about ten yards they spotted each other. And she wasn't alone.

Epimenio.

He lay next to her holding an aged, but still handsome semiautomatic shotgun. Ajax was incensed, but could do no more than shake his head. He broke open the magazine in Rhino's AK; not many left. He looked at Gladys and mouthed, *Ammo?* She handed him a bag stuffed with clips and pointed to the other AK and even a first aid kit she'd fetched from the Jeep. He kissed her on the mouth.

"MARRRRRRRRRTIN!"

She wiped her lips with the back of her hand and mouthed, *Who's that?* He pressed his lips to her ear.

"Krill."

She blanched.

"Martin, my friend! You left so quickly. I have to admit I was angry at first. So many men gone to heaven. And so quietly! But I have come to admire you. We are brothers in our souls, yes?"

"Captain."

Epimenio was an unwelcome burden, but he still seemed to have the hunter's skills that had bagged the jaguar.

"You should be in the house with Gloria."

"No, señor, I have done enough to her already. But the Toyota those three others came in is just over there." He pointed behind them. "None of the Contra are near it and the keys are in it. It's even pointed down the hill."

That was good news. They might be able to make it in a sprint.

"Martin! We have been watching the widow's house. We saw you come yesterday with your pretty friend. We have been debating if she is lesbiana. Is she? But not Red Cross, I think. We were coming for you last night when the other three arrived. They moved like hunters. I thought, this is like a Mexican telenovela. Who loves who, and who is the betrayer! Stay tuned! But I saved you from them. They were going to kill you, yes?"

Ajax's mind was approaching the speed of light, but no matter how fast he thought, the math would not change. They were fucked.

"Epimenio, work your way back to the house."

"No, señor."

Ajax grabbed him by the throat. "Shut up. Get back there. Hide that shotgun. There is a lot of money we took from Evelyn's grave. Tell Gloria to give it to Krill to buy her life."

"I can't."

"You can. Tell Krill we came here with guns to steal the money and forced you to help us. Gladys, you're gonna make for the Land Cruiser. There might be radios in it; either way you get out of here and go to the nearest army base."

"Where?"

"Matagalpa."

"That's hours away."

"I'll keep Krill busy."

"By yourself?"

"No, Cortez and maybe Pissarro are out there somewhere. You've seen that movie—the outlaw and sheriff always join forces to fight the Apache."

"You said *we* were the Indians, remember?"

"Well, then, warring Indians join forces to fight the white man."

"Marrrrrrrrtin! Are you worried about the other two? Don't be.

My men got them, and my other men are already between you and the widow's house."

"Fucking mind-reading piece of shit!" Ajax hissed.

"Listen Martin." Krill's voice rose a notch as he shouted to his men. "Muchachos! Make our new friends sing for Martin."

There was what Ajax would've called a pregnant pause. Then Cortez and Pissarro sang out in horrible screams that went on and on.

Ajax shuddered. "Upside down."

"Upside down, Martin. Remember?" Krill called out.

Still the Conquistadores screamed. Gladys got what some called a deer-in-the-headlights look about her, and Ajax could see how young she was. How afraid. He shook her.

"Don't lose it, Gladys. We gotta move—now. You and Epimenio head for the car, I'll pin them down."

"No, Captain. Let me." Epimenio got to his knees. "Then you two run."

"Fuck no!" Ajax grabbed him by the arm and was shocked when the humble campesino pushed the shotgun to his face.

"It was me, Captain. Me. They made me tell on don Enrique ever since he got back from prison. State Security. Comandante Malhora said if I told him things Enrique would not go back to jail. Gloria would not lose the finca. I've been telling them for years. I told them about the jaguar, the airstrip, that Enrique went to Managua to report the men with the plane. That's why I got to Managua so fast. I got scared they would hurt him. They did. I told them don Mateo had found something, too. Look what I have done to them all."

He broke Ajax's grip and bolted toward the still screaming Conquistadores. Ajax watched in amazed horror as Epimenio threw the shotgun to his shoulder and fired at a dead run.

"Cover him! Cover him!"

He rolled a few yards away from Gladys and opened up with the AK at any shape, sound, or muzzle flash. His first firefight in years and the old feeling returned: One eye shooting straight while the other sought the next target. Shots came from all directions, ripped into the trees and ground around them, but he heard five blasts from the shotgun. When it fell silent, so did the screams.

Then Krill's voice over it all. "Stop! Stop shooting! Hijos de puta! Cease fire!"

Krill's men obeyed but Ajax finished his magazine.

"I want Martin alive!"

Ajax knew they had to make their break now, a mad dash or die. But in the heightened quiet following a firefight he heard a small cry, like a song bird dying.

"Gladys."

He scrambled to her side. She still clutched the AK to her chest, already soaked with blood.

"Gladys! Oh my God, Gladys!"

"Ajax."

"It's okay, it's okay, it's okay."

"I don't think so."

Her voice had the dreamy quality of shock. He had to pry the rifle from her hands before he could pull her shirt open. A bullet had ripped a hole through her side and out her back. He ripped open the first aid kit and pressed two trauma bandages over the entrance and exit wounds. She moaned again.

"Shhhh. Shhhh. You're gonna be okay. I got you. I got you. See? Bandages. Bandages."

"Marrrrrrrrrrrrrtin! Is your dyke leaking? Ha! Ha!"

"Kill that fucker for me, Ajax."

"I will, but first we got to get you out of here. Hold still."

He hurt her tying the bandages off, but it had to be done. She bit down on her lip and took it.

"It must be Saturday."

"Saturday, yes, Gladys, it is. We're going dancing."

"No, idiota. Saturday is for confessions. Epimenio and now me."

"Sure, Gladys, no problem." He got up on one knee. "KRILL! KRILL!"

Gladys grabbed him and the feel of her bony hand in his nearly broke his heart.

"They put me with you to spy."

"I know. Don't talk. Krill!"

"They wanted to know your state of mind, your drinking. I reported on you. Malhora knew. Horacio knew."

"I know. That's good Gladys. That's good. Horacio's my friend. You did good. You want a confession? When you came to my house I was going to blow my brains out. I was gonna eat my gun and you saved me. You saved me! Okay? We're even. Krill!"

"Yeeees, Marrrrrtin! I am holding my fire. I need you alive so we can talk."

Ajax scanned the bush for signs they were moving on him, but all was still.

"Krill, I can stay here and fight it out with you all fucking day. The army will get here eventually."

"I'm listening."

"You want me for an upside-down party. I'll give me to you. You leave my friend and Gloria alone. Me for them."

"Interesting."

Gladys squeezed his hand. "You called me your friend."

"You are my friend. Maybe the only one I've got left. Poor you."

She smiled. "Poor me."

"Krill!"

"It's a deal, Martin!"

Gladys let go of his hand.

"Gladys, Gladys?" He gently slapped her face. "Come on, look at me. Look at me."

Her eyes fluttered open. She reached up and weakly slapped his cheek. "You're a good man, sister."

Her eyes rolled into her head, and she was gone.

"No! No! No! KRILL!!" He leapt to his feet, hands in the air. "Krill! Me for her, you take me and we go. She stays!"

Krill rose from his hiding place and signaled his men to come in. Ajax walked halfway to him.

"You take me. You leave her alive."

"We will take you back to our base in Honduras. I always like to take a present for the muchachos when we return. And you are a much better present than some broken dyke. Get it? I can't stop making that joke. But, Martin, you are too much trouble awake."

Krill signaled to someone behind Ajax. He lowered his hands and let it come. The blow sank him to his knees. He saw stars. As all the world faded to black, he had time to notice that while he had seen stars before, they had never been accompanied by fireworks, for he was sure he heard pyrotechnics all around him. The second blow sent him falling, tumbling, plunging into oblivion. Upside down.

20

1.

Captain Ajax Montoya had a pain in the ass. He didn't know where the pain was, or even where he was. But wherever and whatever, it was a pain in the ass. Then he heard his name being called.

"Ajax. Ajax Montoya. Ajax."

That was the pain in his ass. He just wanted them to shut up and let him alone.

"Ajax? Ajax Montoya?"

Black oblivion gave way to light as the night had to dawn. He needed a winch to raise his eyelids, but eventually they rolled up. A woman's face loomed over him.

"Amelia?"

"Gloria."

"Gladys?"

"Gloria, Ajax. Gloria Cuadra."

A man's face slid into view. Ajax tried to rise.

"I'll kill you, Krill."

Gloria rubbed his face. "Shhhh. Krill's gone. The army's here. This is Colonel Garcia."

"What? *You're* Martin Garcia?"

"No. Josecho Garcia, Seventeenth Light Hunter Battalion."

In the unfocused grayness of his gray matter, Ajax was beginning to understand. "The cavalry saved the Indians."

"I guess. You must have powerful friends, Captain. We got orders from Managua to not come back without you, alive." Colonel Garcia laid a comradely hand on Ajax's chest. "I heard of you; your reputation's deserved, Captain. If you'd lost five minutes we would've missed you."

Through the fog of a blood-clotted brain, Ajax realized that what he'd heard when Krill's man had knocked him out had not been fireworks, but a firefight.

"What about . . ."

"Shhhh, Ajax." Gloria rubbed her smooth hand over his face again; it felt cool and clean. "The colonel got here just as Krill was taking you. The others are all gone, all gone. They took the bodies back to Managua. We buried Epimenio yesterday."

"Yesterday?"

"You've been out a day and a night."

"Señora, we've got to go. He's got to come with us now."

"All right, Colonel."

Ajax did not like people talking about him as if he wasn't here. And he was going to give them a piece of his mind but the cable on the winch holding his eyelids snapped, and down they went.

"Ajax? Take this."

Gloria pressed something into his hand.

"They're going to take you to the clinic in Matagalpa. They're going to take you in the Red Cross Jeep. Can you hear me? I packed your things, *everything,* into the Jeep. Can you hear me?"

Of course he could. He just couldn't keep night from rushing back.

The rest was brief days and long nights, like an Arctic winter. He heard voices, felt himself lifted, set down, lifted again. He saw another woman's face, maybe more than one. But not the woman he wanted to see. The women.

2.

When at last he could open his eyes without a winch, it was night and another woman looked down at him.

"Hello, handsome."

"Marta."

"That's good. You've got some brain cells left."

"I . . ."

"You want to interrogate the world again. Here"—she lifted a large bowl from a bedside table and tucked a straw into his mouth—"drink this. It's Mami's special broth. Drink and I'll tell you what I know."

He did as ordered and the soup seemed to pass directly from the walls of his mouth into every cell of his body.

"You're in Managua, in your own bed at home. Your skull was fractured four days ago."

"Four . . ."

"Shhh. Just keep sucking it down, compa."

He did, greedily. When the broth was gone, she gave him a tall glass of chilled sweet orange juice that seemed to cool the fire in his brain. Greedily, he finished it. *Finish it.* Somewhere in his still fuzzy mind he realized that was the mantra he needed: *Finish it, finish it, finish it.* But the earth seemed to open yet again, and he was falling, sinking, descending.

When Ajax finally awoke as himself, it was night again. He lay for a while, eyes closed, listening. Sensing. A line from somewhere floated into his mind: *The more you sense everything, the more sense everything makes.* He tried to open himself to sense as much as he could, if not everything. Everything. *I packed your things,* everything, *into the Jeep. Can you hear me?* Yes, he could hear Gloria. And now the smell of putrefaction in the Jeep on the long rides to Pantasma and Managua made sense. She must've packed the money. Two hundred and fifty thousand stinking yanqui dollars. Not a hundred and twenty-five, but twice that much, half of five hundred thousand.

Then, quite suddenly, as sometimes happened, he could, fleetingly, sense it all—and it all made sense.

He snapped his eyes open. He half expected to find the ghost looming over him again, and felt a small pang that he did not. A candle burned on the bedside table—it must be Wednesday. Again? Marta slept curled up on the far side of the bed. He sat up slowly, swung his legs over the bedside, and felt the cool concrete under his feet. His head was swaddled in a turban of bandages. He pushed his fingers underneath it and felt the sharp little bristles of his shaved head. He stood slowly. He felt okay, satisfactory, tolerable. He went to his closet and his hand hovered over the clothes there. He knew what he was going to do and he would not do it in his police khakis. He dressed in black pants and a dark T-shirt. He slipped on leather sandals, paused to watch Marta's sleeping face, and then slipped out of his house.

He opened up the Red Cross Jeep and found the two AKs, the ammo pouch, and the reeking money in the rear compartment. One of Gloria's dolls was on the front passenger seat. He searched the rest of the Jeep but did not find the Python or The Needle. Damn. He was a carpenter without tools. He hurried back into his house, retrieved Fortunado Gavilan's Makarov and two clips of 9mm's from the hidey-hole where he kept such things. He paused for a moment: if he'd lost the Python and The Needle, had he lost the ghost? And if he had, had he lost an ally, or a tormentor?

It didn't matter. It was time to finish it.

3.

He parked three blocks away from Sub-comandante Vladimir Malhora's house and watched the street. The house sat behind high walls with a guard post next to iron gates that led to a courtyard. The bad news was that rich neighborhoods like this were the only ones in the entire country with working streetlights, so a stealthy approach on foot was almost impossible. The good news was that with armed guards on patrol few of the residents kept dogs for protection.

The thought of snarling dogs brought back his night with Amelia. The yapping mutts, her pealing laughter, the feel of her arm pressing her to him as she flailed away counting coup. *No! No!* He scolded his weakness. *You've got a lifetime to hate yourself. Finish it. Finish it.*

He rolled up the Jeep's floor mats, rolled down the window, and slipped out. He tucked the floor mats under his arm, the Makarov into the small of his back, and crossed the street. Behind the houses opposite Malhora's ran a darkened alley lined with garbage cans. In Nicaragua, only the rich had alleys in which to store their garbage out of sight. Ajax watched until he was certain there were no strays— dogs or people—lurking about. He made his way in a crouch down the alley until he was behind the house he calculated was directly across from Malhora's. *Calculate. Do the math.* The wealthy might not use dogs, but everyone topped their walls with shards of glass. He tossed the Jeep's floor mats over the glass, then launched himself. This next part was delicate—he'd have to hoist his leg over and straddle the wall without castrating himself. He did so, but his weight crushed some of the glass, which sounded to Ajax like pistol shots.

He lowered himself into the garden and crouched in the darkness. *Don't hurry.* It wasn't the owners he worried about, undoubtedly deeply asleep with visions of Malhora's guards dancing in their heads. But the maid's room was right off the garden, and the maids took robbery as a personal insult, no matter that none of it was theirs and never would be. He crept through the open veranda doors and tiptoed into the house. A light was on outside the front door. He used what illumination it cast inside the house to find the owner's liquor cabinet. He'd decided on a Trojan Horse strategy. He took a bottle of Johnny Walker Red Label and slipped out the front door. He was in a clear pool of light and had to act fast now—fast and natural.

He began to whistle the Sandinista national anthem.

He walked quickly through the main gates, right into the street, made immediate eye contact with Malhora's guard, and waved the bottle at him, whistling the whole time. What nefarious purpose could a man whistling an anthem and waving a whiskey bottle have?

"Compañero, a gift for the lonely guard whose vigil protects us all."

The guard's AK stayed slung on his shoulder while Ajax got within inches. The Makarov was pressed under the young man's chin before he could blink.

"Silence or you will not even hear the bullet I put into your brain. Silence. Hold this."

The guard seemed baffled into paralysis.

"Hold the bottle."

He did. Ajax used his free hand to slip the magazine from the AK and eject the chambered round. Then he pressed the Makarov into the confused guard's pecker.

"Got children?"

"No."

"Want them?"

"Yes."

"Your cooperation guarantees you will have them. What's behind that door?"

"Courtyard."

"Guards?"

"No."

"In the house?"

"Two more."

"The Comandante in?"

"Sleeping."

"Can you open this door?"

"Yes."

"Then open it, walk in front of me to the front door, and an-nounce I am just a neighbor dropping off a gift for the boss. I'll have this gun pointed at your asshole and if you fuck up I will shoot you in such a way that you will never have children to help you change the bag you will shit into for the rest of your life. *Comprendes?*"

"*Comprendo.*"

"Go."

The guard opened the door and Ajax nudged his ass forward to remind him of his options. The courtyard was empty save for two white Land Cruisers and a silver Mercedes. They had not walked four paces when the gate was slammed shut—the metal clang echoing up and down the neighborhood. Six armed men popped up from around the cars and Ajax knew there was a seventh behind him who'd shut the door.

"This is what is known as a Mexican standoff, I believe." An eighth man came out the front door.

Ajax was startled to recognize him.

"Captain Montoya, we are not enemies. Do you remember me? Colonel Garcia-not-Martin?"

It was.

"Josecho Garcia."

"Correct. I was assured that if I gave you the message 'I am commander of the Seventeenth Light Infantry Battalion and Fortunado Gavilan was my radio man,' there would be no gunplay. Well, I *am* commander of the Seventeenth Light Infantry Battalion and Fortunado Gavilan *was* my radio man."

Colonel Garcia signaled his men, who lowered their rifles.

"Will there be no gunplay?"

Ajax saw now they were dressed in the distinctive jungle camo fatigues of the elite hunter-killer troops. But more, he recognized in their eyes and faces that they were combat veterans. He lowered the hammer on his Makarov and raised his hands. The guard stepped away from him, laughed nervously, and adjusted his ball sack for good luck. His compañeros laughed, too. Ajax presented him with the Johnny Walker.

"There will be no gunplay, Colonel."

"Good."

"Where's the Comandante?"

"I'm under orders not to answer any questions. You are to come with me now." The colonel approached and waved a set of keys. "Shall we take the Mercedes?"

4.

The colonel drove them in silence through nearly empty streets. The Mercedes was as quiet and comfortable as a cloud. Ajax ran his hand over the genuine leather, as soft as anything he had felt in recent memory. But then a voice reminded him: *Not as soft as her skin.* He could tell Colonel Garcia was stealing glances at him.

"My orders are not to answer your questions. Will you answer one of mine?"

"Yes."

"What happened to Fortunado?"

"Technically? Sleep deprivation psychosis."

"And untechnically?"

"Guilt. He thought he was being persecuted by the ghosts of friends he'd killed."

"Killed?"

"Krill forced him into a devil's bargain: go on watching his friends be tortured or kill them and end their misery."

The colonel grunted in reply. Ajax knew he was putting himself in Fortunado's place.

"Or he could've broken and talked."

Now it was Ajax who grunted. "Yes."

The colonel stopped at a corner. "So he could not forgive himself for doing his duty as a soldier."

"I guess not."

"He died insane?"

"I don't think so. He charged a line of sharpshooters with an empty gun." Ajax drew the Makarov. "This gun."

"It still empty?"

"No."

Colonel Garcia smiled. "Fortunado was a good soldier. Suicide is a bad end."

He turned right.

"If you take the next left, Colonel, you're taking me to Horacio de la Vega's house."

The colonel smiled.

"It wasn't a question."

"That old man seems very fond of you."

"So he likes to remind me."

5.

Horacio was waiting at the door.

"Ajax! *Mi hijito!* Again you have returned to me."

Ajax hugged him and felt the old man's frail embrace in return. "Maestro."

Horacio took the colonel's hand. "Thank you, Colonel Garcia. You have returned my boy to me."

Garcia returned a casual salute. "We'll drop your Jeep by later, Captain."

Horacio took Ajax's arm and led him inside the house. Horacio's sala was well appointed with wicker and leather furniture. What walls were not covered floor to ceiling with bookshelves were hung with Central American folk art. In one small, elegant glass case were a few mementos of his days with the guerrilleros: one of the original FSLN flags, the first edition of the Sandinistas' insurgent handbook, and a matched pair of .45s said to have belonged to Sandino himself.

It was Ajax's favorite room in all the world, more home than any he had known, maybe ever.

"How's your head." Horacio gently touched the bandage.

"Still on my shoulders."

"I'd like to offer you a drink, but hope I should not."

"You should not."

"What can I get you?"

"Vladimir Malhora. Dead or alive."

Horacio stopped and leaned on his cane. "He's gone."

"Gone as in *fled*?"

"Gone."

"Gone dead?"

"Gone."

"Gone to a cell in El Chipote?"

"Just gone, Ajax."

"You're going to make me hunt him down?"

Horacio said nothing. He did not move a hair, just stared into the middle distance, the kindly eyes in his grizzled head suddenly gone cold. *Shark eyes,* Ajax had called that look. He'd seen it many times before in the mountains, huddled around small fires. It meant it was time, once again, to suck it up and suffer. There was no appeal from the verdict.

Ajax stared for a long ten count.

"What are you thinking, my son?"

"I'm counting the people he murdered who will not see justice."

"Well, the aptly named Conquistadores certainly did all the killing, and they paid before they died. Krill saw to that."

"I'm going to kill Malhora."

"No, my son. You are not." Horacio looked at his watch. "You could not find him if you searched from the bottom of Lake Nicaragua to the top of Momotombo. His crime, his shame, hangs over the city, and over certain political enemies, like a poisoned cloud. But the man is gone. You will have to be satisfied with having destroyed him."

"Destroyed him? You mean destroyed his illustrious career?"

"You have cut out a cancer which endangered the larger organism."

"The Frente?"

"The Revo. *La Patria*. Your country. It will have to do for now."

Ajax knew it would not do, now or ever, but there were more questions to be answered.

"Is there a warrant out for me?"

"No, that was a lie."

"Rhino believed it."

"Poor Rhino. A good compa. But the agreed official story is that the three gringos and the Nica family were killed by unknown bandits robbing Father Jerome of his gold chalice and crucifix. Deserters. Maybe theirs, maybe ours. Here."

Horacio shuffled to a table and picked up a copy of *Barricada*, dated the day before. The headlines were full of the news. Ajax scanned the main story.

"Wait. '*Agreed* official story.' Agreed to by who?"

"Whom. Senator Teal and us."

Ajax crumpled up the newspaper. "Teal the fact-fucker!"

"Ajax, we would not tell him the truth, obviously. He did not want to hear it was the Contra who killed three Americans as he will soon vote them a hundred million in blood money. So, we split the difference. He's back in the States and has stuck to the *agreed* version. *Unknown bandits*."

Ajax felt his head might implode. He pulled off the turban and then gingerly felt the bandage over the wound and rubbed his bristly hair.

"Sit down, mijo. You need to rest your head and I need to get off this leg."

He walked Ajax to the center of the room where antique wicker chairs surrounded an even older mahogany table. On that table were the Python, The Needle, a travel bag, and some kind of strongbox.

"Where did you get those?"

"From the Red Cross Jeep you appropriated. And in this box is what mystery writers call the MacGuffin."

"One hundred and twenty-five thousand dollars in stacks of hundreds."

A smile lit Horacio's face. "That, my boy, is why it had to be you. Now, tell me what you discovered."

"The CIA fronted Jorge Salazar five hundred thousand dollars to bribe members of the Army High Command to overthrow the Revo. But, as a Nica, Salazar knew he didn't need half that. So that's all he brought to Enrique Cuadra's gas station at Los Nubes. Half of five hundred is two hundred and fifty thousand dollars. Malhora, knowing he had secret orders to execute Salazar, kept the rest of the team, like me, away from the car. None of us knew there was any money. Malhora discovered it, but only turned in half. Two hundred fifty thousand divided by two is two sets of one hundred twenty-five thousand. He turned one in—that made the papers." Ajax flipped open the strongbox. "There's the other one and a quarter he kept for himself. With Salazar dead, his widow, who knew all about it or figured it out later, kept the other two hundred fifty thousand, which is right there." Ajax unzipped the travel bag; it was stuffed with cash. "On her death bed she confessed it to Father Jerome, who told Enrique, and they buried the money with her in the false bottom of her coffin."

"From which you disinterred it and put it in your Jeep, which," Horacio pushed himself slowly to his feet and looked outside, into the dark, "I think has just been delivered to us." He patted Ajax on the shoulder and rubbed his cheek with warm affection. "You are the best of us, Ajax." He gave him a little slap. "If not always the wisest."

"You think I want the money?"

"Do what you want with it. It's chicken feed, in the larger scheme of things."

"Yes! Yes it is fucking chicken feed. All this was over a paltry box of money?"

"I need a drink now." Horacio shuffled off. "Can I offer you some fresh orange juice?"

"No." He got to his feet and paced.

Horacio called from his kitchen. "The Dollar store just started carrying a new American invention: alcohol-free beer. Want to try it?"

Ajax paced, then turned to Horacio's bookshelves. "I don't drink oxymorons."

The old man chuckled.

"So." Ajax paced. "Malhora stole the money."

"Yes."

"And he's been hiding it all these years."

"Yes."

"And that's what all of this has been about? The money?"

"You tell me."

Ajax stopped in front of a glass case where Horacio displayed Central American folk art. He looked at his reflection. His shaved head, the stained bandage. He looked into his eyes, but all he saw was a bloodstained shroud topped by wild orange hair. *Money. She died over money?* It couldn't be so base, so cheap. He would never accept that.

Ajax closed his eyes, and when he opened them he looked through the glass at the folk art—a rather nice pre-Columbian cup, Mayan, probably from Honduras. Some cruder clay sculptures Horacio had found himself on Isla El Muerto on the big lake. And half a shelf of Mayan Quiche dolls from Guatemala.

Ajax froze.

Dolls.

One of Gloria Cuadra's dolls sat on his shelf. No, he remembered, Gloria didn't make them, Evelyn Salazar did!

Ajax's head began to pound, his blood hammered in his temples. He doubled over in pain and cried out. He heard glass break in the kitchen as Horacio hobbled out to him.

"You fucker! You old hijo de puta!"

Ajax grabbed the closest thing to him, a first edition of Borges, and hurled it through the glass case. Horacio appeared and Ajax went for the old man's throat. Rage filled him, rage at a world that finally held no more surprises.

He was wrong, again.

With an agility that gave the lie to his infirmity, Horacio ducked Ajax's grasp and drove the head of his cane into Ajax's solar plexus. As Ajax folded, Horacio struck him hard on the kidney. Ajax went down on one knee. Gasping for breath.

"I did not hit you on your head, Ajax. Please notice that."

"You're not even crippled!"

"Sun Tzu says, 'When strong appear weak.'"

"You knew Enrique Cuadra."

"Of course I did."

"And Evelyn, Salazar's widow?"

"I came to know *of* her."

"Enrique was coming to see *you* that night."

"Yes, he was."

"You." Ajax sat up as best he could. He did the math as best he could with a small blood clot still dissolving in his brain and a terrible ache congealing in his heart. But it now added up. There had always been a shadow over this case.

"You." Ajax's eyes went to the table bearing the Python and The Needle. But with a flick of his wrist Horacio had a blade halfway out of his cane. That, Ajax realized, was why it was always so heavy.

"Don't, my son, please."

"You going to kill your boy now, *Papi*? Play Father Abraham? Murderer."

"Don't hystericize the situation, Captain Montoya. You're missing the big picture."

Ajax levered himself flat onto the floor. Horacio took a seat.

"Ajax, we have won. Won a prize you know nothing about."

"Ah, the Jesuit explains it all. Go ahead, maestro. Dazzle me."

"Ajax, this is information so sensitive I need to know your mind before I tell you."

"And Gladys isn't here to report to you."

"You'd be surprised how many people I visit in my unofficial capacity. Gladys, yes. Malhora, too. Matthew. Enrique visited me, true."

"I have never betrayed my country or the revolution."

"And you never will, I know. The secret is this: peace."

"What?"

"Peace. You remember peace, don't you?"

Ajax thought about it, and realized he did not. "Teal will give the Contra the hundred million."

"Let him, let him give them a hundred billion. Teal is a fool." Horacio waved as if at a bee. "A cowboy. He thinks because America is a superpower it has superpowers. It does not. It just looks that way from *inside* America. The big picture is that we are on the verge of a regional peace agreement which will make the Contra orphans."

"The Davids will gang up on Goliath?"

"No, the Davids will ignore Goliath. The President of Costa Rica, who I personally think is only interested in a Nobel Prize, will propose a Central American peace plan which the Central American presidents will approve at a Central American peace summit later this year."

Ajax sat up, slowly, but upright. "Returning El Gordo Sangroso was the first step in normalizing relations."

"Precisely."

"Why would the others help us? I understand the Costa Ricans, they're smug social democrats without an army. But the Hondurans are toadies and the Salvadorans and Guatemalans are as savage as the Contra."

"True. But they are known entities. The Contra are a Frankenstein's monster. Reagan will be gone in two years, and when the Doctor goes what happens to his monster?"

"You tell me."

"There are about ten thousand Contra troops."

"There are?"

"Officially, we say only two. The real number is ten, but only two or three thousand are ever in Nicaragua. The rest are sitting in camps in Honduras, armed to the teeth, getting fat and bored. Reagan has created a militia of mercenaries bigger than the national armies of some countries. The Americans have the attention span of a child. Everyone—and I mean *everyone*—fears what the Contra will become if they are not disarmed *before* the Americans drift away to pull the wings off some other fly."

Ajax got to his feet. He moved nearer to Horacio, who set his cane over Ajax's weapons still on the table.

"I will hear the end of this fairy tale."

"The Contra have become a danger to everyone but the Americans. We will have a Central American peace plan, the Contra will be frozen out, but only if our government will make the concessions, all the concessions, the other presidents demand."

Ajax sat down, and groaned. His kidney hurt more than his head. "And all of our concessions have to be approved by the National Directorate."

"Yes. Thank you for joining the conversation. I had to destroy Malhora not only to sabotage his candidacy, but that of his faction as well. I have. *You* have. And now our side has won and will control the government."

"Our side?"

Horacio rapped his cane on the table. "I explained this to you! Do not be facetious with me! Every nation is divided into the civilized and the barbarian."

"Peaceniks and warmongers."

"Correct. Every nation, us, America, the Cubans, the Soviets."

"Really, the Soviets?"

"More than most. This young premier they have, Gorbachev? He's one of us, you wait and see."

"So the peaceniks run the asylum."

"Yes. Victory."

Ajax studied his mentor. But was he? Had he ever been? Was he just another Doctor Frankenstein, and what did that make Ajax? Ajax calculated the distance to The Needle on the table. "Kings, queens, bishops, and knights."

"Yes, Ajax. Politics *is* like chess. You have to plan your end game long in advance. Some of us have been planning this since '82. And you have been with us all along, you just didn't know it. It began with Chepe Huembes."

Ajax's mind went blank—for a moment. *"El Gordo?"* His head began to ache, throb. His brain, rattled by the fracture, was screaming in pain from the new connections being made. "You? *You* let him escape?"

"I arranged for him to escape into Costa Rican custody. He hasn't been in a resort, you know. But we knew the Ticos would be the first to break with Reagan. And when they did, they would need a symbol, a gesture. But a safe one, unimpeachable. Who better, what better, than a murderer returned to justice?"

To Ajax's alarm, Horacio's chess game started to make sense. But he wouldn't let it. He dragged his mind up and out of the rabbit hole. "So El Gordo was a rook. Let's talk about the pawns. Why did Enrique Cuadra have to die, and did you kill him?"

Horacio touched his hand to his heart. "Of course I did not kill him. But he was coming to see me, not Matthew Connelly, the night he was killed. Possibly about the airstrip, I don't know. But it was the *way* Malhora had him killed that stirred suspicion in my mind—that there might be another motive behind it besides the airstrip. And if there was, it could be the way to destroy him. And I had to destroy him. Me. And I needed *you* to do that."

"Why?"

"Because you carried out every mission I ever gave you and came back alive. You might have come back alone, but you always came back. And here you are again. Victorious and alive."

Ajax turned his head away and gazed into Horacio's garden. That moment had arrived again—when night is gone but dawn not yet come. Horacio's words echoed in his mind: Victorious. Alive. Alone.

"I mean why did *you* have to destroy Malhora?"

Horacio's gaze followed Ajax's into the garden. "Because I created him. He was my monster."

Ajax's head snapped up as if struck. "It all comes back to Salazar. Everything back to him, that night. *You* had Malhora kill him."

"Execute him, yes. On my orders. And don't tell me how you wanted to see justice done. That's why you couldn't be trusted on that mission any more than you could with getting El Gordo to Costa Rica. You see justice in very simple terms. We didn't need justice for Salazar. We needed a dead agent to give the CIA a concrete lesson that they could use espionage against us, but they would never know which of their operations were their own, and which ours. And if that kept them from launching a half, a tenth of the operations they did, it was worth Jorge Salazar's life."

"And your little monster rocketed to power on Salazar's blood."

Horacio looked down at the table. He used his cane to poke and prod the Python and The Needle. "I never saw that outcome. I watched his rise in horror. And when he took over Seguridad, he was almost invincible. When we learned Joaquin was dying and Malhora would ascend, I grabbed at any straw. I reached out to Enrique and he told me that the night after Salazar was killed he went back to his gas station and found Malhora there. 'Caught him,' is how Enrique put it. He didn't know at what, but it was the only thread there was to pull on."

"And you needed me clean and sober to unravel him."

"No. You needed to be sober to survive, as a man. But, yes, you were also my cavalry. I needed foot soldiers, too. I suggested to Matthew Connelly that *he* might reopen his file on *l'affaire Salazar.*"

"Goddamn you. He did, too. I saw that file. He tried to tell me.

I wouldn't listen. I didn't listen. He's the one who figured it all out, not me."

"But you made it happen. You flushed Malhora. When I confronted him with the money from Evelyn's grave, he cracked and confessed. He still had every single dollar he'd stolen. Can you imagine? Never spent a centavo. And yes, his larceny was like the plague. It felled him and everyone who was close to him." Horacio actually rubbed his hands together in glee. "You should have seen them running. No rats ever abandoned a ship so quickly. . . ."

"Connelly's dead!" Ajax was half out of his chair. The words *Amelia is too* rose like lava in his throat. Horacio went for his cane again, but Ajax dropped back into his chair.

"And I am sorry for that. Matthew was a friend, and frankly I treated him better than you did. But he was a sandbag, not a shot caller."

"What about Gladys? Was she a sandbag, too? Gladys? Gladys who was as ardent a believer in your chess game, your big picture, as anyone! A sandbag? We killed her, Horacio. We killed them all as much as Malhora or anyone. You and I."

To his surprise, Horacio made no speech refuting him. He just looked down and rolled his cane in his fingers.

"I don't dispute my part in these deaths. I know Amelia Peck was dear to you. Malhora was my monster. What he did to stay in power is partly my fault. I put him there. But you're wrong about one thing."

"Astonish me."

"Lieutenant Darío isn't dead."

For a moment, Ajax felt like he'd had a stroke. He couldn't make anything move. He couldn't knit his brow or cock his head in a question. Then it passed. "Not dead? But they brought the bodies back."

"Not hers. Krill carried her off. Contra radio chatter makes us think she's still alive. He took her into Honduras."

"Where?"

"The Las Vegas salient."

"Show me."

"Show you?"

"Show me on whatever map you use to keep track of the big picture."

Horacio shuffled over to a locked cabinet.

"Stop hobbling, you're not crippled."

"Habit."

While Horacio fetched the map, Ajax took inventory: he had the two AKs in the Red Cross Jeep, the ammo, and at least a quarter million dollars. That was a start.

Horacio unfurled the most detailed map Ajax had ever seen of the border with Honduras.

"Somewhere here, where the salient dips farthest south." Horacio pointed to a triangle of land, like a thumb sticking down into Nicaragua. "From Wiwili maybe twenty-five miles as a crow flies."

Ajax rolled up the map. "I'm taking this with me."

"Don't be a fool."

Ajax had The Needle unsheathed and at Horacio's throat in the blink of one watery eye. He leaned in so close they could feel each other's breath.

"You listen to me now, old man. I am done with you. All these years of your feeding me poetry and politics and philosophy, they were bones you gave your dog. They were how you scratched between my ears so I would love you. And obey."

"You are my favorite."

"I was a rook you carved from a sapling so you could bash the other pieces on the board. But life is not a game, you're not a grand master. We're not pieces for you to play with. We are flesh and bone and heart. And we do not go quietly off the board. We bleed and weep as we die."

As she died.

His blade quivered in his hand as if begging to do its work. Horacio was as still as the dolls in his glass cabinet. Ajax could see the fear—the old man was *finally* afraid. Finally not sure what his creature would do.

"I am going to get Gladys and if I see anyone in my rearview mirror, I will kill them and come back and peel you like the rotted fruit you are. Say 'I understand.'"

"I understand."

With his free hand, Ajax hurled the cane into the garden. He slid the Python down the small of his back, slipped the Makarov into his pocket and the travel bag with Salazar's money over a shoulder. No, he thought. It's Gladys's money now.

Ajax turned the knife so the blade slid away from Horacio's neck. He pressed the point under his chin until the old man's head arched backward until it could bend no more.

"What was the last thought in her mind before they killed her?"

"Gladys isn't . . ."

"Not Gladys."

"Amel . . ."

"Don't say her name." He pushed the knife point into his chin, not quite breaking the skin. "Did she think her American passport would save her? Did she think *I* would?"

"I don't know."

"Neither do I."

He walked away.

"You're going to die, Ajax. Is that it? A suicide at last? Like Fortunado Gavilan? That's why you've never been happy, never fit in. You're in love with death! You're not going to get Gladys, you just want to go back to the mountains where you think life is simple! 'Live to die, die to live.' You love the simplicity of war. That's why you're a killer. It's not injustice you hate, it's the gray of reality, the fog of life that you can't make your way through." He struggled to his feet, his age showing, and reached out for Ajax. "You're going to die up there with Gladys!"

Ajax stopped and considered that last line. He ran the plan

through his mind. Not in his mind, but in his gut. "You're wrong. I'll get her. I'll save her."

Ajax left and quietly closed the door behind him. He stood near the street in a rosy dawn, and waited. If there were any more surprises, if Horacio wanted to shoot him in the back, he would wait one last minute. The barrio was mostly quiet. Somewhere nearby a bus rolled down the road; the Soviet fuel tanker had come again. He smelled wood smoke. His eyes burned and he realized there were tears. He exhaled long and slow and went to the Jeep, where one final surprise waited.

The ghost of the boy with the long eyelashes sat in the front seat. Very still he sat, looking straight ahead.

Ajax was relieved to see him. He even felt a little giddy and giggled when he muttered, "Well, at least you're not in the driver's seat."

He slid behind the wheel. The Python in the small of his back raised that pain in his ass. He looked sideways at the boy, who looked straight ahead, as if unaware of his killer's presence. Ajax put the Jeep in gear and drove away.

In no time they were on the Carretera Norte, passing the airport toward the Sebaco Valley and the mountains. As the miles unraveled beneath them, as the hum of the wheels soothed him, it was as if Ajax rose higher and higher into the air until the world looked to him as it did on Horacio's map. He looked down and he and the ghost were just specks lost in the green immensity of their homeland. And from this place, he felt he understood at last. The ghost had not come to haunt him. Nor to persecute him. Not even to save him. What the boy had come to give him was absolution, pardon, clemency. He had come to tell Ajax he was forgiven.

At least for all he *had* done.